DEADLIGHT

Deadlight

Library of Congress Control Number: 2021951431

ISBN (hardcover): 978-1-956450-11-8
ISBN (paperback): 978-1-956450-12-5
ISBN (eBook): 978-1-956450-13-2

Published by Thousand Acres, an imprint of Armin Lear Press

215 W Riverside Drive, #4362
Estes Park, CO 80517

DEADLIGHT

Vincent dePaul Lupiano

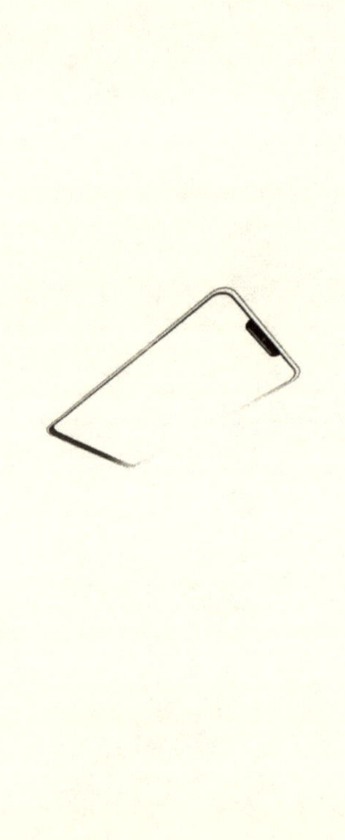

for

"Lovey"

Nancy Scheer-Lupiano

1
SAVED

Lake Constance, Germany, Midnight – Four Days Ago

Rayne Foster, hands and ankles bound taut with nylon rope, has three minutes and thirty-one seconds before she dies aboard a sixty-foot yacht.

The sound from her taped-shut lips is a guttural rage with harmonies of anger and a hymn of fury. All that the science of acoustics will allow through the three-inch patch hastily smeared over her mouth less than three minutes ago by Hans Kesten. Before, he and the Magician precipitously tripped the timers on two digital Silvercup detonators, the catalysts of Rayne's late-night wrath here on this perfect lake in southern Germany.

The Magician, Ernst Schümer, said to Hans in German that there was no need to tape the woman's mouth shut, "*Idiot*! *Wir sind 900 Meter vom Ufer entfernt! Niemand kann sie hören, vergeudet keine*

Zeit!" Idiot! We are 900 yards from the shore! No one can hear her, don't waste your time!"

But Hansi, for the perverse pleasure of seeing her eyes storm with anger, fear, brusquely applied the duct tape over her shivering lips. She did not resist.

Moments after they killed the diesel engine, they primed the Silvercups *after* misplacing the GPS unit. Then Hans lightly caressed the top of her breast, probing for her nipple. Grinning. He wanted this since they captured her earlier at the hotel in the Black Forest. When he went down to her belt buckle, she had enough. Arched her jodhpurs up fast, vicious power, caught him in the scrotum, lifting Hansi off the decking, and bringing tears to his small stone-grey eyes, tearing them. Hans dashing for the railing and puking over the side, pain rippling up, popping out of the top of his head and his torso on fire.

The Magician had to restrain him from strangling her with a coil of rope lying near her head, disregarding the glint of something silver nearby. Then with his sleeve, he wiped the puke from his lips, tore the tape away, and slapped her face.

"*Schwein*!

Pig.

"*Leave her alone*! *We have to find the GPS, now*!"

Kesten thinking that was small revenge for the pain. And then he went for the railing again, retching, gripping his abdomen.

He resented her from the minute he saw her on the mountain top. Haughty, impenetrable to his threats. Too confident for a woman. But, *oh soooo beautiful*. Strong face, luminous blue eyes, her hair cut at the line below her ears. She did not breathe hard with fear and no panic in her eyes that he could sense.

She was, in Deutsche, *formidabillis*. And that is why he respected her.

Kestin and the Magician searching for the Garmin GPS device, shouting in German. Because after they set the Silvercups, they could not shut them down.

Rayne's pulse rate's around one-twenty. Wasting too much muscle energy trying to unleash herself from her bonds.

Keep trying.

If only Rayne could suck more of the black night air into her lungs, enrich the red blood cells and banish the burning in the muscles, then maybe she could tear the bonds and—then what? Swim nine hundred yards to the dock, dry your hair, and kick back with a *Wienerschnitzel* and a *Weissbier*?

Only angels can do that, Rayne knows, angels flying dangerously low to the flame, and Rayne knowing she is no angel.

Perhaps, finally, the answer is simple: what you *want* to do, you sometimes *cannot* do.

Perhaps tonight is the night, Rayne, that you die.

She always wondered how, when, where.

Legs, arms, torso, squirming on the deck.

And then a glance at the time, just above her head, so she can watch her life diminish—lime green digital readout on the detonators clicking down. The detonative the Magician selected uses a TO-5 transistor header composed of the industry-standard Kovar and sealing glass. The detonators, Silvercups, require a relatively low surge of electrical energy for functioning and provide output sufficient to initiate the next stage device. Tonight, a greyish block of the explosive Semtex the Magician meticulously selected neatly into a cruller and shaped inside the car's spare tire.

Efficient, deadly, because the Magician picks his tricks fastidiously. He savors his work. And this is why he needs to stay far, far away from INTERPOL. They have a Red Notice out on him. A Red Notice, not a gold star, advisement to member nations that the Magician needs to be apprehended, that he is armed and dangerous and in possession of wonderfully exquisite tricks that have kept him free as a venomous bird. There is a one-hundred thousand euro reward for his capture.

... 2:59 ...

Now Rayne swallows her panic: maybe this is not as bad as it seems, watching the clock of your life counting down toward your termination and mulling it over, but quickly, please, please, so little time. Think about it, just a few minutes, you lying here in the dark knowing the exact clock click, the precise second when you cease living, and, after all, who knows when we will die. So, Rayne, you are privileged. You can leave life's fandangos that surely will endure if you survive, and you have exact visual proximity to your end, snow cold. You, Rayne, know how it will play, and, God knows, most of us don't, and we care so much about The Conclusion. But you are so blessed, no wondering, no suffering, no pain for weeks or months, no gasping for air on a hospital bed sensing the odor of death and your veins pulsing with morphine to ease your aching, dying from who knows what? **Maybe nothing?** And slowly, agonizingly drifting, drifting off on a mote of dust toward your final star. Twice the speed of light, no less, and, dare say, Rayne, supplicating, accepting a hitch from God's grasp. Because you WILL need HIS muscle, we all do. This finality so close. So close your sleepy eyes... cede to fate.

Take this suddenness with frosty calm.

No?

***NO*!**

***NO*!**

Rayne?!

Hello!

Yes, no?

Maybe?

What?

. . . 2:06 . . .

Same hour:

The FedExField, Cook County, Maryland.

The stadium choked with vitriol, yearning, a sense of raw loyalty: perspiration and hoarse throats.

Maybe fifty, sixty thousand screamers chanting.

The home of the Washington football team. The stadium now holding a small portion of the Movement. Their venom has deluged the field with followers from across America. Nevertheless, the last four years have forged a distinct irate mass seeking national salvation by the man they wait and wail for preparing himself in a dressing room in the basement of this American temple. He is their destiny. The country's future. Their savior. They have waited hours to see him—their leader.

Their hope, chanting.

They scream when a five-minute introductory video of Pug appears on the Jumbotrons.

"***Cé-sar*! *Cé-sar*! *Cé-sar*!**

The chant splits the syllables of his name: an unmusical yelling imploring change, new leadership, hope—the general's appearance at the lectern. The sight of his crisp uniform will cause a volcanic swoon.

Then they will lilt. Listen. Lilting and *then* listening. And then you got the suckers Pug.

In a dressing room below the tumult, General Caesar "Pug" DeJean stands at rigid attention before a full-length mirror. He wears a bespoke U.S. Army uniform, the new, nostalgic "green" WWII design, four glittering stars riding on each epaulet. He glances away from the closed-circuit TV, the shouting crowd chanting his nickname. Examines his posture, the uniform, the brightly colored field of ribbons, his glittering jump badge. He tightens the knot on his tie. His staff standing by in the mirror, showing admiring smiles as the general practices.

Looking good!

The shouting mass is for you.

For you, Pug!

He smiles at himself. A slit cut across a block of aged wood.

Most people do not know how to pronounce his name correctly. He has been called *SEE-ZER* and *SEE-CZAR*.

Those that know Pug know he prefers SEE-ZER. Like Julius *Caesar*. And his nickname, most not sure where Pug originated. The guesses are many. Looks like a Pug, the dog breed, wrinkly, short-muzzled face, a compact, muscled body. Others say the nickname is an abbreviation for pugnacious: confrontational. Truculent, DeJean is, above all.

He glares at the image, studies it a moment.

An image, a symbol that mimics his disdain for the United States government's ineffectiveness.

And you can do so much better for the people, can you not, Pug?

Yes, yes.

He salutes himself, the resolute general in the mirror, a surgically sharp salute honed over many years of practice.

"Looks good, sir," says Colonel Corning. Daring not to say Pug could drop a pound or two.

"Practice and passion, that's what *makes* it righteous, colonel."

"Stirs the pot, sir."

"Indeed."

General DeJean's hand salutes the air several more times. Up, down, up, down. Fusing the gesture into muscle memory. Assuring perfection.

It is Pug. It is *you*.

The salute will give the crowd focus. The unity that they yearn for at these rallies.

And then the suckers will return a shoddy mishmash imitation of the same gesture, fools, all of them.

Patience, Pug, patience.

General DeJean learned the salute, honed it at a southern military prep school, took it with him through his fourth year as Regimental Commander of the cadet corps at the Citadel, the Military College of South Carolina. The salute sliced the air on parade grounds, at ceremonial events, funerals, the president of the United States. At somber ceremonies for the dead. *Too many of those, goddamnit*! And in minutes, to the veneration waiting for him on a football field of American hope.

Their posture will stiffen further when he emerges. The mantra will proceed him, massive wave after wave. Always does. The steel and concrete will quiver with history.

"Cé-***sar*****! *Cé-sar*! *Cé-sar*!"**

Corning says. "They *love* the salute, sir."

"I know. That is why I brandish same with vigor. If you put a little pop into it, Corning, they suck it up. Embodies pride, respect. Integral part of the Movement."

"It's the goose-bump salute, sir. Your signature. That and the four stars."

"*Eight*, Corning. *Four* on each shoulder."

The clamor of the crowd makes DeJean restive.

"Okay, colonel. Let's go kick some civilian ass."

Then he pivots, and his ducks trail.

The whole staff, quack quacking, they go.

Going for some history, they are, yeah.

Rayne!?

Hello!

… 1:38 …

Answer?

What will it be?

FOR GOD'S SAKE, RAYNE!

Of course, you nitwit. Should've known, sorry for the doubt.

Muffled imperative from her mouth: -- *IGHT!*

Do you mean *FIGHT?*

Say it ...

Pronounce it loud in your head.

***Scream it*!**

Yes, fight. That is what you must do.

Rayne, remembering Friedrich Nietzsche's words.

He who has a why to live for can bear almost any how.

Wondering about the *why*, right?

The *how*.

That is the lynchpin.

Not a single note of auditory fear from her. No remaining residual energy in Rayne's breathless acoustic repertoire.

She's done with that.

Never works anyway.

She's grunting. Again, her rage wins. She groans trying to pop the bounds. To live beyond the precepts of time. Beyond the diminishing green ticks on the timers. Hansi and the Magician can't see her, so she struggles to free herself, loosening the rope.

Hell-bent instead, focused truly, on securing her escape from this floundering boat nine-hundred yards from the dock, from the town of Lindau. The luxury vessel afloat on bleak desolation. A petite broach of coastline lights winking faintly, beckoning. Summoning Rayne.

Rayne and the boat lose partners, conjoined on the final seconds of their lives. Rayne, plotting her escape now, while the boat drifts single-minded, independent.

Then she pauses.

She thinks.

When the Semtex initiates, the effect will be so sudden, so devastating you won't have time to register the flash.

You won't know what slammed you.

She can still hear the Magician and Hansi cursing, knocking around the boat's cabin. Doors slamming. Cutlery shattering. A cacophony of anger and frustration storming from the cabin.

The Magician has an apparent low tolerance level for Kesten and blames himself for giving Hansi the Garmin, misplacing it.

Wie blöd! How stupid.

You are a dimwitted dope! the Magician bellows in German.

Hansi cannot understand this hostility. He has been so good to Kurt. So loyal. Hansi has given him all his patience and understanding. Why does he yell at me like this? Then he feels better because he senses the Magician cursing *himself*, taking some of the blame off his shoulders.

Rayne's German—she used it in Munich six days ago—is fluent, conversational, so she strains to interpret their words forming under their stress. Their boots banging fore and aft, crunching glass, cupboard doors slamming.

They are wrecking the boat!

"*Nein*! *Nein!! Nein!* The Magician screaming his frustration.

The interior lights come on.

Now here's Hansi straddling Rayne, chest puffed, self-important with polished Danner jump boots, hands-on-hips. A menacing German firedrake. The catchlight in his irises glinting red, the flashlight's red beam. Then the bastard taking a knee next to Rayne. Hard for him to kneel because his scrota is a scrota aflame and, he imagines black and blue and purple, aching, and he so wants more revenge. He looks at her face and wonders what pain he can inflict. Wants to plunge a knife in her face and twist it around.

"Okay … *Für es nicht aus macht, wem Sie sind, oder wem Sie arbeiten. Nicht mehr*!"

It doesn't matter who you are or who you work for. Not anymore!

He inhales another gallon of air into his lungs to suppress the urge to blow his junk over the transom again. He remains spanned over Rayne's dormant body, gaining his breath and what pain he can put into her body that would surpass his.

Rayne can't understand why he sounds like he *hates* her.

Why?

Then a new onslaught of pain, but Hans manages to overcome the intrusion, leans close, Rayne smelling stale cigarette smoke and cheap cologne. Hearing his gulping for air. He's gagging again.

Give him another nut shot, Rayne? *No, wait.* He will kill you this time.

Chill.

He says, "*Sie sind glücklich.*"

You are lucky.

"*Warum?*"

Wir quälten Sie nicht.

Because we didn't torture you.

Oh, wait, you haven't seen the best of Rayne Foster.

In her mind, Hansi gets the one-finger Rayne salute.

The Magician appears with the Garmin.

He shakes it in front of Hansi's face, gives him a roll of his honey-colored eyes, and Rayne, still now, breathing better—certainly better than the criminal standing over her—and she has no single notion as to what she will do once these two buttholes tumble over into the Zodiac and leave her here to vanish in a ball of fire.

Rayne, you have got to summon your lucky stars.

Reach out to Alpha Centauri A, your favorite.

She can only imagine: they will depart using the GPS and make for the Audi they all arrived in at the doc earlier. Then use the Garmin's software to guide their escape.

The Magician steps closer to Rayne. Hansi's at the railing, bent over, an old rug befouling the lake.

The Magician says to Rayne: "Too bad it ends this way, no? I've come to know you, even though we never met. Between this and the other thing in Florida. Oh, well, *Wiedersehen.*"

The Magician shrugs his shoulders: *I don't care what your name is.*

And then, with Kesten bent over, trailing the Magician, they bail into the Zodiac. Rayne hearing the motor crease the air and skidding off into the blackness, vanishing.

Leaving Rayne alone.

... 1:16 ...

Now she says to herself, *Alles ist leis.*

Everything quiet.

REINVIGORATE, RAYNE!

STRIVE TO STAY ALIVE.

DON'T GIVE UP!

FIGHT!

She's not going to live beyond the timer's parameters anyway because she can't unbridle herself from the tape and the rope they spindled around her wrists and ankles. She can't summon a scream because it will not work. Who the hell's gonna hear her?

Jerking her hands up hard, fast, effecting a slicing, crescent motion, and her wrists come away from the single taped connection they made to her leather belt—the weak link in the chain.

"Goddamn this!"

The words barely mount the railing, skim a few millimeters into the blackness, then subside, and Rayne's hearing what the German had said when they bound earlier.

"Even if you come loose from the tape," Rayne recalls, "you will not escape the blast, the fireball. You cannot swim away fast enough."

Wanna bet!

. . . :59 . . . .

The Magician had it figured spot on, she thinks, looking around the deck, because there's the Silvercup fastidiously connected to that Semtex, the whole thing smiling back at her, an array of pretty yellow and black electrical wiring that's gonna produce the volts to blow you away.

You see, Rayne, the Semtex, the wiring grinning at you, that's just the *initiator*.

Because when the Semtex *initiates*, it will ignite one-hundred gallons of diesel fuel that will fire the night sky with a dazzling orange-red blossom the size of the bomb that slammed Nagasaki. There will be so many pieces of you, the yacht, nothing will be discernible, and the yacht and you commingling, a slick of rainbow-colored greasy fuel, Rayne blood, boat spars, femininity, boat junk. Detritus, all of it.

Recalling the Magician saying: "This is not the only detonator, *Meine fraulein*. We have hidden a second device to coincide with this, a backup, as you say in English—if you should get lucky and dismantle the primary, *verstehen sie*? Please, not waste time and calories looking for it. Hansi has hidden it. Trying to start the engine is futility because we have disabled it, see …."

Then he tossed the ignition coil over the side of the boat, and Rayne heard the splash and the Magician saying, "I am only doing what they paid me to do. *Verstehen*?"

But at 11:35 p.m., one minute and five seconds before detonation, that glint of silver the Magician noted near the coil of rope, but neglected shines in Rayne's eyes.

She focuses on it, refocuses, blinks her tears.

And then sees the wonder gleaming back.

A beacon.

Rayne, on her side, flip-flopping toward the coil of rope where the object rests, the glint beckoning, a fisherman's knife, a crisp serrated upper edge. Perfect for cutting through nylon ropes, yes.

An instrument she can use to escape this deathtrap.

… :50…

An electrical pulse zips from the base of Rayne's neck, down her spine, a delicious electrical thrill popping the hairs in its path, signaling she is alive and forgiving her urge to surrender, giving her a surge to *FIGHT*.

Rayne not wallowing in self-pity, no, no, fighting, trying to feel she will survive this terror.

60 seconds, babe.

Then, *tout à côté de moi*!

With her lips and teeth, she grips the knife's pommel, flicks it over her neck, and the knife arcs and nicks her wrist with pain, cutting through flesh, and then she shimmies her hips closer and grips it between thumb and forefinger near the small of her back, and before she can imagine the notion or make a plan, the knife's serrated edge saws, saws, saws, through the nylon rope and she's free!

Partially.

Rayne now not waiting for the full length of the rope to fall from her legs, but instead hauling herself off the deck and dashing for the transom, leaping off the deathtrap, the rope trailing behind.

. . . :40 . . .

Knifing through the air.

The angel, low flying. Soaring. The Olympian!

Thinking a singular thought as her wings take her up.

God make me safe.

. . . :20 . . .

And cutting the lake's black surface and not looking back and breast stroking away as fast as her limbs can go and using her dormant swimmer's talent. Going for the Gold this time.

. . . :10 . . .

The rope around her ankle summoning her back, a malevolent squid, the boat pulling the angel and her wings down below the surface, twisting around her legs, ankle.

Should've thought of this before diving off the boat, sweetie, doncha think?

But, God, even angels do not have time to do *everything*, do they?

She reaches down, struggling, working to untwine the massive cobweb, Rayne's arms and legs burning, her eyes coal-hot, choking, desperate to unravel the rope twirling around her legs.

The digital readout winking, winking, icy green. And then—

... :*0* ...

Rayne, listen, sweetie, *you are not far enough away from the boat when it*—

... EXPLODES!

The brightest flash she has ever seen. Orange-red. The height, width of a hot air balloon, blossoming, expanding. An atomic monster paining her eardrums and penetrating her sinuses with a massive slamming pressure, lifting a curl of water over her head. A tsunami it is.

Then Rayne sinks below the surface and bobs back up for a gulp of air, the concussive energy wavering out, rippling the water, silvering the surface, bucking her head back, and a nanosecond later, oh shit, the shock wave does an encore and comes rolling again, crashing over her, toward the center of the explosion and then the second pound of Semtex bangs off.

Above the epicenter, above the violence, parts of the boat hit their apex then start a fluttery descent, the mass cascading and twisting and twirling, multi-colored, agleam with reds, oranges against the charcoal sky, the twinkling stars watching the earthly mayhem.

Then. . .

Silence.

Oily surface burning smokey black, flaming.

She stares at the lozenge of lights pale as summer fireflies that speckle the streets and windows along the shoreline that shape the city of Konstanz, Friedrichshafen, Radolfzell am Bodensee, and on around her. A sobering calm creeping over her jangled nerves, the lapping water stifling an inner urge to scream with fright.

Until she hears her mind's voice whisper—

What is your immediate plan here, skipper?

Sleep?

Can't.

Sleep!

If I close my eyes and fall asleep, I will die.

To close her eyes is frightening. Because with eyes closed, the night will be darker, bleaker, less understood, the lake deeper. Infinite deep. The journey from here impossible. If she closes her eyes, she won't see herself. The yacht burns and Rayne imagines a morsel of hope, a splinter of optimism.

You must always have hope, no?

Yes, the voice bleats.

The voice of a woman drowning.

* * *

The Maxwell Maltz theory of psycho-cybernetics recognizes that a patient's self-image includes self-beliefs about their intrinsic abilities and deficiencies. Whether they are popular or not, beautiful, intelligent, confident, so forth, some of those beliefs may have been true at one time. For example, a person might have fallen off a horse and carry that the self-image of a bad rider. Maltz saw such human behavior as a negative feedback (cybernetics) system. Maltz finding he could improve performance by helping an individual mentally see themselves doing the activity correctly. Vague parity with Maltz's theory had won Rayne an Olympic Silver Medal *and* a Bronze in the women's freestyle swimming. Little it did it for her self-esteem. She saw herself finishing first.

Rayne now realizing that Maltz's system must be auditioned *again* right *here* and *now* on this dreadful night. Until that moment, where she can see herself *surviving*, finishing first, Rayne Foster will not win. Rayne will lose. Rayne will die.

Instead, a low-flying angel will succumb to the flames. Rayne, with her wings of self-doubt flailing, sullying the crisp night sky, stirring the dust of her life.

Away with Dr. Maltz, please, away with him and his impracticality.

Because often survival depends on the simplest thing.

A turn of the head.

A good fall of luck.

Blink of an eye.

Tonight, for Rayne, it is a pain.

The one in her wrist where the knife had pierced and bloodied her skin.

The same blade was neglected by the Magician when he passed up a decision to inspect the glare it gave off above Rayne's head. The same blade Hans did not see. Just a blink of his eye distracted him. Much to Rayne's advantage, thank you.

Rayne lifting her wrist, and the small wound inflicted by the knife rivering black blood. Close to the bracelet on her Omega Speedmaster Professional wristwatch. Black blood, Rayne.

Blood of the Alien? Bad, bad, bad joke.

Rayne staring at the slash, her blood washing over the watch's Hesalite crystal.

And then, beyond the wound, she sees *them* in the mid-distance. What is that, Rayne?

Dazzling red stars, two, at ground level. Universe and species unknown.

Could be friends? UFOs?

Planets? No?

And from the red stars, discernible and familiar song lyrics drift to her because Rayne and Elora mimed them last night giggling through an alcoholic smog of sensualness in Elora's hotel room. Elora had her Blackphone. She selected songs. If Rayne guessed the title correctly, Elora had to throw back a shot of Tequila. Or was it the other way? If Rayne did not guess correctly—that and one blunt (maybe two) that they poked at with the Patchouli incense smokin' the whole place up. *Ragin'*!

None shall sleep! Even you, oh Princess. Is that Luciano Pavarotti's voice skimmin' the lake?

Faint, but, *yes*, Pavarotti. *"Act 3, Nessun Dorma,"* from one of your favorite operas, Rayne— *Turandot*!

And high above Rayne, descending to your level, the night sky's night stars Altair and Sirius and Aldebaran and Riegel and Canopus and Cygnus and Lyra and Ursa Minor, and your favorite, Rayne, *look*, *look*, Alpha Centauri A favoring *you*, loving *you*, rendering their brilliant sword rays, a gift of light for *you* to savor, to *see* the night. To *save* you? Bestowing fluency upon your broken angel's wings and shattered heart. Slats of hope unbent. Coming to *you*!

The car's backup lights flaring.

Brake lights lighting up.

Rayne swimming toward the *music*, the Olympic breaststroke, to the dock.

Come to *me*, the dock says. Come. Come.

Or is the dock going to her?

Even you, oh Princess, In your cold room, Watch the stars, That tremble with love.

Are they *growing*, Rayne? The lights? Abiding *your* hope?

On your mouth, I will tell it.

Two red brake lights. Precious rubies.

Then the backups go out, flare again, again. Lighting the way.

Two white earth stars, not brothers or sisters of your mighty master stars, Rayne, but helpful lieges. Similar to the ones in the vaulted chalice of your beckoning heaven. Alpha Centauri A. Your favorite since girlhood. Remember? The one in the telescope that mom gave you winking at *you*? And your mom in the house at night at the piano playing *Claire de Lune*, Claire of the Moon, the notes trilling across the lawn and mingling perfectly with the lovely stars, and how much you loved your mother. She was a gift, Rayne.

When the light shines, My name no one shall know.

Rayne blinks hard, gotta get the water outta my eyes.

And my kiss will dissolve the silence that makes you mine!

A skirl of wind clears the problem.

Yes, and the red lights and the brake lights expanding their focus again.

Coming to her.

From the Audi. Your Audi, Rayne, the one Leland arranged days ago.

Some nut bunny speeding *backward in your car*? Coming toward *you*.

What the— ?

Tires spitting pebble and rock, pummeling the rocker panels, dampening Pavarotti, the lyrics. The vibe.

Audi sliding through a long skid, overshooting the runway, splintering a wooden fence pole, and the thing flailing, skimming, then sinking beyond the dock.

Interior lights on.

Driver's door opens.

One long slick leg jutting out, challenging the door's swing-back.

My name no one shall know.

Running toward *you*, Rayne.

And here she comes.

Running!

To *you*!

Black leotards, the end of the dock, black turtleneck, riding boots. Athletic strides.

Pistol in hand.

Racing to *you*!

Watch the stars, That tremble with love and with hope.

Who is this?

But of course, you know, don't you, Rayne? you daffy ding-donged hopeless mess. God, you have got to get out of this trade!

Stay focused!

The woman is here, and both of you at the dock's ladder—both breathless.

Enough moonlight to comb your hair.

Rayne climbing the mossy steps, soaked, quivering, and the woman's gloved hand going for Rayne's, pulling her up, saving her. *Embracing* Rayne.

Embracing her!

And Rayne, feeling the temperature of the woman's face. Her breath, her lips scuffing Rayne's neck, lingering, hesitant to move away. Taking in her scent. *That* scent. The press of their bodies unrelenting.

Like failed lovers newly conjoined.

Vanish, o, night!

Why?

Now the woman's hand with the pistol pointing to Rayne's most favored star, Alpha Centauri A, beaming its radiance.

Rayne's Walther PPK, the barrel still hot in the woman's hand. The PPK the woman grabbed off the Audi's floormat an hour ago tonight after it fell from Rayne's ankle holster when they shoved her in the car. Safety off, *COCKED* certainly.

Aimed at Rayne's star chalice, *her* universe, and Rayne locked onto the woman's dazzling moon shiny eyes, teary. Neither saying a syllable, lips *soooo* close, wondering *is that the heat of lake water, huh?... or tears blending*?

And my kiss will dissolve the silence that makes you mine!

Oh, they know.

Tears, Rayne, tears. A deluge.

Rayne assured now who this is, her body familiar. *That* cologne. The *scent* of her breath. Squeezing the air from the woman's lungs. Lips so close.

On your mouth, I will tell it.

An archangel of the highest rank, Rayne, saving you from the hellion gods that were banished tonight by your lovely star guards. Those star devils, they were disallowed an imperial descent from your domed chalice. The archangel, *look*! here at the dock for you. She saved you.

Elora Sinner.

In *your* arms.

At dawn, I will win!

Elora Sinner saying, "I killed them both."

Rayne, ignore Elora's words.

Allow yourself instead a passionate consideration.

A stronger embrace.

I will win! I will win!

2
SINNER

Berlin, Germany.

A quarter past noon.

The Lorenz Adlon Esszimmer Restaurant, Adlon Hotel.

A stone's toss from historic Brandenburg Gate.

A lithe woman stands impatiently at the maître d's station, waiting to be seated. She is fidgety. Hair, cut straight above her collar, russet-toned. Her beige linen dress, Tory Burch, neatly trimmed in soft black leather, and the shoes, green suede Rothy driving moccasins. A few diners note her elegance painted against the subdued oak walls. Her eyes prowl the room, and she shifts her weight from one foot to the other, glances down at her cellphone—one of two nestled in her Birkin shoulder bag.

The one with the red cover, Elora.

Saxby's voice.

Remember: *The Silent Circle Blackphone 2, Elora, with unparalleled protection against hacking attempts. The world's most secure smartphone powered by the world's most secure operating system.*

Oh, for God's sake, shut up.

Elora Sinner not too cheery today.

From the Embassy, she took a long way here, scanning as she went, to burn off some time, going up *Wilhelmstrasse*, relishing the cool air, the shop windows, tourists, then right onto *Unter Den Linden* toward the Brandenburg Gate. Unaccustomed and inexperienced in covert situations, she was unsure she was tagged.

Petr the maître d' arrives, escorts her to a table for two.

This morning, Fucking Saxby had asked her for a favor: "Meet with Van Der Leeuwen at noon at the Esszimmer." No further instructions. No, *please*. No, *thank you*. She was incensed, but he persisted, standing taut and trim behind his desk at the CIA's Berlin Station at the American Embassy.

He added, "Look, Sinner, I never liked you. You have too many expensive clothes and not enough brainpower for this work. I'm certain you know that. But we have a task in front of us—at least you do. So, I have to deal with it. And that involves you, irrevocably. I will put aside my reasons and simply ask you to do your duty. Understood?"

She did not even nod. She glared. Turned quietly and left behind a line of indignation and guilt.

Because now she hates herself for walking away from Fucking Saxby in silence and not responding. Pushing back.

At her table stands tall Petr the maître d saying, "Good afternoon, Fraulein Sinner," he enunciates with precision and a shallow bow, the crack of his heels ricocheting off the oak ceiling. He shifts his weight to one leg and folds his arms. This is Petr's relaxed, friendly posture. Not everyone gets this patience from him. El a sucker for this. This elegance stuff. It is just the way she was brought up. Which now is not good. This has beclouded much of her life, part of why she wonders who Elora Sinner is, wondering since she was a child. *Maybe a new you starts today, El? The one you seek. You never know, right*? But what would it be? Certainly wasn't with the man you were commanded to meet here.

Petr is a man with an imperious posture. And his name is *Petr*. Not Peter. A Czech name. It means rock. German, born and raised here in Berlin, speaks all the languages he needs to make his career and presence valuable coin in this international milieu. Thin for his height and age, old-school allure in a bespoke charcoal grey suit, an impeccable high-collared white shirt. Neat nails. Petr smells like fresh cut limes and lemons. He has *gravitas*. Knows all the old and new money in Berlin—the dreamers, the seekers, the almost-dids, knows how to play them. Petr's father was an *Oberstgrüppenführer* in the Waffen SS, captured by Americans after the war, found guilty of war crimes, and hung after a failed appeal. Petr inherited his father's cagey skills. El particularly fond of Petr because he reminds her of Dad a few years ago in his tailored Alan Flusser suits and handmade shirts, and crocodile shoes. Back in the day when she thought of her father fondly as an unconventional billionaire, extremely successful, charming.

Like you, El.

But so much more successful.

Ouch!

Even for Petr, El cannot give up one of her renowned Elora Sinner smiles. Anyone who cannot abide by Elora's smile should be served a subpoena for a Class A misdemeanor and sent to purgatory. The allure seems to skip along through the family's blue blood, but tonight it sits flat.

It is okay today, El, to allow yourself to *wallow* if you want. If you fight, *you will not win*, you know that. You never do. Moods like this spin their sinister webs and are masters of the master's realm. That is the pecking order of the universe. Today, yesterday, always. All philosophers know this.

Petr slides her chair back, removes a handwritten tent card that says "*Van Der Leeuwen.*"

She yearns for a black Sharpie: *Ex-fiancé*!

Petr saying, "How have you been?"

"Good, thank you, Petr, and you?"

"Much to my delight, I have been quite excellent, Miss Sinner, and thank you for asking. Will you have the usual drink with extra salt?"

"Yes, please."

"And you are expecting, , , ?

"A gentleman. Mister Van Der Leeuwen. Should be here soon."

"Oh, yes."

"Do you know him?"

"I believe I do, vaguely." Of course, he knows him.

Van Der Leeuwen's an arms dealer that Petr put together with Chinese businesspeople seeking top-secret drone technology. Meese was here six months ago, and Petr was given a belated five-thousand-dollar tip, a password to a British bank account in Hamilton, Bermuda, and not for his impeccable maître d' skills. A year prior, Petr introduced Meese to a wealthy, obese Chinese patron that loved blonde German teenage girls. Meese was subsequently accused of transferring technology to China that involved highly sophisticated drones, specifically their navigational algorithms. Meese neither admitted to nor denied his involvement. The prosecution's case flopped, and Meese kicked back and went underground and enjoyed the copious benefits of Italy's Cinque Terre—but not before he had passed along half the technology he promised—that he had acquired from Simon Lane, the CEO and sole owner of LaneAero-Tech Systems.

Elora says, "I'm sure he will have the same—a Margarita. But please hold it for a bit. If the ice dilutes, he gets cranky, and you will have to haul it back."

Petr nods.

Elora says, "Wait—bring his drink with mine."

"I will do that."

She thinks, the hell with the dilution. Meese's fault if it's watered down when he arrives.

Petr whirls away, making a mental note of the disdain in Elora's voice because it is a detail he will have to relate later.

And she says to herself: good for you, Elora. Peel away those leaves of self-doubt. Those pestilent petals. Face those clouds of ambiguity that have always plagued your pampered life. Let this day, this new dawn, be scrubbed and clean—a fresh start.

A *new* El starting *now*.

She angles her shoulders. She needs a clear view of the entrance to prepare herself for Meese's arrival. Crosses her legs, then reaches into the Birkin and takes up her chirping BlackBerry.

A Text:

Meese Van Der Leeuwen
Sorry, we caught headwinds. Are you at the restaurant?
I will be there shortly.
Meese xxxx

She does not respond to the Text. Turns the phone to silent mode and places it square near her napkin.

The temperature in this room is chilled, and someone needs to turn it down a notch, and the clinking of cutlery and chatter and the idea of meeting him here is starting to irritate Elora. Sometimes life throws you a couple of shitty things at once besides chilled air and chit-chat, and right now, Elora cannot abide the least of them. Sinner wondering if those things frighten her, or is she excessively anxious? Which? Right now, she has no clue.

So, she surveys the room again.

She has been here at the Esszimmer Restaurant several times; she is familiar with the rich milieu. The tables filled with the lunch crowd from industry and government, the expense account bunch. Businesspeople, journalists, Germans, Americans, power players, diplomats, bespoke business suits, and pricey ties. No tourists. The average meal, €300 without wine.

Elora prefers old places, less intimidating, snug. Or least exude a tone of old school. The way her father taught her to appreciate establishments like this. Aesthetically, she fits in here against the classic dark oak, the precious oil paintings, yes, but her negative thoughts sharpen her anxiety, and she feels distant and lessened. Maybe she's catching a cold?

Or cold feet, El?

Instead, *that* word slams into her brain again with violence.

Deadlight.

She needs time to analyze, to quantify. To breathe.

Then the word disappears.

Time to justify what I am going to do. That's the heart of the matter. *Justification.*

Not another redundant conversation with the man walking to her, gliding into the room, purposeful.

Meese Van Der Leeuwen. Arms dealer, arms smuggler, a mendacious purveyor in weapons systems, ammunition, occasional fighter planes. A man serving death's requirements with pleasure and for profit.

She waves, unenthused.

He bends over, kisses her, a perfunctory smooch, sensing her heat. Her scent still on her. What is that? Creed. *Iris Tubereuse*? Yes. His favorite.

The kiss does nothing for her. Might as well have been from a shoehorn.

Deadlight resonates, distracting her smile, giving Van Der Leeuwen sitting opposite her a negative vibe.

Van Der Leeuwen saying, "So good to see you. You look great. We hit headwinds." Then a two-second pause, and: "Are you okay?"

Already his nose has picked up a sprig of trouble. Elora hates this about herself—unable to disguise how she feels and always at the wrong moments when she needs camouflage to conceal what she must hide.

"I have to tell you; I did not want this."

"This?"

"Us. *Here*. Now," Meese says with his British-Dutch accent.

"I'm not surprised. Nevertheless. Let's give it a go."

She tries a tiny smile, but it vanishes. Knows Van Der Leeuwen can read her like a book.

He selects a breadstick, lathers the tip with warm olive butter.

Petr arrives with the Margaritas. Meese does not acknowledge his presence. And Petr nods a subdued hello.

"So, you are surprised?" Meese asks. "To see me."

"Surprised? Not an appropriate word."

"And that word would be?"

"Annoyed."

"Ah! How so? Do I hear *love lost* playing on this soundtrack?"

"Please, no self-flattery today, Meese. I'm annoyed at *myself*—for not telling Fucking Saxby to go to hell. For making me sit down here now with you—after all these months."

"Oh, harsh words for your master spy, Mister Fucking Saxby, back there in the den of American intrigue. *Tsk, tsk.* Let me ask you something—why does everyone call him *Fucking* Saxby."

"Because he's supercilious, pretentious, and egotistical, and everyone under him hates him. Meese, please, why are we here? Do you want the engagement ring back, is that it?" She twirls it around her finger.

"I'm quite glad you mentioned that, El. I almost forgot. The sixty-eight-thousand-dollar pavé from Van Cleef & Arpels, if I recall. Of course not, El. Yours. Forever. Always."

"So. Why are we sitting here talking about nothing?"

"I'm here on your father's behalf."

She tilts her head, angels it, one of her traits, and laughs. This amuses Meese. He always loved it when El laughed and did that thing with her head, pointing her New York society nose at the clouds.

Then Meese laughs *loudly* and heads turn. He can't figure if he still loves her. Probably not. To bring that up now would be a touchy subject.

"I have a business appointment tomorrow, an important client. I could have Zoomed it, but your father—he asked me for a favor."

"Your appointment—I presume a meeting to discuss who is next up on the killing fields? Perhaps an early bird special? A final clearance sale on artisanal Russian hand grenades?"

"Elora, please, *stop*. Selling arms is no different than selling English Muffins."

"Meese, if I recall, my last English Muffins did not explode in my mouth."

"To us," he says and raises his glass. "And to what might have been?"

She hesitates, then stretches her long body over the table, over her flatware, over her dinner plate, her water glass, but not far enough, and misses tapping Meese's glass by the width of a breadcrumb.

Note here: Van Der Leeuwen does not reach or extend, Van Der Leeuwen only goes halfway, the way he does in most matters, and his hand and glass remain adjourned over the toasty bread rolls, the neutral bread zone, where battles rest dormant, where sadness and anger linger, and that's the furthest distance Van Der Leeuwen extends himself. He can be such a douche bag, she thinks.

So, El rises timidly from her chair, leans, stretches, disappointed in Elora Sinner for yielding to the devious Meese, as she always does, and that's that. Their glasses chirp a dull clink, off-pitch. A metaphor, she thinks.

"Here's to us," he says again.

He waits for a response.

Gets none.

Waits.

But Elora is not looking at Margaritas hanging suspended over the sterling silver breadbasket, no. She is looking into Meese's eyes. They're cold and brittle. Reptilian. She tries to decipher them, burning through his skull, through the back of his head, through the wall behind him, into the parking lot, and not reaching a satisfying stop block. Not seeing anything but the sadness in them that he created in her life.

Because he did not just fly across the Atlantic Ocean in his private jet to simply say hello, buy her lunch, and hope to get laid one last time, oh, God, no.

He signals the waiter, holds up his empty Margarita glass—"*Ein weiterer, bitte.*"

He says, grinning, "I have something—from your father."

"*Finally*. I was afraid I'd have to wait until the Baked Alaska caught fire."

"Impatience was always a subset of your generous arrogance."

"Granted."

"He wants assurance, El. Double, *triple* assurance. Because there's so much riding on this."

"*This*?"

"Deadlight."

"Oh so—you know? He told you?"

"You could say I am an integral part of *it*," he says with a smile. "Big changes coming, El, and you, a key player."

She examines the red gleam on her fingernails and suppresses her surprise—A.G. sharing Deadlight with Meese Van Der Leeuwen.

Elora Sinner sits cold and still, her elbows on the table, face partially hidden by a curtain of half-shadow. Her head pulled down. Slightly, she moves her hand, and the gold chain on her wrist skitters halfway down her slim arm. Her lips are partially pursed, so Van Der Leeuwen supposes she is starting to take this seriously. Van Der Leeuwen almost always able to read Elora's mood transmitted through her lips. She turns her head away from him, her chin still in the air, unwilling to allow him to see her full face, scans the room, then studies his eyes again.

Van Der Leeuwen saying, "I have a room here. Will you stay with me tonight?"

She says nothing. Shakes her head and points her nose at the clouds.

"El, I flew all the way here from New York, and you can't stay with me tonight?"

Grinning, she says, "Meese. Listen to me: I'd eat broken glass first before I'd have sex with you again."

Deadlight pops up.

The word won't leave her.

So that's why he's here.

He opens his menu.

"The Salmon Gravlax sounds good. You?"

"Same."

He signals the waiter.

And then goes on about a deal he is gluing together here in Berlin, the process to salvage it, and the only way to keep it breathing is by throwing more money at it.

Elora not listening. Studying her perfect manicure.

El remembering. She doesn't want to. But it intrudes, uninvited. Undeniable.

They started a year ago at a diplomatic reception at the Museum of Natural History, tuxedos, costly colognes and perfumes, evening gowns, and elegant cocktail dresses. The air awash in power and money and people with Von and Il before their centuries-old names. He spotted Elora standing in front of a herd of wild elephants on a riser stampeding toward her, Elora indifferent to the beasts and the dull words she heard from the two turbans auditioning their disfigured English and insipid politeness. Then there were flirty glances, and she winked, and that knocked him back and started the whole disarrangement between them. But, the glance, her eyes, her coy, aloof smile, sent a spark slithering down Meese's back.

Next, there they were, dancing to a bouncy New York society beat, then a suitable slow number where he could hold her close enough to savor her breasts, pressing his chest, sniffing her hair and her silky skin next to his face. He surprised her. He whisper-sang song lyrics in her ear, and she felt the words lifting from his heart, feeling the heat of his breath on her ear. Knowing she was falling in love with him for all the wrong reasons. He was a charmer—a manipulator.

Oh, God. *That* song.

Now, he's staring at her, sipping a Margarita across the table.

Timid, she is, and still so, so enchanting.

Van Der Leeuwen asking, "Remember the song?"

"'*You Do Something To Me*?'"

"And who wrote it?"

She rolls her eyes, *please*. "Cole Porter."

"I never could trip you up." He leans across his plate, softly off-key recites the lyrics.

She smiles. A brilliance of flowers and happiness and memory and of course, regret, prompted by the lyrical recall.

Later, racing down the museum's steps in the rain without an umbrella, then a cab splashing up Park Avenue to his duplex at 92nd Street. In the foyer, her strapless cocktail dress coming unbound, the hem rising, Elora's muscled shoulders pressed roughly against the Ralph Lauren blue linen wallpaper. Thrusting quickly, drumming into her softness with a stab at the end of each hard thrust, a fevered burst of power, harshness pressing into her pelvis that brought her to the brink, the brink, again, again, and once more. And then she cried out, a shriek coming off the linen walls and beyond until her tremble diminished into a whisper decreeing her finish. Then he proclaimed his eruption, allowing his pleasure to spill from his opened mouth, crying out in pain, a huff-huffing sound, seeking her, finding Elora's waiting mouth there in the half-lit room, and kissing her till their lips ached. Both wanting more now. So much more, yes, yes. Come to me again and do not let me go. *Ever*!

And here, now, in the Essenzimmer, there is a cold drizzle, a snowfall, taking them away and away from that first pleasure, drilling the temperature down and down, subduing the clinking of silverware.

A fat German banker nearby wearing a paisley ascot, red hair flowing over his collar, and an American who-knows-what in a three-piece suit knocking themselves nuts with too much cold seafood, loud laughter, and their second bottle of €200 Wegeler Lenchen German wine, both muddling the air. Elora knows they will drive the waiter crazy when the storied dessert tray arrives.

Then, her stillness leaves her jittery body; she sits straight and robust, a perfect marble statue, leans closer to the towering bread-sticks, and says to him, with stone in her voice: "Exactly what do you want from me?"

"Nothing," he says calmly. "It's not me, it's your father that wants—"

"*Assurance*?"

"Correct."

"You can tell him that he has my"—she ponders for a second—"*promise*. My *assurance*."

"That apparently is not enough, El. If it were, he would not have asked me to sit down with you—despite our *history*.'"

"What else?"

"El, there is no one on earth A.G. trusts more than you. You are the star of his life."

"Thank you for taking me down memory lane. Please take the leash away from my neck. What else?"

"He wants me to. . .well. . .I mean. . .he wants me to *watch* over you. No one knows or has what *you* have. After all, you're the whole trick."

"He wants you to spy on me, is that it?"

"No. *Protect*. Protect is a much *better* word if you will. And from a distance too."

"I could not tolerate that."

He leans forward, over his Margarita.

Says, "El, you don't understand—you have no choice."

"I'm late for an appointment."

She pushes her chair back, stands, folds her napkin neatly, drops it onto her plate.

And before she turns for the exit, Meese says, "And I *will* have *that* back."

That?

The sixty-eight-thousand-dollar Van Cleef & Arpels engagement ring, Elora. With the Pavé diamond band in platinum, glittering. Ha ha'ing at you. The one he lied about a moment ago.

Don't push back—more on your mind than diamonds, Elora.

Deadlight, remember, Elora?

Then she allows a childish grin, and her eyes narrow, and her determination tightens.

Tugs slowly at the ring. Pulling it off her slender finger. Over the sheen. Over their history. All of what it had been fading, ashen.

Neatly positions her fingers over his Margarita.

And permits the ring to freefall.

The distance short between fingers and glass and drawing a short vertical line to the chilly surface. A slow-motion plunge underscored by pain and delight, passion, futility. The diamonds, cleaving the Margarita's cold surface to a definitive conclusion.

An effusive splash the whole world hears, unrestrained, announcing their denouement and what could never be.

Settling atop the peaks and slopes and inclines and crevices of the ice and then skidding down to the bottom of the glass.

And Elora, grinning wider and wider, cherishing the sight.

Saying, "Go fish."

3
NITROPENTA

Munich, Germany – 12:25 p.m.

What the hell just happened?

In the aftermath, there are many residual pieces of Myles Lane's BMW Seven Series, most of the objects no larger than a roasted pepper, and his body remnants scarcely discernible on the sidewalk and walls of the buildings around the Munich Opera House.

Because the blast was so potent, Myles and his Ultimate Driving Machine vanished into the ozone after the primary detonation triggered a blinding, watermelon-shaped mass of fire and smoke. A nanosecond later, the explosive thunder splattered windows on the shops and cars along *Residenzstrasse*, the concussive shock wave rolling out and back, a massive typhoon of scorching air, blowing down pedestrians, the energy punching the air from Rayne Foster's lungs and slamming her to the pavement.

Flat on her stomach, cheek on the pavement, Rayne wonders if she is aflame.

What the hell just—?

Chaos rising.

A chorus of pain.

The streets around the Opera House flocked with bedlam. Pigeons and blackbirds, panicked, scurry in a tumultuous black wing seeking sanctity. Pedestrians, hit by shrapnel and the concussive force of the blast, scattered and writhing. One man is on his back, clothes tattered and smoking, his arm raised, begging. Two women stagger aimlessly, arm-in-arm, bent over, helping each other. One collapses, the other can't pick her up. They are too wounded. Alarms in shops are screaming a massive chorus of urgency. The air a drape of confusion, smokey grays, blacks, and hued blues. Moans begin creasing the air. A song of the wounded reaching a crescendo

The closer to the epicenter the thicker the panic and pain.

In minutes, crime scene teams from the *Bundespolizei* and the Federal Ministry of the Interior will discover a fragment of tobacco brown crocodile strap from Myles's Patek Philippe 18K Calatrava wristwatch nestled improbably beside the tongue from one of his custom-made Church shoes. They'll have their first piece of evidence and then will move painstakingly toward ID'ing the man that Rayne Foster does not want to be linked to.

What the hell just—?

Rayne, dazed, trying to stand so she can run from here and avoid the *Polizei*. First, she has to get the stupor out of her head. Needs to ignore the pain.

Was that—

Entrails and other body parts—muscle, bone, brain tissue—scattered on the sidewalks, mainly on Max-Joseph-Platz across the street from where the BMW just blew. Indiscernible pieces of what had been Myles are glued to the walls of the postal building and adjoining shops on *Maximilianstrasse*, Munich's boulevard deluxe. But the blast has charbroiled the remains in varying degrees, and only forensic technicians from the *Kriminalpolizei* with medically honed forensic skills will discern their provenance.

It was an explosion, Rayne, for God's sake. What it was. An explosion. Myles blew up!

Rayne has seen too much mayhem in the past couple of years—no, wait. In the past twelve months—but she's never seen a human *explode.*

Pain along her jaw, shoulder, pain radiating from her knee.

Just like that, Myles Lane disappeared, and not to the sorrow of the body of people he had been working with at Fort Meade, poor bastard. Friendless Myles misunderstood and under-appreciated, an intellectual, yes, wearing the patience of his peers with his right-wing rants about liberal America and its rotting morals and flooey politics and overwrought political correctness. All too much for Myles to suffer gladly.

The only person now who can ID Myles, Rayne Foster, is attempting a dog crawl near the upended table in front of the discerning *Spatenhaus an der Opera* restaurant where they sat conversing and sipping hot chocolate and buttery croissants less than sixty seconds ago. The place where Leland told her to meet Myles.

Rayne's having trouble turning, rolling over onto her back. She wants urgently to stand, desperate to hobble away. But the searing pain in her knee, her shoulder preoccupies her muscles, freezing them. She wonders if any bones are broken.

She moans—a sorry *oooo*, a sound she's never heard herself

utter before, and she wonders: What day is this? Sunday? The time? *Where the hell am I*?

Tough girl, not tough now.

Oh, for Christ's sake, Rayne, stop nickering and get off your ass!

Before Myles sat down, Rayne had no idea what she was meeting him for. If she consented to the protocols he proposed, she'd undoubtedly set off on another dark journey. Like the others, Leland put her out on. But this was part of her new life. First thing Myles asked Rayne when he sat down with her was if she was available for a few days. And that was the last official thought Myles Lane uttered. Asking like he would if she could saunter down to the grocery store and buy a loaf for him. After that, it was thirty minutes of chit-chat. Myles ranting about the demise of the United States, ill-mannered Americans, the poison of political correctness, dying American morals and incivility, the country's pervasive violence, the cable networks with their gasbags, and on and on—all notions his peers were starting to begrudge, and leading Rayne to think he was a supercilious chatterbox.

But she had a clear notion of his reputation, mainly through rumor and a brief description Leland gave her days ago at an outdoor café in Prague.

Then Myles, thirty minutes later, stood, brusque, Myles a jack-in-the-box in a tailored two-button khaki poplin suit, turned toward the BMW and left Rayne holding her coffee cup in mid-ascent, a croissant crumb tacked to the corner of her lip. Rayne, with furrows in her forehead, wondering, as she observed Myles stride quickly across *Maximillianstrasse* to the spot where he had parked the jade green BMW Seven Series.

Now she can't remember if he took his briefcase?

She wants to get back to her hotel—she can see the façade from here—before the *Polizei* descend on the chaos and start probing, picking, questioning, wanting to know who the man was that had been sitting with her. One or two people probably will remember her sitting with him.

But the damned flaming, smoking, wreckage, that's what's between her and the lobby of the *Hotel Vier Jahreszeiten Kempinski*, halfway down *Maximillianstrasse*. She's going to have to do some zigging and zagging, take a circuitous route, because the police focus is going to be here, at the intersection of *Residenzstrasse* and *Maximillianstrasse*, a perimeter set up immediately around the wreckage. They will be cordoning off the area, surely. But the round-about route's not going to be a hop, skip and jump, no, no—the pain in her knee, the shoulder, the haze in her head, all that. All will hamper her movements. Slow her down.

Rayne, you gotta get a different life for yourself.

What the hell happened after Myles reached the car? She wants to know.

No, wait a second: what happened between them at their table during their conversation that made him leave her so abruptly? Did he maybe sense there was a shooter somewhere with crosshairs on him? Did he see the glint of a rifle barrel— some unforeseen peril?

Too multifarious to sort out now, she thinks. And that's disconcerting because Rayne Foster, former lawyer, Olympic medalist, does not settle for loose ends in her life. Even though God knows there are many.

Gotta gotta gotta get away from this. I gotta get to my hotel room. To the satellite phone.

Rayne still trying to get to her feet, coughing up the smoky particulates drifting down from the blue-domed sky. The universe that Myles created. She glances at the front of her white cotton shirt. Speckles and lines of blood. A road map of red highways going nowhere. Hers or someone else's? Or both?

She taps the ache on her jaw. Her fingers glossy crimson. Then she pries a tiny metal particle shaped like a spider from her wound and flicks it disdainfully and doesn't bother watching where it bounces.

Some of the scene is playing back now, the foggy mayonnaise clearing a bit . Myles rushing across *Residenzstrasse*. Dodging. Taxi. Postal truck. Darting for the BMW's door. Myles's left hand aiming the key fob. Depressing the unlock button. Locks pop up. Myles's right hand extending toward the door handle and then . . .BAM.

Blinding white light. The air shivering. Blizzard of glass. Blistering heat. Car shards bulleting over her head. Swarm of bees snowing the windows of the *Spatenhaus* and zipping over the lovely green table umbrellas, chairs, and then—

That damned familiar strong odor of cordite, Myles's cindered flesh and melting plastic and burning BMW leather, and Rayne realizing she can't hear, not a single sound, not the screaming, not the shouting, not the bleating pleas.

Just a screeching train whistle in her ears.

A silent horror film.

Gotta get outta here.

Rayne overcome with more rage than she's ever felt.

Pure, undistilled hatred for whatever prick blew up the car in the middle of Munich on a pleasant Sunday morning.

She is befuddled.

I am living a nightmare, yes. I am drunk and reeling from a toxic overload of alcohol or some malevolent drug; yes, that must be it.

She jerks her head back and looks up at the sky. Pristine it is not. The sky a cupola, clear blue, shiny bright, vacuous. Then a vast sail filling with dazzling iridescences and drizzles of blues and tarnished greens, simmering through coiling pillars of oily smoke and spirals of indiscernible particulates. But not even this vision can dispel Rayne's worst nightmare: dying on the street because of her incompetence—for getting herself in this situation in the first place. Initially hesitant when Leland asked her to meet Myles. She knows now she made a mistake.

Oh, God, have I ever.

When Myles reached the car and pulled out the handle, thinks Rayne, that was the instant the BMW exploded, not before.

Was it Myles' *hand* that set off the blast—his fingers pulling the handle out? But none of this makes sense now. Not a single scrap of it, no. It's all a bunch of mashed bananas and porridge in her brain. Maybe a coincidence: Myles opening the door and a simultaneous explosion?

What the hell happened, she wants to know, *before* the damned car blew, when Myles was sitting at the table.

What was the trigger?

Bedlam now along *Maximillianstrasse*, sirens ululating in the distance, from all points, playing a disastrous score. Ambulances. Police cars. Under this, the distinct whimper of the wounded, swelling, rising.

Myles Lane was the initiator of all this disorder, says Rayne in her clouded, polluted head. Whether it is was his hand on the handle or some other trigger.

Because when his hand pulled out the door handle, that's what seemed to trigger the detonator connected wirelessly to a one-pound, pale yellow, odorless slab of nitropenta, the German word for pentaerythritol tetranitrate, mixed with aluminum powder—itself not susceptible to exploding, but needing a casual initiator, an electrical signal to cause a lethal result. In this case, Myles's hand being the first step in the collusion of events. This human action—his hand pulling the handle—set off an infrared tone that detonated the nitropenta lounging in the BMW's trunk, molded smartly inside the spare Pirelli tire.

Rayne wondering now if the blast was also meant to take her out?

Maybe the bomber had it figured she'd be here with Myles, and the blast would cut them both apart, Rayne maybe climbing into Myles' Seven Series—saving the killers some time and effort?

A twofer: Myles, Rayne. *Baam*! Gonzo.

But why would they want me dead, she speculates? Might it be data Myles was about to relay? That they thought he *had* dispatched? Some scrap of hypersensitive, noxious data that he would or did share with her.

Rayne doesn't know enough about Myles, his background, whatever, but she's confident that within the hour, she's going to hear more about Myles Lane than she cares to, and that it will all be conveyed to her by Leland Upchurch, her father's best friend, the man who sent her down this dark hole. That's the way it is with these plays: either you never know enough, or you know too damned much for your own good. Or, there are people who *think* you know too much and pose a threat that could trigger some worldwide cataclysm.

This is too much to ponder now, for Chrissake, it really is. I've got to get the hell out of here.

Rayne trying to creep away, clawing at the coarse pavement. Thinking that it was the postal truck that probably saved her life—it passed into the primary blast zone, partially shielding her and most of the other patrons from the main concussion, the bulk absorbing about forty percent of the blast, soaking up shrapnel, car, body parts, stuff like that.

When a shockwave is created by a high explosive, nitropenta in this case, which has a detonation velocity of 6,900 milliseconds, it will always travel at supersonic velocity from its point of origin—in this case, the BMW. This, a fact of physics. So, Rayne saw the flash of the explosive light—a massive, blinding global intensity—then a nanosecond of amnesty before she heard the massive explosion because light travels faster than sound. But shock wave energy dissipates relatively quickly. Especially if a large object is in its path. Like a postal truck, lying on its side now, tattered. The driver's head and arms poking out of the doorway.

Yes, the big bulky truck saved Rayne's life.

Saved by snail mail.

Her stomach begins to roil. She suppresses an urge to vomit.

You gotta get up and figure this out, Rayne! *Now*!

Because the area is filling with clots of *Bundespolizei* in their green and white police BMW sedans and station wagons and their dull black Heckler & Koch automatic weapons pointing here, there, and for sure they're gonna come over here and try to render aid and it won't be the kind she wants, because they're gonna definitely start probing, what'd you see, your name: *Resisepass,bitte. Was ist der Name des Mannes, die mit Dir saß?*

And then —Bingo!

Whatcha gonna say then, Rayne? Whatcha gonna do to extricate yourself from police custody if you don't provide plausible answers and they catch you lying? You, with your phony passport, fake driver's license, artificial smile, bogus airline tickets, and that counterfeit Time *magazine press credential you've been hoarding since Miami.*

Oh, dear Lord.

Leland provided no cover for this.

And that is your fault because you should have pressed him on it.

But why wouldn't he give her some bona fides? He always has.

Rayne wondering if he set her up again as he did in Miami.

Because no one, Rayne, no one on the whole planet will admit they know you—you with your angel's wings that won't flap right now, and all your yearnings and ill-suited dreams and unresponsive lovers that won't take you to the heaven of your dreams.

Because, Rayne, you are now flying sans safety net.

Angel without wings, you are.

And if you believe you can talk your way out of this, Rayne Foster, then you'd assume that four wheels on your grandmother will turn her into a Greyhound bus.

* * *

Halfway down *Theatinerstrasse,* the apothecary where Rayne heads, away from the blowback and the tumultuous pile of smoky bedlam and death.

The pharmacist, dark curly hair cut boyish, wears a doctor's white smock with her name impeccably embroidered in fine blue thread. She's standing outside the door, covering her gaping mouth, her trembling hand clutching a ball of Kleenex, transfixed by the rising calamity of sooty black and brown smoke here in her beloved Munich. Trying to comprehend the explosion, to decipher the horror. The noon sun casts gray shadows under her gray-blue eyes and cuts lines of grief on her face as she stands, awestruck.

A kid on a bicycle gives a fart-like honk on his bike horn, then blurs past Rayne. The pharmacist bobs out of his path and watches in disbelief as the kid pedals *toward* the anarchy, leaving a wake of childish exhilaration.

When the pharmacist sees Rayne tumble into her apothecary, she spins around after her.

As Rayne's bleeding chin registers, the pharmacist spots the bloody knee; her nerves turn to compassion. Her professionalism grips her. She wants to help.

"*Brauchen Sie Hilfe*?" the pharmacist asks.

"*Ja, bitte. Sprechen Sie Englisch*? I need bandages, gauze, peroxide. Neosporin?"

"*Ja, ja*, of course. Did you see what happened?"

"Yes. *Eine Tragödie*. I was there, at the café."

A tragedy, she tells her, thinking about relating what she saw, to expunge the horror and rid herself of her rage. But she doesn't want to relive it now, no, never again.

Something else skips along a blurry neuron in her brain, uninvited but welcomed:

Rayne wants to be on a beach in Hawaii, scanning for seashells, watching a spectacular sunset, worrying about too much sun and not enough sunscreen. Not dodging exploding cars and body parts and shrapnel.

The warbling sirens, penetrating louder and louder, converging, ubiquitous.

The pharmacist's nervous haste causes a roll of surgical tape to spill to the floor and roll out of sight. Then the smell of cordite on the air, the crispy BMW, replacing the scent of a delicate flower-scented Munich summer.

They glance at each other and shake their heads, incredulous.

The pharmacist's eyes are glazed with sorrow.

"*Hast du es gesehen*?" asks the pharmacist.

"Yes, I did—it was a bomb. In a car. Parked at the post office. On *Maximillianstrasse*," Rayne says, trying to suppress the ache the vision provokes. "Near the opera house. The damn thing must have killed a lot of people."

"*Was*?"

"*Das verdammte Ding muss eine Menge Leute getötet haben*."

The pharmacist's face tightens when she hears *getötet*—killed.

"*Terroristen*?"

Rayne shrugs her shoulders—"I don't know," she says. "*Vielleicht*."

Actually, yes, it could have been a terrorist. It could have been Mickey Mouse or Sir Walter Raleigh. Anything is possible. After all, Myles could have antagonized some militant jihadist dickweed bastard while involved in one of his far-flung who-knows-what-the-hell overly aggressive plays, and now here in Munich on a Sunday morning, sudden sweet revenge was the hand he was dealt, punctuated with chaos and death.

Fuck you, Myles, someone might have uttered before the countdown and detonation.

Because Myles, in this trade, with an almost non-existent social life, had made enemies in almost every continent in every bleak cubby hole of every powerful nation, and all the innocuous ones in between. You see, Myles was not a simple piemaker gathering bits and pieces of sexual peccadillos or deciphering and trading military and state secrets for the boys and girls back in Virginia, but rather stole or gathered, amassed, mounds of government confidences—networking, as it were—over a long period of years, while toppling a government or two, and leaving a trail of sensitive detritus in his inscrutable wake. He was an efficient maker of mayhem—Myles the Mayhem Maker. Myles could infiltrate a bee hive and cause havoc. He was bound to piss off someone along his covert journey.

But what over-sensitive conundrum did he take with him, now scattered?

The pharmacist has the first-aid items neatly lined up on the counter, antiseptic salving soldiers neatly aligned. Organized, she is, despite the tremble, the terror she feels.

She says, "*Wer hätte sich vorstellen, eine solche denken konnte hier in München passieren*?"

Who could imagine, she wants to know, how such a thing could happen here in Munich? She glances out the shop window, over Rayne's shoulder—at Munich, her beloved city. She is heartbroken. This *Tragödie* happening here in the city of her birth. This city where she was educated, where she was married. Where she bore her children. She tells Rayne, "Not since the war, nothing like this. . ." She holds her breath, but not her tears.

Rayne saying, "Do you have a bag for this? How much do I owe you?"

"You owe nothing," the pharmacist says sympathetically, handing Rayne a plastic shopping bag and gripping her arm.

"Please, you should allow me to fix your wounds?"

The words don't register with Rayne.

Because the fog is rolling back, a massive, overdue overture smudging the arena of reason, and Rayne's dazzling blue eyes are lathed as if with motor oil and the tears resuming. Her brain is cockeyed. Chicken Little clopped her head. Getting dizzy again, nauseous, the damned ringing in her ears so pervasive she has to strain to understand the pharmacist's words, English to German or German to English—all of it a cat's cradle.

She needs to brace herself on the marble counter. But her sweaty hand misses the edge, and her palm whacks a small confectionary stand and little delicate tins of breath mints and little heart-shaped chocolates in bright silver and crimson tinfoil scatter and hip-hop on the black and white marble floor in a pattern like the one in her head, and she tilts, but the pharmacist is there, agile and wheels around the counter preventing the wingless angel from crashing.

"You should let me help you; you should, please," she says,

holding Rayne steady around her shoulder, trying to comfort her. "Please, sit down." For a moment, Rayne wants to accept the succor the pharmacist offers. She wants her embrace, her comfort. She wants the woman to take her away from what she just saw—Myles shredded into a thousand bloody ribbons.

"Thank you. I have to go to my hotel. Please, let me pay for this," says Rayne, taking the bag and holding out a handful of euros, the number not mattering.

"No, go. I wish the best to you."

Rayne's tears shimmer hot silver in the gold light —"*Vielen Dank.*"

"*Auf Wiedersehen.*"

The pharmacist's tears show her empathy.

They hug.

The pharmacist cannot pronounce any more words—her sadness triumphs.

When Rayne steps onto the sidewalk, the pharmacist is weeping, a profound, shattering grief filled with fright, her soft whimper muted by crying sirens coming to them from all over the world.

* * *

Maximillianstrasse, the upmarket street in Munich, filled with the world's most stylish shops: Gucci, Bulgari, Dolce & Gabbana, Versace, Dior, so on. In the middle, the *Hotel Vier Jahreszeiten Kempinski*, Munich's finest. A blend of trend and tradition, with the cordiality of a grand hotel. Simple, elegant luxury the German way. Up and down the block, the sparkle and flair of Porsches, Ferraris, and Aston Martins are not the exceptions.

A minute ago, when Rayne stepped into the hotel's wood and marble columned entrance, the staff was assembled loosely out front on the sidewalk, too preoccupied with the mayhem up the street, watching Myles Seven Series roasting with a fiery ferocity—all that octane, leather, plastic, and rubber, fabricating a massive conflagration of black smoke and orange and blue flames.

They paid no mind to the guest with the bloody knee, the bloody jaw, as she hobbled through and depressed the elevator button. Up the street, they watched an army of black-clad *Polizei* with automatic weapons and helmets scurrying, scanning the area.

Some other time their heads would have turned and seen the auburn-haired Rayne, the blue eyes, legs like a colt, a graceful woman dressed simply, with an elegance that discreetly matches the tone of this hotel. But not now.

Right now, she is starting to comprehend that this simple operation, without any discernible protocols so far, is headlong for the edge of a cliff, truly. Leland, two weeks ago in a park in Prague, simply told her to meet Myles Lane at eleven o'clock and listen to what he wanted, and that was that.

Now, guests are dashing through the lobby for a look-see outside. But in the perfumed air of the lobby, Diana Krall's voice is singing *Here's That Rainy Day* on the speakers, the piano notes and her soft voice trilling sad, romantic chords on an air of dismay, in a lobby filled with lush scents of expensive perfume and faint, exclusive cologne. What a screwy picture.

Rayne should be sashaying up and down *Maximillianstrasse*, buying everything she sees that she likes in the elegant shop windows, and not suffering from the guilt of overspending on worldly things.

But instead, the screech of sirens fills the elegant lobby with tragedy and fear, and crushes the luxury of her fantasy, and scatters it away. Like so many other things in her life.

Then the elevator doors open, and Rayne steps into a temporary sanctuary.

Away from that thing smoldering down the street, burning into her memory.

The thing she will never forget.

Away.

But only for a moment.

Maybe one day for Rayne, the horror of this will abate and erase the furrows she has on her face, which are starting to be more prevalent now, right, Rayne? The vision of Myles striding—no, dashing—toward his elegant green car will at least minimize, but not even time will allow Myles's visage to escape. Like a morose, fading black and white photograph, the residue of it all will always remain faint and acerbic—she is sure of this. Ever so much of it will remain to disturb her mind at the least appropriate moment. A bit fuzzy, perhaps, but always lingering. The pain of it will subside and dull, yes, but will never be vanquished. The human mind has an irrefutable law against banishing horrors, and this one will not be an exception, not even for her.

Because for now, she is in her hotel room broiling in bathtub water so hot her skin is a maddening vermillion, and what's making her madder is that the hot water's not draining away any of her anger or fear. Instead, one pervasive thought keeps bouncing around her head—the thought that began repeating over and over since she left the pharmacist: *something odd about Myles and the car, aside from the explosion. Something strange about him when he reached the door*, but she can't piece the logic together. Because it is all a tabletop of scattered computer code that her mind's trying to sort, and it's not collating fast enough.

Rayne, dummy, it's not odd at all: when Myles opened the door, the car exploded. Someone in the vicinity had a radio detonator and tickled it when Myles reached the BMW. Start thinking clearly, for God's sake!

Now, if things are not bad enough, she feels impelled to reach for her phone and text out a message to Christian, her Bandit in the night. The idea reinvents an old deep, penetrating wound of love abandoned. She hesitates to tap it out, having to go over the words and correct for errors on the damned tiny keyboard. But the thought is impossible to repel, to convey to him six thousand miles away, there in Miami. Rayne's shaky finger softly tapping while she cries:

I think about you so often that sometimes it hurts when we go so long without talking. I wish I could be there to help you through the decisions about your life. I wish I could be there to make love to you all night long, to feel the heat of you fill the room, the sweat of you. I wish I could be there just to see you and to feel you and to catch the expressions you make when you're happy. I wish I could be there ... I Love You So Much. So much -- R.

And then she stares through the steam at his name in the TO block, and the tears sear her skin, hotter than the hot scented water, and she quivers, touched by a frosty notion of what could be, but might not.

Everything moving.

The walls, the bathwater, and her memories alive with bursts of yearning.

And nothing, nothing can abate the pain his absence evokes. Just the dread that he is not here and that she is without him or anyone else who could assuage the tears, the *desire*.

Why can't *he* let go of *her*? Why is this pain more generous than the tragedy burning out there on the street? Her heart on fire like a wreckage doused with difficulty.

Odd how something so caring can be an intrusion, arriving at the wrong moment and confusing that moment, that second, that day, and muddling one's feelings and logic with images from long ago.

Christian will never go away, Rayne, and you know that. And the only thing keeping him away is Rayne—through choice and indecision and lack of courage. Because she has never walked through life with the certainty that she perceives so many others have.

Things are always grey and indecisive.

She reaches out and grips the satellite phone, encrypted for conveying the deepest of secrets and the holiest of fears and panic. She pushes one button on the phone—the magic one. The one that connects her to the safety net. And then, there's the comforting voice of Leland Upchurch, cranky.

"Yes?"

He's groggy, because he's six hours behind and had been asleep with his wife in their home in Virginia.

"Rayne?"

Her voice raspy, sonorous, feminine.

"Leland, bad stuff here."

"What's wrong?" Leland's voice sounding a slight note of panic, and Rayne's tenor grabbing his attention.

"You don't have the TV on, do you?"

"Rayne, for God's sake, five-thirty in the morning here."

"Turn the TV on, Lee."

"Hold for a sec."

She can hear his pajamas rustle as he moves out of the bedroom, then the TV volume faint.

"CNN?" she asks.

"Yes, story about a train wreck in Georgia last night? Rayne—"

"Myles—"

"Myles? What about Myles?"

"We were talking, and then Myles does a Jack in the Box and takes a sprint across the street and—

On the TV here in Rayne's room, in vivid high definition, a German reporter, breathless, describing the bedlam swelling behind him: Myles's smoldering machine, the chaos, the wounded, the un-believability of the scene.

Leland saying, "What the hell happened, for God's sake."

Now Leland can't hide his dread.

"He pulled on the door handle, and—"

"Hold a second. CNN has—they're pulling in a live sat feed from Munich."

"Lee, that's where I am. *Did you forget*?"

Then he sees a German reporter on the scene and the smoldering wreck in the background.

"Oh, shit."

Leland has been around the block many times, an executive in the secret service of his country, directing more operations than he can recall. But surprises like this are always a jolt. Especially when you're in your pajamas at six a.m. talking to a woman you cherish like a daughter, and you know she can be in jeopardy in a few moments.

"Myles's car?" says Leland.

"Right across from the opera house. Blew me off my chair."

"Car bomb, a missile?"

"I believe it was a bomb in his car. He pulled the door handle, and that seemed to trigger the flash. He just vanished."

"Are you injured?"

"I'm bandaged up a bit, but okay."

Now the clandestine executive, Leland Upchurch, the man with twenty-seven years' experience, that wants to retire but can't let go, allows his professionalism to take over this lousy moment, Leland knowing that if he doesn't get a grip soon, things could go off the tracks, go awry, and become imminently uncontrollable, and possibly lethal for Rayne. And escalate on a political level.

Leland saying, "Listen to me—you've got to get out of the hotel, out of Munich, right away, as soon as possible."

Rayne sits up straight as a corn husk. Water spills over the tub—the furrows in her forehead return deeper. Her stomach clenches.

"What do you mean *right away*? That doesn't—"

"You've got to leave Munich as soon as possible. The police are going to want to question you. They will find witnesses that saw you sitting with Myles. They'll track you to the hotel and get to you straight away. German police are extremely efficient. You're not dealing with a bunch of muffin heads in a third-world nation."

"Shit," says Rayne to the water vapor. Because she knows that *get out of there right away* is an omen of something—she hesitates to use the word, but it pops up—*doomful*.

"Hold for a second," says Leland.

Then she hears him muffle the phone, Leland having hastened from the warmth of his wife and his secure bedroom into a deepening world of chilly subterfuge and uncertainty in his den.

Then, he says, "I'm going to put you on hold for a minute. Standby."

Thirty seconds pass, and he's back on.

"In one hour, there will be an Audi A4, dark blue, parked in front of Reinhard's, a men's clothing boutique on *Marstallstrasse*. Go down to the lobby of your hotel, ask if you have mail. The clerk will give you an envelope with the car keys. Go out of the lobby, turn right, then right again, that's *Marstallstrasse*, the Audi will be there. Under the driver's floor mat will be a packet containing a new ID, a passport—"

"Which you should have given to me in Prague."

He ignores that— "and other self-explanatory items. I want you to start the car, turn on the sat-nav. There will be one address in the address book: Wolfacher Strasse 21. It's in a town named Bad Rippoldsau-Schapbach, in the *Schwarzwald*, the Black Forest. Secluded. About a two-hour drive from where you are. Follow the directions on the sat nav. When you get to the hotel, ask for Juta, she's the owner. She and her family have owned the hotel since eighteen-eighty-eight; she'll be ready for you."

"Yesterday, you made this sound easy, Lee. It was just a meeting with Myles. Now—What the hell's going on— "

"I can't talk anymore; it's too complicated. I'm going to get an Air Force ride from Washington into Munich as soon as possible, maybe in an hour or two. I'll see you at the hotel either tomorrow and will fill in the details. Keep the satellite phone on. When you get to the hotel, lay low. Enjoy the place; it's beautiful."

"You sound brusque."

"Good luck."

Twenty seconds later, Rayne lifts from the tub, and the sat phone rings.

Leland again: "I have to ask you—Myles have anything with him? When he sat down at the table?"

"Yes. Newspaper. Came from the car with it, folded under his arm when he arrived. Put it on the table, then sat down."

"Did he take it with him when he dashed for the car?"

"No. He left it on the table where he placed it."

"Anything else?"

"No—wait. Yes."

"Yes? No? *Which*? Come on, Rayne, this is important for God's sake."

"An expensive brown leather briefcase, one of those with a flap and straps with gold buckles. On the straps, his initials in gold, M.A.L., it was—"

"What did he do with it after he sat down?"

"I guess he either put it down and leaned it against his chair, or the table, I couldn't--"

"And after he ran, did you *see* the briefcase—did he *take* the briefcase with him, or did he leave it?

"I watched him running to the car. I was surprised he jumped up so fast. Then he reached the car, pulled the door handle, and the car blew."

"And the *briefcase*?"

"I have no immediate recollection of what happened to. The blast knocked me off my chair, and I might have been unconscious for a few seconds, so—"

"Rayne—this is important: where do you *think* the briefcase is right now."

"*For God's sake, Lee,* I have no idea! I was knocked on my butt, got hit by shrapnel in my knee and jaw, and—"

Rayne sees herself on the pavement, opening her eyes, defogging her brain, sees the bright blistering flash, feels the concussive force.

She rewinds it for Leland.

"Okay. When Myles arrived at the table, we shook hands. He put the newspaper down on the table, sat, then placed the briefcase against, I think, the leg of his chair leg. That's what he did. I remember seeing him place it there because he was careful about it. He checked it after a moment to see that it was leaning against the leg of his chair because he looked down at it. He was very precise about how he put it down—slowly, easy. He didn't just drop it and forget it.

" She pauses, then: "Come to think of it, he seemed unduly concerned about the briefcase. He did."

"Like he cared for the contents?"

"Yes. Like something valuable. Something *sensitive*."

"Myles was a lot of things, among them minimal bomb-making skills. You're sure he didn't take the briefcase when he ran for the car?"

"Okay, listen to me"—Rayne irate now—"here's the playback one more time: Myles reaches the car *without* the briefcase. Clear? Pulls the passenger door handle and, and the car explodes. Rayne is banged over by the concussion. Rayne on the sidewalk on her back like a dead turtle, staring at the sky, trying to get up."

Then, her mind clearing, she remembers. Hit's her like a thunderbolt.

"*Wait*. He yanked *up* the briefcase and ran to the car."

"You're certain?"

"Sorta."

"*Sorta*! *For God's sake*, Rayne, that's *not* good enough."

"Okay. Coming back to me now."

"Rayne. Please! *Clarity*!"

"Because the moment I opened my mind, the fog cleared a bit, and I saw the briefcase."

"*And*?"

"Myles's hand."

"*Huh*?"

"Attached to the handle of the briefcase, bloody mess. *Just his hand*. Severed at the wrist. Leaning against the wall of the *Spantenhaus Café*."

"Rayne. You have *got* to go back and get the briefcase."

"*Are you crazy*!?"

"No."

"You *must* get the briefcase!"

"It was kind of odd because it was leaning slightly against the wall of the *Spatenhaus*, the restaurant where you told me to meet him, six feet from my head, matter-of-fact as if someone *placed* it there like that. The explosion must've—"

"—Rayne—"

"Maybe it was placed there?"

"Rayne, get the briefcase. National urgency!" Then, Leland adds, "We can't leave the briefcase there. Am I clear on this, Rayne?"

"I saw that coming—you mean *me*, right?"

"Who the hell else!"

A pause, maybe six seconds, because Leland is bulking up his nerves before he speaks the next sentence—an imperative.

"Rayne—you've got to go back to the *Spatenhaus*. Retrieve the briefcase. Take it with you to the Black Forest. *This* is extremely urgent." Another pause, Leland composing, arranging his words, thoughts, then—"The *United States* needs the briefcase."

"And the hand?"

"*Not funny*, Rayne!"

"Hey, skipper, you're not focused on what's going on here—listen to me. The place is overrun with police, first responders, German military, wounded. It's a crime scene. There's blood and guts all over the square. They've set up a perimeter. It's probably completely cordoned off now. No one goes in, and no one goes out. I can't just saunter in and say, 'Excuse me, I need that briefcase over there with the severed hand leaning against the wall because some folks back in the pickle factory want it right away.' And me without any current bona fides, by the way."

"You'll have to use your imagination, is what I'm saying."

"Lee, they'll nail me the minute I go for it. The second I pass through the perimeter."

"You've *got* to get the briefcase. *Use your dammed imagination*!"

"What's in it it's so important, Lee, I have to risk going to jail?"

"Listen to me. Stop being so, so *damned* defiant. You march to a different drummer. You always have, ever since you were a little girl. That's why you're the best at what you do among all the Special Ops guys on our team. Different drummer. Of all the people in this trade, of all the operatives in our group that I know, you have the skills to do this. *Immediately*. So, leave the hotel, now, because that's where the police will be looking for you. They probably already have your description nailed down. If you wait much longer, the next time you open your hotel room door, you're going to be facing German police uniforms."

"And you can't tell me what's in the briefcase?" A few silent seconds, then Rayne adds, "Lee, you are using me as bait again. I see it? Hate to say it, but I'm getting used to it."

"You're paranoid.

"*I am*!"

"Rayne, *please*, I am not on a *clean* phone."

"You didn't answer me, Lee."

"Okay, Myles Lane is—was—a CIA exec, and, during his career, he pissed off a lot of people in our government, in other governments and agencies, and I there probably is something extremely sensitive in the briefcase that could cause a goddamned shit storm. Because that's what kind of man Myles Lane was: he designed and initiated shit storms, do you understand me? He produced more gray propaganda than any ten operatives I know, and he had enough jock strap medals to build a bank vault. That's what he did for a living—it made his career, made his reputation, and it made him a man of venomous repute. That and his aloof, arrogant attitude garnered praise, yes. But at the same time, there is a list of enemies and friendlies back at the pickle factory, throughout the world, that wouldn't mind seeing his head on spike, that doesn't care that he's dead. Clear?" Now Leland's voice rises. "So, keep your head below the parapet and get the damned briefcase! Now! I don't give two nickels how you do it or who you knock over in the process; you do it, just get it. After, call me on the seven-seven number, I'll have a sterile phone, and I'll call you back."

Click, and no goodbye.

Rayne glances at her fingertips. They are showing ridges—the hot water, shaking. She wants to toss the phone against the bathroom tiles, shatter it, book a flight for New York City, and find another life, back to sanity. Away from this torrent of horseshit and get her life straightened.

On my own again. Out here on a plank.

Then, out of nowhere: What is he doing right now, my pilot friend in Miami? My Bandit in the night in Miami. I want him to hold me right now. Is he thinking of me? Is he with someone else? Someone prettier? Does he *yearn* for me as I *long* for him.? Does he know that I *cry* for him, *ache* for him? That I want to have him every night in my arms.

Does he know how much this hurts me?

There will be tears tonight.

In the end, Rayne, you just couldn't hold your man.

She quickly dries herself and peeks out the window through her tears.

Then, she sees them. Emerging. From the core of the chaos.

Big, muscled buffalos. Running.

Four.

Buffalos. Packed with buffalo muscle and buffalo resolve. Jogging toward the hotel lobby. Heckler & Koch SP5K machine pistols swinging from their broad shoulders. Helmeted. Gloved. Serious.

Going for the lobby, Rayne.

Coming for you.

Très rapidement.

The kid on the bicycle is the answer.

Yeah.

He's leaning unsteadily against the bakery shop window, sitting-standing on his bicycle, about as close to the perimeter tape as he can get without being brushed away. The scene here fascinates him: the smoldering BMW, the police cars, multi-colored body parts, fire trucks, the police in black combat gear and thick rubber-soled shiny boots and machine pistols, all military stuff young boys love. All so fascinating. His mouth open taking in the stink and his eyes wide.

And he is soon to embark on a massive favor for Rayne Foster. "*Entschuldigen, sprechen Sie Englisch?*"

The kid's face brightens when Rayne asks if he speaks English—of course, he does!

"*Yes,*" he says, enthused. "I learn in school. You Canadian?"

"*Nein, Amerikaner.*"

The kid struck the mother lode. One of the first real Americans he can trip through his English. Like the ones on American TV shows. *This is soooo cool!*

Rayne wags two, one hundred-euro notes.

To be clear, she says in German, "*Ich möchte, dass du etwas für mich tun*, okay?" She points—"See that briefcase against the wall? I want you to get it. You have to do it fast. Like they do in American movies."

She presses a one hundred euro bill in the kid's hand—"Take the briefcase to the apothecary around the corner, and I will give you this other one hundred euro, *ja*?"

But then the kid sees the severed hand gripping the briefcase handle, and he makes a sound like he's going to puke over his handlebars and score a mess on his bike. *Horrible.* He shakes his head *nein*, then *ja* when Rayne flips over *another* crispy one-hundred euro note. The kid nods his zeal.

He is dazzled. His eyes pop out of his head with excitement.

Honks his fart horn three times.

Then he is off on an adventure. Pedaling his butt off toward the briefcase, slicing through the yellow perimeter tape, doing a bodacious, award-winning wheelie, his *best*, the wind flapping his locks.

Whooaaa! *Yesssssssss*! *Radical*!

The hand and the briefcase there waiting for *snaaaaaaaagging*.

Just like on American television.

4
A CHEERY DARK-EYED SLATE GRAY JUNCO

Washington, D.C. – Sunday Morning - The White House

General Caesar "Pug" DeJean removes a small wad of gum from his mouth. Balls it, molds it into a gum foil, folds it neatly. Slips it into his trouser pocket. He gives his tunic a mannish tug, stands poised, impatient, waiting for the door to open. He's ticking through a list in his mind, action items he thinks the president will voice. Then, rocking on his heels, four-star DeJean is ready to roll. Does he have all his bases covered? Sorta. Pug hoping today that there will be no unanticipated bullets flying over the ramparts of President Rand's brain.

One more lungful of air but certainly not enough to douse his nerves.

The door yawns.

He takes two steps into the Oval Office.

Stands at attention and stares straight ahead.

Behind the Resolute desk, standing, his back to Pug and leaning on the credenza, President John Fitzgerald Kennedy, silhouetted. Dark navy pinstripe suit, stack of auburn hair, the silhouette iconic. Classic pose, yes, weight of the world, yes. Timeless *New York Times* front-page above-the-fold-photo. What's the caption here, Pug? JFK staring at a cheery dark-eyed slate gray Junco tilling the White House lawn, high-chirping while he trolls for a tasty, free snack out there on the people's property. Dirt flying, grass clippings, feathers. So much energy from the little guy. He's just scored some millet, hip-hops, and flies off. Happy, prowling the skies over this, his territory trilling as he goes, the world all his.

Pug!

Kennedy was assassinated nearly sixty years ago.

Even so, I wish JFK *were* here. The country would be in better shape if that *were* JFK standing there, solemn, meditating. Knowing what to do. Just imagine how *he* could bring us together.

President Tom "Tommy" Rand senses the door closing. Pug coughs.

Wearing the legendary smile, the president turns, moves around the Resolute Desk, a nineteenth-century partners' desk used by several presidents of the United States.

The president's arms shoot up like goal posts, straight: *big T.D.*!

"Touchdown! Pug!" yells the president; they howl.

Pug, go out for a long one!

Pug obeys.

Does a tip-toe sprint across the presidential seal, squashing the eagle's eyeball, around a who-knows-how-old precious gold and black antique chair that has supported some historic ass, then a quick shunt at the irreplaceable coffee table that history makers set their ambitions on—dodging, juking every defender. The president throws Pug a *looooooong* pretend bullet pass, a perfect spiral, and Pug lures it into his bemedaled chest and does a flying flop onto one of the couches, rocking the back harsh; they hear a crack come up from the wooden legs.

Pug saying, "*T.R.*! From where I stood, goddamnit, you looked exactly like JFK. *Don't cut your hair*!"

"*Mister* President, please," T.R. chides. (Or does he?). They both laugh, Pug huffing.

They embrace, grip each other's forearms. Then a strong manly hug, back slaps—old college classmates.

Rand saying, "I don't give a hoot what *The New York Times* says Pug, you *still* look like a Pug."

"I do, therefore, my nickname."

"Tenacious. And the demeanor to match. Pug, Pug, Pug. Always loved the nickname. How about a booze or two?"

"Dewar's, if you have?"

"The Dew, I have. And a Cuban?" He points to a humidor—deep blue T.R. initials and the Presidential Seal glimmering on the glossy rosewood.

"Gave them up, T.R. They made me fart. A toot during a meeting at the Pentagon is usually bad form for a four-star."

"Your humor, still intact."

The president opens the door to a credenza below a watchful, pink-faced, wig-less, Benjamin Franklin portrait by Joseph Duplessis. The same portrait on the $100 bill. Franklin looking hip because his hair falls in strands below his shoulders, straggly. Check him out on the one hundred—a hipster before hipsters. When President Tom Rand first came into this office twenty months past, he had a prayer in his heart, doubt in his mind. He was sure Ben Franklin was scowling at him. Not happy with the new face in this hallowed room, *Ben Franklin's* place! Judging him, Tom Rand, the man, the president of the United States.

Occasionally, a chat between them would settle some matter and resolve Tom's peptic stomach, which was always snarling. Six months into his term, T.R. asked Ben, *How am I doing*? Then he looked around *after* the question to be sure no one was in the room. From then on, T.R. felt he could speak freely with Ben, and T.R. wondering if Ben had talked to anyone else here in the Oval Office. He got back a five-minute critique, even-toned, levelheaded. Tom stood and listened, nodding. T.R. won't do that today. Won't ask. He knows what Ben would say. Instead, he will have a man-to-man with his old friend, the general.

Two crystal glasses appear and are stood on a historical silver platter. The president pours a couple of fingers high for both, carries them over to the coffee table. Coasters are dopped bearing the Great Seal next to a bowl of perfect pears. They sit on the opposing couches facing each other. In front of the fireplace where the president and foreign dignitaries take questions from jostling reporters.

Pug says, "You have something on your mind."

"Some*things*. I do."

"And that is why I am here, yes?"

"Yes. *Three* items I'd like to discuss. And first, I want to thank you for taking the time to be here this Sunday morning."

"Hey, always good to see T.R., no matter where no matter when." The president says, staring at the pear mountain: "I've thought about this for. . . a couple of days."

"Deadlight?"

"That and the two other items. So—"

"I thought we were all squared away on—on Deadlight?"

Incoming over the parapet, Pug

The president nods yes. "But there are loose ends, Pug. Lots of loose ends that are troubling. And I want you and me to cut the bullshit between us and get everything out on the table. So, no shitting around, okay? Straight ahead."

"Gotcha. No bullshit. Sounds good. The Pugster hates bullshit."

"I figured it so."

Pug swallows his Dewar's and savors the tingle, flattens his feet on the carpeting, and pushes back hard into the couch. Crushing the puffy pillow with the colorful embroidered presidential seal. Can't push it back far enough, can ya, Pug? Too early in the day for drinking Scotch. His army general's eyes sweeping the field of fire, examining the battle zone evolving, peering into the president's distinguished gray eyes, where the perimeters are. What is about to be breached, Pug? From a ledge in his brain, he hears Barbers *Adagio for Strings*, mournful, despairing. Bringing his mood to an unexpected, dreadful level. Approaching a terrain of political mud and pending harsh disappointment, indeed—that's what he sees stalking the battle zone—deep disappointment.

Pug saying, "Troubling stuff?"

"You... ah... you might say... *very* troubling. Yes. But there are other words I would use."

"Depressing?"

"*Hurtful.*"

Tommy Rand does not want to hear his voice pronounce *that* word. That word roaming around in some fearsome thicket in his head. But he will have to purge it soon, undoubtedly. Cleanse his mind with some strong incense and toxic cleaning solutions. He finishes half his scotch. Hears the happy Junco tweeting. Wants to jump up and check on his carefree buddy out there, where the air is clear, where there is some space to fly, where you can land wherever and not suffer. Instead, he feels cramped. A million ropes binding body and brain, the United States president now finds it harder to breathe. Wig-less, long-faced Ben staring down at him, he knows. Judging the president and saying, you must do this, Tom. Keep going. For the sake of history. Friend or no friend. Former college roommate or not.

Pug says, "You lose sleep?"

"Much. I did. Nothing could put me down. Booze. Xanax. Ambien. Bad. I wanted to climb out of my body and jump off a cliff. Nothing works."

"How 'bout Smith and Wesson?" They grin. "Have you had—?"

"Yes," Tommy says, "of course. I have."

"Perhaps this conversation will allay the matter."

"Fact is, I think it's going to make it *worse*, in the end."

Over the parapet again. Another perimeter busted.

DeJean nods. That does not sound good, does it, Pug? When he stashed his chewing gum and stood at the door, he thought he might be going in for an update on Deadlight, perhaps a big *viva*. No, no viva today. So, now, the tension has not lifted; it has *descended,* thickened. He tilts forward, puts the glass under his nose, settles it softly on the coaster. Then he dips his thumb in the glass, sucks the scotch. His pudgy fingers form a triangle. The nail cuts into his lower lip but stops, Pug afraid of drawing blood. He starts a short prayer, praying for something *not* to be said.

"I'm here, T.R. To listen to what you have to say." He sees a muscle in the president's jaw pulsing. His temples throbbing.

Five seconds of silence.

Then, the president says, fast—"As of right now, I am *disconnecting* from Deadlight."

Gut punch. Busted through the parapet.

There, it's out there. Hanging in the air for dissection.

Five seconds of silence so loud the bulletproof glass's going to shatter.

Then, from Pug, the hiss an angry beast makes before it bares its teeth and rips your head off.

The president has constructed a balanced declaratory sentence for Pug to discern, to digest. No fuzzy-wuzzy grammatical chicanes, not a thicket of words skirting around adverbial potholes, squinty punctuations, no tense confusion. And just one lonesome comma to curate a streamlined bolt into Pug's ears. Succinct. Harsh.

Pen-e-tray-ting.

But Pug's mind has made no effort yet to digest what the president has just stated. He is braindead.

Okay, so, Pug's brain engine is a bit low on motor oil and not fully hitched to the clarity of the words that just ambled over the bowl of pretty pears. The words—particularly *disconnecting*—slam Pug's tympanic membrane, then forge ahead unrestrained, a high-speed bullet train flying over a crumb of ear wax, into the auditory ossicles, and taking, maybe, two nanoseconds to breach the final layer of misunderstanding. An explosive finale in the primary auditory cortex. The place that sorts the mail when the bad news arrives.

Pug has more than a faint notion of what lies ahead. Oh yes, he does.

Even so. The room, the Oval Office, becomes vacuous, foreign. Pug, dangerously low on oxygen, getting that tingle in the solar plexus.

He feels duped.

He leans into the president.

The president thinks Pug's starting to look like a ripe cherry. He could explode and mess up him, Benjamin Franklin, the office.

"I don't believe," says Pug, "what I just heard—*disconnecting* you said?"

"Disconnecting, yes."

At that moment, Pug cannot think of anything expressive to utter his shock. He stares into the president's eyes, tries to pull out a morsel for clarification. For a long time, Pug doesn't move. The president doesn't move. Only the room moves; it spins. Like a Ferris Wheel, the colorful static horses amuck, prancing around in a never-ending crazy, circular pattern going nowhere. Then Pug's left eye twitches, and he feels primitive, abandoned. Something ugly, mulish, has gotten its jaws around his ankle and will not let go. The noisome tone has enveloped the room, the very air.

The president saying, "I know you can't comprehend what I have just said—but..." Now the president puts his body into it, settles his glass on the table, elbows on knees. "For the last six weeks, people in the cabinet, a few three- and four-stars, couple of senators, congressmen, have said to me, 'You have to fire that son-of-a-bitch. Cut this off at the head, Mister President. No Army officer in the history of this country has done what he is doing. He's not *apolitical*!' I really had to bust my ass, preventing that from happening until today. But on the other hand, I have to say: you are undoubtedly the most ambitious general that put on an Army uniform. And, I imagine, aside from General Patton, probably the most egotistical general to take a piss in the Pentagon. Up to now, okay. But no longer. How you ever imagined you could sustain what you will do *beyond* what you *are* doing now and still carry yourself through retirement—I can't... No general has ever gotten away with what you are attempting. And I am sure it's your enormous popularity across this country that lifts your boat every morning to new egotistical heights—Tweets, Facebook,

Podcasts, Instagram. And those damned Movement rallies with that saluting. Bad form, Pug. You farted in the Pentagon."

"Are you dumping out what's keeping you up at night, T.R.?"

"*Mister President, general!*"

"Oh! Okay, *sir*," says Pug, and he stiffens. His knife hand comes up, a vicious blade, and he *salutes* the president of the United States. He stands and looks down at the man he has known for forty years. So, this is where this is going.

The president grins, but the look passes.

The president saying, "*Sit down*, general. Gotta bit of a journey here."

Pug, mortally wounded, the couch awash in Pug blood and fragments of hope.

He flops onto the couch. Grabs his glass and finishes the Dewar's. It is now not too early for a few throwbacks.

President Rand saying, "In the beginning, I thought Deadlight would work, yes, I did, would avoid bloodshed, a larger division across the country. I thought, if contained to the Fourteen if they wanted to secede from the Union, I thought it would have a calming effect, take down some of the heat across the country. But then, I came to see it, under *your* leadership, general, as ascending into insurrection, revolution, treason sedition, and—""Pick one."

"All of the above. All rolled into one big fat, festering shit boil. A lesion growing out of control under your direction that will explode and sully the entire USA."

The general raises his hand.

"Wait a minute. Is this the same president that helped *initiate* Deadlight, that was all in, that I had spent days at Camp David locked in a secret room, feeling his pride swelling in his veins because he thought his vision, that would allow the Fourteen to secede from the Union, that it would be a bold stroke to bring this country together—"

"Don't go any further. The answer is *yes*, the *same* man—but *enlightened.* A man who woke up at night saw a clusterfuck that would benefit one four-star general and *not* the United States. Now. I see you got some Proud Boys spread out in your ranks, chompin' at the bit. Sprinkled here and there throughout the ranks of your National Guard units. Right-wingers, white power wearing Army camouflage, aching for something like this. Can't have that, Pug."

"So now, cold feet. Or you just turned into a plain ol' pussy."

"I've *learned* a lot between then and now. About me. *You.*"

"You mean you have spied on me?"

"Your plan to completely encircle the Fourteen states that want to secede with your National Guard troops and then march across the United States of America—

"Who told you that?"

"Irrelevant. Your plan is out there. I've seen it—a blueprint to take over the United States."

"You're out of your mind. You're crazy."

"You are planning a coup d'état, general, is now plain to see. And prepared to take *me* out—the *hurtful* part. After all these years. You are using your National Guard forces to—"

"You are insane, you really are."

"When I looked at it hard, I saw disloyalty, an egotistical four-star that wants to reestablish the rank of general-in-chief, *above* the presidency, and put the country under his command."

"Where did you conjure this bullshit?"

"Never mind."

"I can't believe this is happening. That you are throwing horse-shit at me, using the words you are using *against* me. We were *one* till this moment. I thought—"

"The Fourteen seceding, yes, but not the rest. It is what it is. And no matter what—" The president stands, takes his glass to the credenza, and fills it, saying, "I'm fucked." And Ben Franklin up there staring at him, *not* disagreeing. No matter what you do, Mister President, you will go down in history as the president who committed treason. You were seditious.

General DeJean says, "You pulled resources on me, didn't you, you duplicitous pussy. You got CIA, NSA, DIA, others, put them on me."

"Incorrect. *They* came to *me* with incriminating—no, *hurtful*—data. Unequivocal. Hardcore."

There, that word is out there, *hurtful*. Slammed your ego, your old friend Pug did.

Pug says, "They gave you—"

"Conversations. Video. Emails. Phone intercepts. They even pulled down some data off the satellites. Incriminating."

The Junco trills again, but not loud enough to distract Pug.

This does not make the general slump back again. No, it stiffens him. The cock bristling his feathers. Showing his talons. "Why are you doing this to me? To *me*?"

"I thought if a group of states wanted to abandon the Union, to secede, so be it. We did; the United States did. Kicked the Brits out, gave them a boot in the ass because we saw a vision for ourselves *without* them—a course of honor. Then, I get these reports, and DeJean, he's squat in the middle, planning to use Deadlight as a springboard and unleash your National Guard troops across the country to assert command and control—you have four-hundred thousand troops, tanks, the Air National Guard air force—and march here, to the White House. Over *four hundred thousand* Guardsmen at your command! You could invade a country."

Pug stands. "I have to leave."

"*Sit* down. Not done here, general!"

"Well, then, *get* done."

"During one of those sleepless nights, I opened my iPad, just casually reading anything. Came across an interesting—a speech from President Kennedy, who you saw a moment ago in this office. You should have taken that visage more to heart, what the man stood for. His grace and the grace he wanted to pass on to all of us. In that speech, he quoted what Pericles said to the Athenians, long true of this commonwealth: 'We do not *imitate*—for we are a *model* to others.' That's what turned it around. That's when I realized I made an irrevocable mistake. The Fourteen, Deadlight, they are *not* models for others. I could not let that happen. Simple as that."

Pug says, "And item number three on the—?"

"You were going to take *me* out and give yourself the title of General-In-Chief, a title not used since General Wilford Gary assigned it to himself during the Civil War."

"'Old Fuss and Feathers.'"

"No. Old *coup d'tat*."

The president reaches into his jacket pocket and takes out a sheet of paper, saying, "You me, we will be found guilty of insurrection against lawful authority. And if that word is not to your liking, you can pick another: coup d'état, or, putsch, one often associated with Hitler and the Nazis." He unfolds the paper and reads, "Insurrection: 'to conspire to overthrow, put down, or to destroy by force the Government of the United States, or to levy war against them, or to oppose by force the authority thereof, or by force to prevent, hinder or delay the execution of any law of the United States, or by force to seize, take or possess any property of the United States contrary to the authority thereof.'"

The president sits down on the couch, throws back another gulp.

Says, "This is the end for me. I'm implicated right down to my socks, no matter what. When you leave here, despite my about-face on the matter, I will be accused of sedition, high treason. Insurrection. Incitement to rebellion. Then marched to a scaffold and hung. Or, shot by firing squad. Me, my presidency—we're finished here. Burnt offerings."

Pug stands, says, "I'm leaving. Deadlight goes ahead with you or without you. That's the way it was formulated. You, A.G., the others—they all know that."

"General, I am ordering you to rescind your orders for Deadlight."

"Can't do that, Mister President."

"*Must* do that."

"Train has *left* the station, *sir*."

"Be mindful. You are disobeying an order from your Commander-in-Chief."

"Sacrifice must be made. Deadlight has a Red N.R. tag, which you also know. A Red No Rescind Order. Soon, the drones will launch, and no one, nothing, will stop them. Not even the hand of the Lord Jesus Christ. And you can't turn me in, you'd implicate yourself."

T.R. nods, says, "I have no intention of turning you in. That's too easy. Too time-consuming. I have something more immediate in mind. Something historic."

General DeJean steps toward the door and the president goes around the Resolute desk and sits in his leather chair and says before Pug can grab the door handle: "I figured you would press on, not listen to me."

"Should I weep now or later?"

General DeJean stops before reaching the door, turns, faces the president, rocking slowly.

"So," the president says, "we have an alternative plan to match your arrogance."

H reaches into a drawer in the Resolute desk, pulls out a mahogany box, places it softly in front of him.

The president saying, "There's a Marine Corps master sergeant outside that door. Name's Neil Paak. Real kick-ass kinda guy all bulked up. Two Purples. One Silver. One Bronze, with Oakleaves. Sniper. Sixty-eight kills. He's got a Beretta on his hip. Devoted to me. Will escort you to *his* limo, *not* yours, sit side-by-side with you and his big gun and take you to your office in the Pentagon"—he checks his watch. "It's ten-fourteen—three-and-a-half miles to the Pentagon. No traffic. You'll be there in fifteen minutes. Do what I am about to tell you to do, and you will be back here in this office around eleven-fifteen. When you arrive at the Pentagon, Paak will escort you to your office. You will draw a sheet of your letterhead stationery and pen your resignation. *Pen it in your hand*, not type it. And no bullshit about resigning to spend more time with your family because we know you don't have a family. Give me something else. Resigning for health reasons—you got shingles, hemorrhoids, or some shit, I don't care, whatever. Then, Paak will escort you here to the Oval Office, and you will hand the letter to me. If I'm not here, pass it to Paak to give to me. Now—and I want you to remember this—"

Pug says, "Deadlight will work with me or without me."

Then he steps to the door.

He almost gets there.

The president opens the lid of the box and lifts a Heckler & Koch P2000 SK automatic pistol.

Then he picks up the telephone and smashes it against his left eyebrow, and a spit of blood flows over his hand onto the desk.

DeJean saying, "*What the hell are you...*?

The president saying, "After your lying there dead, the room's going to fill with security, Secret Service. And I'm going to be standing here holding this pistol saying you threatened me, that we fought, you punched me in the head. I managed to get my gun that I was showing you to protect myself and shot you. They'll check the furniture, the chair you banged into, the couch you fell on. They will see that those pieces of furniture have been moved. Each of the legs sits on a white dot. So they know where to replace them after moving them for photo ops. They'll see the legs off those dots and assume a struggle indeed did occur. They'll find cracks in the couch's legs."

Blood dripping down the president's jaw onto his shirt.

Pug turns, goes for the door handle. To get away from the nightmare.

But then he stops cold.

The general's ear hears the unmistakable sound of steel sliding on oiled steel.

The slide on the H.K.

The sound stops him.

That sound, oh boy, Pug, the Army general doth know *that sound*!

He turns.

Faces the president.

Faces the biggest gun barrel he has ever seen.

Tommy saying, "Touch the door handle, and this bad boy's going to toss a nine-mill, blow your face all over that polished doorknob you're fixing to grab."

Pug grins.

Saying, "Tommy, you don't have stones big enough."

Turns the knob, and the door closes behind him.

The president slumps into his chair.

He puts the pistol down on the desk. Blots his brow with a

handkerchief, swipes the blood dripping from his chin. He swivels away from DeJean's exit. Banishes the picture in his mind.

Wondering what happened to the Junco, his buddy?

Where did he go?

How lucky. To just *leave* like that. On a whim. A little bird. Away.

But no trilling, Tom, says Ben Franklin.

Then T.R. pulls the oily slide back again for a peek.

Enough to see, *yes*, there is a round in the pipe ready to go, Tommy.

5
DEFENDER

Rayne, exhausted, behind the wheel of the Audi A4 Leland provided while she boiled in the tub at the *Vier Jahreszeiten Kempinski* hotel. Two blocks from where Myles did his jack-in-the-box and entered the ionosphere. His BMW exploding, pedestrians torn. Body parts pasted to walls, the street, but somehow leaving the lovely Opera Fountain intact.

Dissolve that thought—eyes on the road.

The *Wolfacherstrasse* road on the sat nav leading to Bad Rippoldsau-Shapbach, the site of the Ochsenwirtshof Hotel. She glances down at the passenger side footwell. There, Myles's blood-stained briefcase. The stains could pass for a splash or two of coffee. No hand attached. The tenacious grip would not let go, but the kid on the bike wiggled it off, and it flopped and skidded along, slathering the sidewalk.

And Rayne, instead of mourning for the dead and the man detached from the hand, Myles Lane, sat with watery eyes over lost love and tapping out a futile text in water hot enough to melt a grilled cheese sandwich. Lotta empathy. Thinking of yourself. Still no response from him, and that was, what, two hours ago. Probably with someone prettier, the perfect shade of lipstick, and smells *erogenous*.

You do not smell erogenous. Not now.

What, Rayne wonders, is worse than waiting for a text when you want one, huh? Waiting for love to *return*? Waiting for a chilly kiss? A frosty hug?

She checks the rearview mirror and thinks she sees herself reflected

Oh no!

But certainly not you. Not Rayne Foster.

Nausea coming on. The pain where the spider shrapnel hit her in the jaw throbbing. The wound in the knee, hot. The meds dwindling. She needs a Tylenol. No! A Xanax *and* a Bushmills *and someone* to drop their arms around me. But who would fall in love with someone looking like that woman in the mirror? Who would offer comfort?

Lightheaded now.

Okay, Rayne, just keep driving and get ready for another cock-eyed day. You can do that. Just don't look at the rearview mirror.

She looks again.

And here is the green Defender again—or is it black?—tagging along, or just coincidence? Far enough back to vanish after a curve, then back again in the rearview mirror, and no way Rayne can determine who is driving. The intention? The driver's skills at the wheel? So, she evaluates the vehicle based on what it appears to be: a 1994 Land Rover Defender, four-door. Transmission type: unknown. Question: can it outrun Rayne's Audi AF. Probably not.

Rayne, why not give it a shot—try to blow off the vehicle. Revisit your driving skills.

Checks the mirror. Defender absent.

She double-clutches, drops the gear, slams the accelerator.

Ahead, a blue and white sign says *Reutlingen*, and just beyond a sweeping curve in the road, something she can handle, the speedometer hitting 150 kph and the engine giving her the sound she *loves*—a high-whine, refined exhaust notes. Looking for an opportunity. And then a dirt road for farm equipment cutting over a stream and through a berm.

Braking hard, the ABS stuttering, tires smoking. Then she yanks it hard right, and she's on the road and skidding on the grass and stopping under a drooping White Pine.

Silence.

Five seconds.

Nothing.

A Meadow Pipit flies off a branch.

Four seconds.

Rayne breathing a little harder, thinking when she gets to the hotel, she has to call Leland.

Three seconds.

And there flies the Defender, over the horizon, and gone. Green it is, yes.

She slumps, drifts onto another plateau. One equally imprecise as the Defender's intention.

Five items circling her brain, five persistent planets in her universe trying to gain priority (1) the jaw pain and knee throb (2) No bona fides issued in Prague (3) Who was driving the Defender, and what was the driver's intent? (4) Was he/she following me? Just coincidence? And (5) No Text message from Christian Largo. Maybe I'll never get one ever again or hear his voice. This is crushing me.

Then the excuses abound: The wound in her chin and knee will dwindle and care for themselves. No bona fides from Lee is a significant issue. It could only mean he put this private operation together so quickly he had no time to issue Rayne the protection of a cover: Passport, driver's license, Social Security card, Medicare, counterfeit employee badge, ID, and so on. But not in Prague. Her paranoia tells her Leland Upchurch is off on his own. This thing he has set her off on is out of *his* pocket. Rayne, you know how dangerous this is? Of course, you do. Perhaps Leland wants no record of this mission he's set you off on.

As soon as she left the Munich city limits, she drove onto E52, following the sat nav, going west by northwest, the pre-programmed instructions Leland gave one of his ghosts to input. After a mile or so out of the city limits, she pushed her foot down on the accelerator and cranked it until the speedometer hit 175 kph—110 mph

She forgets the Defender and drives back onto E52.

Eyes on the road, and she opens a mental note pad in her brain—a pen. No, wait, use a pencil with an eraser to make changes. Then, she starts writing in her head while she drives:

- L meets R in Prague
- L normal? ~~Yes~~? No. Fidgety. Stress?
- Happy to see me? ~~Yes~~. Sorta
- A bit ~~apprehensive~~? Nervous, jittery? Yes?
- Chitchat, etc. ~~Normal~~? No. Clipped. Distant.
- Lunch, sandwiches
- L ~~Asks~~ Wants favor. Can you do L big favor? Something personal?

- ~~L says "not exactly~~" Is business or personal. No responsibility
- What favor
- Can you meet a friend of L's in Munich
- L does not know what he wants but needs help
- College classmate
- Myles Lane. Good man
- Myles and Simon Lane, brothers
- Inherited LaneAeroTech from father
- Myles silent partner w/Simon
- Major mil. drone manufact
- Was CIA whole career. Now… loan to NSA. What's that about?
- Air kiss then bye
- R leaves Prague. No bona fides
- THIS ONE IS OFF THE BOARDS!! CAUTION!!!!!!!!!
- Lee rogue!!!!
- No SAFETY net!!!!
- Personal favor!!
- R bait?!!???
- CAUTION!!
- R bait!!

She puts away the imaginary pad and pencil—Peeks at the mirror.

Still scary. You look like a German rabbit—a Rhinelander Buck. Butterfly markings, cheek spots, eye circles.

And the other question, Rayne: Why are you working a *favor*? And why didn't *you* ask Leland for bona fides before *you* left Prague, because now you are out here flying around like a damned raggedy Ann flipping flopping thoughts and no real idea what's up, what's down. So, if shit happens, who's to blame? The Rhinelander rabbit. Oh yeah!

If Leland did this arranging so fast, this car you are driving and provided *partial* bona fides because he did not have that much time, then why didn't he arrange a complete profile in Prague when he had time? Leland is more efficient than that.

But the wound in her jaw throbbing back, like a toothache, numbing the right side of her face and going down her neck to her shoulder.

She thinks of her apartment in New York City. She could pull the sheets over her head and sleep for a quarter-century.

Back to the driving.

The A4 is a sleek and thoroughly competent vehicle suited to her driving skills, trolling the pancake-flat L96 roadway twenty-five miles east of Bad Rippoldsau-Schapbach, twin towns in the Black Forest. Rayne thinking of wine and bedsheets, not even a shower. Just sleep.

That destination is indicated on the sat-nav system, noting her passage now through the picturesque town of *Freudenstadt*, with its ginger-bready window-planter-box homes snugging the sloping mountains either side of the manicured road. The dense, towering Christmas tree scented Silver Junipers and Scots Pines.

Then within ten seconds, Rayne is beyond *Freudnstadt's* Christmas card margins, batting away a craving for a massive wedge of Black Forest chocolate cake in the charming bakery that just blurred past.

Rayne recalling that character in August Wilson's play *Joe Turner's Come and Gone* who says:

> everyone's got a song inside of him or her, and you can lose sight of that song at your peril. And if you get out of touch with your song or forget how to sing the song or forget the lyrics, you're bound to end up frustrated and displeased, because you have no tune or lyric to follow.

A character in that play recollects a time when he was out of touch with his song, and he says, "Something wasn't making my heart smooth and easy."

Okay.

Right now, there is something more substantial to ponder than a distant lover.

Rayne thinking after I get to the hotel, I'm calling Leland.

Tell him that, yes, I know the lyrics, but I just can't sing them anymore.

Because I keep hearing that *other* song.

I'm in a New York state of mind.

* * *

Presently at 2:10 p.m., a Lufthansa Airbus brakes to a halt at a passenger portal at Munich Airport. The cabin door swings open, and the first passenger steps out—a short man, a redhead, lightly freckled with a five-inch quiff. He's stocky, late-fifties, wearing a grey hounds-tooth jacket, no tie. He is sullen, has a slight waddle in his steps, a mannerism that distinguishes him from the other passengers hastening behind.

Simon Lane is impatient and insolent. Shows it with a quick inhale, sort of a grumble and a grunt. His staff at LaneAeroSystems in Yonkers, New York, know the sound. They run for cover when they hear it like they would from an impending bombing attack from the air.

Now, exiting the airway, he takes up his smartphone, notes the time—fifteen minutes late—taps into the Munich Airport app showing the Fly Away Café, the place he arranged to meet Meese Van Der Leeuwen.

Look at him: collegial traits, an intellect superior to people moving around him. After graduating from Harvard, he taught there for one year. There, he earned a Master's in engineering. Enrolled at the Massachusetts Institute of Technology. Received a Masters of Aeronautical Science, immersing himself in such intricate subjects as Aerodynamics of Viscous Fluids, Stochastic Estimation and Control, Rocket and Space Propulsion, and Numerical Methods for Partial Differential Equations, and so on. This immersion in the impenetrable and cryptic subjects that he relished did not burden his interest in chemical engineering and the mysteries of explosive formulas and nuclear fission; it was his hobby. He was brainsick for chemistry, science, and mathematics. He took an around-the-world cruise on a tramp steamer working as a freight handler and dishwasher when he was done with this abundance and scope of learning.

Upon returning, he deposited all his clothes in a Salvation Army dumpster, took a train down to Manhattan, and bought a new wardrobe at J. Press, just across the street from Brooks Brothers. Three days later, on Thanksgiving Day, his father ate an ample helping of turkey and dressing at the family's dining room table, burped loudly, then fell face flat in a bowl of delicious homemade gravy. One month later, Simon and his younger brother, Myles Lane, inherited their father's faltering business, LaneAeroTech, in Yonkers, New York.

Simon reluctantly takes a seat at the café but does not have time to eat.

Less than a minute later, Meese Van Der Leeuwen looks down at him, says, "You're late."

"I'm always late. Get used to it."

Van Der Leeuwen starts to pull a chair for himself. Could use a pretzel and a beer.

Simon Lane stands, says, "Don't. Let's get going."

Three minutes to walk through the passenger terminal and they arrive at Van Der Leeuwen's olive green Mercedes G 550 SUV *Geländewagen*, a polish on it could light a baseball stadium. The license plates are the standard German blue and white with an M designation for a *München* registration. As they go, Meese notes Simon's peculiar five-inch quiff bobbing in synch with each stride. It seems to have ascended since they last met.

Meese pays the toll, drives them out of the garage, follows a road sign that says the Black Forest.

"Maybe," Meese says, turning the radio on, "after you take a nap, you can update me on Deadlight."

Simon nods, barely.

After a minute, Simon thinks he hears Meese softly humming *The Music of the Night* from *Phantom of the Opera*.

Simon says, looking out over the hood, "Would you do me a favor?"

"What?"

"Stop humming. It's annoying and musically inaccurate."

"In a terrific mood today, Simon? Morning sunlight warmed your soul?"

"Get used to it."

Meese reaches for the radio dial and settles on Munich's Hardest Hits—an eclectic taste Meese has. This, not to Simon's liking. He looks at Meese like he is crazy for choosing that music. He calls it "innocuous rabble-rousing music. Unnecessary."

Simon saying, "Let me. . ."

His fingers play a staccato with the radio dial, left, right, finally settling on BR *Klassik* FM 103.2 – Munich. *Zeit für Musik* (Time for Music). Ah, yes! Ravel's *Pavane for a Dead Princess*, the London Symphony. Perfect. Finally. His favorite rendering. He's happy.

Meese saying, "I'm going to fall asleep with that on."

"Let me know before you do." He closes his eyes, slips down on the creamy black leather, loosens his knit tie.

Meese saying, "Did you ever think your business could do better if you had a more pleasant demeanor?"

Simon shakes his head, *no*.

They will be close to the underground bunker in two hours, where the drones sleep in secret side-by-side with their odd names painted on their vicious, razor-sharp noses.

The drones Simon Lane and his company took two years to manufacture.

Drones Simon designed himself.

Going to score the biggest score of his life.

* * *

Twenty minutes later, Rayne turns into the parking area of the Hotel-Ochsenwirtshof.

The structure sits on the side of a gently sloping hill in a shallow valley of tall, svelte pines and firs. Either side of the hotel, a meandering tree line and occasional mountain homes with cheerful window boxes and blooming flowers. The area trimmed with perfectness.

Parked next to the main entrance, there it is, the green Defender. So, it wasn't following you Rayne, you paranoid puppy. Merely a coincidence coming here, the same hotel.

She turns in, parks next to the Defender, grabs her bags. Hobbles up a short flight of stone steps into the lobby area. At the receptionist's desk, she drops her bags and rings the bell.

Juta, the owner, dressed in a dirndl, appears. Not the usual cheery reception.

"Rayne Foster?"

"Yes."

"Your friend called ahead for you. You are all checked in. Please, fill this card out, and I will need your passport. Also, he said you would give me something to put into my safe."

Rayne hands Juta a paper shopping bag containing Myles' briefcase. Then she places the passport on the desk

And Juta says, "I am sorry for your loss."

Rayne looks up into Juta's teary eyes. "What loss? What are you talking about?"

Juta says, "Oh, I mean—"

Then she reaches for the television remote, aims it, and the TV on the desk lights up, showing CNN.

Juta saying, "Oh, God, you didn't know? I'm so sorry. Your president, he has committed suicide."

6
TEN-THOUSAND SIOUX, LAKOTA, APACHE, AND ONE BREVET GENERAL GOLDIE LOCKS

New York City, NY – 10:16 p.m.

A courier from C.D.L. Breakaway Courier Services halts his motor scooter at the Fox News building, Forty-Seventh, and Sixth, opposite Radio City Music Hall where the Easter Bunny hops in seasonally.

He parks the scooter in a space saved for bicycles and scooters. Removes the strap attached to his facsimile World War I gas mask bag, containing one item—a white Number 10 envelope without a return address.

Then, he dashes through torrential rain toward the lobby—circles through the revolving door. Three uniformed security guards stiffen as he walks up to them at the reception desk; they don't take their eyes off him. He flops the dripping wet bag on the marble top.

"Got somethin for a Mister Gilbert Scott."

"Okay," the guard behind the counter says, dropping a clipboard and pen next to the courier pouch. "Fill this out, sign it, we'll get it to him ASAP."

The courier says, "Can't do that."

"What do you mean, 'can't do that?' That's Fox protocol."

"You got Fox protocol, and I got *me* protocol. Have to *hand* it to Mister Scott direct. Gotta see his employee ID, driver's license, then *he* has to sign. He signs he gets the prize in the Cracker Jack box."

"That's not the way it's done here, bro'."

"Then Mister Gilbert Scott's gonna be disappointed he didn't get whatever it is he's supposed to get, and who knows where it flies from there."

Courier points his finger to the ceiling, where the suits work.

Oh. Guard nods, *okay, I get it.* Picks up a house phone, taps four digits.

Everybody standing there picking their noses, checking their nails.

The courier takes out a handkerchief, soaks rainwater dripping from his face, dries his goggles, saying, "It's a bitch out there."

Behind them, the largest TV monitor the courier has ever seen showing the story of the president's suicide.

The courier looking at the TV, says, "Terrible. Just terrible."

Everyone doing the donkey nod, *yes.*

Then the guard says into the phone, "Is this Gilbert Scott?" Silence. "Sir, there's a courier here has something for you." Silence. "No, no. He won't do that. Says he needs to *hand* it to you *after* you show employee ID. Oh, and he also needs your driver's license too."

Then the guard looks at the courier— "Mister Scott wants to know what it is you have for him."

Courier says, "Hey, not my monkey, not my circus. I only *dee-liver.*"

Guard says, "Can you give him a solid, a good *general* idea of what it is you have for Mister Scott?"

Courier says, "Sure." He opens the flap on the courier bag, reaches in, slides out a white, sealed, Scotch-taped Number 10 Envelope addressed to G. Scott in black Sharpie, no return address. Places it on the courier pouch. Like he's handling dynamite.

Guard stares at it like it's a urine sample.

Courier says, "That's it, my man. No bomb. No anthrax."

Guard says, "I understand."

Courier says, "I deliver to you, what, two, three times a week, why you giving me a rash here?"

"No rash. It's not *you*. Don't take this personally."

"Just doing my job. What they taught me at Harvard Business School."

Everyone thinks that's the funniest thing they ever heard from a courier; they laugh.

Guard says into the phone to Mr. Scott, "It's a standard white envelope, sealed. Says G. Scott. I don't think it's a document inside. Might be a USB flash drive the way the outline is shaped on the envelope," Pause. "Yes, sir."

The guard hangs up.

"He's coming down. Want some caffeine?"

"No, thanks, I'm good."

Forty-five seconds pass, the courier watching the orange status floor numbers decreasing. Then, bingo, the shiny steel doors slide open, and, *ladies and gentlemen, please give it up for Gilbert Scott, anchor of* FoxNewsNow! Here's Gilbert, stepping out of the elevator walking to the reception desk, wearing red suspenders and Fox News cufflinks. Hair too perfect.

Gilbert's not holding down a two-hour weekday gig like Hannity or Ingraham. His gig's a two-minute news insert at ten, twenty, forty, and fifty on the clock with a commercial break into the middle, then news heads, financial, weather, and the latest whack-a-doodle conspiracy theory they are plying that evening. And for that, Scott nails down about a buck ninety a year. Glorious gig. No stress. But he wants an anchor gig. Not for the coin. The prestige. And those gigs, they are impossible to score. He's worried. He is getting dangerously close to his sell-before-date.

Unless.

Because only the best, handsomest, most beautiful with the best dentistry and the bluest of blue eyes get those gigs and grab millions of bucks, and Gil's indeed not down for one at the network. The line goes all way to Radio City Music Hall. Probably includes the Easter Bunny before Gil. So, Gil's professionally hungry, and perhaps that's why he's so thin. He thinks *maybe* he should bulk up, eat more. Get away from the scarecrow silhouette look and that gooseneck he has. Looks good on the beach, Gil, but in front of a camera? You like a bone a vulture forgot on a road.

Gilbert Scott walking to the guards' station now like a ghost that hasn't eaten in weeks. He is sorta wispy, thinks the courier. Got a head on his shoulders, looks like a muffin top, high hair. Still has makeup and a bib because he's down for three more inserts before he shifts out. The courier's seen him a hundred times on Fox. But this dude looks thinner, and behind his back, they call him the Goose. Has a coupla pock marks made years ago by, the courier guesses, serious acne. But ten pounds of makeup fill the craters in nicely for HD TV, the lighting, the camera angle, little things like that cover up flaws in television. These days with the technology, you can see nose hairs curling at you.

Scott approaches the courier.

Before he comes to a halt, the courier notes way too much Walmart cologne preceding Gil Scott. And the courier is sure Scott's head is a pedestal for a costly rug, probably more than the courier makes in three months.

"Whatcha got?"

The courier taps the thin envelope resting on his pouch. A drop of rainwater or snot falls from the tip of his nose and splotches the **S**, so now the **S** looks like a drunken ***8***.

Gilbert Scott reaches for the envelope.

"*Whoa, dude*!" says the courier, hands up like stop signs. "Gotta sign for this puppy first, my man."

"*Oh*. Yeah."

Scott places his driver's license on the counter.

Courier goes inside his anorak and pulls out a wrinkled receipt with the C.D.L. Breakaway Courier Services logo.

Gilbert Scott has pen in hand, a gold Cross ballpoint for outstanding news reporting or something he cannot remember. Twisting the top of the barrel to get the ball exposed, signs the receipt, holds up the envelope to the ceiling lights so he can see inside. Then saying, "No nuclear device in there!"

All laugh. Except the courier. Heard that a dozen times.

Courier says, "Have a good night, guys."

"Thanks. You too."

Satisfied, the courier throws the pouch strap over his head and hastens to the downpour and his water-soaked scooter. Before he gets to the revolving doors before, he grabs his scooter key, he stops, glances at the TV monitor showing a smiling President Tommy Rand caught mid-wave somewhere in a parking lot in Houston, Texas, days before he let his brains loose all over the historic Resolute Desk. The courier decides to take a break, wait out the downpour. He presses his back against a column and slides down. He settles on the Lotus position on the floor, starts to meditate. His sadness swelling: *why would a dude like that kill himself?*

Then he closes his eyes.

Yeah, man, that's what the entire planet wants to know.

Why did the President of the United States kill himself?

At the tenth floor, the Goose steps off the elevator, wondering what's so essential it's delivered at 10 p.m. He wants his Manhattan apartment and a couple of Bud Lites and the leftover cold anchovy pizza he had saved for when he got home tonight, too lazy to heat it.

He enters his office, closes the door, rips open the envelope.

He jiggles it and out slides a black USB SanDisk memory stick. Written in black Sharpie the letters **CJ 1 of 1**. Scotch-taped to it, a Post It Note: ***Raw, uncut.*** Meaning, as is or unedited. No B roll or any effects.

He grins.

Maybe he's got a scoop going here in his hand. A scoop would be good. Would look great on his show reel. Work him towards the big desk somewhere.

And Gilbert Scott, the Goose, will take a feather for his rug, too, thank you. And—*hold on for a sec, Gil.*

Doncha' think you better check out what's on the memory stick before you—

Yeah, thinking I better.

He stuffs the memory stick into his pant's pocket and hastens to the elevator. Checks his watch. Only eighty-eight seconds before his next 'cast.

At 11:03, Gilbert Scott closes the door to his office.

He reaches into his pants pocket, takes up the SanDisk, and goes to insert it into his desktop computer.

He's so excited, he's a got a little finger shake.

Then he puts on the brakes. *Screeeeeeeech.*

Whoa!

Think about this, Gil: You stick the stick in the drive, fire up the PC, the world, sooner or later, will have access to it—to *you*. It goes out there, and it never comes back. And your ass will look and smell like ten-day-old roadkill no matter what. Besides, you have no idea what's on the stick yet. You could be down for some looney-headed moron wanting to blackmail you and Fox News. Then you can say tooloo to the career. No anchor gig, and you'll be reading news heads on the overnight at a Mom and Pop ten-thousand-watter in Slow-poke, Maine.

Chill.

Gilbert does not insert the SanDisk into his desktop.

He pulls up his personal black Lenovo he bought a week ago, twenty off, at Best Buy on Third Avenue. Places it on his desk, flips the top open, fires it up.

Thirty seconds and he's got the screen demanding his password, and *damnation*! he can't remember it! *God damn passwords*!

He rummages around in his brain, and by a landslide miracle, he nails the password:

Pussyaintcheap$$

Then: if someone comes into my office now, they're gonna wonder what I'm doing here after my shift because I usually leave here faster than the Tōkaidō Shinkansen bullet train in Japan shooting for a coast-to-coast record.

Slams the laptop lid, calls for an Uber, takes the elevator down to the lobby, waves goodnight to the guard reading the *Post*.

Ten minutes later, Gil, the Goose's in his apartment at Sixty-eighth and Third. A bit sterile. Sorta like his life.

He gets comfy, cozy at his dining room table, pops a Bud Lite, turns on the laptop, waits a minute. Then—

He inserts the SanDisk into a USB port—

The screen's black then flickers snowy white. The USB port's pulsing tiny green. Yes, he's got activity, and then—

He can hear the small drive purring, the little fan fanning.

He waits.

Nothing.

Maybe this's a joke?

Hey, there's no slate at the head of this video, Gil, no ID, no date, no time code. No camera roll data. You got cow poop here, pal!

This is *not* a pro job.

This has been shot by some bunny rabbit with a simple iPhone, a 35 mm camera—*a toaster oven, maybe*!

Just raw video shot with who-knows-what and showing a flickering black screen.

Gil getting mightily pissed off here!

But then—

Bingo.

There, four-star General César "Pug" DeJean on Gilbert Scott's twenty off Lenovo from Best Buy. DeJean kicked back in a blue terry bathrobe. Bare feet on a hassock, sitting on a couch hoisting a glass half-filled with—looks like orange juice. Lighting subdued, a soft taste of romantic music playing.

And then, as if on cue, a monster flash of lighting flares the whole room, enhancing General DeJean. It's a scene out of a German opera. Gil's truly digging this, yes.

No doubt, it *is* United States Army General César "Pug" DeJean, Chief, National Guard Bureau.

Gil taps the Pause button. Goes into mull mode. Recollecting.

Gilbert Scott knows this guy on the couch, this Army general. And he cannot recall why. His brain lingers on the name, and some of the known data start rolling up on shore.

Four stars, Chief of the National Guard Bureau, member of the Joint Chief of Staff, serves as military adviser to the president, Secretary of Defense, National Security Council, and is the Department of Defense's official channel to the Governors and State Adjutant Generals on all matters pertaining to the National Guard—one of 231 four stars in the U.S. Army. Graduate of the Citadel, Bachelor of Sciences, Mechanical Engineer (Aerospace).

The Goose presses the Forward button.

Hears music, faint. What the hell is that? Sounds like Johnny Mathis?

Behind DeJean, sliding doors, a balcony looking out onto—*wait*, that's the Washington, D.C. skyline out there behind DeJean, city lights twinkling like a bed of diamonds and rubies, Abe Lincoln sitting patiently. Still laid back in that uncomfortable stone chair at the Lincoln Memorial, all lit up bright white. Maybe this video shot in an apartment at the Watergate, Gil? Could be. From the viewer's perspective, the lower third of the frame is filled with a woman's slender thighs. Her knees half-covered with a silky teddy. One perfect leg crossed over the other, and a flawless foot with polished navy blue toenails shaking nervously from side to side. Scott cannot tell what time of day it is. Maybe dusk. The camera hidden somewhere behind the woman and to her right and placed over her right shoulder. DeJean oblivious to the recording. The video is of excellent quality.

Wait a sec.

Scott presses Pause.

A wedge of memories skids along a neural track in his brain. Particles of memories. DeJean's background goes flip-flopping through his mind. Scott has a difficult time latching on to one. But a clip of DeJean speaking before a crowd of people known as The Movement—their only credo allows states to secede from the Union and form their own country. But their motivations and plans are more sinister. They want their own constitution. Their own laws *and* their own Army. It's coming back: The man with the biggest Army in the United States is the president. The man with the *second* biggest Army is General César "Pug" DeJean. Three-hundred and fifty-thousand guardsmen currently serving. And every National Guard unit in the country is under his command. Scott thinking, you can go places with a group that size.

You can make waves, Gil imagines.

But then a detour in his neuronal network, and he's back to Bud Lite, pizza, and the video. And those tootsies tipped in navy, more enchanting than DeJean sipping orange juice and tightening the sash on his rob.

Gilbert presses the Forward button. *God, let there be something here.*

First, a woman's voice. We do not see her.

Then, Gilbert Scott kicks back. Watches as he works on the can of Bud and last night's cold pepperoni pizza with not enough tomato sauce:

WOMAN: So what time did you get there? You said—?

CESAR DeJEAN (C.D.): Eh, ten-oh-one, I checked my

watch before entering the Oval Office. The place, like a morgue, compared to a usual weekday.

WOMAN: And?

C.D.: Tommy has his back to me, leaning on the credenza, staring out the window. Looked like JFK from the back. I take two steps in. He hears me cough, turns, laughs. He says, "touchdown," throws a pretend pass at the Pugster. I pretend to run, catch the pass, and flop down on the couch. Big laughs, both of us. It was a fun moment. Brought a wave of yesterdays back at the Citadel. I might've busted one of the legs on the couch. *In the Oval Office*! Can you imagine? The Pugster mighta crushed the couch!

WOMAN: Were you in your new uni I bought?

C.D.: All of it, Blake. Top to bottom. Wanted to look official—stars on the shoulders, salad on the chest. And I want to thank you again for giving it to me. A very special gift, I must say. [He throws her an air kiss.]

WOMAN: [She throws one back] And?

C.D.: We bullshitted around, reminisced a bit, and—

WOMAN: And then he—?

C.D.: Sat on the sofas there in front of the fireplace, you know, where they all sit when they have those impromptu photo ops, a foreign dignitary and…

WOMAN: Yes, yes.

C.D.: Then offered me, ah, he offers me a Scotch—crystal glass with the presidential seal. First-class.

WOMAN: At ten in the morning? On a Sunday? Scotch? Jesus, Pug.

C.D.: Yeah, but in retrospect, he was all nerves, so I went with it and threw back, ah, I think it was a Dewar's. [Sips his orange juice.] The Pugster does not like drinking in the morning, I'll tell ya.

WOMAN: I would think not. So, then what? Did he—?

C.D.: He told me he had three things on his mind.

WOMAN: So, everything was sorta normal with you and him.

C.D.: Almost, yes. I mean. . .

WOMAN: Pug? What? Tell me—

C.D.: I mean, outta nowhere, he tells me he's pulling out of—he said *disconnecting*—from Deadlight. Shocked the hell out of me. He said he didn't want to hold back, but—

WOMAN: You sure, Pug, that's what he said—*disconnecting*?

C.D.: I asked him why. He said he realized it was against his conscience. It was immoral and would ruin the whole country. Second thoughts, nightmares, all that psycho nonsense. He was goddamned serious.

WOMAN: Then?

C.D.: Then? What then?

WOMAN: Then, I mean, where did it go from there, you said.

C.D.: Oh. From there, well, from there, it goes *prickly*.

WOMAN: Prickly? The hell does that mean?

C.D.: It means, Blake, that he pointed a gun at my head. Can you imagine! An automatic. But first, he wanted me to resign for health reasons. Assigns a Marine Corps master sergeant, a former sniper, to escort me back to the Pentagon, where he wants me to write a handwritten letter of resignation. I refused. Then, he orders me to shut down Deadlight. I tell him no, Pug cannot do that. Train left the station. No recall option available. He says unless I agree to shut down Deadlight, he's going to blow my brains out all over the door I'm trying to get out. I'm a bit tightened up here, Blake. Can you see it?

WOMAN: I see it in your eyes. Pug, I just gave you my body five minutes ago. I know you like a favorite lollipop. Like a book. I can see you're nervous about something else.

C.D.: Speaking of books, Blake, I'm down on the visitor book for being his last visitor. Last guy there before signing in and signing out. They have me down. No way General DeJean wasn't there, I—

WOMAN; He shot *him*self, Pug.

C.D.: Yes.

WOMAN: So? You were the last visitor he had. So what?

C.D.: I have a meeting with the chief. He's going to put my ass under the microscope. Then there's the press.

WOMAN: Screw the press, Pug.

C.D.: I guess, yeah. Not that easy, but—

WOMAN: Pug, you did not shoot President Rand. President Rand shot President Rand.

C.D.: That is not the point, my sweet pussycat. The point is this could open a barrel of snakes. Once they start pokin' around—

WOMAN: After your chat, after you finished talking. What occurred?

C.D.: I told you, I went to leave, and just before I reach the door, I hear him rack a round in an H&K autoloader. I turn, and he's pointing it at me—nothing in the world like facing a man with an automatic in a shaky hand. I never saw a muzzle that big.

WOMAN: Hard to believe! I can imagine. Well, he did not shoot you.

C.D.: Ya' think!

WOMAN: So, what's to worry?

C.D.: He told me he *would* shoot if I didn't rescind the order to launch. Then I told him he didn't have the balls, and I left.

WOMAN: Then, you're good, you're clear. He's dead. You are alive. So far, Jim Acosta, that CNN correspondent that gets the details before everyone else on CNN, says sources say he shot himself in the *right* temple. Classic, 'cause he was right-handed. No do-overs. Must of messed up the gold drapes. Haven't you watched any TV?

C.D.: No.

WOMAN: Well, maybe you should, Pug.

C.D.: Yes.

WOMAN: The shot triggered an alarm, and within seconds security, Secret Service was in there, placed filled with EMS. He was slumped over in his chair, a pistol in his hand. They tried to revive him, but—on a stretcher, down to the infirmary in the basement, but by that time he was gone. They are going to have a press conference.

C.D.: When?

WOMAN: They said soon.

C.D.: That guy, Acosta, said this?

WOMAN: Acosta said this. His *source* said it.

C.D.: I'm thinking, suppose he left a suicide note saying that I initiated Deadlight—that the Fourteen States seceding was a red herring, a springboard *to* Deadlight, that I would put the troops out throughout the States? Shifting the plan to me *away* from him? Suppose—you know, he can say anything in the note and implicate me any which way he wants. Then I am genuinely and richly screwed over because a dead man's words in a note'll stick for a while. A long while.

WOMAN: Why would he do that?

C.D.: Haven't the slightest idea what goes through a person's head prior to a nine-millimeter bullet, do you?

WOMAN: Pug, you guys were roommates at the Citadel. A friendship that goes deep, lasts a long time.

C.D.: For two years, we were roommates—friendship change.

WOMAN: Still. That friendship has to have some value here, no?

C.D.: So?

WOMAN: I'm saying, is all. Also, what about Elora? She's still—

C.D.: What *about* Elora?

WOMAN: She's *over* there. Maybe you should—

C.D.: Blake, forget Elora. She's got one job to do assigned by your father. One job. One button to push, and whatever the hell else A.G. has her down for. Bring her further into this? Things can get *gummy*. Leave her be.

WOMAN: Pug, let me ask you a question? When does Deadlight kickoff?

C.D.: As soon as I say it does.

WOMAN: Pug, it takes them longer than three days to unzip their flies, get their peckers aired out, and take a leak. By that time, Deadlight's off and running, and *you* are the man. You have nothing to worry about, sweetie.

C.D.: Not to worry? Ha! Are you kidding me? That's what General Custer said to his boys at the Little Big Horn—"Boy's, follow me, not to worry, just a small group of cranky Indians." On the day of the attack, June 25, 1876—listen to this—there are *ten-thousand* Indians, *ten-thousand warriors* of the Lakota, Sioux, Northern Cheyenne, and Arapaho tribes, along the flats, teepees all the way to the horizon, the largest gathering of tribal nations ever, a gathering storm, waiting for that egomaniacal Brevet Major General Goldie Locks, to run into their trap. Hungry, the tribes were, to *engage. Annihilate.* Goldie Locks got *too* complacent. A coupla hours later and, all of 'em, two-hundred and sixty-eight Federal troops, slaughtered, their nuts cut off, eviscerated, and scalped.

WOMAN: You're good. Not to worry. There are no Indians this time, Pug. Look out the window. No threats. No teepees. [long pause]. So, let's go back to bed. I'm a wee bit steamy.

C.D.: *Again*? Whoa! *Blake*! Good for you, sweetie. Love it when you're all *steamy*. And the Pugster, he seconds that emotion. [visual/audio ends, screen goes black].

* * *

Scott chews off a piece of pizza too big to chew politely, thinks, grabs his friend, Mister Bud Lite.

Then, he wonders: who the hell sent this to me and why?

The Goose speculating, parachuting down to reality, having no idea what he'll do with the memory stick.

Where to take it, Gil?

Seems like something unlawful going on there.

How to leverage to my advantage?

Hey, listen, you nit-witted skinny soda straw pencil-headed toe rag, if you want the gold ring, my man, you gotta work it. Do something drastic. Cause some chaos. Because sitting on your skinny ass adding to your hemorrhoidal itch night after night reading what other people write off a TelePrompTer doing two-minute inserts sponsored by Cheerios and Japanese automobiles ain't gonna cut it, so get your dick straightened out and start work on slamming yourself a significant gig.

Now!

Whatever you're imagining, Gilbert, if you think hard enough, work it hard enough, you could end up in the Museum of Television and Radio Broadcasting after all. And you could stop eating cold pizza and Bud Lite and go for a slab of Beef Wellington. And *stop* reading articles in Reader Digest magazine.

Maybe you should partner up with someone, Gil? Someone who has been out in the woods a lot? Down in the weeds.

Maybe this flash drive could score you an anchor gig somewhere sunny, Florida, anywhere in Florida, or Arizona; you love all the Zip Codes in AZ., right? This is opportunity knocking!

Get hip!

But how do you pull it to your advantage, Gil?

How do you make a buck out of it *somehow*?

This is big-time stuff here, Gil.

Use it to springboard to an anchor desk.

Tough. Question. To. Ask. Harder. To. Answer.

Gil!

WHAT?

Wait a damned simple pimple minute here, my friend!

Gill, saying to himself: I think I just crash-landed on *one* teeny-weeny tasty idea.

7
MISSING IN BUSHMILLS

Rayne, at the Hotel-Ochsenwirtshof bar, watching the television over the bar dissecting the suicide of President Tommy Rand. His popularity had been dwindling. Heartbroken is the nation. How many equate, the nation queries itself? Too many know. There is an array of live television feeds from correspondents around Washington, D.C., New York City, Sudbury, Massachusetts, where Tommy was born and raised. All the cable networks—American, Trans-European, Far East—shuffling panels of "experts," Zooming their stunned reactions. Enunciating their drop-jawed notions. Some scratchy, snowy feeds are aborted or momentarily abandoned because of technical problems electricity and algorithms cannot unravel. A montage of images showing President Rand's career pops up: attended the Citadel for two years, transferred to Boston College Law School, joined the U.S. Army, achieved the rank of captain, awarded the Medal of Honor in Afghanistan, the Senate. Countless words of speculation over these images, while lower-third graphics on the screen showing Tommy Rand facts from the day he was born. The motive? Speculation. All of it over the top praise now that Tommy is dead. Too much of the lauding is hollow. Several correspondents and clutches of cameraman in front of Rand's childhood home in Burlington, elbowing for *the* shot doing standups in hushed tones. Some of the windbags on the panels sounding omniscient, masterful. An anchor on MSNBC saying they will soon hear from Rand's former roommate at the Citadel, US Army General Cesar "Pug" DeJean, head of the country's National Guard. Fox News, never a Tommy Rand fan, covers all the angles anyway because, well, this is major news. The cable stations using the same live, master feed, a wide establishing shot of the White House, the Portico, raw tape, unedited packages from field reporters doing hurried standups on the White House lawn. In the background, flickering police emergency lights gushing red around the Portico driveway. The cry of sirens the song *du jour*. An anchor introduces Heather Bellizzi, psychologist, standing on the campus of New York University, a subdued attractive woman wearing a plain blue baseball cap talking the arcane subject of suicide. Plying academic speculation as to why people surrender themselves over to the Lord. Broad strokes again. Tip of the iceberg. The television monitor chocked with conjecture. Lawyers, doctors, psychologists, psychiatrists, authors. Facts have not been collated. Everybody's sort of flying loose out there. Yet, one or two panelists produce thin-ice reasons Tommy Rand jerked the trigger, having no notion what tormented the man enough to off himself in the Oval Office. And, please, tell us why, Tommy, why did you have an automatic pistol in your historic desk? Impending attack of the Proud Boys? Neo-Nazis? The Movement? QAnon? White Supremacy dudes running amok? Bounding overprotective perimeters on the Lawn, smashing White

House bulletproof glass. Coming for *you*? Take over America? Some say perhaps it was Rand's *fuck you* to a nation that did not fully appreciate his *body of work* going back to his days as a senator, a decorated officer in the U.S. Army. For not *loving* him enough. Rayne mindful that suffering and heartache are intricately woven into the fabric of all our lives. Many simply cannot bear the vitriol, the enduring. Tommy ran out of gas, Rayne thinks. He killed in Afghanistan and now had to take down one more enemy, the most threatening—himself. The biggest one. He had to crash somewhere. So his office was the cabbage patch he figured best to auger in. Rayne watching now with equanimity as one buck correspondent with plentiful hair and appearing just to have been handed her high school sheepskin, describes the U.S. Navy ambulance she saw skimming out the main gate to Georgetown University Hospital bearing Tommy Rand's body. She glances down at her cellphone—her notes—recounting that the president was first gurneyed from the Oval Office to the White House Medical Unit inside the Eisenhower Executive Office where, she speculates, doctors attempted *valiantly* to keep him alive. *Valiantly*? What? Odd word choice that one, Rayne observes. Maybe she means *vainly*? Then Rayne herself makes a mild effort to conjure what Tommy Rand had within the boundaries of his mind. Did his morals exempt him from guilt, from some major shame until he could not hold back? Was that cornfield of brainpower too thick for you, Tommy, to set aflame and watch the smoke take away your pain—that you had to blow your brains away using the force of a 9mm to finalize a convoluted problem. No other way, Tommy? Were you lost in guilt of some kind? What alien insects were boring into your head coming to you. For total consumption? What horrific wave after horrific wave went on with no respite? How burdensome, Thomas, could the onus have been? Could you not have traded your chips in for fresh stacks. A few bottles of Dewar's? A million voices in the wind asking the same questions. Rayne does not know the answers. But she wants to guess. The country will move on. It will stumble and shuffle and fall forward. It will hurt. It will disregard for a moment their new president, the former vice-president. It will criticize and analyze and prioritize and minimize hopes and fears, and doubts. But it *will* move on. Because there will *always* be a race for gold and glory. And in summary, President Tommy Rand was *exceedingly* selfish, Rayne feels because he put his misery above that of country. Still, Rayne Foster is compassionate, understanding of Tommy's unknown, unrelenting agony burgeoning in his head up to the impact of the bullet. The country mourns, yes. Flags half-masted, yes. But the nation flounders. Where's the oxygen? And everywhere, the USA is set off onto a higher altitude of national chaos and grief. All not deserving their president's apostasy. Rayne, mostly, angry at the President of the United States of America for turning nation and people into a coffin of heartache and misery.

I have an opinion. Does anyone want to hear? Of course not, Rayne. Well, here it is anyway.

Rayne puts her notion out there for herself to hear, raising her brain voice, saying to herself: *Tommy, you killed yourself because of an inescapable guilt, a profound shame. So big that death seemed as pure and as white as the roses that will adorn your coffin tomorrow.*

Rayne switches thoughts: after this beer, after this drink, after the buzz anoints me and vanishes, I'll call Lee. Tell him I can't sing the damned song anymore, that I want to get the hell out.

Out of *this*.

Juta appears behind the bar. "Drink? What would you like?" She asks quietly, a reverence reserved for a departed relative. She drops a coaster in front of Rayne.

"Do you have Bushmills? And a beer this tall"—one hand two feet above the tiled bar. Juta spins around, searching the shelves.

And before Juta can get her hand on the Bushmills, Elora Sinner, a cloud of radiance, settles on a barstool in this romantic Bavarian bar not too many centimeters from where Rayne studies her movements. Elora glancing at Rayne.

Elora afloat. Unmoored. Not expecting to see a woman she is attracted to in a bar in the Black Forest. How fortuitous you are, Elora, that you have sat on the right barstool and at the right moment.

Now what?

Isn't that always the question?

Do I give her *the* famous smile and then the nod, Elora wonders? Or do I just sit here and wait to see if she will acknowledge me? Maybe if I make eye contact, she will say something first?

They nod and show faint hello smiles.

Juta serves Rayne and moves to Elora. "What can I get you.

"I'll have what she's having."

Rayne says, "Not afraid of the unknown?"

"Only sometimes." She winks.

"But not now?" says Rayne, pointing at the TV.

"No. I welcome it."

"I could be drinking cyanide."

Elora throws her chin in the air, musters a chuckle. "You don't look like you want to exit the rodeo just yet."

"Well, perhaps a change of horses." Then quickly switching thoughts, Rayne asks, "If you *could* guess, what would you think I'm drinking?"

"Ah, a contest. I love contests."

"So?"

"The beer is certainly a *Weissbier*."

"Why?"

"Because I know beer. And yours is cloudy."

"Correct. But what brand?"

"*Weihenstephaner Hefeweissbier.*"

"Excellent, and so is your German. But how did you know that this was *that* brand?"

"Simple," Elora says, pointing at the taps, "It's the only *Weiss* Juta serves here."

"You cheated! I curtail my amazement." Rayne raiser her glass in a salute.

"I always cheat. That's how you win. Playing fair these days is for losers. Besides, I can tell by looking into your eyes that you are a woman of superb taste, the way you dress, the way you hold yourself. *Weihenstephaner* is *Beste in der Klasse*, won many gold medals. So, the two of you go together well—the woman and the beer. Congratulations. Three cheers. At least for now. One never knows."

Juta places the beer, the Bushmills, in front of Elora, taps the shot glass, says, "*Und dieses, was ist das*?"

Elora says, "Bushmills."

Rayne feigns defeat, frowns, saying, "How did you know *that*?"

Elora grins, showing off her world-famous Elora Sinner smile, saying, "I saw Juta pour it."

Rayne raises her stein, "Here's to you—*Wie heißt du*?"

"Elora. *El*—if Elora is *too* complicated to pronounce, too many syllables. Elora Sinner. And—?"

"Rayne. Rayne Foster"

"And I am sure it is not spelled R-A-I-N? Could not be."

"Of course not."

"Capital R-A-Y-N-E."

"Nicely done." Then, it hits her, Rayne asking, "Sinner is an unusual name. Is your father A.G. Sinner, the former American ambassador to Germany?"

Elora holds back for a second, then reluctantly answers, "Yes."

Already Elora's hooked on Rayne's magical blue eyes. An unusual tingle starts a-buzzin' in the nape of her neck. Struggling to keep her delight bottled.

But Rayne sees herself in her room at her iPad typing a report to Leland. Because he is going to press her for details, particularly about this woman at the bar:

> From the Ochsenwirsthof bar1410 hrs: A woman entered and sat two barstools from me. Just Juta, the owner/bartender, me, and the woman who introduced herself as Elora Sinner (ES). Attractive, hair cut severely at ear level, strawberry blondish, sophisticated She saw what I was drinking ordered the same. We started a silly guessing contest about beer/whiskey. Like two teenage girls. She is likable. Elegant. Seems to have knack for expensive clothes. Juta hit mute on TV because she saw it was bumming us all out (she was right), the suicide.

Rayne holds up her stein. "Here's to you."

Elora can't reach the stein, reminds her of Meese at the Essenzimmer. Here is different. She moves her lithe figure to a barstool closer to Rayne. The motion, the grace of a wave washing a beach. Both delighted with the proximity.

They click glasses, Elora saying, "*To us*! *Cheers*! And especially you for taking our minds off that." She throws her chin at the television.

Rayne saying, "There are other things that need our attention."

"Like?"

"*You.*"

"Me. How so?

"Has anyone ever told you that you look like—?"

"Rosamunde Pike? Not lately. But six months ago, on a flight, a woman sitting next to me said, 'Excuse me, Miss Pike, do you mind?' and she handed me a small pad and pen. 'An autograph?'"

"Did you sign?"

"What would you have done?"

"Signed."

"I did. Somewhere in some town in some house with a picket fence in a drawer rests Rosamunde Pike's autograph signed by Elora Sinner. I feel famous."

Rayne saying, "And you made that woman incredibly happy. That's wonderful."

Rayne's cellphone vibrates. She glances down. A text message come through via WhatsApp:

Leland Upchurch
Landing Munich your time 1800 hrs. Need to meet ASAP. Contact info, hotel, etc., to follow. Keep me up on everything you see, do. ~ Leland

Rayne looks down at her watch. Thinks, this is unusual: Leland never appears in person on a mission.

Then Elora pulls an odd thought out of nowhere, saying, "I'm starting to wonder what's more therapeutic: therapy or alcohol?" She holds up her Bushmills, stares at it. "You know—that whole ritual: the selection, the uncorking, picking the right glass, the pouring, holding it up against the light, smelling it, then, *bang*, throwing it back?"

"You mean the *drinking* of alcohol? You're comparing that to therapy?" asks Rayne, not having a clear picture of where Elora is going with her newly constructed out-of-left field thought. It is the

Bushmills, Rayne. You are getting lost in the vapors. Elora getting a bit lost in it too. And the *Weissbier*. But that's good, Rayne, both of you exploring your philosopher's minds and learning more. And trying to find something both of you knew you never had. Is that it?

Rayne saying softly, "I sorta think I know what you mean, sorta."

"I mean, wait, no. I mean the whole *ritual* of it. What do you think?"

Rayne shrugs her shoulders, thinks for a second. "The ritual of it? Never thought about it."

Elora saying, "And then, of course, getting the *buzzerino*." She sniffs the fresh Bushmills, then throws the glass back. Places the shot glass on the coaster. Peeks into the bottom. Turns it upside down—"Nothin' in it." She signals, and Juta's there with a refill. Then she stares into Rayne's eyes, deep as she can, challenging Rayne to avert her glance. Rayne does not accede, does not blink. "I'm saying," says Elora, "it can be sorta like sex: lots and lots of foreplay is good, right? and then—you know—you can't hold back any longer, you can't bear it one nanosecond more, the tension, your back arching, short breaths, and then—pardon the pun—*bang*, you accede to *it*, can't resist anymore. It's like a sneeze—try to hold back, and you hurt yourself, yes? And then, *it* can be wonderful, sure, you've arrived. *Arrivé*, as the French say. Don't take me wrong, but the journey from here to *it* is—it is just *too* marvelous for words."

"Sounds like a song."

"That's because it is a song."

Rayne listening, can't hold back. In perfect harmony, Elora and Rayne finish out the lyrics, rising slightly from their barstools. *Too marvelous for words. . .*

And with gusto neither has seen, they slam their palms in the strongest, highest high-fives, almost knocking themselves off their barstools—their joy reaches the heavens.

Elora, saying, "That was *wonderful*. You, Miss Rayne Foster, have a wonderful voice."

Rayne saying, "You too. Too *marvelous* for words!"

There is a fly buzzing the around the bar, and Juta picks up a swatter and goes off hunting, following it into the kitchen.

Rayne and Elora, boozy, alone with each other.

They hear Juta swatting and swatting again.

"Can I ask you a personal question?" asks Elora, red-eyed, staring at a wall.

Hear it comes.

"Shoot."

"Are you seeing a therapist?"

No response.

Rayne has heard this tone before. When she hears this tone, she knows she is facing a problem. In her trade, Rayne Foster realizes there is a lot of pain that cannot be faked. The woman sitting next to her can hide a lot of things with her elegance, her poise, and singing, but she can't hide the pain that's falling on a tiled bar.

Rayne saying, "I really should hurry."

"Why?"

"I have to call a man."

"Why?"

"Tell him I can't sing anymore."

"What? You just did, Foster."

Elora turns and faces Rayne, her eyes glinting. The cocktail napkin balled in her hand.

Rayne saying, "Long story. But never mind. Contests are more fun." Rayne picks up her Blackphone. "Excuse me, I have to answer this text, and then we can get back to knocking ourselves out …."

She types:

To: Leland Upchurch
Sitting with the daughter of A.G. Sinner, No idea why she is here yet. Drives a 1992 Land Rover Defender, green. Arrived this afternoon. Very affable. Think she is here alone. Seems saddened over something. Pls advise ASAP. More to follow. Rayne Foster

Elora, saying: "That's an unusual phone you have there, and I happen to have one too.

"You can't get better encryption."

Elora wondering why Rayne has a $2,000 cellphone known for encryption "Before you go, let me ask you another question? What happened to your chin?"

Rayne laughs. "Cut myself shaving."

Juta returns, waving the fly swatter. "I scored! Add me to the list of great Luftwaffe fighter Aces! I should be awarded the Knights Cross *Mit Brillianten*!"

Everyone laughs.

Compared to her, the lady sitting next to you, and you in your cargo pants and hair need a comb, and your jaw looking like you caught a right hook. Yes, Rayne, you are that Rhineland Buck rabbit you saw staring back. Comparing yourself to Miss Fashionista over there in her Milano stitch sweater jacket and dot smock neck top. Rayne, at the very least, before you came into this bar, you should have combed your hair. How the hell can I look attractive feeling this way?

Rayne takes a deep breath.

Another mélange of prickly thoughts circles in her head: who is Elora Sinner? Why am I hooked onto her green eyes? I have to talk to Lee. Something strange going on here. First, I have to get out of here. Second, maybe Elora is a trap? Could that be? In this trade, Rayne, one never knows.

Rayne asks Elora, "What do you do? For a living."

"I work at the American Embassy in Berlin?"

"Doing?"

"Chips and dips.

"Parties for diplomats and businesspeople?"

"Yes. I went to Bryn Mawr sort of, if you know what I mean. I majored in amenities. I arrange Embassy parties for diplomats," and she says, holding her head up with her hand, "my father got me the job."

"And that is part of what made you cry?"

Elora touches Rayne's lips, saying, "And these."

And then, from Rayne, a trickle of unannounced juices right here at the bar.

"Sounds like a fun job."

"If you like to low IQ jobs, yes. Miles of smiles and head nodding. And you?

"Photojournalist. Freelance, mostly. I take pictures of assignments, write stories. I like automotive subjects. Indy Five Hundred. Twenty-Four Hours of LeMans,

"Rayne Foster. Nice to meet an expert in something. *Sprechen Sie Deutsch*?

"*Aber natürlich. Fließend. Und du*?"

"Sure."

"*Ja. Das ist gut*! I assume you are from the U.S."

"New York City, born and raised."

"Really! Me, too."

"Where?"

"Greenwich Village."

"This is a coincidence. I can't believe it."

They shake hands.

Then, Rayne opens her mouth to say something, and Elora raises her hand, Stop.

They look up at the TV.

Elora saying to Juta, "Can you turn that up, please."

There he is, in his new pinks and greens, the gift from Blake, the Pugster, General César DeJean, bemedaled, stars glittering on an olive-green heaven, his ribbons an illustrative collage of colors, row upon row. The lower frame of the TV monitor now too high to project the badges, awards from other countries, plentiful.

The young CNN correspondent has scored a significant piece of breaking news—she's live on worldwide TV with Pug. Becky Watson, five-foot-three, has stopped the five-foot-ten pugnacious Army general because her feet happened to be planted in the right spot on the White House lawn. Becky Watson's got the mike in Pug's nose, and he has no end-run opportunity:

Becky Watson: General, it is understood that you were the last visitor President Rand had this morning?

CD: I have been told.

BW: And how did the president seem to you?

CD: Fine. He seemed his usual self to me.

BW: Can you tell us anything about the *nature* of your visit, especially on a Sunday morning?

CD: Well, that's primarily privileged information. But It was a combination business and—we were roommates at the Citadel for two years, then he transferred to Boston College. And I've known him ever since. So, it was a social visit, and it was on the books for a long time that we occasionally have over the years, mixed with, this morning, ah, government topics relating to the National Guard.

BW: General, did your visit have anything to do with your controversial appearances at the Movement rallies.

CD: Again, it was a social. . . catching up. . . some matters pertaining to the Guard.

BW: As you know, there has been talk of a possible Department of Defense investigation involving your appearances at the Movement—

CD: Becky, let me say this about that: My appearances at the Movement rallies were invitations, nothing that *I* initiated. The leaders of the Movement contacted me on several occasions, invited me to speak—which I did without receiving an honorarium. They were merely asking for information on the strength of our military.

BW: General, excuse me—CNN's Jim Acosta has, ah, just been with a source who says the president was found with a bloody wound over his left eye, a cut under his eyebrow—

CD: Well, he did shoot himself in the head and—

BW: According to Acosta's source, this is a *separate* wound from the one the gunshot caused. And there was a bit of blood found on his telephone earpiece.
CD: I have no—I cannot comment on that, Becky—

BW: The source says the president seems to have been hit above the eye by a blunt object of, perhaps a fist, and—

CD: Listen, I appreciate the interview, but I have an appointment—

BW: When you were there, General, you didn't—

CD: Punch him in the head? Of course not. Now, I've got to go. But I do want to say this: we had a wonderfully long relationship that dates to our days at the Citadel, and I am going to sorely miss him. He was a man of great integrity, and the nation will surely miss him too, may he rest in peace, and I have his family in my heart and prayers, thank you."

Watson turns it over to the anchor in the studio, and Juta hits the mute button.

Rayne studies Elora's face after the interview with Pug. Winter in her eyes. "You okay?"

No response. Elora is off into the stratosphere.

Starts to come off her barstool, and as she moves to step away, she says, "I forgot, I have an appointment."

Then El steps toward the door, wobbly, saying to Rayne. "Hope to see you again."

8
WAR ZONE ROGER DOES A SOLID

Gilbert Scott in his Hertz rental, Newark Liberty Airport, waiting for CNN war correspondent, journalist, Roger Kitchens.

He is parked in Short Term Parking, spot 29, Lot B, the coordinates he will Text Kitchens after he lands—forty minutes late now. He lets it ride. Probably the weather. It's a good parking spot, a short walk for Kitchens from the Delta terminal.

After checking out his Chevy Malibu, Gil walked back to the rental counter, taking a little protestation as he walked, saying: "The color sucks. It looks like barf yellow. Reminds me of my ex-wife's eyes." Hertz told him they were out of blues and grays today, said it wasn't their policy to match customers' eyes to cars they rent, so please accept our apologies.

Gil sitting behind the wheel, drizzle slathering the windshield. Drizzle soaking Gil's anxious mind. Gil hoping for sunny weather when Kitchens arrives.

Gilbert's listening to Rick Braun on the car radio. A hard jamming jazz arrangement, *Coolsville*, and it's lifting his spirits up and down like a yoyo. The sax solos bring him down, and the swells and harmonies give him a feeling of soaring confidence. The car's windows rattle, the dash quivers, the rearview mirror trembles, and Gil the Goose's having a hard time thumb-drumming on the steering wheel and toe-tapping the accelerator because he's not the most rhythmic broadcaster on the planet. And he curses himself because he left Manhattan without grabbing a pastrami and rye and fries from the Manhattan deli around the corner from his apartment. Could have been sitting here in a drizzle, listening to the radio, eating his favorite sandwich with a Dr. Brown's Cel Ray soda. Daydreaming his anchor gig somewhere.

In his jacket pocket, in a Zip-Lock bag, the precious SanDisk memory stick nestled nice and cozy, water-tight, scratch-proof. Happy as a clam waiting for answers from Roger once he squeezes body and reputation into the Chevy.

Gil Scott sits starving, waiting for Roger Kitchens, Senior CNN Correspondent, journalist, currently based in Beirut, but temporarily assigned to CNN's military desk in the Pentagon, his favorite beat. Kitchens savors gunfire. The esteemed Kitchens. The archetype of the modern war correspondent. The legend. *The man.* Winner of multiple Emmy and Edward R. Murrow awards for team reporting. Growing up, he attended boarding schools in Beirut, Tangier, and Windsor, Connecticut. He graduated from the University of Texas at Austin with a bachelor's in Asiatic Language and Linguistics and from the University of London's School of Oriental and African Studies with a master's in Middle Eastern Studies. Has been a war corresponded and journalist with CNN for twenty-seven years. In and out of Iran and Iraq on a variety of dangerous assignments.

Roger, moving with a ten-man Marine patrol in Helmand Province, close to both the Taliban's spiritual center in Kandahar and the Pakistani border, imprudently stuck his head around a revetment for one more peek at the tracer rounds blistering the elephant grass. Bad move, Rog. A red-hot chunk of shrapnel from a 60mm mortar round, Russian manufacture caught him. Sliced through his helmet, slammed him near his eyebrow where it remained lodged for five blood-spurting seconds until his cameraman, Emmy winner Burt Talley, fingered it out. Roger unconscious for nearly fifteen minutes. There was so much blood, Talley couldn't make out if Roger was Roger or Roger was some disfigured sock puppet. Roger could have eventually turned the wound over to a skilled plastic surgeon at Walter Reed, but no. The scar shaped like the state of Florida, thirty-five millimeters of jagged coastline silhouetted from St. Augustine down to Key Largo—Roger's *insigne de Guerre*. Kitchens, then in his late fifties, said, "The chicks dig it, so the scar stays."

CNN initially hired Roger as a local Jordanian employee. The job title: "fixer/producer/sound technician." One of his duties was helping reporting staff get through checkpoints since he is fluent in multiple Arabic dialects. He eventually rose to CNN's Bureau Chief in Amman. Then he moved on to bureau chief in Cairo, where he led CNN's coverage of the uprising of then-President Hosni Mubarak.

He was the only Western journalist granted access for an interview with the ruthless, fucked-up Uday Hussein. Uday's thank you was plentiful, over-the-top, and *supremo weirdo psycho*. For the interview and subsequent CNN exposure, Uday offered a beefsteak dinner, French wine, Series P Partagas Cuban cigars; and for an evening of debauchery, two thin, wacky, stoned-out Russian teenage girls with rusty gold teeth and pony legs. Rog chowed down on beefsteak flown in from Paris that day aboard Uday's private jet, a Gulfstream, selected a surreal *Château Latour Pauillac* (17,00 USD), but declined the teenagers saying, "I have a splitting migraine." Uday's English/ Arabic translation of "migraine" came out as "cracked open head," so Uday did not flip the rejection into an insult. And, although Roger Kitchens had never been involved in a *menage à trois* he would not have been at his peak anyway come bedtime. And Uday must've had the crazy button turned off that day. Uday understanding, being a connoisseur and consumer of the legendary three-way, that only the luckiest of lucky males score. One should be in top mental form to enjoy a three-way, Roger imagined.

Then three years later, in Sabah, Libya, covering the 2011 war that overthrew Muammar Gaddafi, Kitchens was slammed in the back with a 7.62 mike-mike round from an AK-47 Kalashnikov just as he was slipping into his undies after taking a shower. Almost died of blood loss and embarrassment.

Kitchens, some say, has a gunpowder jones. The smell of cordite and spent munitions and hot shell casings give him a buzz. Since he has seen much combat, colleagues and friends refer to him as War Zone Roger. Others think Roger "The Dodger" is more suitable because hundreds of bullets and shrapnel have gone astray avoiding him.

But while doing a standup package for the London bureau on the new F-35 multi-role fighter, Roger's luck fell fallow: He was given an erroneous fact by a part-time CNN intern, a tiny incorrect factoid that embarrassed a US senator.

Roger Kitchens was almost fired. Instead, because of his illustrious career, he evaded firing, received censure, and wound up in purgatory, Miami Beach, doing gun shows, bank robberies, beached whales, one escaped orangutan, several vanished boaters, and a few Little League games of national import. Although pissed, he said it was okay because he loved the beach and boating. Roger did the news in Miami for one year before he crawled back with his mike between his legs to the five-sided building in Washington, D.C., where CNN had an office. He was welcomed by colleagues with a robust party at the Old Ebbitt Grill on 15th Street, in D.C., and presented with a hefty plastic bag holding one pound of shrapnel, spent shell casings of various calibers, and miscellaneous rounds that had been collected for his return.

And there in the distance, coming toward the Goose from the Delta Terminal, is Kitchens in his trademark bush jacket, shirt open at the collar, navy blue rep tie. His straw-colored hair flittering in the wet breeze, flopping over his gray-blue eyes. He swears he will shoot himself first before he sprays Adorn on his locks, unlike his colleagues. Over his shoulder, his black Tumi duffel. He walks toward the car carrying a medium-size Dominos pizza box and two beverages he just picked up in the Terminal.

He glances up at the Parking Lot letter on the light stanchion, "B," then starts scouting for parking space 29.

The Goose flashes the lights and blows the horn. Excited to see Rog.

Roger moves toward the rental like an agile bulldozer.

Roger covered with dew. His body bejeweled, tiny diamonds glittering on his hair, clothes. Tall, six-feet-four, big-boned, when Roger Kitchens enters a space, there's a legend in the room.

Gil lowers the passenger window, shouts, "Hey, Rog! Over here!"

Kitchens makes a U-turn and hands Gil the pizza and drinks.

He bends down, squints sharply at Gil.

Gil squints back.

Recognition noted.

Then, with a loud growl and an "oh fuck me," Roger the Dodger squeezes into the passenger seat of Gil the Goose's Hertz rental having no solid idea why he's here. But figuring he has to do a favor for an old news radio colleague.

It is now a sentimental meeting of former radio buddies. Once a radio buddy, always a radio buddy.

Gil saying, "Power the seat back."

Roger fingers the button, cursing modern automotive design, and the seat hums back far as technology will allow, and Roger's knees still crush the glove box. He wiggles a bit till he's snug.

Gil saying, "Great seeing you! How long has it been?"

"I counted on the flight—ten years down there on WJIN, '*WJIN… all news, all day, all the tiiiiiiime*,'" sings Roger.

"Kripes sake, you remember that?"

"All of it, I do. I still have the jingles on my PC. Loved news radio. When I retire, I'm going for a part-time gig, this time spinnin' tunes."

"They don't spin 'em anymore, Rog. They use a mouse and click on 'em."

Roger flips the top on the box, and pepperoni and cheese and warm bread flavor the interior.

"I brought you this, and I'm damned hungry too."

"Man, you remember?"

"Dig in. I always remember. You were the pizza man at JIN." He picks up a slice. "The food was not too enticing flying up on the Starship Enterprise, so this ought to hit the spot. In the meantime, we can chat. I figured that since you did not go into detail on the phone, it's gotta be big, else you wouldn't have asked."

Gil shakes his head. "Big and top secret." Nearly through his first slice, Gil's eyeing the next one, ignoring a napkin, going for number two, the one with the big pepperoni slices and the extra layer of cheese.

Gil asking, "When's your flight back?"

Roger bites half the slice, checks his Rolex GMT watch, chews, says, "Plenty of time—four hours, only a one-minute walk to the terminal."

"We're good."

"Yeah. So, tell me, whatcha got."

Gil reaching for a napkin, "Last night I'm in the studio between 'casts—"

Roger interrupts, "Refresh my memory: you do what at Fox News?"

"Nightly inserts: eight to eleven, ten, twenty, forty, fifty on the clock face: headlines, weather, sports. A monkey could call it in. Weekends I'm anchoring overnights on Saturday and Sunday—the death valley of TV news. Only people watching are my mother and father, and they're both in the grave."

"And that's why it's called the graveyard shift. So. . .?"

Gilbert tells Roger, "Last night, a courier delivers direct to me a flash drive, flash stick, whatever the hell you call 'em. Has me sign personally. Rather than check it out on my Fox PC, I figure I'd take it home, view it on my laptop."

"Any markings on it?" asks Roger, going sucking on his beverage.

"Not really. In Sharpie is written 'CD one of one.' It had a Post-It Note attached to it." Gil pauses, finishes munching the crust.

Roger saying, "First, *massively* smart move not copying to a Fox PC. As soon as the copy's complete, it's all over the internet. Then, you enter the twilight zone. And there's no crawling back from the twilight zone. Anything else?"

"Yes. A Post-It Note taped to it. In Sharpie, says, 'raw, uncut.'"

"So, you got the SanDisk last night? Lemme see it."

Gilbert does a thorough finger wipe with a napkin, balls it, drops it on the floormat, reaches into his pocket for the Zip Loc, pulls out the SanDisk, shows it to Roger.

Gil saying, "I brought my iPad. Shot a copy this morning."

Roger asking, "Just give me an overview of what you *think* you've got here."

"Honestly, I don't have a clear idea what this is. The only thing I know, I feel, it looks—you know what, Rog, I don't want to cloud things up, so why don't I play it and let you see for yourself, without me shading it up, understand?"

"Understood."

Gil consumes his last slice, wipes his fingers. Then he reaches behind Roger's seat and takes up an iPad from his briefcase. He sets it on the console, hits the Play button, and—

Blank screen, some snow, and there's General DeJean in his white terry, about to grip his OJ glass.

"Pause," commands Roger.

DeJean on-screen, frozen mid-reach.

Roger gets in close to the iPad, saying, "Whatcha got here is four-star general César DeJean. Nicknamed the Pug. Shit, this could be interesting. Do you mind?" Roger sets the iPad on his thighs, taps the Play button.

On screen, the woman's bare legs, bare feet, navy-blue toenails, her foot nervously jiggling from side-to-side.

Roger saying, "Oh, baby! Here we go! The Pugster, terry robe, bare feet, seems to be drinking a Screwdriver, and a woman. Romance music is in the background. Very tasty. *What could go wrong here*!"

Gil asks, "You know this guy?"

Roger looks at Gil as if he's nuts, rolls his eyes, saying, "Gil, you seem to forget, I'm *the man,* CNN's military dude, you get it, I know. I know all these guys. Some of them I've known since they were buck-ass lieutenants, now they're generals. Back in the day, the Pugster and I crossed paths—Iraq, Afghanistan—I used him for background intel. Did a few beers. Long time ago. Probably has no idea who I am."

"Oh, yeah."

"Ok."

Roger taps Play again.

Silence for the next thirty seconds. Gil and Roger watching the conversation unfold, sucking on their beverages. The pepperoni pie is gone; they're satiated, so nothing to divert them—complete attention to the video.

The Pause button again, and Roger saying, "Okay, so far we have DeJean in an apartment in D.C. Probably his."

"How come?"

"Over his shoulder, see that, the Lincoln Memorial. And from that angle—he lives in the Watergate, that's a fact, over there on Virginia Ave. I think we're sitting in the Watergate here. And besides, if you look close, there's some kind of award plaque on the bookshelf"—he broadens the screen, reads off the plaque— "Lt . Gen. César DeJean. Presented a few years back before he made four-star, I suspect. And there are several military choochkies on the shelves. This is DeJean, and this is his apartment."

"Sherlock Holmes, here."

Roger presses the Play button.

Roger saying, "That woman, DeJean calls her by her first name—Blake. So, she has to be Blake Sinner. A.K.A. Blake the Flake.

"Who is Blake Sinner?"

"Okay, Pug never married, said he was married to the Army. So, he was always dating. Had a fine eye for the ladies. But lately, he's been seeing one woman for the past year, Blake Sinner. He's seen a lot in town at various events with her, and there was talk of marriage, but that seems to have fizzled."

"It appears she's familiar with everything he's been talking about."

Roger picking away on a thought, then, saying, "My friend, this here general is playing with a dangerous lady. Powerful, rich, if she is who I think she is. Always has had the hots for general officers. Nothing less than two stars. A woman who loves a uniform. Definitely Blake Sinner."

"And the significance of that is—?"

"'*The significance*!' You know, for a news dude, you don't get around much. Doesn't the name *Sinner* ring a bell. How could you *miss* that, Gill?"

"Hold on—A.G. Sinner, billionaire, former Ambassador to Germany."

"Bingo! You make the first round of *Jeopardy*. Yes. Forbes says A.G.'s worth around eighteen *billion*. Has two daughters, Blake the eldest, and one other. Blake's supposed to be worth around seventy-five mill herself. Don't ask me anything about the other daughter. I don't even recall her name. But this one—his main squeeze right now. When you get home, Google her."

Roger taps the Play button.

They listen and watch for the next three minutes.

Rogers stops the playback.

Saying, "Okay. News quiz time—what do you know about General DeJean."

"Okay, so he's in a bit of trouble for appearing at those Movement rallies, and there's talk about initiating either a Congressional or Pentagon investigation into his association with the group."

"And what do you know about this Deadlight thing he's referring to?"

"Haven't clue?"

"Neither do I. Sounds like some kind of military ops."

"That's why you get the big bucks."

"So, it seems," Roger says, "that DeJean is involved in something bigger than attending the Movement rallies and the secession of fourteen states, maybe using that as a springboard into the Deadlight operation. Or as a cover."

"Starting to sound complicated. What do you think you can do?"

"Soon as I get back to D.C., I'll get my team started on this."

"Well, you have to be fast because the video says it's imminent, whatever that means."

"You have a safe deposit box?

"Yes."

"Put the SanDisk disc there. Send the file to me via WhatsApp. You got WhatsApp?"

"Yes."

"Good. Here," Roger slides the iPad back to Gil.

Gil sends the file. Roger checks his cellphone. "Got it."

"What else?" asks Gil.

"What are you looking to get out of this?"

"I want the desk, the big desk. Anchor. Good weather. Five days a week. Reasonable hours."

Roger's got his eyes on the coming and going passenger planes. Inside his head, the wheels are turning, wondering what this Deadlight is about. Not a Boy Scout Jamboree, deduces Roger Kitchens.

He looks over at Gilbert, his face twisted into a grin, waiting for Roger's response.

Roger saying, "Remember my son-in-law."

"Tall, good-looking guy?"

"Yeah, well, he's living la dolce vita down there in Miami.

President of Pulse Broadcasting. They have seven AM and FM's throughout Florida. I might be able to do something there. Not promising. Let's see where this goes."

"Of course, and I am most appreciative."

Gil sucks out the last of his beverage.

Kitchens watching a passenger jet lifting off the runway.

Saying to Gil, "You own a gun?"

"Matter of fact, I do. Not registered in New York City."

"Get it registered. Get a CCC real quick today. Now."

"What's a CCC?"

"Concealed Carry Certification. Tell 'em you're with the press at Fox News. Give them some bullshit about the Mafia threatening you. Should be able to expedite one for you. In the meantime, as soon as I have any news, I'll get in touch."

"Why?"

"Why what?"

"Why do I need a concealed carry gun permit?"

"Because," Roger says, opening the passenger door, "This entire country could turn into a shitshow at any minute. So, saddle up, cowboy."

9
THE WOMAN ON THE GLASS CANVAS

"I'm not getting the whole picture from you," Leland says, savoring the loamy air.

Rayne shrugs her shoulders.

They're on a gently sloping hill, looking down at the Hotel -Ochsenwirtshof in the mid-distance.

Rayne, sitting on a bench, watching Leland pacing, chucking pebbles in the air toward the hotel. Got a handful in his left hand. Flips one to his right, pitches it. They watch it vanish.

Leland saying, "This trade, you never know where things are going to land."

"I smell a metaphor."

One, two more deep breaths don't clear out his brain.

"What part don't you grasp?" asks Rayne, nibbling on a blade of grass, resting her forearms on her thighs, watching Leland.

"The whole part. I don't grasp what you are saying. The logic." Leland says, not looking at Rayne. "Or you're doing a incomprehensible job trying to explain what you're trying to explain."

Another pebble launches toward the hotel. They watch the arc.

Rayne says, "If you're trying to hit the hotel, you're doing a lousy job."

"I'm not trying to hit the hotel. I'm trying to reach a clear understanding of my number one operative. And she's not being clear."

A minute crawls by.

Rayne continues chewing.

Leland stops, faces Rayne: "Give it to me again."

Patiently, she says, "Are you familiar with August Wilson's play Joe Turner's *Come and Gone*?

"Vaguely. Help me."

"One of the characters says everybody's got a song inside of them, and you can lose sight of that song at your peril. And if you get out of touch with your song or forget how to sing the song or forget the lyrics, you're bound to end up frustrated and displeased because you have no tune or lyric to follow."

"And? The point, please?"

"The character recalls a time when he was out of touch with his song, and he says, 'Something wasn't making my heart smooth and easy.'"

"So, rocket scientist that I am, something's making you feel uneasy." Not a question, a statement.

"Correct."

"And that is?"

She tilts her head back and looks up into his eyes, says, "*You.*"

"Not honest enough?"

"So it seems. Not open enough."

"Because?"

"Your demeanor, mostly."

Leland pacing again stops, says, "In this trade, Rayne, no one's demeanor is always honest, always truthful."

Rayne does not respond.

Leland says, "I'm getting two bullet points out of this: One, Rayne is tired, wants to go home. Two, Rayne does not trust Leland Upchurch. Correct?"

"Dishonesty in this trade can lead to lethal consequences." Rayne does a slight twitch of her mouth. Leland recognizes this. It tells him that Rayne's disappointed, angry. At him.

She says, "In Prague, you asked me to meet up with Myles Lane in Munich. I agreed. It seemed like an 'unofficial' request, a favor. To me, a favor is unofficial business. Off the boards. And I foolishly left you without asking for the usual package, I mean, it wasn't until I hit the airport that I realized you *didn't* give me a solid pile of bona fides, protocols, as—"

"I was jammed up and never thought meeting with Myles was a full-blown mission, that it would require all the basic elements of a cover. It was a favor, Rayne. I asked you to meet with Myles as a favor. That was the basis of it. Sorry for the confusion."

"Yes, and that's the hurtful part. Because I think there's more to it than that."

"Hurtful?"

"Yes, the part where you were less than honest—after all these years. After our family relationship, my father—"

"How so?"

"Because to me," says Rayne, standing and looking down at the hotel and calculating, assessing, assuring herself that what she is about to tell could be damaging to their relationship. "To me, a favor of this kind could mean you have gone—rogue."

So, there Leland Upchurch, it's out there.

His head whips around, and with squinty eyes, he peers into Rayne's face, saying with force, "And what does that mean!"

Rayne has pricked a nerve.

"This time is different, Leland. This time, now, today, I think—I think you're playing me."

"And you have, you have proof of that, Rayne?"

"No. No proof. Rayne has a trusty bag of intuition. I am drunk with intuition. A feeling."

"And say why, please?"

"First, you sent me off to this hotel. You didn't have to do that."

"The police were coming for you."

"But I had nothing to hide from the police. I was merely sitting at a table having cocoa with a friend of yours, and I had no idea who he was."

"A former CIA executive and a man associated with every intelligence agency in the USA."

"But still, they—"

"The only person that had something to hide was Myles Lane. And they could not question him. So, why would you send me here?"

"To keep you safe?"

"From what?" She picks up a stone, tosses it at the fir tree, misses.

"This is where the action is, right, Leland. This is where you had me going after I met Myles, and I suspect—"

"Rayne, please!"

"The intent was—your intent—was for me to come here after

my meeting with Myles. The purpose of the meeting with Myles was—you wanted me to act as a courier to take his briefcase, and after that, I don't know. I mean, why would you insist that I almost get arrested trying to get the briefcase—with his bloody hand still attached. That was the purpose of the trip to Munich—Rayne meets with Myles. Myles gives Rayne his briefcase and instructs Rayne to come here to the Hotel-Ochsenwirtshof, and pass it along to you or someone you designated."

"Rayne. Please. Stop. Now."

"But, for some unknown reason, Myles has a change of heart—or, I think he does—and dashes back to his BMW and—I am speculating now—blows *himself* up. Suicide? Thoughtful soul that he was, he figured the BMW was the furthest place in the plaza where he could detonate the explosion with the least damage to buildings and casualties. I told you, after he used his key fob to open the locks, he pulled on the handle, and that triggered the explosion."

"Sometimes, you are too damned good for your own safety."

"How're my doing?"

"Can't say."

"Can't say. Because I'm on the money, right?"

Leland picks another stone, one the size of a walnut. Aims for a tree. Hits it, and the sound cracks off down into the valley.

Down at the Ochswirtshof parking area, a Mercedes *Gelendewagen* slips to halt in a parking space. The driver's door opens. A man's legs come out. His shoe touches the pavement. He scans the area, the parking lot, the road. He walks to the hotel entrance.

Meese Van Der Leeuwen opens the lobby door and moves to the reception desk.

Leland saying, "Do you know who that is?'

"Haven't a clue."

"I think I might. Can you do me a favor?"

"Another one? Off the boards?"

"Please! Can we take this off the table, put it in abeyance for now?"

"Yes," Rayne says. Hating herself for acquiescing. Then she spins quickly, aims for the hotel, and leaves Leland alone. She wants to scream. Tries. Nothing comes out.

Down the dirt road. Taking risky strides on the gravel. Two steps at a time. Almost slips. Passes a perfect tomato patch. Sunflowers bow hello. Leaves spinning on a trout stream. A house with flower boxes. A barking German Shorthaired Pointer. She almost slips again into a mud puddle. Chickens cluck their annoyance. She waves. Somehow, she keeps her balance on the slippery ground. Then two red Rhenish Warmblood horses, sisters, amble toward her. Noses over the fence. They smile. Their heads bob, *touch us*. The sputtering wind flutters their manes, Rayne's hair. Her hand goes to their faces. Their braying and snorting give her comfort. She reaches for their noses, soothes them. Presses her face to their warm snouts and strokes their big ears. She takes comfort in their fur. They turn and leave her. Then a stretch of flat road and over the small bridge. She crosses the trout stream, crosses the road, and here she is at the Hotel-Ochsenwirtshof. A second or two later and she rings the desk bell for Juta.

Juta appears: "Rayne, *Guten Tag*."

"*Guten Tag*, Juta. Do you know the man that just came in?"

"No. He asked to see Fräulein Sinner. I dialed her room number but no answer. He thanks me, then he leaves."

* * *

Elora steps out of the shower, and in the steamy sink mirror, she sees the haze of her nakedness.

For a moment, she gazes at herself. Wondering.

Humble lines painted with care by an old-school master. Elora's muggy image on a glass canvas. The artist knew how to select his brushes. His colors. His paints. The pinks borrowed from wispy clouds at sunset. The golds and rose tones squeezed and crumpled from tubes of long-ago hues. Burnishing your lines, Elora, muted but real. A classic photograph, you are on the hazy glass. The artist using masterstrokes with nimble care to make you pretty, beguiling. You can see that, can you not? The artist's hand a master of light using brushstrokes that meld the portrait's shadows. Banishing the blemishes. His hand will never repaint this picture; you know that. The artist painted you from *within*. A masterpiece. The one you yearn to be. So that you can see yourself as you wish. Not as you are. That is the challenge. The one within. A new Elora. The sage abides time with tolerance and perseverance. And then only the sage, Elora, can anoint a new path. A new you. The air must take time to dry your image before the new image is redrawn. Can you allow that time to pass? Can you wait that long, Elora?

She wraps a towel around her head. When her hand picks up the terry robe, there is a knock at the door.

In the peephole, vulpine cheekbones, predatory eyes.

A viper wants to enter your room, Elora. Peering at you.

Maybe you should avoid the door?

Meese Van Der Leeuwen knocks again. Harsh.

El opens the door.

Van Der Leeuwen says, "Busy?"

"What's it look like." The towel on her head, and she wrapped in the terry robe.

"I called from the desk, knocked three times. What were you doing?"

"Masturbating thinking of you."

"*Putz*!"

"If I were, I'd be stroking a dead raccoon. What do you want?"

"A quick chat."

"Forty-five seconds."

He steps into the room, moves toward a chair.

"Easy, big boy. Don't bother settling down that Dutch ass of yours."

"A.G. Wants an update."

"On? My health? My happiness?"

Meese grins: "Your masturbatory preferences."

Asshole.

"Always convivial, aren't you, El. Always, always was. A.G. would like an update. Specifically, where's the red cell phone? And not too happy you haven't checked in. Starting to get a bad vibe from his daughter."

Elora points to the briefcase. The briefcase with Myles Lane's gold initials sitting on the credenza.

Meese says, "That's the only one now. Let me take a peek?"

The "only one" duly noted.

She presses the lock, the leather flap pops, opens the briefcase. Rummages through files and papers, a pack of Wrigley's, file folders, Chapstick, bills, receipts. Under this, a Blackphone with a red leather cover.

Meese says, "Please take the phone out."

She hands it to him. On the bottom right of the cover, barely discernible, the letter **E** scratched in. He drops it back into the briefcase, and Elora snaps it shut.

Meese saying, "Take it out again. A.G wants an examination."

"Of?"

"The software in the phone."

"Oh! Thank God! I thought you were about to squeeze into a pair of latex gloves and ask me to bend over."

"El, I would stick my finger up an elephant's ass before I—"

She yanks the towel on her head, drops it to the floor.

Meese says, "Should have left it on."

She places the phone on the credenza, and Meese hands her his phone.

Side-by-side, she turns them on.

On the red phone, she taps on an app: DL-77. The two phones start talking with each other. He takes three minutes, and they stand in silence, watching the screens scrolling, checking this and that.

TEST PASSED.

Elora says, "You can tell A.G. that the red one is still a go."

Meese says, "They also wanted me to tell you that the Wi-Fi signal has been expanded to one hundred feet, understand?"

She shakes her head: "Where's Myles?"

"Myles's got suddenly redistributed into the ionosphere yesterday. In Munich. Didn't you hear the news?"

"Why bother? Same old shit."

"Not this time, sweet pea. Myles went for the door handle on his car, his car exploded. Found him no bigger than a well-done beef roast under his rather crispy driver's seat. We have no idea how or why it happened."

"I'm heartbroken."

"I sense that."

"A.G. just wants to be certain that you *have* the second red phone. So, I am confirming that you do. And he sends his heartfelt best wishes and says he misses you."

"Hey, I can hold it up, drop the rob, snap a selfie."

"Also, one more item: Myles was sitting at a table with a woman in Munich before he left the planet. We have no idea where *his* briefcase is. So, we have no idea where his duplicate cell might be. A.G. is concerned about Myles's cellphone floating around unaccounted for. The probability of finding it, much less intact, is highly improbable. Probably destroyed in the explosion. We have pictures of him and the woman at an outdoor café near the opera house. Not particularly good ones. But we think she might be checked in here at the hotel."

Meese holds up his cellphone: a picture of Rayne and Myles at the outdoor table at the *Spatenhaus*. Meese asking, "If you happen to see her, or someone that looks like her, let me know?"

She nods reluctantly.

Meese says, "Maybe you should drop the one-hundred percent Egyptian cotton robe and the New York attitude, cover up your sweet ass with the latest fashions and find out. For A.G., not me. ASAP, okay? Name, rank, serial number, the whole nine yards. Quick, please." Then he adds, "Elora, I'm getting a sense of reluctance on your part—a less than enthused attitude here."

"The only enthusiasm I have right now is for you leaving this room." She moves toward the door.

Of course, I know her, you chuckleheaded slug—Rayne Foster. The bar? How could I forget? Trading shots and beer. Never quite felt that before. The two of us flirty-flirty. Putting on a buzz. I would have stayed longer at the bar, but that joker general on TV with his misguided politics in Washington, D.C., showed up on TV, harshed the whole buzz.

Elora ponders. Maybe you should ask yourself: Who is Rayne Foster, and why was she with Myles lane before he died in Munich. Why is A.G. looking for Rayne now? And why didn't I admit to Meese that I think I know who the woman is? Am I protecting her?

Yes, you puppy face moron, you *are* protecting her. Why? Tell me, why am I protecting her? You know why! Because you have a little tickle-wickle down there in the *looove* zone. Simple. And how many times in your life has *that* happened? Huh? How many? I don't hear an answer, El.

She opens the door.

Meese saying, "I'll be in touch."

"My anxiety is overwhelming."

Meese, thumb and pinky phone to his ear, says, "I'll give you a ring later."

"Don't bother—you'll be talking to a dial tone."

"Hey," Meese says, grinning, "Now you can finish polishing your you-know-what-skills," and he winks and leaves.

Elora thinks, "What have I gotten myself into?"

* * *

Rayne, one hour later, jogging up the hill she had slip-slided down earlier. Leotards, sneakers. Good cover.

She finds herself glancing up the hill for her friends, the Rhenish Warmblood horses. They sought her touch before. Now she wants to pet them again, give them a warm hug. Rub her face against their muscular jowls. And she is looking for the swaying sunflowers she admired and the perfect tomato patch and the chickens warily watching her stride. Wants to hear the Pointer barking.

Right now, she's looking for Elora Sinner. She watched her earlier walk up the dirt road. Maybe around the next curve?

Up the hill she continues.

A while ago, she had been on her bed with her iPad researching Elora Sinner and the Sinner dynasty when she heard Elora's door close across the hall. She slammed the cover shut. Jumped off the bed.

Her iPad had started to give her what she sought: Elora, the second daughter of A.G. Sinner, five years younger than her sister, Blake Wentworth Sinner (*aka* "Blake the Flake"). She made a penciled note to find out more about Blake. Both girls were born in New York City, Manhattan, raised in Bedford, New York in Westchester County.

Elora was named after her grandmother, Elora Elisabeth Sinner. Completed her secondary education at the Brearley School in New York City and graduated (straight Bs) with a bachelor's degree from Bryn Mawr. She loved birding since she was a child, took numerous courses on the subject until she could ID the obscure from the most obscure, "almost an expert." A.G. gently steered her away from birding because "you might have it difficult path to earn good money. Birds only produce songs and eggs." A.G. owned many businesses for Elora to join: supermarkets, multiple TV and radio stations, automobile agencies, a piece of a Formula 1 racing team, upscale restaurants, and multiple shopping centers. And he was massively connected to the strata of society that ran many global businesses.

Elora picked television. The only experience she had in TV broadcasting was deciding which streaming films to watch with her friends on weekends.

So, Elora discovered she desired a career as a manager of program acquisitions at her father's StarBright Networks, a cable television unit based in Manhattan. Seemed like "a fun gig." She had no grasp for "program acquisitions," a subjective notion, having worked at a StarBright property as an unpaid intern in Topeka, Kansas. Mostly acquiring take-out lunches for staffers, getting their cars washed, and polishing water glasses in the executive dining room prior to the arrival of guests.

Sooner than later, Elora got tired of the deadbeat routine. She wanted "action." Wanted to "sink my teeth into something creatively major." Since both Blake and Elora, at an early age, knew how to play A.G., Blake the Flake mostly got everything she wanted and was drastically more ambitious than Elora, who seldom asked for anything because it made her feel somewhat "obsequious (her word choice). Every chance he took, A.G. doted on them (their mother died two years after Elora was born).

Soon, Elora expressed interest in buying a sleepy about-to-go-dark, mom-and-pop daytime FM'er in Vineland, N.J. for $220,000. Elora was ecstatic. She would have an entire radio station to play with. Instead, she was momentarily sidetracked by Dad who steered the buying matter toward a much larger proposition: buying a pair of revenue busting NBC-affiliate television stations with big sticks (antennas) in Nevada on a $35 million loan secured personally by A.G. Within eighteen months, A.G. and Elora decided the best move was the sell move. They reorganized the stations and took two days to sell them for a $12 million profit. Publicly, Elora was touted as a financial genius in the broadcasting industry. Who knew? In one sense, she did offer a pivotal contribution to the sale: she picked the ink color for the Mont Blanc fountain pens (Sage Green) used to sign the contracts. And she showed her organizational skills and put together a memorable celebratory party after the signing.

A.G. had realized that daughter El was talented at organizing chips and dips rather than TV spot sales and make-or-break programming. And she was a *fashionista* with a brilliant smile that dazzled the universe. After, with nothing more to show for her efforts than a $12 million windfall, and no certain path to follow, Elora showed up daily at dad's New York City office in the MetLife building on Park Avenue around ten each morning, "learning the biz." Mostly organizing dinner parties and social events for her father and StarBright.

A short time later, A.G., his influence in political and social circles at its peak, secured her a "top secret" job at the American Embassy in London, where he had multiple connections. London, too damp and rainy for El, requested a transfer to the CIA's Berlin Station, specifically in the public affairs section where her organizational chops were put to use, putting together diplomatic receptions, cocktails parties, and selecting delectable hors d'oeuvres that few had ever seen before or could pronounce their names,

Now, after hearing Elora's door close across the hall, Rayne watches her cross Wolfacher Strasse, the road separating the hotel and the dirt road that goes up the hill. Rayne watches the way she moves, holds herself. Why, Rayne? What's the attraction? She cannot explain the feeling. El has a camera strapped over her neck and a pair of binoculars. Rayne changes into her jogging clothes and sprints out of the hotel for the dirt road.

Watch Rayne now, approaching the chicken pen. They come to her again clacking. Then she passes the horses with regret. Can't stop, boys. Must proceed up the hill.

She starts an easy trot.

Ahead, a curve where one side of the road dips into a shallow valley with sparse trees.

And there is the chips and dips queen, Elora Sinner, camera around her neck and a lightweight pair of binoculars in hand scanning a wide-open field of short grass opposite the stunted firs. She's wearing white slim ankle jeans, a band collar blue-stripe shirt, and a navy-blue blazer. Pure white, untarnished Converse sneakers. Tasty. Rayne respects the combo. Rayne can't ID the binoculars, but even from this distance, she knows the lightweight Leica camera (what else?).

Before Rayne takes two more steps, Elora turns and faces her and raises her hand. From this distance, Rayne sees Elora mouthed, "Hey!"

Rayne waves back, hastening to reach Elora. Wondering what's the quick step for, Rayne. Oh, shut up and be still. I'm just anxious to get this thing over with, book a flight back home. Rayne not convinced she believes that.

Before Rayne is ten feet away from Elora Sinner, she says, "Catch anything?"

"Oh, you are such a delight! Funny, girl. Yes, I have: two Brown Trout."

"And where might they be?"

"I ate them."

"Here?"

"Of course, nice and fresh. What would you have done?

"The same."

"You see: we have so much in common, Foster."

Rayne says, "Hey, how come you always call me Foster?"

"That's your name, isn't it?"

Rayne rolls her eyes, scans the trees. "What birds are out today?"

"Nothing special. So far. But then again, you have arrived."

"And what species am I."

Elora aims her binoculars at Rayne, moves them down from head to toe. "You might be a Ring Ouzel, Raven, Citril Finch, Water Pipit or Three-toed Woodpecker. Which would you prefer to be?"

Rayne does not hesitate. "A Citril Finch."

"Why so?"

"I know what they look like. Lime green, olive tones."

"And they are pretty, like you." She winks.

For the next five minutes they discuss birding. Elora's preference for the Leica (it's the best money can buy). Her binoculars (Nikon Monarch HG 8x42mm. Near $1,000).

Then they sit at the same bench where Rayne sat earlier where

Rayne hit up against a failed attempt (at least for now) to tell Leland she wanted to go home.

There, they talk about the beautiful landscape, the scenery, the purity. How much further could we climb up the hill? Whatcha think, Foster? What, Elora, might there be at the top for us to see? Maybe they should explore the topmost area, but on hiking boots, Rayne, and two of those cool German hiking canes and get lost in the forest and have a rescue team find us, coming with dogs and helicopters and carabiners and climbing rope. They laugh at that notion until there are tears in their eyes. The horses down the hill, aren't they beautiful. Where were you born (both in New York City but raised in Westchester? What a coincidence!). And this continues. So easy and so non-stop, and time has created no boundaries. They are getting lost in each other (picking up from when they were lost in Bushmills). Lost now without that drink. Not part of the past. Not seeing ahead. *Now*! And nothing around them that is peculiar, not the forest, not the trees and the flowers and the sunlight scent of the air and the joy they both feel. They skim across President Rand's suicide (neither can make sense of it, nor do they want to now). A brief pause does not hold them back, and they continue. A fly buzzes between them, and they wonder if it is related to the one Juta nailed in the kitchen. Another burst of laughter. Then, two bumblebees settle on the posies near them. So ponderous the bees that it bows the stalk. A butterfly chases it away, and Rayne and El amuse themselves, listening to the refined buzz until the sound fades, leaving a memory trail. The sun feels good, doesn't it, yes. Lovely.

But then Rayne says, bluntly, "What are you doing here?" The sentence comes from nowhere. For a moment, the sky collapses for both.

"What do you mean?" asks El.

"Here," says Rayne, waving her hand across the trees, "I mean, here at this spot, this hotel?"

"Birding. As you can see." A pause. Then, "Why did you ask me that, like you just did?"

Rayne, thinking for a moment, saying, "I don't know."

And they both smile, and that is what takes them back to where they just were.

Elora saying, "Hey—how 'bout dinner tonight? I have a table reserved at the hotel. Just for me. We could go crazy eating and drinking!"

Rayne thinks of Leland. Just for a millisecond.

She will have to tell him.

Tell him what, Rayne?

That, for now, Leland, I do not think I want to go home—to New York City.

And I'm starting to think I know why. Sorta.

I want to stay here. In this place. And maybe forever?

So, Rayne has to hold a tear from appearing, a tear before she answers El's invitation.

"I think that would be lovely," says Rayne.

"Seven o'clock? I'll tell Juta?"

Rayne nods happily. She cannot enunciate the word *yes*.

It would make her cry.

10
THE THIRD OPTION

Gilbert Scott, a glass of Crush Grape in hand, standing at his apartment window gazing at foggy lower Manhattan, waiting for Roger Kitchen's WhatsApp call.

Manhattan almost empty at this hour, Sunday morning. But Gil does not see the buildings, the streets. The geometric glory of the city. He checks his watch. The only thing he sees on his brain screen is an anchor desk and Roger Kitchens ten minutes past due. If you tell me you're going to call me at such-and-such time, fahchrissake, call me at such-and-such time.

Gil can never imagine any good excuses for not calling on time anywhere on the planet earth. Except maybe if someone's being beheaded by a Jihadist down the block and obviously can't get to their cellphone. *That* would be a good excuse. Roger said nine o'clock and Gils's watch says nine-twenty. For shit's sake, where the hell is he? This, one of the most important appointments of Gil's broadcasting career. In broadcasting, this doesn't happen. In broadcasting, this is mortal sin punishable by death.

He turns for the Crush bottle, pours another glass, checks his watch again: nine-twenty-one.

Now, in a whisper, he starts cursing Roger with a string of words he has never strung together before. He leaves out the classics. Instead, he stiches together never-before-used words to stir his anger. You should write a book, Gil. He comes up with prick face, brainless cow turd, and one of his faves, dickwad. But none beam the heat he needs.

So, he settles on one, his go-to phase.

Fucking asshole!

That, for now, is supremely satisfying. He pronounces it two more times. Then he takes it to the window and shouts it to the City. To his City. That sprawling steel and cement landscape. The place of endless dreams. Endless heartache.

"*Fucking asshole*," he shouts at the City. The City does not respond. This is good for Gil because it convinces him that you can throw a lot of bad shit at Manhattan, and Manhattan will ignore it and keep ticking day and night. The City, he knows, is steadfast. And so, Gil must remain strong for himself and his career,

And the name-calling is magical! Refreshing.

Roger's coming in over there on Gil's laptop on the dining room table.

Gil so excited he spills Crush on the beige rug and must hold himself from peeing his pants.

He plops down on a dining room chair and adjusts the laptop's screen.

There's Roger in a Brooks Brothers blue oxford cloth button-down shirt. Sleeves rolled up to his biceps, looking like he's really digging into this thing. Looking good, Rog!

Behind Roger Kitchens, a books case stuffed with lopsided, piles of magazines, an F-35 fighter model in steep climb mode, a porcelain Mickey Mouse statue. Roger appears to be at his Pentagon office.

Gilbert Scott (GS): Hey, can you hear me?

Roger Kitchens (RK): Yes, good morning, Gil. How goes it?

GK: Good. You?

RK: I got some good stuff, not as much as I would like, and me and my group have sources providing us with, at least, a start.

GS: What does it look like?

RK: A lot of things. The video file you received came off an iPhone, which I suspected.

GS: Belonging to?

RK: Blake Sinner. A.G. Sinner's oldest daughter. She's the one with the pretty feet. She more than likely set up the iPhone and started the recording.

GS: Oh, boy.

RK: Around Washington, DC, she is often referred to as Blake the Flake. Married once to an Arab *brazillionaire*. Lasted seven months. Since then, Blake Sinner dates only millionaires. Made a name for herself two years ago at a society party in Miami. Got drunk, challenged the hoity-toity crowd at midnight to a swimming contest—in the pool—*naked*. At first no one took up the challenge, so the Flake, she jumps in first. *Nude*. When the men there see the Flake's killer body *sans* the latest fashion, they dive in. Some of the women followed. Made all the newspapers around the world. About two years ago, she discovered General Cesar DeJean.

GS: The same DeJean involved—?

RK: You got it. Likes guy in unis. She visited Afghanistan as part of a PR trip for one of her companies. Has a couple of contracts with Uncle Sam. Met DeJean. Since then has been seen a lot around the social-slash-charity scene in D.C. A month ago, they were dinning at the Le Pavilion, super upper-crusty restaurant, you know, where they serve sirloin the size of saltine crackers and charge a hundred bucks. Something happened, they got into it, and the Flake tosses a glass of wine at DeJean, the wine *still* in the glass, followed it with a napkin, told him to "get your shit together," then stormed out. The patrons thought the place was slammed by an earthquake. DeJean, lucky boy, was not in his uni, which saved much embarrassment and diminished the negative PR impact. Sources say, the Flake wants to marry DeJean, and he won't have it. Hell hath no fury like a woman scorned.

GS: So, we have some revenge brewing here?

RK: That, or blackmail. Could be, yes. She's got a reputation for intolerance, not suffering fools gladly, and won't hesitate to bite your head off if you piss her off. Because she's ambitious and her father dotes on her, she's gone off and shown the world what she can do on her own. A.G. set her up in a lot of businesses since she graduated college, but she has worked hard toward branching off from him. Net worth's around seventy-five million. Drives a red 911 Porsche Carrera. Races sometimes on weekends out at the Hamptons.

GS: Question?

RK: Shoot.

GS: Why'd she send the flash drive to me?

RK: No idea. And who says *she* sent it to you. Also, she *lives* in Manhattan. Probably sees you doing the news and you were the first thing she thought of. What's also important is—

GS: Yes?

RS: The revenge-slash-blackmail factor: maybe she's getting set to tell him about the flash drive and stick it to him, and if you don't marry me—well, you get the drift?

GS: I do. Bad drift.

RK: Now, on the DeJean side. Boys and I have been digging, contacting some reliable sources. Not much love was lost between many Congressional types and DeJean. They say, on the surface, a nice guy that has a personality can melt a crocodile's ass. Underneath, a prick. So, there are a lot of people that want to see DeJean go down, and that's one reason I got the info I got. Plenty of people will give up some wild shit if they think it will take down a dickweed.

GS: So, she figures into this somehow? I mean, he's talking to her about something called Deadlight, and she's reacting like she knows exactly what he's talking about. This thing is like an artichoke. Gotta peel one petal at a time.

RK: Seems that way, yes.

GS: Yes.

RK: The Pugster it seems—and I emphasize *seems*—to be planning a coup d'état of the United States.

GS: Jesus! Hard to drag that into my head.

RK: Yeah, how big an ego has a guy have to have to pull *that* off? We are sure he's using the secession of the red Fourteen States as a jumping off point, or, as a cover for Deadlight. He's got a lot of crazy white supremacists and other ding-dong brains in the National Guard, QAnon, Proud Boys, a spattering of the always denigrated, reviled, that *everyone* loves to hate, the New-Nazis—all awaiting his command, all on his leash. *Bow wow* and off they go!

GS: And how is he going to put this—this coup?

RK: That, my friend, is the sixty-four-million-dollar question. We are working it. But, for the time being, do you recall Operation Valkyrie?

GS: The 20 July plot to overthrow Hitler?

RK: Because Germany had so many foreign workers, the Nazis were afraid they could revolt and take over the country. So, they built up a home army—a reserve force—in case the foreign workers revolted. The code word to activate was Valkyrie. The home army had prearranged assignments, such as taking over SS headquarters, taking over the radio stations, roadblocks, taking over Paris. But the plotters used that action to shut down and take over the entire country as cover to kill Hitler and install their own government.

GS: Didn't work.

RK: But it came damn close. And, we're thinking, set an example for DeJean and his National Guard. Now, instead of Valkyrie, we have Deadlight.

GS: Big question now is, when?

RK: You got a magic wand there in that apartment?

GS: I do not.

RK: Then, my friend, you will have to wait until the fat lady sings her last aria.

GS: So, what else?

RK: As you know, the Pugster was the last warm body to visit President Rand in the Oval Office. We have no idea why he was there on a Sunday morning. Shortly after, the president pulled the trigger.

GS: They went to school together.

RK: They were cadets, roommates at the Citadel. Two years marching to and from class and everywhere else was enough for Tommy Rand. He transferred to Boston College, got a law degree. One of my people did some research this morning, came up with something *extremely* interesting. While Rand was at Boston College, he roomed for two years with Myles Lane and his brother, Simon. Yesterday, Myles Lane was killed in a car bombing in Munich. He also roomed with a guy named Leland Upchurch, who is a first-rate spymaster at the CIA. The Lanes studied aeronautical engineering. Upchurch went for a law degree but never practiced. He was also recruited by the CIA. After graduating, both Lanes went to work for their father's aerospace company name of LaneAirTech.

GS: Missiles and drones and aeronautical guidance systems for the US military.

RK: After a couple of years, old man Lane passes away on Thanksgiving, goes face-first into his Turkey dinner. Simon Lane stated that was a total embarrassment to the family and never forgot his father for dying like that. The boys inherited the company. Myles apparently needed more wind in his sail and was recruited by CIA. Highly efficient he was, but insufferable at times. Eventually, he gets pulled into the CIA's Special Activities Center, specifically the Special Operations Group, one of the smallest components of the Agency, their clandestine arm. And Upchurch soon follows, and they forge a deep friendship. SOG, as it is referred to, is responsible for clandestine or covert operations that include covert ops and paramilitary "options" that the US government does not want to be overtly associated—AKA "black ops." Upchurch is one of their most outstanding assets. He's got a group of Paramilitary Operations Officers and Specialized Skills Officers. Obviously, they do not wear uniforms. One of Upchurch's top operatives is a woman, name of Rayne Foster. Graduated Marymount High School in Manhattan, the valedictorian of her high school class, attended The Catholic University of America, has an MA, BA. Proficient in several languages. Served as sports editor of the university newspaper during her senior year. Attended Columbia Law ostensibly to go into her father's law practice. Because her father and Upchurch were close friends, Upchurch recruited her into the Agency because he knew she hated working at a desk. Has a pilot's license, scuba dives, and has 182 parachute jumps. Because she flips flops from flying to skydiving, she is sometimes referred to as Airhead. Had a vanity plate with that on it.

GS: And another petal of the artichoke is peeled away.

RK: The reason I'm passing all this detail onto you is this: in case something should happen to me, you have as much intel as I have. And I want you to know the caliber of people involved in this.

GS: All of it intertwining into a big political operation.

RK: Yes. SOG is the most secretive special operation force with fewer than one hundred operatives. One of the oldest members today is Leland Upchurch, a major spymaster, who operates his own small, elite group of highly specialized operatives. If these SOG guys get into your shorts, your wonderful day in the neighborhood's gonna turn into corned beef hash.

GS: How far out are you from finding what DeJean's up to?

RK: Not sure. But what scares the shit out of me is two items—

GS: C'mon, nothing scares War Zone Roger,

RK: First, SOG's motto is *Tertia Optio* means "Third Option." In other words, the third option is a *covert* option when diplomacy and military action are not feasible. And that means knives and gunpowder. SOG might be preparing to go head-to-head with Deadlight.

GS: And number two—?

RK: No one, not a single one of my sources, knows the whereabouts of Leland Upchurch. That is very scary. The tiger is loose. So, I'll keep in touch. In the meantime, there's nothing you can do except clean your weapon.

GS: Anything on the anchor situation?

RK: Hate to disappoint, Gil, but no. Have been on this since I met you at the airport. Also, I don't want to harsh your buzz there. But you gotta know the line goes around the block three or four times. Anchors usually die in those charts, then they will the slot. You understand that, don't you? you?

GS: I sure do.

RK: Okay, buddy. Talk to you soon.

* * *

They click off Signal.

Gil picks up his Crush. Rattles the ice around. Sucks the last drops through a straw. The sputtering, watery jangle pierces his ears, his nerves.

Then he drifts to his window—the fog clearing.

"Screw you, New York City," and then thinking, what do I care about DeJean and all that other cow crap I just heard from Roger?

Then a practical response bangs around his brain cells: Well, Gilbert, perhaps you had best clean your weapon. Maybe, just maybe, Roger the Dodger knows what he's talking about.

And maybe he's not telling you everything he knows.

After all, he *is* Roger the Dodger.

11
FÜR EINE LANGE ZEIT

Rayne walks into the Hotel-Ochsenwirtshof dining room, hungry as a puppy and rag tired.

German décor here. Pine and dark woods blend with ruffled red and white curtains and white linen and beeswax candles and sparkling cutlery and the fragrance of the forest coming through the windows.

There is a dance floor and when Rayne sees the polished wood, she wishes for a dreamy twirl in the half-light with someone whispering to her in any language. She will understand. Holding her so close that the air leaves her breathless. Wishing.

Frank Sinatra is in the room, Rayne, singing to you, asking what you're doing the rest of your life. Yes, Rayne, you need to start again.

Rayne wants romance. Her Bandit in Miami, what happened to him? Still no text. Abandoned you, he did. Or has he just misplaced you? How could he have the courage to do that? Maybe you ought to contrive to keep your eyes dry. Start by replacing him with this evening, and whatever this evening brings to mind and heart? Give it a go? Sure.

Rayne wants to embrace an adventure of the heart and hold it forever. Might be difficult to do. Instead, for a silly moment, she sees herself unequivocally elegant, desirable. The thought makes her walk taller than she has walked a long time.

Oh, what the heart can do to us.

She wants her head scrubbed clean and fresh with food and alcohol and a challenging conversation, and to rid herself of looming responsibility. Shelve it for now, Rayne, it shall come back.

Now, what about Leland? What shall I say to Lee?

Hey, Lee, can you hear me, dear friend? I have something to tell you. Please, listen to me. I'm so tired and I think I want no more of this. I think I want to go home, Lee. Climb into my comfy bed, pull the blankets up close under my chin, which I have been sticking out much too much for you, and hope it is snowing and I can look out my window and see snow breaching my window ledge. No, wait. Maybe that is not what I *really* want. I'm so confused, Lee, please bear with me. I'm in a strange place right now. Can you give me another second to ponder? Another week? Another lifetime. Thank you, Lee. You are dear to me.

Rayne wants her head on a shoulder. Her fingers on a smiling face. A beckoning kiss. She wants to show the diners that she, Rayne Foster, is as beautiful as *she* thinks she is. Or wants to be.

When she sits down, she places her napkin on her lap and wants someone to lean into her and whisper in her ear—Rayne, yes, you are the most beautiful woman in the room. In the world.

She glances around the room and wonders about the lives of the diners. How do they compare to my life? Have they achieved what they set out to achieve? All the tables and booths are filled, mostly Germans. There are two German couples at one table buttering their bread, waiting for their appetizers. The men are partners, bankers, owning a parcel of small banks throughout Germany. Established couples relishing the comfort of an enduring relationship. They are in non-stop conversation, not staring at the pinewood walls wondering what to say. They speak softly. They seem happy. In the corner, alone at a table for two, an American who works in Munich for Siemens and vacations at the Hotel-Ochsenwirtshof alone every year for two weeks. Is he happier than the German bankers? She sees him sitting by the sea, reading a paperback and eating an apple. He appears pensive. Rayne feels sad for him.

A waitress in a dirndl asks if Rayne would like a drink. She will wait for her dining partner.

And then here she comes toward Rayne. Bringing that smile no one can ever forget.

Elora waves. Heads turn subtlety as she moves to their table and follow the beauty walking cross the room..

And there she is, Rayne. Give her a big wave back. Show your enthusiasm.

Elora, moving without pretense.

Rayne savors watching Elora walk.

Is liking this depraved, my fascination with her movements? Rayne can't answer the question—she does not want to know the answer. Not now.

Elora almost at the table, and Rayne thinking *comment merveilleux de la voir.* Her heart jumps.

Rayne feels something flutter. What the hell is *that*? She ignores it.

The feeling will stay with you for a long time, Rayne, so allow it to flourish. Savor it. These feelings seldom arrive pre-announced. They come like lightning. They are life's tender souvenirs. One of the surprises we cherish. They are presented in a box with a bow and left unopened until appropriate. Keep it close to you. Examine it in the future. At least until after dinner. Because whoever knows what happens after dessert.

Rayne rises from the table, and they embrace and air kiss. It is comforting and pretty.

Elora slips into the booth. It is the smoothest slide into a booth Rayne has ever seen. Rayne thinking, how can she move that elegantly? Tall women are usually gawky. Like baby giraffes. Maybe I should give that a go sometime? It's a perfect ocean wave sliding on shore and then slowly sliding back into the ocean. So fluid. Effortless.

Rayne and Elora at their table, shielded from the eyes of the restaurant.

Elora in black turtleneck. Chocolate brown leggings. Simple gold earrings. Stainless-steel Rolex GMT. Her hair is so cute, cut severe just above her collar. Understated sophistication. What did the great master architect Ludwig Mies van der Rohe say, Rayne? Less is more.

Rayne, with a big grin, saying to Elora, "There is a wonderful French expression, *dépouille*, which means 'without ornament.'"

"Yes?"

"That, in a word, explains you. Particularly the way you dress. Without ornament."

"Well, thank you, Foster! Sweet of you. You're not so bad either in the clothing department."

The waitress takes a request for a bottle of *Chateau De Saint Cosme Gigondas*.

Elora and Rayne flummoxed for a second for words.

Where to start, right?

"So," says Elora, you never told me about your background. What you do."

"Long story."

"Time is on our side."

"What do you think I do?"

"Another contest? I love it!"

"Guess. Three guesses."

Elora takes a few seconds.

"A dentist."

They howl. Heads turn. The German bankers and their wives glance over with a frown—*Amerikaners.*

Rayne says, "Go again. But first, you have to drink that whole glass of wine."

"That's the penalty? Didn't we do this at the bar? We're going to need a bank loan."

"A painter?"

"House?"

"Artist."

"*Nein, mein Freund.* Drink the whole glass of wine. And you get one more guess."

"And if I don't get it right?"

"We'll figure that out later."

"Okay, Foster, here's my best shot." A pause, then. "You are a jewel thief."

Rayne rolls her eyes. "No. But let me ask you, *why* do you say that?"

"You look like a woman in an Alfred Hitchcock movie—Ilsa Lund slash Ingrid Bergman, playing opposite Cary Grant in *Notorious* or with Humphrey Bogart in *Casablanca*. Or maybe Grace Kelly but with a bit more edge. You have that strong, I can-handle-anything look with a douse of, as the Germans say, *Eleganz*. But you also seem to have—how should I say?—a softness, a side you can't hide, that is vulnerable, that you dislike about yourself. And you work out. I can see that. A bit of an athlete in you. Good for scaling French castles and walking away with gobs of jewels, then putting on an evening gown and joining the merry party in the ballroom. How right am I?"

"You hit the wine bottle right on the cork," says Rayne.

"Thank you."

Rayne, saying, "I was going to be a lawyer. I mean, I am a lawyer. I graduated from law school, passed the Bar. My father had a great practice in New York City, and I joined right after graduation. A year later, I left. I liked cameras and photography more."

"Then what? I enjoy listening to you."

"I managed to make my way through freelance photo-journalism. I love the Grand Prix, Formula One, the Indy Series. If it has wheels and is loud, I'm down for it. And I've published two books, one on the Grand Prix—mainly because I love Monte Carlo and love taking pictures there—and the other book's on the Indy Five Hundred."

"I've been there! For the race!"

"Indianapolis?"

"No, Foster, Monte Carlo."

"I bet you have! Should have known better."

"What?"

"Classy you. You fit right in there. With the yachts and endless lines of Ferraris and Porsches."

The wine arrives. They don't take a moment to taste the ninety-five-dollar bottle of fine French wine. Other more important things to ponder.

They raise their glasses.

Saying, softly, "To our friendship."

"*Für eine lange Zeit*! For a long time!" says Elora. "So, what else? Tell me more. Ever been—?"

"Married? Close."

"Out there on your own?"

"And sorta liking it. You?"

"Was engaged to a jerk. Somehow, someway, I came to my own rescue."

"Painful?"

"Delightful when it crashed. I mean, literally. I dopped the engagement ring into his Margarita glass. Ice met ice."

"Classic move."

"Not sure about that. It antagonized him. And he's not the type you want to antagonize. He can get a grip on revenge and won't let go."

Rayne takes up the menu. "Want to order? They have a good menu."

"No," Elora says staring into Rayne's face. "Let's just talk and drink forever."

"Oh my God! They'll have to hire a crane and dump truck to get us out of here."

"Foster, let me ask you a question: compared to what's going on in the rest of the world, how bad would *that* be? Have you ever been picked up in a dump truck or hauled off in a crane?"

They don't ponder the menu for long. They both have the same dishes: Pancake soup, roast pork rib with fingerling potatoes, German red cabbage, and for dessert, red berry pudding.

Then Elora looks into Rayne's eyes and says, "I researched you."

"I'm not surprised. We all do."

Before the appetizer and the second bottle of wine arrives, Elora spills the data she picked up on the internet. Pictures of Rayne. What schools she attended. Her favorite books, the usual litany of half-made-up details and approximate dates. Rayne listens cautiously. She feels heat on her cheek. Wondering if Leland had enough time to "adjust" her credentials, her background for the current version of her Facebook page. She's relying on his professionalism and the speed the team spent on her new cover to match what Elora has read. If they don't get it right, Rayne knows, this whole mission could be blown.

Halfway through their pancake soup, Rayne says, "And you and your happy life? What do you do in the daylight hours?"

"I work at the American Embassy in Berlin."

"Doing?"

"Unlike you, nothing exciting. I'm at a desk most of the time, planning. I'm the social director for the Embassy. I plan diplomatic parties, teas, receptions." Elora rests her spoon and signals the waitress.

Rayne saying, "And that seems to make you sad?"

"Does it? Well, Foster, you're charming, smart, *and* perceptive. I don't like my job. Good at it, but don't relish it. It was handed to me, like most things in my pampered life. My father, A.G., got me into it ahead of dozens of others more deserving. And this breeds resentment that is palpable among my peers."

Elora summons the waitress for the wine menu.

"Another bottle?" asks Elora.

Rayne grins.

"Riesling okay with you? They have a J.J. Prüm, very tasty."

"You're the wine boss."

The waitress takes the menu.

A song on the speakers brings the German couples to the dance floor—Jimmy Durante, singing *I'll See You in My Dreams*. The song is romantic, slow, and the German couples are joined by a few more dancers. Amusement and delight lift the room.

I'll see you in my dreams
And I'll hold you in my dreams
Someone took you right out of my arms
Still, I feel the thrill of your charms

Rayne finishes her red wine and looks up at the ceiling, at the music. "Know who that is singing?"

"Of course," Elora says. "I know the song—Jimmy Durante, *I'll See You in My Dreams.*"

"*Get out*! How the hell did you know that?"

"My father. He loved all sorts of music. That song is a classic. Listened to it all the time when I was a kid. The first time I kissed a boy, that song was playing. Released on Brunswick Records, it charted for sixteen weeks during 1925. Seven weeks at number one in the United States. JimmyDurante, the Great Schnoozola, later took it to new heights."

"Your musical knowledge is astounding."

Elora, winking: "So are you, Foster."

The Prüm arrives. They don't watch the waitress pull the cork or pour.

Silently, they sip, listening to the music, pondering.

Elora glances at the tablecloth. Moves her fingers toward Rayne's, stealthy, slowly, her fingers feeling the heat of Rayne's, listening to Jimmy trilling.

Lips that once were mine
Tender eyes that shine
They will light my way tonight
I'll see you in my dreams

Rayne finds to her surprise that Elora's fingers are welcome.

Elora smiles. Sips half the Prüm. Their stares meet. *Lock.*

Then she raises Rayne's hand to her nose, savoring the charm of her scent. And with their hands against Elora's lips partially hiding her face, Elora says:

"Kiss me, Foster. Kiss me right here at this table."

"Here?" Rayne giggles.

"Dance floor then. Let's go."

The tone urgent. Impulsive. Determined.

Five seconds later Elora has decided the time is right, and the music makes her embrace Rayne on the floor. Rayne in her arms now. The only sound is the music. Not the chatter of the restaurant. Not the shuffle of shoes. Not the drop of a dinner plate. Elora presses her way through Rayne's hair, and she whispers on her cheek into her ear, "Kiss me here."

Rayne says nothing. A jolt slams through her. Was that a tiny gulp you just made, Rayne, huh? Regulate your breathing, please? At least close your eyes.

She brings Elora in closer, not as close as she wants, just enough to feel her breasts pressing hers, and they both let Jimmy Durante take them away, as far away as far away is, and then further and further away.

Soon my eyes will close
Soon I'll find repose
And in dreams you're always near to me

Then Jimmy evaporates, and they're back at their table and going at the second bottle of wine and thinking about a third, and is that the room tilting this way and that? No, silly. It's the planet Earth, girls. It's moving off trajectory, like you. But you can bear under it. Take another sip.

Rayne's eyes are on Elora's.

Rayne saying, "You said your father got you the job?"

"Yes. And so many other things. Too many and with my hand out without guilt."

"So, what are you going to do about it?"

Elora shrugs her shoulders.

The entrees arrive, and the surprise is they're both hungry and start eating. Thinking maybe the food will cut the haze of expensive wine. Probably not. And why try to banish the buzz right now, Rayne. Both of you are eight inches off your seats and about to bounce off the coffered ceiling.

Elora takes a bit of time pronouncing her words, saying, "My father got me a lot of things in my life. And that giving taught me a lesson: taking for me is a lot harder now than giving. But taking is like a drug: you can't stop when it's as simple as drinking water. My sister, on the other hand—"

"You have a sister?

"Yes, older. Her name is Blake. We're about as opposite as a spoon and fork. Haven't talked in years. Remember yesterday at the bar, how I walked out when that army general was being interviewed on TV? Well, Blake the Flake—that's her nickname—is dating him and I think he wants to marry her. He must be as whacky as she is. He's got to be intrigued by her wealth."

The wine arrives and they watch wordlessly as the waitress cuts the foil at the neck, unscrews the cork. Both using the moment to ponder what Elora's been saying.

Rayne, you better start taking notes on what's going on here. Leland, remember? He's going to want to know about this Elora Sinner. And you're getting your head soaked in expensive wine and fluttering sensations you can't or won't describe (denial?).

And, coincidentally, her cellphone beeps. She glances down at a text message from Leland. She has to blink twice to give to read the message—the wine taking an intricate serpentine pattern in her brain.

Leland Upchurch
Pls meet me tomorrow morning 9 a.m. at the Wolf and Bear Park in Bad Rippoldsau-Schapbach. Easy to find. Bring briefcase. ~ LU

So, Rayne is now trying to unscramble the brambles and vines coiling in her head. Leland and the increasingly complex operation. Her indecision (or not?) regarding returning to Manhattan. And there, across from the table, Elora staring at her (*that* stare), boring through her eyes.

Rayne asking, "Do you have money of your own?"

"Ha! Plenty."

"Then what's the other problem."

"My father. It would break his heart if I broke away."

"Broke away. What's that mean?"

"He owns a fifty-five-million-dollar mansion on sixty-eighth street in Manhattan. I have two floors to myself, including a Porsche in the garage at street level," Elora says, taking a pause. "You know what, Foster, I don't want to talk about it for now, and I appreciate you lissenen—I *mean lis-e-ning*. It's bringing me down and taking me away from here. We can talk about this when there's less brain in my wine."

"You mean less wine in your brain."

"No. I meant what I said." They laugh.

Thirty minutes later, the second bottle of wine has vanished, and the third is diminishing. The red berry dessert absent from their bowls, their speech feathery.

Elora saying, "Time for beddy-bye."

"Me too."

"Where's your room, Foster?"

"In this hotel."

"No! I mean where? Where is—?"

"Second floor. In *this* hotel."

"Me too. Less go."

"To where?"

"Second floor."

"Oh, *lord*. I jus' said that."

"Okay. Less go again. The second floor. After you, Foster."

"After you, Sinner."

So they go.

Rayne cups Elora's elbow and guides her toward the restaurant's door.

They pass over the dance floor, where Elora whispered in Rayne's ear, felt the heat coming off her chin. They both nod at the Germans, who nod politely smiled back at them. Everybody's happy. Joy aplenty. Alcohol effective.

Then they are at the stairs, Rayne gripping one banister, Elora locked on the other until step-by-slow-step they manage the ascent to the second floor and waver down the hallway toward their rooms.

Elora asking, "Foster? Where you going?"

"My room. Right here."

"Come to mine. It's right here. Come. Less go in. We can—"

"Look," Rayne says, dangling her room key, "see, this is my room. Right here. One zero eight."

"Hey, Foster! Your room is right across from mine! One zero nine! We're hotel buds." They giggle. "Come into mine for a delicious tequila. Please, please. We can put on our jammies, PA-JA-MAS. Have a sleepover. I have tequila in there, the bes' you've ever drunk, drank" says Elora knocking on her door. "Hell-owe mister tequila, can you hear me in there. It is Elora; let me in. I want you."

They are frozen in the hall between their opposing rooms.

When Elora takes Rayne's wrist in her hands, she shuts her eyes to allow the touch, the power, to linger. A second later, she opens her eyes and sees Rayne's head tilted back, reveling in Elora's touch.

Rayne allowing the tide to tumble, hoping for the next wave.

Saying to herself, she is almost damned sure she has never felt this way before. What the hell is this?

Then slammed against the wall.

Splayed.

Elora's hands around Rayne's wrists, pinning her. Then their fingers intertwined, gripping.

The butterfly cannot escape.

Does not want to.

This is all out of place Rayne, out of character. Where goes this?

Saying to herself, Rayne, *it's called being drunk*. But not certain. Is that it?

And why are you allowing Elora to do this?

Letting Elora press her vagina into Rayne's, pressing it, pushing, and feeling the heat triple as she presses harder and harder, sharpens, feeling her wetness swelling into a cascade. So hungry. Wants to pull down Rayne's pants and slide her finger in over and over, drumming up and down, until she quivers, and Rayne's mouth feeding on Elora's and wanting her hand, all of it, every finger, flat against her stomach and going down, sliding. Elora crushing her, and all they feel now are their lips, the scent of their breath, the taste of their tongues.

Elora saying, "Don't stop kissing me, please, don't stop."

Rayne's arms wrapping around Elora's neck. Pulling in. No handhold. She's never had an orgasm standing up, and she's not going to have one now, but this is so, so close. This is *further* than an orgasm. This is lost-my-mind-outta-control-going-to-hell-and-not-coming-back. This *woman*. This *Elora*.

"Don't stop."

It hurts, the kissing, and they cannot breathe, stopping only to stare into their eyes.

"Don't stop. Please."

Rayne bringing her knees around Elora's waist. Gotta jam into her. Squeeze her.

Then, they hear the German couples trudging up the stairs, and they jolt away.

Unlocked, taking a swell of their juices.

Rayne, stepping toward her room, saying, "See you tomorrow?"

And El parting with an air kiss.

Winking, whispering: "I'll see you in my dreams."

And disappearing behind her door.

And before she closes she realizes:

Rayne did not return the air kiss.

And Rayne in her room, wondering.

The next morning, not far from the Hotel-Ochsenwirtshof, at the Bear and Wolf Park on Rippoldsauer Strasse, Rayne waits for Leland Upchurch. She's sitting on a bench watching the people in the admissions area.

Atop the hill, the massive enclosure where the bears and wolfs mingle and draw people. It is caged topography, man-made, and the wolves and bears observe the patrons observing them. The bears and wolves love it. Rayne envies them. They're cared for and admired. The two species live in harmony.

What were you last night, Rayne? A bear or a wolf? What was Elora? How do you feel about hallways now and the dangers they cannot suppress?

Last night's encounter ended precariously, suddenly.

And maybe seeing it over in your mind is what's making your stomach tighten now.

Rayne imagines being caught by the conservative banking couples climbing the stairs the same time the two of you were simultaneously attempting your ascent. Perverted *Amerikaners* humping in the hallway of a hotel. The *polizei* would have been summoned had they caught you in an arduous lip lock. Wouldn't that have been joyful for all back at the police station. And if they caught Elora with her hand down your pants, dear Jesus, you would've been arrested and, according to German law, beheaded in the town square. No trial. Bad end to a good evening, no?

So, last night, a bear and a wolf engaged in a *danse de l'amour* in a hallway of a hotel in the Black Forest. Endlessly breathless, the two of you. Squishing and squashing. Elora feeding on your kisses. You made her so happy.

Can you imagine? You? Rayne Foster? The questions cause her to grin. Then more from the playback reel brings a broader grin, and she murmurs her name. "*Elora.*" As if she is an eloquent, revered visage from a fairy tale. From the same lips, torched and charred last night, right, Rayne? *Burned. Burned, Burned.*

And lest we forget the *heat* of the moment.

So, what were you last night, Rayne Foster? You have not answered. What was Elora last night?

Rayne, she slammed you against a wall, a crucified butterfly you were, with your arms supplicating. Your wrists bound with her fingers. Yearning? Of course.

Je me rends!

Well, I did surrender to her. I did.

Was there anything wrong with that?

Only a bear would have the power to take the kind of push you took. Elora, grinding into your pelvis, feeding off your mouth like a ravenous wolf with unimagined power and thirst. Devouring you. Thinking about it gives Rayne a low-grade fever.

She forbids the images. Not wanting to see them right now. But then asking herself, why don't you want to play that scene back again in your mind? Why? Maybe later? After Leland leaves you here alone again.

Next to Rayne on the bench, a brown shopping bag holding Myles Lane's briefcase, the one she took out of the safe at the hotel. She hadn't looked at it since she gave it to Juta to put in the hotel safe and never looked inside. So, she decides to take a peek. Vows not to open it, not to peer inside the briefcase until Lee is with her.

Rayne knows that there must be a million variations on men's briefcases, and that so many appear similar. But this one's a Lorenzo Scott. A reddish-brown leather with a V shaped flap, the clasp at the crux of the V. She opens the paper bag wide enough to look down at the briefcase. It's tattered. Brownish blood stains, furrows caused by shrapnel from the car. One end shows a smokey black burn mark. It smells like gunpowder and blood. The flap is not secured in the lock. The handle intact because Myles's and was wrapped around it when the blast kicked in. She sees the kid on his bike again, snagging it, pedaling away. She doesn't want to look at it anymore.

She crumples the paper bag closed, and when she looks up, there's Leland looking down at her.

Rayne says, "Did you take the tour?"

"Not yet."

"Want to?"

"Let's do this first," he says, tapping the paper bag.

They walk to Leland's BMW, a maroon X5, the Alpina model with 345 horsepower.

"Treating yourself nicely, Lee?"

"I convinced accounting I might need something for hot pursuit over hills and valleys, so they okayed the rental." He winks at her.

Leland has directed big and small operations involving the life and death of men and women who worked for him. And the idea that it seems Rayne is the only operative working for him now says much about his professionalism. He gives whatever he has to every mission working from the smallest, most sacrosanct slice of covert ops. For many years now, he has been considered "the main man" in the Special Operations Group. Revered and sought after, Leland Upchurch, master spy, seldom gives away his feelings. But Rayne has known him since the day she was born. She can read him more than anyone. And today, she sees something in his spy's eyes that is troubling. He's working too fast, too burdened by fault and doubt. Whatever the hell this is about, Rayne figures if anyone's going to figure it quickly, it's her.

He's sitting behind the wheel, rolls back the seat as far as it will go. The paper bag is sitting on the console between Rayne and Leland. He opens it, tosses the bag on the back seat, and peers inside.

Rayne asks, "What are you looking for?"

"A Blackphone with a red leather cover."

"And that's what he wanted to give me to give to you?"

"Yes."

"Well, skipper, now we're making some progress. However, I must say Mister Lane had a major change of heart, wouldn't you agree?"

"I would."

Leland opens the briefcase. He grips four file folders, pulls them out, and places them on Rayne's lap. Inside are sales receipts, blood work from a laboratory, a TV manual, crumpled gum wrappers. He does the proforma search for anything clandestine: GPS devices, AirTags, hidden microphones. He finds a pen.

"Here," he says and hands the pen to Rayne. "See if this works, then open it up and check it." She clicks it, scribbles on paper; it works. Unscrews it, no spook stuff inside.

He stares out the window. "The briefcase is clean." Then, under his breath, he murmurs three words he has never uttered in Rayne's presence: "Pissed I am."

"Odd combo," she says.

"It does not truly express how pissed off I am."

"Okay, skipper, why don't you tell your best friend's daughter what this is *really* all about."

"This is not good," Leland says, slamming the briefcase shut. He reaches back, snatches the bag, slams the briefcase inside. Then he presses back on the seat.

He reclines, gazes through the sunroof, then the windshield. Taps the steering wheel three times with his finger. Folds his arms and says, "Okay, let's talk a bit about your friend."

"My friend?"

"Elora. Elora Blythe Sinner. Scion to billions."

Since earlier this morning, Rayne was content, starting to mellow a bit. Because Lee seemed eager to provide a bit of information about Myles and the briefcase and the Blackphone, but she had not thought about how deep he would go about Elora Sinner. About last night? Do you reveal, or do you not reveal, Rayne?

"She works at the American Embassy in Berlin in the—"

"I know all about Elora Sinner's background and her father. I want to know more about present-day Elora Sinner, present day.

Why's she here? What's she up to, okay? I want your professional impression, and assessment." He abruptly pulls the door handle. "Let's take a walk."

They head toward the ticket window. Then they stop, and Leland looks into Rayne's eyes.

Leland asking, "How does she seem to you?"

"Very wealthy. Conflicted about who she is—signs of self-loathing, which seem to be some anguish in her life. A bit immature. She has been pampered all her life by her father and is getting a sense of being worthless—in other words, she doesn't seem to think she's accomplished anything on her own, without her father. And she's trying to find a new direction."

"Did she seem fidgety, nervous?"

"No."

"Have you seen her with anyone?"

"No."

"When were you with her last?"

"Yesterday, she left her room and walked up the hill across from the hotel. I changed into my jogger clothes and surprised her. She had a camera and a pair of binoculars."

"She's a birder. What else?

"We talked. About birds. Nothing special."

"Yes."

"Then she invited me to dinner. Said she had a table, would I like to join her. I did."

"And?"

"We ate and drank a lot."

Here it comes, Rayne: tell or no tell.

"Then?"

Rayne? Can you answer?

"Then?"

Okay, here comes the tricky part.

"We wobbled back upstairs to our rooms—they're opposite each other—and said goodnight. Before that, she asked if I'd like to go hiking today. I said yes."

"Good. Try to find out who the man was that visited her. What else?"

"I think she's falling in love with me."

Leland tries to hold his surprise, but he's not successful. He raises his left eyebrow.

"Say again?" Leland falls back a step.

"I believe she's falling in love with me."

"Well," he says, with a grin, "I can't blame her if she is. That's good news, Rayne. Advantage *us*. We can use this. We might have a good cards here. This could be a big break."

But Rayne, you haven't told the boss the whole truth, have you? You have not revealed all the fervent minutia. Can you utter why? To yourself, of course. No? Figured as such. Maybe later. Could be difficult describing Elora's heated yearning, devouring you pinned against the wall in the hallway. Oh, wait! What about your reciprocation. No?

They're standing at the ticket booth waiting their turn for tickets, Leland off on some interplanetary star wondering. A kid with a lopsided ice cream cone skips by, and Lee steps out of the way, annoyed.

Leland saying, "This is a not first for me," he says, shaking his head. "In fact, now that I think about it, we can probably work this to our advantage. When did you come to this 'falling in love' conclusion?"

"Last night. At dinner. Two and a half bottles of wine.

"And?"

"We did a lot of talking, our backgrounds. Usual stuff people discuss when they first meet."

"And?"

"Well, after two and half bottles of wine, we were pretty zoned out. We helped each other upstairs, and when we got to our rooms, we slurred through 'good night', and she asked me to go hiking today."

Leland purchases two tickets, and they start the walking tour, not speaking.

Then Rayne says, "During dinner. That's when."

A second before a gray wolf spots them, Leland stops abruptly, "Myles Lane committed suicide."

Rayne has a vague look of surprise on her face.

"How do you know?" she asks.

"Same way you think Sinner's falling for you. Gut instinct. Which more often than not seems to cut the mustard."

They move along the beaten path, and the wolf remains still, but his eyes stay on them. Then he takes two short steps, slow, keeping pace with them as they move up the hill.

"Why?" asks Rayne.

"Long story."

This operation initiated by Upchurch is exclusive.

Only one executive in the intelligence community knows of its existence. No one else in the intelligence community has any awareness of what specifically Leland Upchurch is on to right now. Worse, he is not back in Virginia watching over this. He is out in the field thousands of miles from a safety net with Rayne not fully trusting him, and he can't find fault with that. Worse still, he has persuaded SOG to allow him to kick off an operation that, marginally, belonged to other parties. But, in essence, Leland Upchurch admitted that he would be a wildcat, a rogue (as Rayne suspects). Fully sanctioned to commit homicide without pushback of any kind. And they went with it, full tilt. But this is what SOG does. Operates outside protocols. If necessary, Leland Upchurch will initiate the third option and without blowback.

And only because he had convinced the executive entirely that this was "the most sensitive operation that I have ever seen" did he let Leland go unbound. At the same time, assuring him that all the resources of SOG would be his if needed. He could ask for the world now and get it.

Leland and Rayne stop and gaze at the gray wolf. He is majestic and pure and muscular. Blessed by nature with a thick, beautiful coat. His bright eyes are curious, and his foot-long bushy tail flicks a big fury fan slowly. He won't take his eyes off them. Not until something innate signals, then he will move on to some other leisure.

Rayne can feel Leland's puzzlement. She senses his frustration. And not surprisingly, she wants to help him.

Leland saying, "Two things happened in Munich: Myles either didn't put the phone in the briefcase, or he did, and the explosion blew it out. In that case, we'll never find it."

"What was he supposed to do?"

"He asked me to send you because he had something to give you. At that time, I had no idea what it was. But I found out. He said he would explain it all to you and ask you to pass it along to me. He said it was so sensitive that the only way to convey it was verbal—not in writing, not via text, not decoded. Verbally."

"Lee, you're never going to find the phone. Myles Lane is dead. You'll never know what he did with the phone before the bomb went off."

"Tell me again what he did at the table."

"He jumped up and jogged to his car. He took the briefcase with him. He reached into his pocket, took out the key fob. When he reached the car, he pointed it at the door handle. And then—"

"The car blew."

"All of this ignores the elephant in the room: Why would he commit suicide?"

Leland says nothing.

"And," asks Rayne, "Why is the phone so central to this?"

"I'm going to hold back on that for a while."

"Why?"

"I don't want to jeopardize you. If you know the importance of the phone, someone would be able to pry it out of you. There will come a time."

Up ahead on the path, the kid with the ice cream cone is trying to push a French fry through the fencing. His father tells him to stop. The kid wants to attract a bear. His mother yanks him away, and he starts bawling. His mother says French fries go into your mouth, not the bear's, and oddly that turns the kid silent.

Leland, Rayne notes, has an odd look in his eyes. He's pondering, saying something he does not want to say.

Before she can start to guess what, he says, "There are two phones, identical in every aspect. One is backup for the other. We—you—have got to get the second phone."

"From?"

"Elora Sinner."

Then Rayne feels it's time to tell him.

She says, "I've decided to unpack."

"I knew that you would," says Lee, grinning for the first time this morning.

Rayne wondering, am I staying for the operation? Or something else?

She can't answer her questions.

12
THE BUNKER

Meese van der Leeuwen at the wheel of his Mercedes-Benz *Geländewagen*, Simon Lane in the passenger seat driving higher and higher up the mountain. No headlights.

Elora Sinner on the backseat, squirmy, sullen, and slumped.

If she could, she would bale now. But A.G. keeps the leash on. Where would you go anyway, Elora? Back to your humble desk at Berlin Station and prioritize your list of lovely canapés and select wines. Watch the tropical fish lap the fish tank? You have no idea, so shut up and use your brain. Amuse yourself with a lantern of thoughts. Whisper sing the Giacomo Puccini aria from La Boehme: *O Mio Bambino Caro*. Think of Rayne. *O Mio Bambino Caro*. How beguiled the angels must've been painting Rayne's lips and sketching her sky blue eyes, her hair. To perfection. Close yours and gaze at hers. Smell her. Keep the music strong. The angels, El, heard the same aria you hear and felt the same joy your thoughts crave. Ignore the knuckle-brain driving them up the mountain. He is not a philosopher. You are, El. Delight in those pebbles darting against his precious door panels.

Meese asking, "How much further?"

Silence.

Elora saying, "I have to pee."

Silence.

Brooding at the wheel because he's driving his $160,000 Jade Green German constructed G-wagon to do the climb up the hill. Meese knowing the drive up's going to sully the lacquer with a veil of dust and speckles of pebble knicks. It might be offered as off-road capable at the showroom, but Meese can't think of anyone except the Exalted Prince of All Light and President for Life of Botswana that would go off-pavement with a ride like this.

Elora refused to allow them in her Defender. Her vehicle twenty-five years old, but El has it suited to showroom new shape. Mechanically it is a dreamboat—a classic, like you, Elora Sinner. No way I'm driving up that pebble-layered dirt road with my car.

After a sixty-second verbal battle of nonsensical proportions, Meese's resistance collapsed, and they climbed in the G, the rear door slamming too hard for his liking. Elora, in her mind, doing two victory laps, one fist-pump followed by two satisfying *yes, yeses.*

Simon in the passenger seat happy as a drake on a lake in sunlight, paddling his way to a new beginning. A state-of-the-art SatMap GPS device is on his lap, indicating, yes, Simon, you are on course here. You know where you are going. Take your pleasure and let these two daffy-ducks to their own devices. He smiles and nods to himself. Feel the dream, Simon. Not to worry. A few more minutes past clusters of trees and you'll arrive. You will. And then LaneAirTech will blossom fresh and money-green again.

El again: "I *said* I have to pee."

They push past the bench where Elora and Rayne chatted yesterday. That poignant bench. She can barely see the outline, the spot where the bee vibrated the air, and the colorful butterfly flew between them. She senses the bench more than she sees the bench. She sits up, slides across the Nappa leather, and presses her nose against the window making a smudge on the glass shaped like Cuba. There it is, Elora. The sight of the bench brings back yesterday's delights. Now she feels saddened. Rolls the window down and enjoys the cloddy air. Then inhales again and again and again and again. And once more before the outline recedes.

Meese saying, "I can't see a damn thing. Where the hell're we going?"

"Keep going. You're doing quite well," Simon says. Both of them concentrating on the road, landmarks.

From the backseat: "Keep going, and I'm going to soil your leather."

Slow going, not because they cannot see but because they do not want to be seen or heard.

Meese van der Leeuwen wondering how high up this pile of trees and scrub he has to drive to cop a major score. A once and for all score.

There is always a mountain, isn't there, Meese? And you always have to strive for the top, not the middle. Why is it never the middle? That would be too damned easy. Like finding the key to your door. Always the last one on the ring. That's where the big, big, score's live, beckoning, dangerous—at the top of some mountain top that you can hardly breach.

Black trees, black gravel. The grass is black. The road is black. At night, that's when it was named the Black Forest.

Meese again: "Difficult to see. How much longer?"

Meese just wishes they would get to where Simon is leading them and then get down off the mountain. Meese, with his murky background and ersatz credentials. An INTERPOL person of interest for a litany of questions. If they're stopped and questioned by the police on this dirt road with the CEO of LaneAirTech; the daughter of A.G. Sinner, former American ambassador, Elora an employee of God knows what—what a hard-blowing storm that would be.

Simon never told either one of them they would be driving up a mountain in the dark.

Elora glances at the glow of her Rolex. She's supposed to be having a drink now with Rayne.

From the darkness, again: "I have to pee."

But with the sputtering pebbles and crunch of the Pirellis on the dirt path and the concentration upfront, no one hears about Elora and her urinary urgency.

Meese has wanted to deal with Simon for a long time. But there's a lot to pay to deal with Simon. To buy his in-demand weapons direct from the billionaire owner of LaneAirTech and bypass the US government's labyrinth of regulations is one more thing that no one ever brings up in his presence: Another thing: Simon's snotty attitude and go-to-hell-arrogance is another. Oh, and there's one more thing: Simon reminds Meese of a squirrel. He's never dealt with a rodent before. Rats, yes, but not a squirrel.

"I had no idea this is where we were going," Meese says.

"You should've asked me, I would have told you."

Simon's fingers are wrapped around a high-tech SatMap GPS device that looks like it dropped down from the StarShip Enterprise, that only a tech-head like Simon would have. That gives him assurances. Gives him the power. He could have managed this with an Apple Watch.

Every few seconds, when the screen refreshes and the coordinates on the screen change, the squirrel snickers. He is loving this, yes, holding the device clamped between his knees, smiling. Know the little journey is driving Meese crazy. The screen so detailed Meese wonders how Simon can read the data.

Meese, to the windshield, says, "This is painstaking; it is."

Simon starting to lose his patience with Meese's wariness. "You wanted to come. You wanted proof, and I can't blame you. But this is how we do this. In the dark. We always come up here in the dark."

And again, from the back seat, "Meese, if you don't care, I'll just let loose on the leather."

Meese, in his trade, has been on many risky kicks where a slight misstatement or teeny bit of mistrust could creep into the conversation, and some teenage terrorist cowboy trying to make a name for himself suddenly shoots your scrotum off because he didn't like your haircut—something Simon and his quiff should be aware of.

Meese glances at Simon. For the last few seconds, he has been silent, concentrating. Then whispering to himself as the numbers on the screen change rapidly, the satellite doing a happy boy dance up there in the twilight zone.

Right now, Simon could be an alien devil down here to sprinkle some spooky alien devil juju on the planet. But the faint smile says the drive up the mountain feels good to him. We are going the right way.

"Keep going. The altitude's coming up. We're good."

We're good? Who says?

Meese could use a Martini. A big one. Big as a swimming pool. A fireplace. Getting toasty and mellow. Because he has several governments counting on him. He didn't exactly promise them, but he said it is almost a sure thing. Give him a few days more. They all agreed.

"Take a left now."

"Before you do that," says Elora, calmly, "Stop the car, or I let loose here, right on this two-thousand dollar option I'm sitting on, and you'll have to replace the whole seat."

Meese hears the rustle of clothes, turns. There's Elora, long legs stretched out, thumbing down her panties, saying, "Don't want to ruin my Ralph Lauren's."

Meese stabs the brake pedal. "What the hell're you—" They jolt forward. The SatNav falls to the mat—"There! Happy now!"

Elora kicks the door open, takes off like a jackrabbit into the dark.

Simon glances down at the SatMap. He's looking for an altitude of 842 feet and some longitude and latitude coordinates he has scribed in his brain to match those scrolling on the screen.

Simon saying, "Yeah, we have to take a left here. This *is* it."

"Here? It? What're you talking about" says Meese, looking through the windows.

There is no left to take here, squirrel face, or so Meese thinks because he only sees the shrub and dead tree limbs on the ground and the walls of black fir and impenetrable brush. Now, his trust meter's fallen off to zero. There could be a falloff here, he imagines.

And the Geländewagen—driving through the brush. Scratching the green finish. The thousand-dollar five-spoke rims.

Simon has to be skull crazy. He's got the coordinates screwed up or something, or the SatMap's busted. He struggles to keep his anger bolted. You had a two-hour drive here from the airport, and you could have gotten a bit more info out of Simon. You jerk.

They might drive over a cliff, Meese thinks. He has goose bumps. He feels a chill.

He sees them doing a nose over into an abyss, freefalling, and they don't have seat belts on, and Meese's vulpine face, there it goes, busting through the windshield and spraying glop over the G-Wagon's hood.

"There is no left!" Meese shouts.

Elora opens the door, jumps back in, slams the door. "You boys miss your chaperon?"

Meese hurts his neck turning, and he glares at her. "Are you happy?"

"Happier than you, cowboy," she says, grinning.

"Okay," says Simon, "slowly move the vehicle forward.

Meese says, "We could go over a cliff here, you know."

They all hear the brush scrabbling the door panels. Like running a finger down a blackboard. Elora takes delight in the sound. The damage. The pebbles are her friend tonight.

"No cliff."

Simon takes a deep breath, sucks every atom of air inside the *Geländewagen* into his lungs, releases it like a punctured tire going flat—his patience escaping.

Then Meese hears the thud of the SatMap hitting the rubber mat and sees a pair of squirrel claws coming at him, one claw on his shoulder, feeling the heat of the nails, the other claw reaching out for the leather steering wheel, hissing, the squirrel's breath lathering his ear. The claw gripping the wheel and coming down in a half-circle, firm, slow.

Simon, even-toned, saying, "See, left, I said, do you hear me? Do you understand English? *Left*."

"There is no …."

But there is, Meese, there is a left. It's just that there's *no left in your* brain map.

Simon's hand on the steering wheel and the *Geländewagen* abiding Simon's command.

"I said left," and the claw guides it down, and the *Geländewagen* makes a lazy left through the razor-sharp shrub, and they hear the crunch of the tires munching over whatever the hell is under them—pine needles, gravel. Alien monsters. Branches scratching the door panels, fenders.

For all Meese knows, they could be floating in outer space right now, nearing the third ring of Saturn. A capsule because maybe Simon did not input the correct numbers in his magical SatMap, and he's got the coordinates crazy messed up. Meese hates the dark. Oh, boy, he does, hates deals in the dark. Swears to himself that he will never, ever again, do a deal in the dark, no way.

"There," Simon says. "Left. I said left."

Meese, dubious. "Here?"

They go straight, slowly.

"Here. Yes."

Elora grabs onto the headrest in front of her anticipating, what? Panicked. But she keeps her mouth shut. Because she wants to show Meese she has a set of balls bigger than his.

Meese cannot figure it, though, because his mind can't see anything, and that means he cannot believe Simon. Have faith, Meese. Give your soul to the hand of the squirrel sitting next to you.

Simon saying, "Yes. Go. Just go. Straight and slow."

And so there they go. Abiding the squirrel's command.

Meese can't compute that squirrel face has them slicing through the scrub and onto another dirt road. A pathway that runs perpendicular to the one they were on. They have easily cleaved their way in the right direction. Simon was right. Yes, the squirrel knows what he is doing! Relief abounds! Elora takes her hands off the headrest and settles back. She glances at her watch.

Off to the right, a gently sloping hill of short-cut crass goes on into the mid-distance and then edges into taller evergreens. They sweep up higher and higher on the slope forming an abrupt thicket—charcoal black and forbidden.

"Just follow the grass strip in the middle of the road here. You're doing good. If you saw this place in daylight, you'd say what the hell was so alien. It's all peaceful and beautiful."

"Lights?" asks Meese, more relaxed.

"No. Keep it at five miles-an-hour. GPS says two minutes and fifteen seconds."

Meese more willing to obey at this moment. More trusting. He keeps the speed at five miles-an-hour like Simon requested. The goosebumps subsiding.

Ahead, the path scribes a shallow dogleg to the right, slight because Meese cannot make out too much. Everything out there a Rorschach test. But now he is comfortable abiding the squirrel's directions. Squirrels, he acknowledges to himself, work well in the dark.

Gently, they take the curve.

Two minutes later, Simon throws his hand up.

"Stop here."

What the hell is *here*?

There's nothing *here*.

He slowly presses the brake pedal, and the *Geländewagen* obeys.

"Shut it down."

Meese turns the ignition key, applies the parking brake. He's being dutiful now.

Elora has her eyes closed. She really does not want to be here. Wants to get this "sightseeing" over and get back to worrying about other things.

See how peaceful it is here, Meese? He hears Simon's beard grazing his shirt collar looking around for more landmarks.

Meese asking for the SatNav.

"What for?"

"I just want to get a feel."

"For what? Plastic and glass?"

"The area. What planet I'm on."

Simon rests the SatMap on the steering wheel for Meese to peer at, keeps his hand on it like he's afraid Meese might steal it. The SatMap lights Meese's face. His eyes sparkle with delight. In the windshield, there is a heavily shadowed circus clown squinting at the SatMap screen. But having no fundamental notion of where the hell they are except the cold numbers coming off the screen.

"This is one hell've secret spot you've got here, Simon," says Meese. They are 1.6 miles up the hill from *Wolfacherlstrasse*, from the Hotel-Ochsenwirtshof.

"Okay," he says, and Simon takes back the SatMap. "So. This is it? Now what?"

"Almost."

Meese slumps, grunts his annoyance. "I don't see anything out there. But I trust you know what you're doing."

"I do, I do," Simon says, nodding, a happy donkey.

Then he reaches into the glove box and takes up a Surefire flashlight with a red filter, turns it on for a test. Red light splashes the dashboard. He beams it through the windshield. Out there, a variety of trees. Common Junipers, Douglas firs. And, wow, look at that: a magnificent specimen of Scots pine. A majestic beauty. Meese thinking they must be having a Christmas tree sale out there.

Simon saying, "You, sir, have arrived at a billion-dollar deal."

"I see trees. Not dollar bills."

"You will soon," says Simon.

Elora leans forward, says, "Can we get this over with? I have an appointment."

Simon's red light scans a flat, neatly trimmed grassy area four times the size of a football field. Now he's certain he's in the right spot. Been about eight months since his last visit. But now he is sure that the tunnels, the whole facility he's striving to get to tonight, are forty feet below that massive area of grass. This is what they came for.

This is Deadlight.

Simon and Meese exit the G-wagon, come around to the vehicle's nose. Elora slams the door. Meese glares at her. "You are a *ballbuster*," he says. She answers, "I do my best, Meese, to make your life happy whenever I can. I always did."

Simon has the SatMap dangling on a strap around his neck, and he turns off the screen. He sweeps the flashlight around the area, down the path they just left. Because the beam is red, it has a shorter wavelength than white light and can't go out as far. Less detectable from a distance. He splashes the beam around. Everything it falls on is horror-movie red. At any moment, a demon will jump out and eat them all.

Ten feet ahead on the left side of the path, Simon lights up a clump of junipers. A Three-toed Woodpecker flitters off into the dark. Then Simon's light lingers at the base of a juniper and slowly moves up the bark.

There it is.

A "V" shaped branch, inverted four feet in height, two feet wide. The crux caught on a nub.

"That's it," Simon says, grinning.

"That's what? I see a tree and a branch."

"The branch," says Simon, jiggling the light. "That's what we want."

Simon's raw wish right now is to banish his impatience with Meese van der Leeuwen and to get down underground, get to Deadlight and move on.

They walk to the branch, and Simon presses the bark between the legs of the inverted Y.

A spring-loaded door the size of a playing card snaps out, reveals a backlit keypad, easy to read.

Simon shaking his head, yes, yes, yes. If he was monkey, he would be swinging from the firs.

He presses a five-digit code into the keypad.

The beam of the spotlight falls across the field. There, a panel the size and shape of a bed, opening, the top a carpet of matching grass. Slowly, silently it yawns open. The jaw of an alligator, ominous. Simon is so excited he thinks he's going to pee himself.

But this is it, why they came here.

A door at the top of a mountain in the Black Forest, undetectable that could possibly change the history of the entire planet. How simple it seems.

They walk to the door, and Meese thinks Deadlight is going to make a lot of people happy.

If the operation is a success, Simon and LaneAirTech will significantly improve the faltering sales of the company, and new customers will arrive at his door. War makes money, he thinks. The more war, the more money. Meese, the transnational prince of illicit arms and ammunition to some of the world's most repugnant arms buyers, will become a billionaire. He has customers lined up. A.G Sinner and his phantasmagorical collection of right-wing theories and his eccentric proclivities will thrive. And that United States Army general, DeJean the buffoon, a delusional critter who sees Julius César talking to him in the mirror when he shaves, will theoretically command the entire United States of America. And Miss Elora Sinner, there in the backseat, what about her? Simon knows her role and hopes she plays it out well. Else, they all fail. And it finally hits him: the whole intricate plan could ride on the proficiency of A.G. Sinner's daughter in the backseat of this overpriced SUV. Who, Simon is starting to wonder, is dangerously disinterested and possibly incapable of fulfilling her role? But she is A.G.'s choice. So, Simon, be gentle with her. Treat her like you would a new puppy.

Simone says, "Let's take a walk. Follow me."

Both Simon and Meese know that the United Nations Sustainable Development Goal has targeted 2030 as the year to reduce the $1 billion in illegal arms flow. And they had best move quickly. Simon and Meese knowing that when Deadlight's gunpowder lights off, there will be one massive, incomparable event. Meese does not give one small canary's ass, as long as they fulfill their mission. It's all about money, isn't it, Meese. Success is nearly at hand.

And when it arrives, Simon, shrewd technologist, master mathematician, will let out an orgasmic monkey howl that will rattle the whole jungle.

Simon says, "We're going to walk down into history."

Simon's got the Surefire's filter changed over to white light and beams it down a long flight of musty steps that have not heard the clop of shoes in quite some time. At the end, a landing, then another flight of stairs. The people that built this were thoughtful enough to install an iron railing into the stone wall. The tunnel, six feet wide, eight feet tall, is painted smooth white, and history has not blemished the finish.

They start down, their footsteps echoing.

The further down the stairs they go, the more confident Meese feels.

Simon reaches into his pocket and lifts out a cell phone. He taps it a few times, and a schematic drawing of the bunker glows.

As they walk, Simon talks: "Since the Nazis were getting bombed day and night, their factories were getting decimated. So, they started Project Riese—"

"Project Giant."

"Yes, correct. They made a decision to move parts of their armaments and production infrastructure underground. There were seven bunker complexes like this all over Germany. One was under Tempelhof Airfield in Berlin, where they were assembling Focke-Wulf Fw 190 fighters. Because of a lack of documentation, it is not precisely known what this complex was meant for. This one was built by the Hochtief company. Some think it was going to be used to assemble Hitler's failed 'wonder weapon,' the Messerschmidt Me 262. I could not possibly build what you are going to see in US or anywhere else in the world. A perfect location that half the residents have forgotten about. All of it hiding in plain sight."

Simon's flashlight picks out a rusted wall box. When he pulls the door out, it creaks, and rust particles pepper the floor. He flips a switch, and the overhead lights glow.

They walk to a fork in the tunnel, and Simon's cellphone tells him to take the next right. This fork is finished as the others: smooth, plain white, eight-feet wide, nine-feet high.

They come to an open door, and Simon's light brightens a room. "This," he says, was the main office." There's a long table with discarded dinner plates and cutlery.

Meese is shuffling along behind a confident Simon. Sure, he's been down in this labyrinth a dozen times. Okay for him to be confident. But I think, Meese, this is weird, in a Nazi tunnel designed to contain technological wonders.

After walking seventy feet, Simon stops.

He says, "We call this area the hangar."

Oh yes, and you shall soon know why.

The place is a sprawl. Smooth concrete walls, beams, columns painted white.

And against one long wall opposite them, five floor-to-ceiling brick partitions perfectly formed to contain what they came here to inspect.

Simon takes in the view as he would a rapturous sunset. On a shelf in his intellect's brain, he hears a musical sound: Vivaldi. Violin Concerto in G Minor, *L'Estate*—his favorite. The bows singeing the strings. He feels their vibrations skimming his flesh, delighting him. Those creatures there that he faces, five of them, are his. His invention.

Meese says, "My God!"

Elora says nothing.

Look at her face now, the disdain. She turns so they can't see how she feels about this.

And then, for a minute or so, the three of them just stand and stare.

The five drones squatting side-by-side are separated by brick floor-to-ceiling partitions fifteen feet high. Splotches of subtle greys mark the diamond-shaped bodies. The edges razor-sharp. Angular. Efficient. They sit on tricycle landing gear and dare someone to approach.

Their designer and manufacturer, Simon Lane, has designated the model SS4-ML.

"For Supreme Stealth," he says to Meese and Elora.

Simon Lane, the maestro, standing before his audience, baton in hand about to launch into a spiel featuring his warbirds. Meese, eager to listen. Because he has five customers lined up. That is if they work. Elora, she doesn't want to hear this. She has her appointment to keep with Rayne.

Now, Simon lifts his baton and goes to work: "The 'SS' stands for silent and steal. Took four years to design and build. ML is for my brother, Myles Lane. I love him very much. Sad he won't be around to see what these boys are going to do."

Elora says, rolling her eyes, "Havoc. That's why everything is havoc these days. Maybe the havoc of it all made him choose a suicidal path. Blowing himself up in public. By the way, Simon, I don't see you filled with too much grief."

Meese says, "You know, Elora, sometimes I wish you'd just keep your yuppy mouth shut."

"Meese, the last time we had sex, you didn't say that."

Says Simon, "Myles lived a precarious life, Elora. I'm quite glad and surprised he lived as long as he did in his trade."

Simon starts his presentation with the names of his drones.

The first one has its name painted on both sides of the nose.

Tommy Tells Tales

Elora asks, "And the meaning … ?"

Simon says, "We have a guy at the plant in Stuttgart name's Tommy, always telling tall stories. Gives it some living character. Better than Grim Reaper or Avenger or Predator."

Simon continues: "Each drone will be carrying five EMP devices—an EMP—is a nuclear electromagnetic pulse, a massive burst of radiation created by a nuclear explosion. The result is a rapidly varying electric and magnetic field that couples with electrical and electronic systems. It produces damaging current and voltage surges. Specific characteristics of nuclear EMP events vary according to a number of factors: the most important—the altitude of detonation. We are going to use five-thousand feet. It's a real jolt in the butt."

Elora shakes her head. "To do what, kill people?"

"Oh, God, no dear," says Simon, dismayed at Elora's ignorance.

Meese says, "To knock out all the electricity, my dear. In the contiguous US—cars, house, businesses, anything that uses electricity."

In July 1962, the United States carried out the Starfish Prime test. They exploded 1.44 megaton bomb 400 kilometers above the mid-Pacific Ocean. The effect caused electrical damage in Hawaii, nine hundred miles away from the detonation point. It knocked out 300 streetlights. Set off numerous burglar alarms. Damaged a major microwave link. The effect was quickly repaired because the device was relatively weak. Only three percent of streetlights were extinguished. Later, calculations showed that if the Starfish Prime warhead had been detonated over the northern continental United States, the magnitude of the EMP would have been larger because of the greater strength of the Earth's magnetic field over the United States.

Meese says, "The EMPs on these drones are ten times more powerful."

"They are pilotless," Simon says, "have a service ceiling of 58,000 feet, a range of 10,000 miles, have refueling capacity, and are silent. They were constructed at two of my factories here in Germany."

Meese asks, "Then how did you get them here?"

"Flew them at night, undetected."

"No noise."

"No, they have silent engines. That technology alone, which I invented, is worth billions of dollars."

"And the targets?" asks Elora.

Meese says, "The top twenty-five cities in the United States. After the EMPs are set off, we estimated it will take months, if not longer, to restore things. Everything will eventually come back, but very slowly."

Elora says, "And you, Meese, I suspect you have something in mind if these drones work? Something you can put on your 'for sale' menu, if you don't already have a line forming at the door."

Meese shakes his head.

Simon says, "This is what the group wanted; this is what the group is going to get."

"The group?"

"The Deadlight group. Your father. General DeJean. Tommy Lane, former president of the United States, and my brother, Myles. All college buddies at one time or another. Back in the day, DeJean said the country needed a 'freshening up.' So, he's initiating one himself."

Meese says, "One more name you forgot—Leland Upchurch. We have no idea where he is or if he's still part of Deadlight."

They walk to the second drone.

Oh, Gosh Golly!

Simon says, "Same as the first one, technically. Name's a bit different. One of the techs misassembled the FAR—the Forward Looking Radar—on this. Assembled it backward, which I warned him about several times. Some people never listen. When he discovered it, he shouted out, 'Oh, gosh golly!' Once aloft, they will fly in formation to the US at an altitude of fifty feet over the Atlantic, silently, undetected, of course."

"Of course," Elora says.

Simon continues: "If along the way then sense a threat that could degrade the mission, they'll abort to the Puerto Rican Trench—the deepest part of the Atlantic. Once there, they nose dive over the Trench. The impact won't bust them up because they're so stealthy and will be flying diving under fifty kilometers per hour. Then, once they reach a dept of one-thousand feet, they'll self-destruct."

"Why?" asks Elora.

Then they move to the third drone. The nose is draped in cloth:

Dear Elizabeth Anne

"An old, dear friend of mine," says Simon.

Looking up at the nose, further back than Meese and Simon, Elora says, "Simon, thanks for the Air and Space Museum tour, but I have to get back to the hotel. Now."

Meese says, "But Elora, I have one for you."

He jerks the cloth off the fourth drone's nose:

Elora

Meese saying, "Thoughtful, right, Elora? How considerate of me."

"Trust me. I'm beside myself."

"You are quite welcome."

Elora says, "It isn't every day that a woman gets a drone named after her."

"And this one," Simon says, "I saved for last because without it, we would not be standing here. We would be cast alone on a sea without a rudder."

They move to the fifth drone.

Elora says, "Maybe tomorrow we can come back for some selfies."

"I never thought of that, Elora. Wonderful notion."

"But right now, I have to go."

Smiles abound.

And then, Simon turning to Meese, says, "And dear Meese,

have I told you how much I have enjoyed your company and participation. Your financial skills. Your mind. Even that little friction over the radio station at the airport. Thank you for introducing me to the concept of Deadlight. Introducing me to General DeJean, a hollow-brained turtle he is. But despite that—what a pleasure to know you. But I am thinking I want to do a solo."

"A what?"

"A solo."

"Huh?"

"To reap *all* the benefits of my efforts. When I was a kid, I never liked sharing my toys, even with brother, Myles."

"What are you talking about?"

Elora saying, "I think I know," oh, yeah, she does, and then hastening three quick steps back from what she sees coming. To get out of the way.

Simon yanking the cord down off the drone:

Meese, Dear, Meese

Then Simon scrabbles for his Beretta Centurion in his cargo pocket and pours three rounds into Meese's carotid artery and ropes of blood spume.

Rayne and Simon step back further. To avoid the spurting.

Meese reeling. Like he's drunk. Wondering. Hand in the air. Doing some quirky new dance craze? He yearns for words to come to him. Come to me, *please*. Explain what that was that just punched so harshly. *Please*. But his mouth is befouled. Filled with gluey mulch and stomach bile.

He doesn't make a sound. A slight gurgle, maybe. He's halfway down. Hand seeking the cement floor.

And the walls hear everything. Gunshots that echoed fiercely.

The tinkle of the brass shell casing. The drones knowing the sound of lethal gunfire waving over their gaunt shapes. The sharp, painful cracks of the rounds snapping through Meese's neck and ricocheting willy-nilly off the walls, the shells bouncing away. Stunning their ears. Mixing with the corrosive odor of gun smoke and Meese's plentiful blood.

"God *damn*," says Meese. His words soggy. Looking at his blood smeared hand.

Simon saying, "Oh gosh golly, how can you possibly talk after that?"

"I thought," Meese says, doing his shaky-shake dance, grabbing at his neck, and examining his blood-washed palm. He spits a rope of blood, saying, "I *thought* that we had a deal. We were going to make billions."

Trying to snag Simon's sleeve.

"Meese, my friend, we *did* have a deal. An excellent one. But your sandcastles are not as purely constructed as mine. They don't match. We simply have to part ways. Nothing more complex than that. Can you understand? Can you forgive me? I'm sorry I made such a mess here."

"Shut up. I will *never* partner with you again. You fucking intellectual asshole. I won't work with you for shit anymore," and then his eyes lolling back into his bloody head, and he bends forward, and his face slams the cement.

13
"IF YOU HAVE TO, GO DEEP."

"You didn't have to kill the bastard."

"But I did, Elora. I did have to kill him. He was cheating me."

Elora and Simon in Meese's G-wagon driving down the hill to the Hotel-Ochsenwirtshof. Simon at the wheel, driving warily.

"Everyone has to die sometime," says Simon. "Wouldn't it be terrible if Meese was lying in a hospital bed dying from nothing?"

"Oh, *please*. Don't crush me with your bullshit, Simon."

How can he be this callous, she wonders? How could he jerk out a pistol and just shoot and kill without feeling something? Without *showing* something. Look at him: impassive. She pities him. He's sitting driving the murdered man's car. As if he dropped off his laundry and is heading home to dinner. Elora, *he designs machines*. He *is a machine*. She's appalled. She feels her rage surging. Heat swarming her temples. Not because Meese Van Der Leeuwen is dead. There are no tears for that, but because she feels a fury over her lack of sorrow for a man she was engaged to. Or are you just so damned egotistical, Elora, that you only think of Elora? Then her voice relents. She gives up. She surrenders. She focuses on her assignment. What A.G. wants her to do. *Let's please, Daddy.* Suddenly, Meese lying dead in the bunker; well, someone will apply a cleanser and a polish to that.

"In my head, I did," Simon says. "I had to. The man would be stealing from me if I allowed the relationship to continue. I worked four years as hard as I could. That name on one of the drones, 'Elizabeth Anne'? She left me. I was deeply in love with her. It was my work or her. Off she went. Meese wanted half of the sales we made. Half."

"Why didn't you think of that before?" asks Elora, raising her eyebrows.

"Because he came to me with wealthy customers. Eighty-eight million dollars apiece to design and manufacture just one drone. You think they fall from the heavens? I want more than my money back."

"You wanted his blood."

She hates everything about this man. Hates his manner of speaking. Hates hearing his voice, his breathing as they drive down the dusty road. If she could, she would throw him over a cliff and end the hatred she has for him—*bigheaded monster*.

"By the way," Simon says, "you don't seem that saddened—you and your history with each other."

"Murder's murder, Simon."

Now they pass the chicken coup and the coral where the horses are. She doesn't hear them. She wants to hear them. The yard where the German Shorthaired Pointer barked. Wants his bark. The bench. Sitting close to Rayne. The bee. She wants to hear the horses sneeze. The dog's bark. Sit on the bench now where Rayne sat with her. Those sights, sounds. So safe and friendly. So comforting. But Simon takes them away.

Simon says, "I don't know too many people willing to pay that kind of money for a drone, do you? Mister Van Der Leeuwen had customers lined up. We only had to prove the drones worked. And we will in the coming days—with your help, I might add. Arabs, our friends from Iraq and Afghanistan and, moneyed people from the Emirates. China interested, too, I might add."

"And you don't care about the politics of it, the drones. The havoc. The thousands they could kill."

"Simple answer: No."

"There's was no other way? You could have told him just to get lost. I mean—"

"I couldn't take that chance. Elora, please. He could have soured the relationship with those customers. Everything is going to be okay."

"It's all about money, isn't it?" She shakes her head. She needs a drink. There's tequila in her room.

"I'm afraid it is all about money."

"What?"

"Money. Power."

"Just like my father. Money. That's all it's about. People's lives are insignificant as long as he satisfies himself."

"If you don't mind, my dear, you don't look like you're living on a particularly paltry budget."

"I'm doing something to fix that if it matters."

"It doesn't, dear."

"I would think not "

"Well, if you don't mind me saying: please tend to whatever it is *after* you set off changing your life after this is concluded, after your participation terminates, okay?"

"Now what? What are you going to do about this?" she asks, tapping the dashboard.

"It's fixed, don't worry. I will drop you off at the hotel and drive off into the night. Not to worry about anything. You just stick to the plan, okay."

"What will A.G. say?"

"A.G.! Girl, A.G. won't say a thing. If anything, he will sing my praises. Sing them off that balcony of that townhouse in Manhattan."

"You don't know what A.G. will say."

Simon looks at her.

He says, fast, "Elora, A.G. *sanctioned* this."

"Not surprised."

He pulls into the hotel parking lot, and Elora exits the car. Slams the door, punctuating her irritability. She heads for the hotel lobby.

Through the window, Simon says, "Hey, I'll be in touch." And then he squeals the tires and is off into the night.

Elora takes the lobby steps two at time, hastening to the second floor. To Rayne's door.

She wants to knock on 108. To feel her comfort. To thaw her guilt. For not crying over those first spits of blood. To withdraw from the horror she has just seen.

She knocks on Rayne's. Waits. Knocks again. No answer.

With key in hand, she turns for her room.

* * *

Leland Upchurch is sitting at the wheel in his parked BMW at the *Glasswaldsee* nature park not far from Hotel-Ochsenwirtshof. As he glances down at his watch, Rayne's Audi pulls alongside his car. She douses her lights, turns the engine off. They remain in their cars and start talking through the open windows.

Leland saying, "We've peeled away another layer of the onion. Clawed through it rather quickly, with urgency. But before I get into that, I want you to know that, as is always the case, you can bale anytime you want, pull the ejection handles, I'll understand."

Rayne nods. "I'm here. Whatcha got, skipper?"

"I mean, you seemed to approach this with a bit more *trepidation* than usual and, I might add, a certain measurable amount of distrust for me. I understand that. That said, do you have any reservations whatsoever? Because from this point on, you might need a big umbrella."

"For?"

"A major shitstorm."

"Lee, I always pack an umbrella."

"Just asking. Good. Consider this an official briefing, okay?

Rayne nods yes.

"We have gained access to President Rand's suicide note."

Rayne 's face lights up.

"Really?" she says, surprised.

"About two hours ago, I received a Tier One intelligence flash that came to me through an abbreviated report chain—practically direct. Top secret crypto. Utmost importance. It was a black bag job by one of my controllers. He has been working with a most reliable asset—a raven. That asset is a close 'friend' of General César DeJean's. Name's Blake Sinner, AKA Blake the Flake, the sister of your friend, Elora, your fan. You've probably heard about Blake Sinner through the media. President Rand gave her his suicide note on a SanDisk. Through all her years floating around Washington, Lane and Blake Sinner had remained close friends—that's the kind of circles she's in. His suicide note is a long, concise, well-written missive, dated the day before yesterday, passed along to old friend Blake with a list of instructions. First, she couried the SanDisk to a TV newsman in Manhattan. But we haven't heard a peep from the news media about it. The guy she sent it to is a low-level news guy on Fox that she occasionally watches every night. He's without any connections, and he hasn't a clue how to peddle stuff like this. Then, she gave it to our controller. Sources say Blake has a major issue with César DeJean. She thought she wanted to marry him, and he does not. She believes he's in it purely for sex and having a trophy woman on his arm, which doesn't sit right with her. In his note, Rand outlines the specific plans for Operation Deadlight. First, he confesses that he was initially an enthused participant. But apparently, guilt and gnarly things got the better part of him. He includes names, timelines, the chain of command. General DeJean has a specific plan to take over United States radio and TV stations, newspapers, using 'his' National Guard troops. DeJean is using Operation Valkyrie in 1944 as an exemplar—the plot to kill Hitler and take over the Nazi government. The objective of Deadlight is similar—insurrection, revolt, call it what you want. DeJean intends to takeover the United States government, physically and otherwise. In the Guard, he's got some Proud Boys, QAnon, the Boogaloo Bois, Antifa, New-Nazis, etcetera, etcetera. There's anarchy in the streets, and these groups, waiting throughout the United States and hidden in the Army and the National Guard, are waiting to explode, waiting for a leader to show them the way.

"Might be easier with Rand out of the way and a vacuum of chaos in D.C. These groups will fill the void. In addition, Rand instructed Blake to made copies of DeJean's battle plan, his call-to-action speech, and the entire chain of command instructions for Deadlight 'in case something happens to me.' Blake made a copy, gave it to our controller. Rand is obviously seeking partial justification for his participation, a revision to his legacy. I guess he thought a 9mm to the temple could settle things—at least for himself."

"So, this is why we want the Blackphone?"

"Good guess, but I am not sure. The Blackphone with the red leather cover, it seems, is simply a tool to communicate with the drones—to abort their mission, to recall them, or destroy them while in the air. Elora has the code to access the app that does all this."

"Once over the US, they will launch their EMP devices and shut down the whole country."

"Where are they launching from?"

"Not sure. But it would seem they are here, around the hotel, in the Black Forest."

"Lee, the Black Forest is twenty-three hundred square miles. It got its name from the one-mile stretch of pine trees so dense the sun barely reaches the forest floor. By the way, what are the drones tasked to do?"

"They will be flying with EMP devices. The EMP devices will be detonated over the top twenty-five cities in the U.S. at an altitude of five-thousand feet and knock out all the electricity in the U.S. Giving DeJean a perfect opportunity, a week of so, to implement his plan. Feeling like a bloodhound?"

"Wanting to feel like a bloodhound. But—"

"First call of action is—"

"Get the Blackphone."

"Since this is an A.G. Sinner affair, we're certain the Blackphone is in the hands of Elora Sinner, who, according to you, has a stone-cold crush on you, right? So you're halfway there. Knowing that, you've got good cards here. You play that anyway you want. Even if you have to reach deep down inside those panties—"

"Lee! That's gross!"

"But it might be necessary. *To save the United States, Rayne*! I mean, what wouldn't you do to save your country from Deadlight?"

Rayne rolls her eyes. "This is a big ask, Lee."

He says, "If we're right, she has a Silent Circle 2 Blackphone, one of the most secure cellphones in the world, this one with a red leather cover. It's probably in her room as we speak. In a bag. One exactly like the one in Myles's briefcase. Or maybe not."

"Without a hand attached, I hope."

"Myles had the same phone, which he intended to give to you and pass along to me. He knew about the whole plan. Was an integral part of the plan. Until, like President Rand, he changed his mind, wanted me to have the phone and stop the Deadlight drones. We believe Elora Sinner is operating naked on this—in other words, bypassing the Berlin Station, and working directly with her father, A.G. Sinner, who's pulling all the levers."

Lee pauses, takes up a stick of chewing gum, unwraps it. "Want one?"

Rayne shakes her head no.

"So, Elora's not a spy?" asks Rayne.

"No. She's out there naked on her own. Doing, we believe, what A.G. is directing her to do."

He starts chomping on his gum.

Rayne saying, "And her sister, Blake?"

"Blake Sinner is what we in call a female raven. She has been employed by us to gather intelligence mainly about César DeJean since he started his involvement with the Movement. For some reason, she has had an on-going fascination with high-ranking military people. Nothing below a brigadier general."

"Okay, so I'm after the Blackphone with the red cover and the location of the drones."

Before she starts to roll back, Leland signals her, and she pulls up to his window again.

Leland saying, "Don't forget—if you have to, go deep."

* * *

Gilbert Scott has just completed lining up his laptop at his Manhattan apartment, a glass of iced Crush Grape, a lined notepad, his gold Cross pen, and his favorite snack, a bag of cheddar Goldfish for his indulgence.

Gil, earlier today, put in his third call to Roger Kitchens since they did WhatsApp. When was that, Gil? Three days ago. Oh, boy, amigo, it does not look good when the calls, they go unanswered. But what could that mean: no news is good news, or no news is bad news? He never figured that damned expression.

Either way, to soothe his nerves, Gil sips the icy grape beverage and eats one Goldfish at a time to make the bag last and stares out his window at a couple of tugboats going south on the Hudson River. That's an excellent job, working on a tug on the Hudson. Around Manhattan pushing boats into their berths. Ships' captains eager for your appearance. The salty air. Views of the City. Thankful for your expertise. Just like your gig, right, Gil?

Then, there's the Signal alert from Roger Kitchens, and they're connected.

> **Roger Kitchen (R.K.):** Hey, Gil, how're things up there in the apple.
>
> **Gilbert Scott (G.S.):** Hey, Rog. Ah, not that great. First, I called you three times, no return. Second, I'm sitting here nervous because you have the SanDisk, and I got Jack shit. So, where are we with everything?
>
> **R.K.:** First, my apologies for not returning the calls. I've been jammin' on this story day and night, and I was figuring when I got an update, I'd give you a buzz, okay. So, I'm sorry. Not that I am not thinking of you. At first,

we were making good progress, but then things hit a brick wall.

G.S.: Do you have anything?

R.K.: Crumbs. We do have a definite connection between Blake Sinner, A.G. Sinner's daughter, and President Rand. They have been social friends for a long time. And we have a relationship between Blake and General DeJean—

G.S.: Rog, that's a stale sack a shit. Everybody there in D.C. knows about the Blake-DeJean relationship. Do you have anything on Deadlight?

R.K.: Talk is there is something brewing. DeJean at the center.

G.S.: And?

R.K.: Okay, the Guard, like the U.S. Army, has a good share of radical groups, QAnon, the Proud Boys, and quite a few others.

G.S.: Such as?

R.K.: The Constitutional Sheriffs, Oath Keepers, the Three Percenters, and the Not Fucking Around Coalition, a black nationalist paramilitary organization that advocates for black liberation and separatism. It has been described by news outlets as a "black militia," and it denies any connection to the Black Panther Party or Black Lives Matter. DeJean seems to be one of the first politically "straight" people to advocate the overthrow of the U.S. government. He has coalesced these radical groups and others under one new flag, his, and they're planning some type of coup. There are people in the government that have a similarly vague idea. And then there are others that want to see DeJean dead. There are members of the intelligence community that know what he's up to, but they won't release details because they first have no hardcore evidence and, second, they don't want to look foolish if they're wrong.

G.S.: When?

R.K.: At this point, all I can say is that it appears imminent. We're working on it. And that's all I have.

G.S.: And anything on—?

R.K.: The anchor job? No. Gil, I'm sorry, but I've been hung up on this. I did call my son-in-law, and he said he'd start looking around. Anything happens on that front, and I'll be in touch ASAP. Sorry, I don't have more. I gotta go.

G.S.: Yes, talk soon.

Gil has an instant notion that if he picks up his laptop and holds it high, then smashes it down on his dining room table that the splatter will scatter the rubble ambling around in his brain.

What you do not understand, Roger, is, I do not give one piece of cow dung about this Deadlight bullshit. What I care about is *my career*. Do I make myself clear? Guess not. I mean, you can take five thousand years figuring this insurrection and revolution and General DeJean. All I care about is *me*. Now. Anchor desk.

Gil, you must be brain numb, you moron. You gave away your

leverage on this, so stop complaining. You lack the brainpower a chipmunk has in figuring out strategy. How to play your cards.

What silly idea, Gil, made you think Roger was your solution to moving over to an anchor job. Now, you dumb-witted disappointment, you have given Roger control, all the marbles, and left yourself with one thumb in your nose and one-up your butt. Terrific move. You know what, Gil, you deserve staying where you are, you skinny-necked newsreader. For the rest of your career.

You are not worthy of an anchor spot!

Instead of his laptop, Gil the Goose picks up his blank notepad and sails it, and it slams into the wall.

After it lands on the floor, Gil, thinking to himself, yeah, I gave up my leverage.

And best you start cobbling together another work plan.

14
SHE TURNED THE TABLES ON ME, AND NOW I'M FALLING FOR HER

Rayne in her hotel room. Pondering.

As she changes into her pajamas, she writes herself a mental email: How much will you be willing to give of yourself to this mission? Is there anything disposable that you won't regret giving away forever? To surrender willingly or unwillingly? Is there anything left for you to chip away at without leaving ashes of remorse? I can't answer these questions now. Later, when I run out of time and it's too damned late to question how much I've compromised without hurting myself. Maybe this is just part of this operation. Remember Leland's crude joke a while ago: *Don't forget—if you have to, go deep.* Said with a grin. That hurt you, didn't it? You found it offensive, didn't you? Why? Let's see if we can dig down to the answer.

The knock on her door initiates the onset of a settlement in her mind.

"Yes?" says Rayne.

"Room service," Elora says through the door.

"Hold on."

Dinner last night flashing back. Taking your hand in her hand. Dancing to that song. Slowly sliding her lips along your jaw line and up to your ear. Giving it a little sniff there, remember? What did she say softly, Rayne? You remember. Recall it. *Kiss me now*. Yes! Right there at the table. Seldom taking her eyes away from yours. You can't take those things back, Rayne. Keep digging. If this is what it will take to get the phone, you might have to take Lee's advice—go deep. But that bothers Rayne.

Rayne grabs her cellphone. Has to steer herself into Elora's room. Where the red covered Blackphone is (she presumes).

And a few seconds later Rayne opens the door, and there's Elora smiling. She has two glasses in one hand and an unopened bottle of tequila in the other.

"How much tequila can you drink in one sitting, Foster."

"Enough to make me feel I drank too much."

"Can I come in?"

"Room service is not allowed in this room. It's too messy." She grabs her key and phone, and they walk across the hall to Elora's room. Elora locks the door, chains it.

She says, "I've captured the butterfly. Finally. Have a seat." She indicates the bed.

Rayne saying, "You've captured lightning in a bottle."

They sit cross-legged, facing each other, their toes almost touching.

Elora hands Rayne the bottle— "It's a cork, not a twist, and I can never get a grip on the damned things."

Rayne saying, "What is it we have here." She inspects the label. "*Hecho en Mexico. Casa Amigos Tequila Blanco*. It's got George Clooney's signature on the label."

"Wow!"

"He owns this brand. It says, 'Notes of a smooth vanilla finish.' And it warns according to the Surgeon General that women—that's us—should not drink alcoholic beverages during pregnancy.' Do we have a concern here?"

"Oh, God, no! I'm just wondering if Mister George Clooney went all out and signed this bottle just for us. For tonight."

"Why?"

"Because I feel special right now. You and me here, sharing a bottle of white thunder in my room. And approaching storm."

Rayne pries the cork, pours two glasses.

Elora saying, "Here's to our friendship."

"Here's to our *feelings* and friendship. May they always be true."

"Feelings and friendship. Yes."

They click glasses and throw back the first shots.

Elora saying, "It certainly does have a smooth vanilla finish."

Under the desk, a Birkin bag and the Myles Lane's duplicate briefcase with gold initials M.L. lined up next to the other. *How am I going to get over there and see if the phone's in there*? The operation depends on this. On you getting the damned phone. Maybe you're not going to get it. And what if you don't, Rayne?

How, Rayne, are you going to get your puss into those bags to see if the red phone is there? It could be anyplace in this room. You can't just bend over and say, excuse me, Elora, mind if I take a peek there for a red phone? What are you going to do? Compromise? How will that affect you later?

And will it take a compromise you had not thought of a short while ago?

"Hey, Foster, let's have another contest. We're supposed to have severe thunderstorms all night, and we could pass the time listening to music and the rain. Fun, right?"

"Good idea."

"Okay, you know what the rules are. If the other person does not guess the title, the loser throws back a shot. How's that?"

Rayne gives Elora the thumb's up.

And Elora says, "This is a toughie. I'll give you a clue. It pertains to *us*—I think. Another clue: it's about two lovers and a *huge* piece of real estate. And ya know what, Foster, this just could be *our* song,"

Elora presses the play button.

From the phone's speaker, a distinctive female voice, soft, alluring:

I've a cozy little flat in
What is known as old Manhattan
We'll settle down
Right here in town!

We'll have Manhattan
The Bronx and Staten
Island too.
It's lovely going through
The zoo!

"Wait!" says Rayne, "I know it."

"Name it?"

Rayne shakes her head. "Give me a sec."

Elora says, "Stumped? Oh, come on—this is *you*, Foster, this song is *you*!"

It's very fancy
On old Delancy
Street you know.
The subway charms us so
When balmy breezes blow
To and fro.

The song plays on.

Elora sips tequila. She closes her eyes, moves slowly to the lyrical picture.

But she's losing her contentment. The sight of the bloody ropes and Meese going down face first. It takes her mind away for a moment.

Then, smiling, she drifts back to *them*.

Rayne says, "The singer is Blossom Dearie."

"One hundred percent correct, Foster! So proud of you! Only a musical aficionado would know that. Bravo for you!

They both throw back shots. The burning makes them squint, shiver.

And so, the song goes on:

We'll go to Yonkers
Where true love conquers
In the whiles
And starve together dear, in Chiles

We'll go to Coney
And eat baloney on a roll
In Central Park we'll stroll
Where our first kiss we stole
Soul to soul

Elora saying, "You too are a musical genius. You *can* name the song; I *know* you can! I'm rooting for you!"

And after the fire subsides, Elora locks into Rayne's bright blue eyes. Wants to get lost in them. Wants them to lead her away from the bunker.

They're sitting cross-legged facing each other, so it's easy for Elora to reach down and pull on Rayne's big toe and giggle, pleading for a smile in return. Trying to cover the echo of the three shots up there.

Rayne's face brightens, and Elora gets the smile she yearned.

"Rayne," Elora, says, after closing her eyes and then opening them. "This could be *our* song—both of us from New York City."

Rayne saying, "I got it!"

"Give it to me!"

"*Manhattan*!"

"Oh, my God!"

Elora looks into Foster's eyes. Yearning to kiss her, to celebrate their momentary happiness—she doesn't. Wants to hold her hand—doesn't. Tell her she's daffy about her—doesn't.

And they just sit and listen. Both their yes half closed. Adrift.

Rayne fills their glasses, and they throw back another shot.

And Blossom finishes the lyric—her wispy, lilting voice giving tingles to Rayne and Elora.

The city's glamour can never spoil
The dreams of a boy and girl
We'll turn Manhattan
Into an isle of joy!

Then Elora tells Rayne: "Foster. It's official: *Manhattan* is *our* song. It's *you. It's me.* It's *us*!"

A couple more songs, a few more shots, Rayne, and the only thing you will be able to identify is a pillow. And here you are, squandering a moment to get that red cellphone and focusing on the woman sitting opposite you cross-legged. Replacing it, yes, *replacing* it with a mission unfamiliar to you with a woman you are not sure about in your heart, your dreams, your reality. Did you ever think, maybe she's playing *you*? You can't go forward, and you can't go back. Leland again: *You've just got to reach down deep inside those panties.* Too much thistle and prickly shrub crawling through her neurons and synapse mixing with Mister Clooney's brand.

The distant sound of thunder.

Elora saying, "Nothing like thunder at night."

Rayne saying, "Okay, here's one of the most beautiful songs ever written. If you guess this, I'll do two shots and tickle your toe and crown you a musical maven."

Rayne feeling the fever in Elora's eyes.

The compromise, Rayne? Is this part of something you must do. That you might regret? That you have never done before?

Rayne saying, "You know what—I don't think I want to play the songs anymore. Okay."

Elora nods.

More refills. More throwbacks.

Rayne saying, "Are we getting drunk?"

"Too soon. But we're off to the races, Foster."

Elora leans forward. "You always smell so. . . beautiful."

Triumph or failure. What will it be for Rayne tonight? Exulting or cussing?

Elora watches Rayne grab the bottle and pour. The rainbow optic of the fluid flowing captures her attention. She does not see Rayne glance at the Birkin bag or Myles's briefcase.

How are you going to get at them? Maybe if she goes to the bathroom? Enough time?

Hey, how about helping her to get drunk till she passes out? That could work. But is that better than the alternative? What El wants—you?

Are you playing, Elora? Are you abusing her so you can get to the salvation of the United States?

Oh, how the flush of passion almost always overrides. Corrodes everything else.

Then a slam of thunder. A ragged bolt of lightning in the distant night sky. Their fear abates when they grasp each other's hands. They laugh. The rain ticking the windows, the ground.

Is that the room moving a bit? What's causing the walls to ripple?

Through the rising fog in Rayne's head, a manta with a barb at the tip—*it's all up to you.* The voice is Leland's said a few times over and over. This unfolding dilemma. The drones. DeJean. The overthrow of the government. *It's all up to you.*

Elora asking, "Another song."

Says Rayne, "Just one. My head is moving off into another zip code."

"You pick one."

"No. I want *you* to pick one from your heart and play it. From your heart. Play it for *us*." And she presses her finger over Elora's heart— "Pick it from there. Play it before the thunder is so loud, we won't hear the lyrics. We won't hear ourselves talk. Before time comes and takes away everything we have at this moment. Pick one. From the heart."

Elora thinks. Her shoulders slide left, and she catches herself.

She takes up her cellphone and starts searching. Scrolling. Scrolling. Scrolling.

Rayne pours two more tequilas. Then she glances at the briefcase, the Birkin. Too far to reach, Rayne?

Thunder bangs the air. Lightning glows the pines.

Then they throw back their five-hundredth tequila. Or is it the six hundredth. Their brains not keeping track of shots. Tequila fog keeping track of *them*.

Through the haze in Rayne's eyes, she sees the red around Elora's irises.

Sees her finger pause.

What is she going to play?

Their. This one, yes. The music starts. The slowness of *I Wanna Be Loved by You*, the girlish voice of Marylin Monroe singing:

I wanna be kissed by you, just you
Nobody else but you
I wanna be kissed by you, alone!

I couldn't aspire
To anything higher
Than, to fill the desire
To make you my own!

Elora saying, listening to the lyrics, "I'm just thinking. . ."

"What? What're you thinking."

"That I'm gettin' drunk."

"Getting?"

"Am. Jus' a teeny bit. See." She makes a drunken face.

"So, say what were you thinking?"

"That I care for you very much." She reaches for Rayne's hand.

"And I know that, and I care for *you* very much. But—thas not what you were thinkin'."

"No. Wasn't."

"What then?

"Can't. Will make me cry."

"You're already crying, El."

Then she blurts it out: "What will happen when we leave here, leave each other?"

"I don't know."

"But I know."

"What?"

"I'll cry all day and all night."

Rayne glances away. Away from Elora. She doesn't let her hand go. The bags, Rayne, please! You have got to get your hands in *them*, not Elora's.

Go deep.

Can't.

Why?

And look, Rayne, Elora is caressing you tootsies—she must be falling in love. Ya' think?

Then Elora falls onto her side on the bed. Rayne wants to soothe her. Take away her tears. She lies quietly opposite Elora. Rayne wanting to say some balmy words. But none engage her brain.

Because there isn't a bit of compassion in your selfish bones, you bitch.

The only thing Rayne's thinking of is that damned cellphone that she can't get.

Because if you do, Elora will never talk to you again. Rayne feeling Elora's fingers on her shoulder.

Rayne, smiling, saying, "And you are not getting laid tonight." And she closes her eyes.

Maybe you ought to write another email. To Leland. Tell him: Dear Lee, I just can't do what you want of me. It's, well, it's so duplicitous and deceitful and misleading.

Then he will ask you why. And you won't have a *why* answer for him.

Oh, wait a second. You will. You will!

You just tell Lee *Elora turned the tables on me, and now I'm falling for her.*

15
ONE SHOT KILL

Washington, D.C.

A rifle is only as good as its telescope.

The shooter knows this.

He knows that he must kill.

That he might fail to kill.

That he would not kill for nothing.

This time more crucial than any other time.

He knows he is the best in his trade.

His name is Neil Paak.

He was a United States Marine Corps sniper.

The cardboard shipping box on the floor next to his improvised shooting platform says Colony Florists, Arlington, VA.

In the box, a Heckler & Koch PSG1, sniper rifle, German manufacture—a *Präzisionsschützengewehr*, "precision shooting rifle."

Developed in response to the Munich massacre at the 1972 Summer Olympics. Weight's 7.2 kg. Forty-eight point four inches long. A 7.62x51mm NATO cartridge. Effective firing range, 3,281 feet. Today that is an excellent number. Because the target exiting the building will be 900 feet from the rifle's muzzle.

This PSG1 model he is prepping now had been used in the Iraqi Civil War, Yemeni Civil War, and the Saudi Arabian-led intervention in Yemen. Efficient, extremely reliable. Today, it will be historical.

The building he's setting up in is near completion as an upscale apartment complex in Washington, DC. It sits on Nevada Street N.W and is named The Nevada.

On the tenth floor at unfinished Apartment 9 West, the shooter's concealed position is in the living room. First, before entering here, he put on a pair of ShuBee paper booties doctors wear in surgery. No footprints from his Danner boots. They have plastic pull-string collars for easy-on-easy-off.

He will not shoot from the apartment's window. He will shoot four feet back in the room. This way there will be no glint from the scope's lens. No muzzle picture. He will engage his target as the target moves from the main entrance of The Croydon apartments across the street to that waiting black Chevrolet Tahoe. The Croydon is the target's residence—two bedroom luxury apartment with an office, a balcony, and an expansive view of Washington, D.C.

Right now, the sniper's using compact Predator 10X binoculars to examine the area down there for threats, anomalies, scanning slowly. A surgical process. So far, nothing out there trips him.

He has been up here since 4 a.m. It is now 6 p.m., and the target is set to appear now; walk from the entrance and step into the Tahoe. The sniper does not care where the target goes after entering the limo. He would not have been told that because it has no relevance to his main purpose: the kill-shot. He is laser-focused.

He knows: no matter how much he preps, the unexpected can always happen. He keeps this in his head. He knows he cannot be a perfect shooter. But that's what he aims for.

Before he left Afghanistan, he had sixty-three. Then, he joined the staff of President Tommy Rand. He worked for the president as an ad hoc bodyguard, confidant, friend. Rand loved having him around. Others on the staff were envious but understanding. When he learned Rand killed himself, he cried for four hours. He has two Purple Hearts, a Bronze Star and Silver Star. He would give them all away if it would bring Rand back. Currently, he is attached to the CIA's secret Special Operations Group.

He has incorporated ballistic protection (cover) and suitable terrain over which to withdraw after firing. His position inside the building's a solid cover. But equally important, his egress after the kill shot. For a short prep, he has drawn a meticulously detailed escape option. He is systematic. He is cautious. He is a sniper addict.

This is a nail-up job. In civilian terms, last minute. Which is always precarious. Takes the talent and expertise of only the best.

From the cardboard box, he takes up a Sig Sauer Tango 6 3-18x44mm rifle scope. He places it on the rifle's base mount. Checks the hex screws for a snug fit. Triple checks.

The shockwaves and sound force from his first round will be partially absorbed by the empty room he is firing from. This is further lessened by the Tango 6 suppressor bringing the sound down to the level of cap gun. He knows what he will do with his rifle and clothes after he fires. The booties and surgical gloves will also disappear.

He does not know the political consequences of his bullet. He does not lose any yarn over an unnecessary burden. His focus first is the first shot to the target. Second, getting out, leaving no trace. Third, erasing the kill shot from mind and heart. Almost always the most difficult aspect, but he will work hard at it.

Question: How can any government admit to the sniper's action? They can't. Therefore, he is known to no one, to no agency, to no country. If captured, he will say nothing. He will be a cipher. That is his journey.

The sniper is mindful that violence and suffering are woven into the distortions of our lives, but it is the philosopher that embraces these things. He goes about securing weapon and scope with equanimity. Inserts the magazine with poise. But as he goes on, more important is what he learns about himself, that equanimity cannot acquit what he is about to do.

This will be the last shoot of his life. He pledged himself to that. To the man that asked him to do this.

Then, once and for all, he will destroy his old friends, his rifle and telescope, and his residual tools and never see them again. Except in his mind where they will never be purged.

The PSG1 is set to go. The scope securely attached. The Sig Sauer Tango 6, the key to a successful shot, is a spiritual part of his body.

He sets the rifle down on a beanbag atop a drop cloth that he had draped over three cinder blocks. Now, he presses the rifle's butt against his shoulder, peeks through the telescope. He calculates external ballistics, the bullet's travel path before impacting the target. The figure he will be tracking, a moving target—walking from the lobby on the pathway to the SUV. He will swing with and ahead of the target, holding an appropriate lead for the target's speed and range. This demands more talent, more experience than firing at a stationary target. Old salts are familiar with this. His calculations whir through his brain. The lead is the side width of the human body—about 12 inches—and is used to estimate how far a sniper should lead a moving target. At 300 yards, a sniper must aim one-and-a-half leads ahead of the target.

He estimates that the target will be at point-blank range, less than 400 yards. This assures him that the bullet's trajectory will be flat because the bullet will start plunging after 400 yards. So the scope has been set for 300 yards.

At 6:02 p.m., through the lobby's glass windows, the shooter spots the target stepping out of the elevator. But he follows a woman out. Not a casual passenger, the woman seems to be accompanying the target. The doorman approaches, and they talk briefly, then the doorman disappears.

This is the first unanticipated event: he was told nothing of a woman accompanying the target. "Shit," he says. This could be a failed mission. The woman could unwittingly act as a shield preventing a clear shot.

The target and the woman remain in the lobby staring out through the tall glass windows, observing the weather. The woman wearing a black cocktail dress with thin straps over her shoulders. She holds a small, glittering purse.

Then the second unforeseen event happens.

The unanticipated. Drizzle.

Earlier, he checked the forecast: rain starting at 7 p.m., not 6:02. The shooter knows this about shooting in the rain: bullets *impact* higher in the rain. Changes in barometric pressure affect everything. In general, fair weather is accompanied by a high barometer, which means more air density and more resistance to the bullet. Likewise, rainy weather is likely to occur at times of low barometer readings when air pressure is low, producing less air density and resistance to the bullet. A drop of one inch in the barometric reading will increase the ballistic coefficient by about 3.33 percent. His conclusion: The drizzle at present will not alter his shot.

He will go for a catastrophic brain shot. A special one-shot kill to the brain stem or neural motor strips. Kills instantly. The body reflexes have no time to react. The target drops like a sandbag. The best kind of kill shot.

The glass door in the lobby opens, the target and the woman step to the doorway, and the doorman holds the door open. The doorman comes to them, unfurls the umbrella, holding it over the woman.

Then the target and the woman, and the doorman start toward the limo.

The limo driver swings the rear door open and gives the couple a gracious head nod.

The couple has sixty-five feet to go to the limo.

In an instant, the sniper decides: He's going for a side shot.

Between the temporal bone and the squamous suture, slightly above the ear. This, just as effective as a rear shot to the occipital bone.

And that's where the cross-hairs go.

He sucks it in a, deep draw and holds his lungs still.

The scent of the gun oil is strong and masculine, a good, clean scent.

The rifle moving slowly right to left.

Take your shot!

Not yet.

Take your shot!

Not now.

Take...

Shut up.

He continues tracking right to left, slow. Smoothly.

So focused.

Moving the barrel, flicking the safety off. Becalmed.

Take your shot now!

Hold.

Hold.

Hold.

Then his finger takes up the tension in the preliminary spring and goes on squeezing, and when the Heckler & Koch kicks, Paak keeps the scope on the target and sees a pillow of red mist and the sonic shock cone on the other side of the target's skull, the cap cartwheeling in the drizzle. The woman diving inside the limo, and the target dropping and slamming the pavement, and Paak assuring himself indisputably that he has just taken down General César DeJean.

16
PILGRIM IN A CATHEDRAL

Rayne's sitting on the bench at the Bear and Fox Park waiting for Leland Upchurch. Thick, low clouds, stark day. He said noon. Now he's twenty minutes late. Unlike him.

A German couple strolls by, dropping a speck of conversation for her to ponder. One word stays with her—*Ermordung*. In English, *assassination*. She pulls out her cellphone, taps on CNN. The BREAKING NEWS graphic fades in and out above the banner the bottom of the screen:

US Army General César DeJean Nat'l Guard Chf Killed

Reading this, she is not surprised.

But she culls the sparse details.

General César DeJean, commanding officer of the United States National Guard killed at such-and such time yesterday. Walked from his apartment lobby in Washington D.C. toward his waiting limo.

He and his companion, Blake Sinner, the daughter of A.G. Sinner, the former billionaire ambassador to Germany, was at his side when a bullet struck him in the head. No warning. No sign of pending violence. Witnesses could not recall the sound of a gunshot. Before DeJean and Sinner reached the limo, DeJean was hit and fell dead to the sidewalk. Ms. Sinner slightly injured when her shoulder smacked the door jamb diving into the back of the limo. The doorman accompanying Sinner and holding an umbrella for her said he had not seen nor heard anything significant. Authorities have no clear notion as to where the shot originated. The correspondent notes DeJean's controversial appearances, his speeches at the Movement. Rallies throughout the United States. Adds that a Congressional hearing was about to occur into DeJean's political activities and "aspirations." Correspondent uses the word "kill." Not "assassination."

Nearly noon now, and the clouds are stacking up over Rayne's head. At the far end of the park, Upchurch exits his BMW and walks toward Rayne. The gray sky a backdrop for his slouch, his head down, watching his footsteps.

As he nears the bench, Rayne holds up her cellphone—the CNN story.

He peers at it. Nods.

Yes, I have.

"Neil Paak? Neil *the* Paak?

Yes.

"You sent the Paak in?" Rayne not really surprised.

Upchurch does not respond. He takes one more small step toward Rayne and stops.

Looks down at her—"The *full* Paak," he says.

Fidgety. Hands in the pockets of his tweed blazer. Far, far away.

And not looking at Rayne. Gazing into the distance. At the

storied clouds. Approaching, burgeoning. Angry blue-black. Coming for them.

Thinks Rayne, he must be communicating with someone in heaven.

Upchurch saying, "Rayne. Rayne. Dear, dear, Rayne. Lifeguard to the Drowning. Keeper of the Hidden Sins. Observer of Chaos and Madness—sleeves rolled up—hole in the boat—glue and putty in hand—dustpan and broom—serving your country well—sacrificing. But anarchy remains immutable and America is despairing, democracy unraveling, disobedience growing, heartache and relapse thrive. No new America here, coated it is with a patina of political and social puke. No partitions between old America and new—chaos endemic—gunfire in the schools—gun sales rising. Okay, we have occasional hallucinatory euphoria, but we have to continue to carve coffins and dig graves. Let us take a knee for Shiva the God of Destruction and pray to him to wipe our slates clean, destroy everything and start anew. And this is why I called Paak in. To begin fresh. To cleanse and polish And to turn to you, Rayne."

"Are you okay?"

He's pale.

"Lee?"

A pilgrim in a cathedral. Let him go on, Rayne. Allow him to make his way through the candlelight, unobstructed.

Leland: "In my twenty-seven years I sought to make a difference—maybe did, maybe didn't—but tumult never concludes. Two impeachments, no justice, riot at the Capital—New Nazis, old Nazis—all gravitating, yearning for another mindless insect to lead them with a barge of lies in tow. He's waiting in the wings, you know—this insect, whoever he or it is. Walking behind the elephant in a parade—the broom, the dustpan—always something to pick up the shit because the parade never stops."

He turns from the clouds, the gloom. Gazes down into Rayne's eyes. He worries for her.

"Yes, I put the Paak out there. Last minute. Start of a new beginning, I thought. Sixty-eight sanctioned kills, and the Paak reached for one more pull of the trigger. You have enough spirit for this, Neil? Tell me. Can you slip one more shiny round into the chamber? Bear *one more* guilt? I knew he wanted a wave of calm to anoint his tired body. To *anesthetize* himself. To move on to his Vermont cabin. So, I asked Paak, 'Neil, my man, one more pop for the flag?' Paak nodded. One more purging. Just enough operational energy and skill left in a jar he secretly holds to pull the trigger in a disquieting career. Of course, I pulled the trigger too. I gave Neil the go order. Felt it was a new phase for me also. Paak knew too he had opportunity facing him. To purify *himself* with the Holy Water of shot number sixty-nine. A sad landmark. Because Neil the Paak needed to purge *himself* of all the killings that provoked his guilt. You know, Rayne, Paak had a personal connection to his last shot. He knew the face of the target, which I am told makes it much more difficult. It becomes *personal.* Neil knew the face. He was at the White House on his final active-duty day when DeJean visited. President Rand ordered Paak to drive DeJean to the Pentagon. He wanted DeJean to write his letter of resignation on his stationary and have Paak drive him back and give the letter to the president in the Oval Office. A formal presentation for the record. Perhaps with photographers memorializing the moment. Paak told me he would have shot the bastard in the face if he thought he'd get away with it. The kill shot was Paak's closing curtain, and he hoped to use it to end his own insanity, to distance himself from those sixty-eight kills—and end some of the lunacy in our nation and in his own head. He wanted to see more than a signature on a letter of resignation from DeJean. He wanted *complete* termination—he wanted a bullet and blood to do the job."

Rayne never heard Leland speak like this. He is frightening her.

Leland saying, "I might call Paak once more."

"*For*? *For*?"

"To cleanse. To purge. To rid the puke and excrement that remains. That seems so pervasive. All at once. To terminate Deadlight. And everyone associated with it: A.G. Sinner. Simon Lane, Elora Sinner. Kill the entire hive. All the breeding insects that occupy the darkness. Light some incense and call down Shiva. He will come. He will take his pleasure in eradicating. Exterminating. I believe that. Don't you, Rayne?"

Pilgrim in the cathedral. Finding his way to the altar. And the choir singing vigorously.

Leland lighting candles as he probes the darkened aisle. Going to the Altar of Truth, not Mayhem.

"Leland, *please*—"

"Rayne, I realized the moment I contacted Paak that I had *emerged* for the first time in my twenty-seven years, not through the doors of the Central Intelligence Agency but from the asshole of a repulsive darkness, and into a sepulcher of light and truth. That showed me evil presides and we must try to change. And only small strands of hope and effort can save us. We kill wantonly what we eat. We kill what we feed our young. We must nick and pick at the pimples of wickedness. Do you see what I am saying, Rayne? We have to do what we are here to do: We have to ascend from the blackness—the comfort and solace—and go off on our own, despite the challenges. A new journey. Even if we think we cannot make a difference. We must strive. The stink must be cleared at all costs. Burn our bridges. Burn our boats. No turning back."

"Skipper, take a deep breath, *please*."

"Tired of it."

"Well, then retire."

"Boring."

"Go to the beach."

"Hate the sand."

"Take a nap and start all over again!" She throws her shoulders back, and Lee looks at Rayne and sympathizes. *He* sympathizes with *her*.

He says, "One last push?"

And she says, loud, "Do what you have to do. But leave me aside." She turns her head away from him, trying to ignore him; it doesn't work.

He says, "All right, all the gloom and doom aside, what has to be done has to be done immediately. It's the last nail, Rayne—if the last nail on the deck isn't hammered in tight, the boat floats fallow."

She glances back at him. Sees it coming. Doesn't want to hear it.

And Leland telling her, "Again, I am asking *you* to get Elora's phone—the red phone. As soon as possible. Even if it is a Faustian bargain. He takes a short rest. "And you *can* take the shortcuts we discussed and suppress any guilt."

"If I can't? What does the Keeper of the Hidden Sins, Observer of Chaos and Madness do? Wave her magic wand?"

"But you can. If you try. You do have a magic wand—you just don't know it."

"How do you know?"

"I know you. I've known you since the day you were born. I can see it all the time."

Leland rests his elbows on his knees. Braces his chin with his hands.

"If you can't, then I would call in Paak for one more scrubbing. One more polished brass shell. Put him in on a special Air Force cargo flight out of Andrews into Munich."

"*What*!?

"Alternatively," Leland says with reluctance, "If you find that repugnant and ignore the pain of Mister Faust, then I would ask *you* to make a cold call."

"In other words, you want me to *term*inate Elora."

"To *get* the phone, Rayne. Not for me, for God's sake. For the United States of America."

Rayne pulls in a deep breath, sucks the oxygen out of the Forest. "And how do you think that will make *me* feel. That and *pretending* I'm falling in love with her. How duplicitous is—"

Leland saying, "I know, I know, I know. Stop!"

She looks at him again. His bushy eyebrows do not distract her. She peers right through his pupils. Saying, "Go ahead. *Say it, Lee.* You've wanted to say it for the past two days. *Say it now*! Go!"

"Okay, you want me to say it? *You want me to say it*! You want me to say that you don't have to pretend. You don't *need* a Faustian bargain—you *are falling* in love with Elora Sinner. So, there I said it. You are falling in love with Elora Sinner—*so what*!"

"You are *sooooo* wrong!"

"Why? Convince me!"

"You have no idea what you are talking about. No idea how I feel about her."

"I have an excellent idea. Ashamed to admit it? Or you don't want to fall in love with her—one of the most beautiful women in the world? We all fall in love with beauty. I know I could. And maybe that's all there is. And that's okay, Rayne. But don't, please, please, *don't* let it get in the way of this, what we have to do here—the red phone."

"Honestly, I don't even know what love is. I've been messed over more times than I can remember."

"Oh, poor, poor Rayne. We all have. Should I take up my violin now? I think you *fell* for the *charm*. The *allure*. The *wardrobe*. She's a woman who stepped out of a dream, and they are few and far between. And that's fine, Rayne. But this is not about love. Not about you. Me. It's about *hatred*. We have to *hate* A.G. Sinner. We have to *hate* Deadlight. We have to *hate* Simon Lane. Enough to squash it and kill it and everything clinging to it. That's what it takes to make this succeed—*hatred*. And if she's part of it, so be it. It is about saving the United States from revolution. From a new-day Hitler. Can't you see that?"

"I can, and I'm not going to argue with you."

Leland stands. He wants to say something. Then not. Then nothing. A variety of options arranging themselves around his heart. Because he knows Rayne's feelings.

A change of subject, and Rayne saying, "Do we want to see the bears and foxes again?"

Leland shakes his head: "I think they have seen enough of us."

Rayne saying: "So then?"

Leland needs a few seconds, then says to a fat black cloud, "I am going to call Paak. I think he has enough bloodlust and operational energy left to pull the trigger a few more times. For the United States. For himself."

"A *few*?"

"Indeed."

The air and the clouds have now turned frosty and harshly hostile. All the friendship and the relationship they had before now gloomy and limp. But, thinks Rayne, it appears Lee's finding the strength to tell the truth. To open up about something he has wanted to divulge days ago.

Leland saying, "I have a responsibility. A personal responsibility to clean the whole mess up myself."

"Why don't you get it off your chest, Lee. The whole thing. Going back to you and me in Prague."

He sits on the bench. Puts his face in his hands. Then looks up at Rayne. "Why don't you sit. I'll tell you a story. A good one."

He starts from the beginning: When youthful paths crossed from dreams into idealism into reality in his college days: He tells her about DeJean, the Lane brothers, Tommy Rand. Back when the idea started to gestate, then fester, then arise again and be met with renewed enthusiasm and vigor. And hope. Lots of hope back then.

Rayne has a general idea of what's coming. She watches his eyes going back for the details. She doesn't want to hear it. Doesn't want it to soil her relationship, the relationship he had with her father.

Leland tells her, "We weren't going to burn the schoolhouse down. Nothing like that. It started out we were just going to give it a new coat of paint, maybe do some essential repairs. But as time wore on—"

Rayne, he's going to tell you details you don't want to hear. But you can't allow your discomfort to cover your ears. You must listen, Rayne. Allow Leland to purge himself. To tell you about his participation. His guilt. Be a good girl to your father's memory. Let Leland Upchurch confess.

Leland saying, "The country was imploding, falling in on itself, and the landscape was turning toxic. We were baling water. For every bucket of water out, two came in. The planning, the theory, was to devise a gentle approach for a makeover of the government. Time worn on until we discovered that, politically, there was nothing we could do. We were too idealistic. Then DeJean, he asserted himself, egotistical bastard told us that we were either all in or out. Tommy said he had to think about it. I said the same. Then DeJean found a tool he did not have up to that point. The secessionist idea had started to float around various areas of the country, spurred on by divisiveness, and DeJean jumped on that and started making his speeches in front of The Movement's gatherings. It was make or break for him. If it didn't work, the Army, the government, would have arrested him for perfidious behavior, treason, and a multitude of other crimes and hung him in the Rotunda. By that time, Myles, myself, and Tommy were no longer privy to DeJean's plans to take over the government. But we knew that that's where he was going. Communication between DeJean and us ceased."

"And you never thought he could pull it off, did you."

"Up until a few months ago, no."

"But now he's dead."

"He has backup upon backup. We'd have to call in Paak and have him go out and pull the trigger a thousand times. It might be too late. I see lots of damage on the horizon."

"So when you and I met in Prague, that was the beginning for you in your own small way to stop it."

"I was hoping Myles wanted me to have the phone to shut it down before it started. He had no idea how to use the phone. A.G. gave it to him as a backup. He trusted Myles almost as much as he trusts Elora. I think he figured that since I was running the Special Operations Group I could figure things out, including the codes on the phone."

"And Myles Lane? Why? When he got up from the table and ran back to his car, he had the briefcase and, presumably, the phone in his hand."

"Guilt. Abhorrence for allowing Deadlight to grow."

"Suicide?"

"Of course. I believe he wired his car to explode when he pulled the handle. Get the blame away from him and make it seem like a terrorist act. Great way to end his career and polish his legacy. Killed by a terrorist bomb on a street in Munich."

"And President Rand?"

"He had a lot of head problems to begin with. Deadlight broke the camel's back. I am sure he knew that no matter what, he'd be implicated in Deadlight. He didn't' want that as part of his legacy."

"Guilt?"

"Yes. He knew his legacy would be in shambles once he was implicated in Deadlight. And he would be implicated. So, he pulled the trigger. He could have done more for his country if he hadn't killed himself—if he told the world what Deadlight was and how to avoid it in the future. Do you know what a deadlight is, Rayne? Tommy got the idea one summer when we were all sailing on Myles's sailboat. He was fixing one of the portholes on the boat and asked us if we knew what a deadlight was. None of us knew. A deadlight is a protective cover or shutter fitted over a porthole or window on a ship. A skylight designed not to be opened."

How could you have let this go this far, Rayne? Think about it. You knew that Leland knew too much about Deadlight. You knew he was operating on his own, employing loyal members of his team to get intelligence for him. You knew this was not sanctioned by the people in Virginia. Allow that to gel a bit while the two of you conjure up what's next.

Leland stands. He looms over Rayne. Getting back some of his strength. Throwing his shoulders back.

Saying, "Rayne, if you get the phone we might be able to save the day. We stand a chance."

"The phone. Save the day. At any cost? Faust again? You want me to give away my soul to the flag?"

Winter, in his words. "Yes. If you can, *please*. You're the only one that can get into her room. And if that means getting into her pants, then, goddamnit, do it. Just get the phone out. At any cost." Says it like he's reciting a recipe for bread pudding. But this is what Leland does, Rayne. He directs with a cold spray of ice.

"At any cost."

"Yes."

"Even if I have to make a cold call?"

Rayne, what do you think? Can you do what Leland is asking you? He seems so chilly about it, but he has to be that way. Perhaps you should adopt that attitude and get this over with and get back to a normal life. Can you put aside your feelings for Elora and kill her.

Lee saying, "I can give you something. You put it into her drink, and the matter is over in less than a minute. No pain. Closes her eyes, goes to sleep."

The two of them, Rayne and Elora, in the hallway, embracing, kissing with a passion. Do you see them? Do you see yourselves? She smells her cologne. Their breath.

"She goes to sleep. But I stay awake for a long time after."

"Count your blessings."

And then Rayne breaks from the kiss in the hall, the embrace, Elora, strides to her room.

Now Rayne pops up from the bench and screams out:

"*No*!"

Her face red.

Birds panic, wheel away.

A child in the parking lot stares at her, his jaw open.

She tells Leland, "You give me bad cards, Lee. There's no play here for me."

"Bad cards, yes. But there is play. You have choices. You can stay, or you can leave."

Rayne, there are a thousand excuses you can use here that will allow you to leave. So, what is yours?

Leland wants to say something. He wants to smile. He wants to chastise. But the only person he can think of berating is himself, and he has already done that and not enough.

So, he watches Rayne turn from him and take her ache and silence and doubt with her. A small blizzard of gloom trailing. She walks toward the parking lot, her car. Head down. Collar up. And as the distance grows, Leland knows clearly what a terrible business he's been in all these years. What a terrible business he has taken Rayne into. What an appalling choice he just threw at Rayne's feet. He keeps his eyes on her as she moves away. Watching over her as long as he can as if she were his own daughter. The steps she takes, plodding. Her jaw tightened. He imagines doing her a favor: go home, Rayne Foster. Put this out of your mind. Put away the legend of Half Face. The terrible choice I have given you. Forgive me? Focus on photography. Set up a law practice. Stay safe. Curl up with a blanket and allow a snowfall to comfort you. Stay warm. Stay away from the mayhem, this life. I care for you too much, my best friend's daughter, that I fear that I might be setting you off on a train into a darkness with a pitiful destiny.

But then Rayne stops, pivots, starts walking back to Lee. She feels alone and helpless, under siege. She hears Elora speak her name for the first time, *Foster*! and she notes the distinct way it sung from her mouth, assertive, friendly. Stamped forever in Rayne's memory. I want to hear it *again* and *again* and *again*. Mumble it to me, El. *I miss you*! Shout it! Whisper *Foster*, like you would the word from a poem that lilts and whispers. Rayne does not know how or where she will find the courage she has selected. But just for a moment, Rayne, just for a single solitary moment, *please*, *please* pretend this *isn't* madness.

Her eyes locked open as wide as wide can be to see now that, yes, this *isn't* insanity. This *isn't* chaos. This is the *truth* of the moment.

To be suffered later when debentures come due.

Rayne whispering to Leland. "Please don't call Paak."

* * *

At the same hour, Simon Lane is dancing in the drone hangar in the bunker.

He's figured a surreptitious way to get to the secret backdoor during daylight without using the dirt road they came up a couple of nights ago. He had to hack a path through the pines and thick brush. Slow going but mostly undetectable.

The ceiling speakers are cranked up. Peter Gabriel's *Sledgehammer* bouncing off the cement walls, the throbbing bass pounding the sharp angles of his drones. Simon dancing with himself and as his inventions look on. The drones, he imagines, are casting him a sharp look watching him Tutting and Breaking in their refuge. How disrespectful!

His quiff, the five-inch red wave atop his lightly freckled face, is bouncing in tune to the Gabriel beat. Jiggling like fiery Jell-O. What more is music than mathematics, and he is, after all, a brilliant mathematician—recalling his college days teaching some the beauties of his moves. It was not the storied quiff that attracted the young beauties, not the bounce, not the red sheen—it was the weirdness of Simon Lane. The girls did not gaze at Simon: they inspected him.

Oh, his youth! The delights of the isosceles triangle. That's what started *this*. The challenges found in Wolfram's Mathworld. Lovely! It was indeed the isosceles that inspired his drone designs. All those groovy, angular, razor-sharp lines. The sight of them alone made others fall to their knees. He preoccupied his time learning the theorems evolving into cutting-edge aeronautical designs. Some in his classes thought him to be eccentric. Well, time to say *fuck'em*. And give them a lusty one-finger tribute. Go ahead, challenge me. Many aeronautical companies begged him to join their ranks; why should he? His father's company, always on the edge of collapse, would come around once he and Myles set about with new designs governments would beg for. And now, Simon Lane, you are on the cusp of a fantastic success. Dance to your delight.

He makes a few moves in front of *Elizabeth Anne*, looks over her faultless frame. Then, without pause, presents her with the one-finger tribute—for deserting me, a genius.

He dances on to the next drone. A musical inspection of the babies he created from scratch. However, he thinks they find his gyrations odd and the music syncopations relics. They are weaponry, after all. They are severely complex systems that can kill people. That's what he imagines they think. But he doesn't care. He is elated. The drones will be flying soon, and their flight, the success of the mission, will prove their efficacy to many, many customers. Joy swells the cement hangar.

How, he thinks, could Meese Van Der Leeuwen possibly have been a part of this tapestry of achievement? This poetic construction of aerodynamics and geometric perfection. *How could I have justified giving him one cent of this, my effort?*

Now twirling before the watchful gaze of the drones, he pauses and does a Michael Jackson backstep at "Meese's" pointy nose. He stops, grins at "Meese," and blesses him too with the bird. He feels he can do now only something Superman can do: he performs a rudimentary ballet move, a *grand jeté*, over the dark bloodstain that Meese so rudely left besmeared on his surgically clean, nearly a century-old hanger floor.

Then his cellphone rings, and he pauses Peter Gabriel. Thinking this is the beginning.

Saying, "Yes?" and allowing himself to listen to the man with the German accent for a couple of seconds.

Then, glancing at his watch, saying, "Very good. I will be there in one hour."

He taps off. Reaches down into his cargo pocket and takes up his Beretta, his friend.

Checks the magazine, pulls back the slide to be sure there's a round in the pipe. Pops the safety on.

He's all set to meet them. Just wanting to be sure he's protected.

Just in case things start going wrong and the genius's work gets sidelined.

17
THERE CAN BE NO SHILLY-SHALLY STUFF HERE

In her New York City duplex penthouse, socialite Blake Sinner is sitting in a half-lotus position, brooding, staring out through the floor-to-ceiling windows at Central Park fifteen stories below.

The view of the Park is vast. Green everywhere. Cuddled by high-rise towers of eminence and grace. The Ramble Arch and the Delacorte Theatre, and Strawberry Fields. It is visual poetry, Blake says to herself, taking a sip of tea. The view temporarily alleviates a storm of worries. Makes her concentrate on what she will relate to the man who will ring her doorbell in a minute or so.

For Blake, today is a confusing day. From the kitchen TV, multitudes of stories on the president's suicide intertwining with the death of General DeJean. The cable stations are stretched thin. Every correspondent and qualified part-timers are out there gathering and reporting every spec they can grab.

After researching, Blake realizes she will be meeting with a legend. A CNN senior international correspondent. Has no idea why she did not go to him first. Should have done that before, right, Blake? Sometimes you move too fast for your own good. Then you tumble and fall and have to tend to scraped knees and a diminished ego. When will you learn? Probably never.

Then she thinks about the hot cocktail dress she had on walking to the limo, the one with blood spatter. The vision pops into her mind. The brain matter. Not a sound came out of his mouth. He just dropped. Next day, she arrived at her apartment and took the dress out on the terrace, placed it in a metal garbage can. Emptied a five-hundred dollar bottle of Drambuie she got from Pug onto the black fabric. She needed a piece of paper to ignite the clump.

She picked up British *Vogue*, scanned the pages. Paused on "Princess Beatrice Is Expecting Her First Baby With Husband Edoardo Mapelli Mozzi." But wanted to re-read that. Weddings of this sort fascinate Blake. Her wedding to an Arabian prince was a glittering mass of bling and overdone everything. Lasted nine months, cost one million dollars, and never "consumated" the marriage—something about a holy vow he took.

She thumbed more pages. Stopped briefly at "The Best Fairytale Royal Wedding Gowns Of All Time." That was a keeper. Fanned to another page. Stopped, read the headline: "Platforms Are The Ultimate Reemergence Shoes." Who the hell cares? Mildly interesting. Off it came from the spine. She lit the page with a gold Dunhill lighter Pug gave her and dropped the flaming page onto the Drambuie soaked dress. A huge WHOOSH and an orange ball of fire set her back. In a couple of minutes, the dress became ash—his ash, Pug's. Who would have ever imagined that pieces of the egotistical general's brain splatter would end up as smoke particulates floating over sunny Manhattan? Above the taxis, the buses, Department of Sanitation trucks, and hot dog vendors.

She recalls saying to him months ago: "I see us in Lahaina soon at my place on the beach. Beautiful. We could watch the sun set and barbeque and drink Hawaiian beer."

Pug was not interested. In the sunset or the barbeque or the beer. He was focused on his iPad. Planning, he said, a history-making event. It would freshen up the whole planet.

Now the only thing she recalls of that sprig of memory is watching the smoke from the burgers drifting off over the white sand and frothy waves and shooing a few hungry flies. And now, Pug's smoke wilts and spirals over Manhattan. Over Strawberry Fields, the Boat House. Until Pug no longer exists, and Blake can turn the memory off and on whenever she wants.

She sips tea. Wants to get go into the kitchen and turn off the TV. But her thoughts hold her here on the couch, the view.

Now hopscotch to another thought: Tries to analyze what she sees in military officers, generals, and their uniforms and their stars. Authority? Manly substance? A fervor for country? Pug always said he had eight stars, four on each shoulder. Giving himself exaggerated prominence. There were three generals in the past four years—all debacles, right Blake? Love sought—the tickle of it. Love lost. Pug the biggest fiasco, undoubtedly. But the most stars. He was overweight. Shorter than Blake at five-foot-eight. She liked them leaner too. Nimble. Let's be honest, Blake, weight, height, girth, that was a turnoff that you thought you could climb over. But no. Hard to suppress. All the generals unquestionably great on the battlefield or wherever they fought their wars. But such disappointing soldiers on the field of sheets. Where they were expected to stand erect for their own self-worth. Everything by the numbers. No adlibbing. Position

One. Then Position Two. Let's try Three and Four—a military drill. And if Blake was lucky and felt a tickle, the firecrackers went off through her efforts before Position Five exploded.

She rises from the view and answers the intercom.

"There is a Mister Kitchens here, Miss Sinner."

"Please send him up."

"Yes, ma'am."

A minute passes, and she opens the door, and there they are staring at each other. The enduring War Zone Roger and Blake the Flake. Celebrities on the landscape of renowned people. At a loss for something fruity to say. Both have seen the other over the years in newspapers, magazines, documentaries, news pieces. But in person, they appear different, peculiar. Roger, she thinks, has a crusty face of a cynical war correspondent. She sees muzzle flashes in his brown eyes. The crack of cannon fire blaring from his ears.

She takes in a slight breath to gather herself and stands straighter to give Rog the gift of her height—a lady cobra fanning the hood.

Roger Kitchens is staring at a six-foot-tall Blake Sinner, a statue in her apartment with Central Park a tableau behind her. A skirl of perfumed air drifts between them. Did not expect this, Rog, did ya'? The reality does not match the rigid picture he has had that the press has shown. Which was in the last series of pics of her and General DeJean at a White House black-tie event. Blake in a simple dark gray cocktail dress, one strap lingering off a shoulder and too much décolletage for the White House hobnobs. Both stunning the crowd to Bruno Mars' *I'm Gonna Leave the Door Open.* The scene reminiscent of Princess Diana and John Travolta twirling around, delighting all. Not often, a four-star dances with someone of Blake the Flake's repute.

They smile. The six-foot-four Roger standing over the six-foot Blake. Her primary weapon with men is her height. Then the raspy voice. When she is with someone taller, things even up. Unusual for her to be outflanked by stature and fame. Roger the Dodger impresses her. Hard to do.

"*You*," she says, pointing to the scar on his temple. "*You* were wounded doing a news piece. Under fire. Now I remember. Saw your bloody face on TV. The *famous* Roger Kitchens. Marine patrol. Helmand Province. You were wounded there. In the head. I remember. Nice scar you have there. Please, come in."

"Some suggested plastic surgery. I tell them soldiers get medals; war correspondents get scars."

Roger's *son charme* brightens her face.

They walk into a ramble of luxury seen only in *Architectural Digest*.

"Very impressive," he says. His broadcast voice noted.

"Thank you. Welcome. Nice day to sit outside." She leads the way. "Can I get you something to drink? I'm having tea."

"That's perfect," Kitchens says, moving out onto the wraparound terrace.

The dazzling view. The sound of traffic spiking up from below, the sound of Manhattan.

They sit, and five seconds later, out of nowhere, a maid appears with a tray holding a pitcher of tea.

He says, "First, I want to thank you for the interview. I was a bit surprised you agreed to see me."

"Why wouldn't I?"

"I guess seeing a man killed two feet from your face might have an effect."

"It was horrible, but life goes on. I cared for General DeJean. I was *not* in love with General DeJean. And General DeJean was *not* in love with me. DeJean loved DeJean. I was a detour. A sack buddy, if you get my drift. Another ribbon he could wear on his arm at social functions."

"I understand. And I would guess that's why you consented to this interview—to clear the air?"

"That's part of it, Mister Kitchens. And by the way, my hand was approaching the phone to call *you*. But you beat me to it, Mister Kitchens. Fact is, I have something for you to mull on."

"Please. Call me Roger."

"Not War Zone Roger? Or Roger the Dodger? I did my research."

He smiles. "All of the above is okay."

"And you can call me Blake."

"Ground rules established," he says, grinning.

Blake says, "Before we begin, let me set the record straight. Most things you heard about me, 'Black the Flake,' etcetera—I've heard all that—they are either not true, made up, or exaggerations. Can you appreciate that? Because powerful, single women with lots of money attract the best and worst in everything, which includes the press."

"Being a journalist, I understand."

"Good. You must also understand that I was not vindictive—despite The New York times piece. I never threw a glass filled with wine at César. I stood up to go to the ladies' room and knocked over my glass of wine."

"I don't believe everything I read."

"César and I spoke about marriage, and César was against it. I respected that. After a couple of months, I came to realize that, thank God, he did not say yes. I could never marry him. But the press, they wanted something sexier. So, all this negative publicity about marriage and revenge—bullshit."

Roger nods, reaches into his pocket, and takes out a small pad and pen.

Blake asks, "Are you recording this. I don't see a recorder."

"No. Not recording," says Roger, lying. He has a DynoTech transmitter mic the size of a peanut attached under the knot on his tie. "Taking notes, the old-fashioned way," he adds.

Blake says, "I'm glad you called me. I checked you out on the internet, and I realized I made a mistake."

"And that was?"

"I sent a surreptitious recording—a video file—of a conversation I had with Pug to that local Fox newscaster. I watch him at night sometimes. I recorded it on a smartphone in César's apartment at the Croydon. César had no idea I was taking it. I sent it to—"

"Gilbert Scott."

"Not realizing he did not have the impact—the credibility you have."

"Thank you."

"How did you know I sent it to him?"

"He called me and told me. He had no idea what to do with it. We worked at the same radio station years ago."

She pours tea for both.

"I want the world to see what a treasonous, egotistical man DeJean was—that he was setting out to do something destructive and selfish. People in the United States feel like they understand all this. That's not enough. They should be outraged in this post-Trump era, and César outraged me. One does not think too clearly when one thinks they are in love, no? So, marriage was the last thing on my mind." She drops a sugar cube into her tea. "I dodged a bullet."

"You seemed to be with him for a long time—years.

"Eighteen months is not years."

"You know, he was going to be investigated and more than likely convicted of conduct unbecoming an officer at the very least, besides treason and sedition, to name a few. Dishonorably discharged. Prison time. No pension, no benefits."

"He knew that, but he said Deadlight would be in play before the government got around to that. He had no idea a bullet would end it all. But then again, he knew he was a controversial figure, and you either loved his politics or hated them."

"Do you have a specific idea what he was setting out to do?"

"Yes. I mean, no."

"Can't be both, Blake, yes or no. Which?"

"He spoke about it in vague, general terms, if you know what I mean. He was planning a coup to take over the US government. Never explained exactly how or when. Does that make sense?"

"Not from my perspective."

"He'd come back from meetings and generally say this and that, but in general terms. It was usually about him, what *he* said, what *he* did. He never seemed to tire of hearing himself talk about himself. One of the things he mentioned that I'll never forget was, he—I mean the National Guard—would be poised to take over all the radio and TV stations in the United States. That was the first move. Then he'd have a platform to get his intentions out to the people. That was only the real specific I can recall. I think he saw himself as a savior, a general who would save the country. They would erect statues of him."

"To start an uprising among the people and follow through with the National Guard. Would you say that that's accurate?"

She takes a sip of tea and silently rests the cup on the saucer. "He has four military people in his organization that can, will, pick up where he left off. Zealots. Things will be less smooth without him, but they will go on. I've met all four of them, and they are more than taking over for him."

Roger leans forward. He puts his pad and pen down.

"Did General DeJean have plans—I mean written, typed."

"Yes. He did most of that on an iPad."

He leans back, asks, "And the iPad, where is it?"

She can hear the impatience in his voice. She slouches back and searches her mind.

Blake, this is the moment of truth. If you want this information out, if want to help save democracy for at least the next few minutes, you have to tell Roger the Dodger where the iPad is. Can you do that? Or is this all a paltry pale of bird shit, and you are losing your courage?

She closes her eyes and says softly, "In his safe at the Croydon apartment."

"You have the combo?"

"No? It's digital, by the way."

"Of course, you don't have the combo; that would be too easy. How about the key to the apartment? Got that?

"Yes."

"Good. And how serious are you about this matter?"

She squints her eyes and stares at him. Blake Sinner hates to be challenged.

She slouches back again and feels her nerves tingle. Her breathing hastens. "Very serious," she says. And she knows what Rodger will say next.

"Serious enough to get into the apartment, open the safe, and get the iPad?"

Blake Sinner nods yes.

She says, "I could get into the apartment, but I can't get into the safe."

"Blake, let me ask you a question: if you were me, what would you want me to do with those plans, that is if I were to obtain them?"

"I'd want you to do something to stop Deadlight."

Kitchens finishes his tea, slouches into his chair, and stares out at the Hudson River. Reminds him of that airliner that landed there. Everyone got out alive. This might be different. Roger now feeling he is starting to deal with some risky odds.

Kitchens says, "I know people that can get into the safe. That's not a problem. The doormen, they know you?"

"They adore me. I take care of them year-round. They knew Pug wasn't married. They knew we were a couple. They treated me like I was his wife."

"Good. Then we could get you and the safecracker into the apartment."

"A bit risky, no?"

"I can pose the safecracker, make him an estate appraiser. The safecracker busts the safe, gets the iPad."

In a hesitant voice Blake asks, "Okay, now what? We have—you have—the iPad. What's next?"

Roger starts thinking. He didn't focus on the end game. Too busy tracking down sources and facts. Blake Sinner wants to know what Roger will do with the biggest political story in US history. Right now, Roger has no clear answer. Because he has not collated all the facts.

He sits up. "I don't know what's next. First, we have to get the iPad."

"How so? You know people, powerful people. In the Pentagon and elsewhere."

"They would have nothing to do with this. I'd have to put together what is known as package—the story, with a narrative, graphics, facts and quotes. It could be as secretive as possible. Or I could string the facts out like Woodward and Bernstein—little bits and pieces over a period of days. It would get out, what I was doing. In this instance, that could be very dangerous."

"How so?"

"A person, a radical group could want it squashed. Do you understand what I'm saying?"

Of course, she knows.

After a first rush of dizziness Blake's brain clears. "You could get killed," she declares. She doesn't know what else to say, and those words were not easy to get out of her mouth.

Roger says, "If there is anything you don't understand about this, let me know."

She shakes her head. There's so much to ask; where do I start?

Rodger adding, "And it would require triple management permission before they'd give me a studio and airtime. Before that, I'd have to present the story to management from beginning to end, double and triple-check sources, and if it doesn't pass their smell test, could confiscate all my notes, interview footage and ask for the iPad. It could drag on for months."

If Blake was emboldened before by her stance against DeJean's whacky-crazy-scary plan, now she's stunned. Not so simple is it, Blake. All these things, you, Pug, Deadlight.

The blood rushes up to her neck, prickles her scalp. Blake, you simpleton: you thought you'd hand Roger these tidbits, and Roger the Dodger would hop skip and jump to a refrigerated CNN studio down in D.C., open a mike and present a Pulitzer Prize piece, and the nation would be safe again. Oh, sweet Blake. You have got to climb out of your insulated, isolated, unrelated bubble and take a dash toward reality. Perhaps this apartment, the view, the altitude too high for your daily oxygen requirement. Get down to earth!

Blake says, "I said that I have something that I want to give you." She walks to a desk, picks up an iPad, and sits next to Roger.

Roger says, "And this is?"

"Show and tell."

They wait in silence while the iPad configures.

Blake starts to reminisce: "Back in my junior year of high school, I met an attractive boy, and we dated for a while. He was my prom date, and I was his prom date. It began and continued as a friendship. Then he went off to college. I went off to college. And that was it until a few years later I turn the TV, and I see that he's running for Congress."

"And his name was Tommy Rand."

"Not too hard to figure out."

"No."

"So, we of course, reconnected. I mean via phone. It wasn't until after he won a seat in Congress that we'd see each other occasionally, mostly lunches, walks in the park. It was one of the best friendships I ever had. Then he got married, Texting became popular, and we'd send notes to each other—infrequently, I might add. Then, about three months ago, he called me and asked for a favor. He said that he wanted to send me two documents, and I said, of course. One was his Last Will and Testament, the other would be self-evident."

Her hands flutter around the keyboard and she shows Roger two files:

Rand – Last Will & Testament
Rand – In the Event of My Demise

Roger's eyes widen. They look like hockey pucks.

"Tommy asked me not to open this one," she says, tapping on "In the Event of My Demise,' until after his death."

"You've read it, of course?"

"Yes. Essentially, it's a suicide note—"

"Saying?"

"Well, you can have a copy and read it for yourself. Bare-bones, it's an act of contrition, a *mea culpa*."

"Saying?"

"Saying that he was one of four people, the nucleus of Deadlight when it started years ago. There are no plans outlined in it, no specifics. The point he was making is that it was a big mistake and that he saw how wrong he was, how destructive it could be. The only person he mentions in general terms is DeJean, the man carrying the flag, and how he begged him to shut the whole thing down. In the margin of the note, he wrote, 'DeJean refuses to stop Deadlight.' He dated it the day he shot himself, which was the same day DeJean visited the Oval Office. He goes on to apologize for ever getting involved. Knows that his legacy will be nothing but vilification and loathing."

"Okay, you have a historic document there. What are you going to do with it?"

They stand and walk silently into the living, sit on the couch. Blake slumps down.

She says, "I haven't stopped thinking about it. What would you do?"

"I have no doubt whatsoever what I'd do."

"What?"

"Absolutely nothing."

"Nothing?"

"I'd pack it up and put it into my safe deposit box until the right time. You have nothing to gain exposing it now. It won't change a thing. It'll hit the news cycle, spin around for twenty-four hours, and then be forgotten. In the process, it would only go further to besmirch President Rand's reputation. Only inspire more questions about him."

Roger says, "First, we have to get the iPad. Are you up for a trip to our nation's capital?"

"Yes."

"Get dressed," he says, reaching for his cellphone and starting to dial.

Blake asks, "What are you doing?"

"Calling the airlines."

"You don't need to do that, Roger. My corporate jet's at Teterboro Airport, thirty minutes from here. We'll be in D.C. in time to beat the traffic and have dinner at Yardbird Southern Table and bar."

* * *

Two men seated at a sunlight table at the Hotel Der Junge Albon. Enjoying the food, the pleasant weather.

The hotel sits in the twin towns of Bad Rippoldsau-Schapbach and not far from Rayne's hotel, the Ochsenwirtshof. Both men wearing sports jackets, shirts, no tie. Looking like two German businessmen on lunch break. Eating silently.

And in possession of illegal firearms.

Look at the thinner man, Hans Kesten, cutting and dicing a humble German Cottage Potato with *Bratkartoffeln*, a green salad, and two perfectly fried eggs. He adds a sprinkle of pepper. In front of his plate, a frosty glass of iced Coca-Cola. In a bespoke leather shoulder holster, his Glock G-199 mm with extra magazines in his jacket pockets. Hansi, most assume incorrectly, is a serious German gangster—until he opens his mouth. Then, they discover he is a wannabe that someday will shoot himself in the foot with his Glock. He will be his first victim.

The man to his right has concluded his Bratwurst with cabbage and beans. Now he is savoring his dessert: Black Forest chocolate cake, whipped cream, and cherries troweled delicately between each layer. He is a stocky, powerful man with an anachronistic flattop haircut fastidiously trimmed. Like a bear from the forest behind him, he has honey-colored eyes. He exercises. Jogs. He thinks of himself as fit for any fight with any weapon. His name is Ernst Schumer. Assassin. Bank robber. Known to most police and criminal organizations as The Magician. He feels secure with the Sig-Sauer P365 stuffed into his belt. A couple of extra magazines add to his confidence. A thousand psychologists in a thousand years could never figure this man's pestilence.

Both men are on the INTERPOL's Red Notice. A Red Notice is an international wanted persons notice, but it is not an arrest warrant.

Finding yourself on the Red Notice indicates that you are screwed—once the police catch up to you. Impossible to walk about without constantly looking over your shoulder. Having your name plastered on Interpol's database means that any law enforcement agency in the world can arrest you, regardless of where you've fled to. These boys are two steps ahead of the German police. The fee offered by the man pulling into the parking lot now can provide some respite for them. But not for long

Now, the car they watch, a silver Jaguar F-Pace, stops. A few seconds later, the man they agreed to meet swings the door open and starts toward their table.

The man walks like a duck. He has freckles, and his red quiff jiggles. He thinks about waving to them, throws up his hand. They don't wave back. Simon, he thinks, these are not the kind of men one waves to. Especially with the business at hand.

Hansi says to the Magician: "*Dieser Mann, seine Haare sind zu hoch. Er sieht aus wie ein Clown.*" That man, his hair is too high. He looks like a clown."

The Magician nods his agreement.

The high-haired man's name is Simon Lane. Coming here today with his trademark quiff. Today set in place with a gentle spray of Adorn.

Like the men at the table, Simon comes armed with his Beretta Centurion, which renders some comfort.

He reaches the table, and the Magician stands, and they shake hands. This is their first in-person meeting. Several phone calls a few days ago familiarized them with each other.

Hansi remains seated; he signals the waitress.

Hansi saying, "*Möchten Sie ein Bier*?"

Simon says, "Yes, I would. Could we speak English, please?"

They agree.

The Magician says, "So, do you have a pleasant drive to here?"

"It took about one hour."

"Ah, easy trip. Where are you staying?"

"Strasburg."

The waitress takes the order. When she leaves, Hansi indicates his sexual attraction to her. The Magician looks at him; he loathes this and rolls his eyes. It is hard to keep Hansi focused. He figures he's got his hands full with Hansi. "So," he says, to Simon, "where are we?"

"We are," Simon says, "at the beginning."

The Magician says, "I realize that. But *where* at the beginning?"

"Did you get the pictures I sent you?'

"*Ja*. I assume you are talking about the woman. Not the location."

"The bunker area, you mean?"

"Yes. I got the pictures of her. And the bunker area too."

"Good. The woman is the target."

"Where is the woman staying."

"At the Hotel-Ochsenwirtshof."

"Okay. But before we go any further, Mister Lane. We should get the fee out of the way."

"I understand that. And I just wired the deposit to the banking coordinates you gave me."

The Magician takes out his cellphone. Scrolls through it: "This is not satisfactory."

"I didn't think it would be."

"This is only twenty-five percent here. *Ich bat um fünfzig*. I asked for fifty."

"Fifty is risky for me, Mister Schumer. Up front. This is a special job. There can be no shilly-shally stuff here."

"*Was*? *Was bedeutet das schilly-schally*?"

"It means, Mister Schumer, I do not want to spend time spinning my wheels doing something or making a decision because you do not want to do the right thing."

"Spinning what wheels. I don't understand. I know what the right thing to do is. You come to me asking for a big job. Unusual. You are asking me to—this is not a stroll in the beach. This is a matter of—"

"Making a situation disappear. Disappear forever. *Verschwinden*. I know perfectly well what it is."

The Magician saying, "Big job, big money. Fifty now. Fifty after. *Dann sind alle glücklich, nein*?"

"Incorrect. I will not be happy with that deal." Simon settles back in his chair, crosses his arms. "For God's sake," he says, looking at a cloud. "I thought we had all this settled. If not, I would not have wired the twenty-five percent, and I would not have driven here today."

The waitress arrives with the beers. Sets down a basket of

pretzels and mustard. Hansi smiles at her. The Magician rolls his eye. He is starting to loathe him.

Hansi takes out a cigarette, says to Simons, "You could always go to somewhere else, no?"

Simon says to Hansi, "I am somewhere else."

Hansi, lighting his cigarette, says, "Ha! You Americans. How do you say in English, You are such bullshit painters."

Simon, giggles, says, "Bullshit *artists* is the English."

"I like mine better."

The Magician glances at Hansi. "W*ould you keep your mouth shut.*" Then saying to Simon, "We cannot do this deal," and stands away from the table.

With firmness on his face, Simon says, "Sit down. I have some news for you."

He moves his chair closer to the table, leans in. "This morning, I get up around six. I have scrambled eggs, beans, a slice of Black Forest Ham. I take a piece of black German bread. Coffee, black. I flip open my laptop, and I check the headlines. All dreadful news. Nothing good anymore. Everything is bad. The President of the United States killed himself. A prominent United States Army general was assassinated coming out of his apartment building. Terrible times. I scroll to INTERPOL's site—the International Criminal Police Commission. I am sure you know INTERPOL Between my eggs and beans, I help myself to a big slice of INTERPOL news. Very tasty. Very compelling. I scrool down—and if I were you, Ernst, I'd take my chair and slide it under my ass right now because this might shake you up a bit—and after I butter my homemade black bread with sweet German butter, *mein Gott im Himmel*!"—the Magician resumes his seat— "and there is a picture of someone I know. Name of Ernst Earhardt Schumer, AKA the Magician. *You*! You are very popular. In

Germany. The world. The most serious item: the suspected assassination of a Peruvian minister. How sinister if I might be judgmental. Also, something in Miami, Florida. Dear lord, that can't be true. Also, instrumental in political corruption. Theft of precious, significant artwork in Belgium. Stealing four-hundred and fifty thousand dollars' worth of raw DeBeers diamonds. My, that's impressive. Killing is easy, isn't it, Ernst. I've discovered that myself. I mean—my weapons. But stealing raw diamonds—now *that* is an art. Now, if INTERPOL knew you were here, that would make life very hash for you, no?"

The Magician raises his hand. "Stop. I know where you are going with this exercise—you are extorting me."

"Ernst, trust me—I don't give a *damn* what you think I'm doing to you. I am *dealing* with you on a finite level. And from where I sit, you, Hansi with the roaming eyes, do not have good cards. You have a bad hand here."

"So, what deal is it you want."

"A fair one. The original deal. Twenty-five percent in your bank account now. Twenty-five percent when you relate to me your final plans. And fifty percent when the matter is concluded. The balance wired to your account in Bermuda as stipulated by the coordinates you have already given me."

Hansi says, "I do not think I like that deal, Ernst."

"He did not ask you what you think," the Magician says to Hans. He glances at his cellphone. At the deposit Simon made earlier today.

Simon says, "Cash there, right? American dollars? Untraceable."

Ernst Schumer grins, extends his hand, and they shake. "So, this woman, he says, holding up picture on his cellphone. I am not going to ask who she is because I do not care."

"I want her to disappear, do you know what I mean? *Keine Spur*."

"No trace, of course. That is what you pay me for."

"No need for you to know anything about her—except her face. *Also, alles ist gut*?"

"*Ja*, all is good. One more thing."

"Yes?"

"Her name, *bitte*?"

"Rayne Foster."

18
THE RACE BETWEEN A FLOATING FIVER AND A VERY LOVELY FRUIT BASKET

Gilbert Scott in his Manhattan living room watching a couple of tug boats lugging a gravel barge down the Hudson River. He wishes he were out there with them. Out there for a few days on the Hudson. Your own kitchen. Great views. All to yourself. He notes the wind pushing and shoving. Sliding through the frothy white caps. Challenging for the tug captains because wind moves what it wants to move when it wants to move it. The two tugs straining their ropes, trying to coordinate their tracks to keep the path straight down the middle of the choppy river. You and the tugs and the barge, Gil, just like you. Tugging and pushing and pulling. Tough doings sometimes.

Gil's got something going on in his stomach. Either that or Gil the Goose is having a heart attack. He stands up, belches, sits down. Heads for the medicine cabinet and takes his second Tagamet in the past forty minutes. The first a flop. Bile erupts. There must be a new volcano emerging down there. Lightheadedness. It's nerves, Gil. So much on your mind. So hard for you to chill. You thought you had things all coiled up with Roger.

Unmoored now. Afloat in space. Looking down at the planet.

Two bad pieces of news in the past two days singeing his brain. One would have been a kick in the head. The other a kick in the head, too, but less bloody.

The first, a meeting with the Fox News director in his office.

"I just want to give you a heads up," said Jack Tambrey," the news director, "that there could be some changes coming that might affect you."

"When?" Gil asked.

"Next week. Maybe two weeks from now."

Gil walks back to the living room and stares at the view again. The tugs are still aching out there. So is Gil. He figures maybe if he vomits, he will feel better.

He wishes Tambrey didn't say anything. No heads up crap. Now, I won't sleep until the changes pop up and surprise me. I'll have to buy a years' supply of Tagamet. What could the changes mean? They get rid of me and replace me with brighter teeth. Bluer eyes. Award-winning hairstyles. They stick me on the graveyard overnight, midnight to six a.m. Who the hell's watching then? Probably a pay cut. This business sucks, thinks Gil.

The second event took place at nine this morning—a Zoom call from Roger Kitchens.

The Goose's face lit up like a basketball on fire when he saw Roger's ID.

After the elation, the first rush of dizziness, Gil dove for his lap, and there was Roger on the screen. Big grin on his face. Good sign for Gil? This time Roger did not appear to be at the Pentagon; there were bookshelves surrounding a fireplace in Roger's Connecticut place, Rog wearing a plain gray T-shirt.

GS (Gilbert Scott): Hey, Rog, good to see you. What's up, my man!

RK (Roger Kitchens): Little bit a this, little bit a that. Good news, bad news. Bad news is, I haven't been able to scour up an anchor gig for you, but I'm on it, stay tight. We'll get you there, okay?

GS: Got it. So's what's the good news?

RK: Well, the good news is really a combo sandwich, bad news *and* a good situation, understand? But still very tasty, okay?

GS: Ah, yeah. Sorta.

RK: I just wanna tell you that I—I mean me, personally, Roger Kitchens—can't put the story out there, not the way I want. First of all, I'm a foreign correspondent with a heavy military background, understand. I'd sorta be stepping on toes.

GS: So, who cares?

RK: I have too big a reputation, and management at CNN will want the facts double, triple checked, and that will take five centuries. And there are some things that I had to do while looking into this that, well, I don't want out there, if you get my drift? A few less-than-legal moves. Understand?

GD: Shit! This sucks.

GS: Yeah, I know. But listen to this: Yesterday, I visited Blake Sinner. 'member her? Blake the Flake?

GS: Yes.

RK: She has a key to DeJean's D.C. apartment. We flew down, and I had a friend from CIA get into his safe. Pulled out a stack of plans he had for Deadlight. And listen to this, we got his iPad. It's all there, Gil, all the plans, everything. All out for the world to see.

GS: I'm not getting this. The connection. You. Me. What the shits this got to do with me? Gil and his anchor gig?

RK: Gil, my man, It has everything to do with you. It has to do with your reputation. *Your future*. Advancing it.

GS: How so?

RK: In a few minutes, a FedEx box will arrive there at your apartment. It has been sent by an anonymous source, so it can't be traced to me. In the box, all DeJean's plans, plus his iPad.

GS: You're kidding me.

RK: I shit you not. So, all you have to do is take—maybe you go with it to your news director. Say, someone dropped it on you anonymously, that you went through it, and that it's a bomb shell. News director—what's his name?

GS: Jack Trombley.

RK: Jack wants to be a hero too. Sees opportunity here. So, he takes the package and runs with it. Who gave it to Jack? *You*, Gilbert Scott. Promotion. Maybe a part-time anchor desk to start with there at Fox. Your name on the cover of the New York Times, The Washington Post. Do you see what I'm saying here, Gil? It's *clean*. In, out. You have supreme leverage. Simple.

GS: I'm liking this. Yeah. And you? It's—you're cool with this?

RK: Gil, I have more than my share of accolades. And besides, I'm thinking of retiring soon. This one's for you, pal. This is the right play. For both of us.

GS: I think it is!

RK: Yes. Keep your eye out for Fed Ex.

GS: Yep.

RK: Okay. Let's stay close.

Gil might have to change his shorts he's so happy. This could be the answer. And, Gil, you have your leverage back.

He rushes into the bathroom, shaves, showers, heads for the refrigerator, and throws back a big gulp of milk to chase the bile.

Before he takes his second gulp, the intercom rings.

The doorman saying, "Mister Scott, FedEx down here for you."

"Send it up, please."

A minute later, Gil opens his door, and there's the FedEx box. He opens it, glances at the contents. All there, just like Roger said. Even the iPad.

He calls Fox, asks for Jack Tambrey, tells him he has a bombshell for him, can he come down right now for a meeting? Of course. A bombshell. When you say that in broadcasting alarms go off, sirens start singing—a hard-cranking boost to Gil's brain cells.

Starting to chase some of the demons out of his head. Taking a deep breath in the elevator going down to the lobby of his building.

But when he steps out onto the sidewalk, Gil wonders about a few things. Why would Roger give up a good story like this? Sounds a little *bullshitty*, doesn't it, Gil. All those years of experience in the news biz and Roger could say God is visiting the planet tomorrow and will say mass at Madison Square Garden, and the world would go out for tickets. Gil thinking there's something else, another layer. Gil wondering if he's starting to smell some stale tuna here.

Also, another thought pierces his brain: Maybe I'm in over my head here? Maybe I should say screw the anchor gig. Live the dull life. Read the news on the prompters, and sleep tight every night.

Thirty minutes later, Gil steps out of a cab at Fox headquarters on Sixth Avenue with the Fed Ex box. He doesn't exactly have the spring in his walk he thought he'd have. Takes the elevator up to Jack's. They spend the next hour, just Jack and Gilbert, going over Gil's bombshell. They play the Blake Sinner video with DeJean a couple of times. Jack whispering "Holy shit" over and over. Scorching through DeJean's plans. Handwritten notes. Telephone contacts. They have his leather-covered phone directory with a zillion handwritten notes. Tambrey himself will personally map out a plan of attack, he tells Gil, a press release with the other networks notified. No designated players. Jack will do it himself. They'll trounce CNN, MSNBC,

CBS, NBC for the next week or so. Gil has to keep his mouth shut till it's time to shout it out.

Gil stands up, proud, and for the third time, Jack, with a little more intensity, asks him, "Where'd you say you got this again?" His eyebrows furrow—dog hunting for a bone.

"*I* didn't get it; *it* got me."

"How so? Tell me again."

"A few nights ago, a messenger arrives in the lobby. Security calls me down says, you have a package down here. Messenger needs to hand it over in person with ID. So, I go down to the lobby, show ID, sign for it, and that's that."

"Tell me again what you did with it."

"I was going to watch it on my desktop in my office. Thought better of it."

"Yeah, good move. You never know, right? Once out there, you never can get it back."

"Later, at my apartment, I check it out, and there's General DeJean with the unknown woman."

"As I said, probably Blake Sinner. He's been seeing her lately."

"You know this?"

"Six, seven years ago, I was News Director at WTOP, in Washington, D.C. and I did two stories on DeJean. Since then, I perk up whenever I see something about him, her."

"So. What do you think?"

"It's got massive potential. But let me ask you something. Anyone else knows you have this, family, friends, colleagues?"

"Nope. Just me. Now you," says Gil, lying. "Why do you ask?"

"Because. This is dangerous material. Number ten on the Richter Scale." Then silence, Jack Trambley checking his fingernails. "Careers can skyrocket. People could get hurt. Or worse."

"Some people might want it suppressed, you mean."

"Exactly." Gil sits down. A new burden. Nothing is easy, is it, Gil?

"I'm just saying. These days, anything goes. Maybe there are people who don't want this exposed, see what I'm saying. Don't want to scare you, Gil, but them's the facts." Gil nods. Inhales. Exhales. A little worry flickers across his eyes.

Jack saying, "Anyway. This is why I want to mull this a bit. Not too long, but I don't want to jump the shark here. See what I'm saying?

"I do."

"Good. Then we're on the same page?"

"Same page."

"Top secret."

"Lips sealed."

"So, keep it to yourself, and I'll give you a buzz."

Gil does not walk out of Tambrey's office like he hoped he would. He does not float out. He goes numb before the elevator doors open to the lobby.

Why he wonders, is he not jumping with joy?

Maybe, just maybe, Gil, you just got knocked clueless by Roger the Dodger.

* * *

Four hours later, Gil's in his apartment.

He's dressed in his favorite comfy clothes and dials Joe's Home of Soup Dumplings. He's starved. Nerves. Tonight, no Bud Lite. Needs hard stuff. He goes to the refrigerator, grabs a bottle of chilled vodka, takes it to the coffee table and turns on the TV. Pours himself a double, figures this should mellow the negative vibe rippling through his body.

The vodka's fire brings warm comfort. Now, Gilbert Scott is simply taking care of himself. Abolishing unpleasant household chores, bills, vacuuming. All can wait while Gil views the awful movie on TV. Soft distraction while he thinks and eats. He lets the drivel run on, too worried and lazy on his couch to fumble around groping for the TV remote. Focuses on what matters: The delicious dumplings and pork fried rice displacing the unpleasantries of the moment. Another double vodka will lift you to embrace the angels of comfort and solace. For now, Gilbert Scott does not have to face the darkness. The darkness will leave him to himself. You are now, Gil, the Emboldened God of Contentment. And this dumping in your mouth simple reward for cunning and intelligent thinking. Finally, perhaps, Trambley recognizing true broadcast talent.

He finishes the second glass of vodka. Pours another, lifts the glass, saying, "Here's to you Roger Kitchens."

Then the intercom buzzes. He looks at his watch—who the hell's here now?

"Yes?"

"Sir, a delivery down here for you."

"Send 'er up."

Good. A bouquet, about to descend upon him with good wishes and the scent of heartfelt appreciation. He walks to the coffee table. Throws back another big gulp. His toes have vanished, replaced by a slight tilt to his walk. A pleasant buzzing in his ears. Yeah, a congratulatory bunch of flowers from Jack Trambley, that's what it probably is.

The doorbell rings and Gil opens the door.

And there's a shadow standing there in the hallway. Tall guy dressed in black, hooded.

He's holding a fruit basket. A massive grouping of oranges, pears, nuts, peaches, and his favorite, plumbs. Jack knows I love firm plumbs.

Gil reaches for the basket, but the shadow says, "I can put it down on that table for you."

"Okay."

They walk to the table in the dining room, and the shadow places the basket down. It's heavy, and it thumps the wood. Could have laid a scratch down on Gil's table.

Gil says, "Hold on a sec," and he hops to the kitchen drawer to pull out some tip money, and when he comes back, the shadow is standing there facing him. When Gil extends the tip money, the shadow takes Gil's wrist as if he wants to dance with him. Pulls him in close. He wants to kiss me? What?

Then the shadow twirls Gil like he would a dance partner. Ropes his arm, his elbow, around Gil's throat, cutting off oxygen, pulls him in tight to his muscular torso.

Then he presses an ether-soaked rag over Gil's face—*anesthetic diethyl.* The kind that makes you unconscious, and you see all the planets and all the stars for free right there in the auditorium in your head.

One inhale, and the living room turns downside up and begins to vibrate and buzz like a million honey bees. The walls wiggly.

Gil thinking he's had too much chilled Tito's, maybe? The bile swishing in his stomach. Thas what it is. No, Gil. Better check into Cam Realitiy here. It's the rag on your face. I ought to be finishing the dumplings and watchin' date lousy movie. If you didn't throw back so many vodkas, you coulda thrown the lovely fruit basket at the shadow, freed myself.

The rag has a pleasant but foreboding odor. The more he inhales, the smaller the room becomes, the size of a walnut shell until Gil seems crushed, can't seem to fit inside. And the auditorium filling with blue and green sparkles and silver rain and the smell of seaweed and red waves slamming a beach made of pomegranate seeds.

Gil's eyelids at half-staff.

He feels something smash his toes because the shadow has just stepped on one of his feet with his boot. But the pain's not that bad, is it, Gil? Dull, overtones of sparking nerves, red and blue lightning bolts, and the devil's red eyes, sending unheeded emergency signals to the brain. How can that be? Well, Gil, your brain is filled with an auditorium of kaleidoscopic colors. It sorta roots him to reality which is slowly dribbling away.

The shadow is strong. Duck walks Gil to the dining room window, the one with the splendid view of Manhattan.

The looming window has Gil concerned. Not open. But still? Why there?

Gil struggles.

The shadow has such a grip on Gil, the ether rag, that Gil can't speak. He can't cough. He wants to get rid of the thick phlegm clogging everything.

The shadow's arms cutting off oxygen flow from Gil's nose to his lungs. Gil knowing it would be useless. Figuring before they get to the window, he will think of something slippery and work his way loose. The Goose Needs to Be Loose! But the only thing Gil Scott manages is a little girly ass wiggle and the sound a puppy makes when it has to wee-wee. Not the storm of muscle he imagined he could muster. Because he's going limp. Gil thinking, maybe I should have worked out more.

Gil wondering, is all this because Gilbert Scott wants an anchor gig? What I gotta go through for a major gig? Or, could this be—?

Wait a second.

Could this be because Roger figured this story was so hot that whoever puts it out there's going to get killed? That Rodger the

Dodger didn't get his nickname for nothing. Dodging bullets. Could Roger be that cruel?

Gil starting to think that maybe Roger played him. Saw what *could* happen to him and did a handoff, *and I fell for it*.

There at the window, the shadow reaches out, yanks up the window as far up as it can go, and a bellow of Manhattan air and diesel exhaust and a sprite of salty Hudson air presses presses Gil's nostrils. The window wide enough to—shit, Gil, dis is dangerous, near an open window—

Fourteen stories up.

Ah, finally, the shadow unhooks his grip around Goose's neck. Gil thinking, thank you, God, the shadow has had second thoughts. This was a bad joke. He's going to let me go and tell me to keep the tip which Gil still has clutched in his hand.

But then the shadow slides that outta-the-universe strong arm, that hand, down between Gil's butt and his pant's belt. Gil feeling the shadow's knuckles pressing the base of his spine.

Gil knows he's going for a late-night test flight over Manhattan's streets. Gil sorta glad he had three tall vodkas to help mellow him. But the buzz, it's thinning.

Then without much huffing and heaving, the shadow ups Gil's torso over the windowsill.

And there goes the Goose into the night air.

Over Manhattan!

It hits him: That son-of-a-bitch tossed me outta my fourteenth-floor window, my *own* window. *Before* I finished the dumplings.

The ether, the vodka, Gil, a strange combo. Bet no one before has done both together.

Gil, in outer space, on his back, arms supplicating. There are the bountiful stars. No rhyme or reason to the spatial picture. Everything whirling, changing. Seeing his window at 14A growing smaller and smaller. Gil hitting terminal velocity at 120 mph. He'll meet the pavement, cars, people, garbage cans in 3.8 seconds. Those are the rules. Not a second before. Not a second after. Rules are rules. You fall out of a fourteenth-story window, and 3.8 seconds you come to a sudden conclusion. Remember, Gil, what pilots know about falling: it's not the fall that gets you; it's the sudden stop.

He opens his fist, and there, floating away, is the neatly folded fiver he took out of the kitchen drawer to give to that demon that delivered that very lovely fruit basket.

And just behind the floating fiver, *Hey*! There's the Chrysler Building, Battery Park, the Staten Island Ferry sliding into a berth in lower Manhattan. And, too, Lady Liberty holding her arm up just like you. She's watching you!

And look, Gil! Plowing the air and passing the spinning fiver, the fruit basket, the contents ripping through the flapping yellow cellophane. The bananas, the peaches, your plumbs, descending in a chaotic image.

Fruit over Manhattan kills bystanders, reads *The New York Post*.

Who could imagine getting decked by a ripe banana, writes *The New York Times*? CNN: French Poodle almost killed by a falling plumb.

Or seriously wounded by a bulbous apple, says MSNBC?

And Gil finally realizing, *finally*, saying to himself, *Roger, you scumbag dickwad*! *You used the shit out of me*! You dodged a bullet.

I'M THE FALL GUY!

Of all the lights in the City, the brightest glowing presently is inside Gilbert Scott's kaleidoscopic mass of neurons and synapses. Converging. Simultaneously.

Then this isn't so bad after all. Think about it, Gil: no more worries about anchor gigs. No jealousies. No bills to pay. No what's-for-dinner decisions. No Gill the Goose jokes at the studio.

You just stay like you are on your back, the stars, curious, twinkling at you, carefully watching you descend.

Featuring you in their cold bright thoughts, and then. . .

Splat.

19
CHERCHEZ LE FEMME – SEEK THE WOMAN

At the Ochsenwirtshof parking lot, noon, Elora standing at the Defender peering into the engine bay. Large question mark on her face. Hands-on hips, one hand holding a Phillips screwdriver. She rocks on her heels, walks around the vehicle, and sticks her head closer to the carburetor.

Rayne has been watching through the lobby window. She walks to the lobby stairs and walks up to Elora.

"What's going on?"

Elora coming up for air. "I think the fuel line's got crap in it, and I can't open this clamp to clear it out. Engine starts then coughs then stops."

Rayne casts her eyes around the engine bay, spots the fuel line going into the carburetor. There, speckles of dirt, the clamp, and the screw clamping the fuel line tight around the carb nipple. Rayne extends her hand, and Elora gives her the screwdriver.

Rayne saying to the clamp, "Left loosey, right tighty. Which way were you turning?"

"Can't remember. Trying both, maybe."

Rayne turns the screwdriver left, and the screw starts coming away from the clamp. A few more turns and the clamp comes undone, and residual fuel drips out. She applies the screwdriver to the opposite end and frees the clamp. When she holds up the line, she sees the dirt, puts one end to her lips, and blows out the tiny clump.

"It's clean now," she says and starts putting it back. "You have to know which way to screw to tighten and loosen."

"Trust me, I—"

"I know, I'm sure you do. Start 'er up," she says abruptly.

Elora clambers in, turns the key, and after a few coughs, the Defender's engine's singing.

She says, "Let's go for a test spin."

"Only if I drive."

Rayne gets behind the wheel, Elora in the passenger seat.

Elora saying, "Do you have any idea how privileged you are—driving *my* Defender?"

"Where do you want to go?" says Rayne, stone in her voice.

"Up the mountain—to the bench."

"I want to see the horses again."

"Hey, Foster, we're really starting to know each other, aren't we?"

"It seems that way," Rayne says, flat. Distant.

Rayne grabs the gear shifter, slams into reverse, and they're out of the parking lot, up the dirt road, and bouncing up the mountain.

"Hey, cowboy, take it easy on the clutch."

After a few hundred yards, Rayne pulls over and turns the engine off.

She stares into Elora's eyes. Silent for ten seconds. She wants to tell her here.

"Let's walk," she says. "I want to see the horses."

They go to the corral where the horses roam but no horses today.

Rayne leans over the fence and makes a clacking noise, and the horses appear around a chamomile bush. Then they stop, peer at Rayne and Elora. *Oh, you again*! They clomp forward eagerly toward Rayne, their heads nodding up and down. They know Rayne; they like Rayne's touch. *Maybe she has sugar*?

She does. She sticks her hand out with sugar cubes she took from the hotel, and their big lips slurp them up.

Elora looks at Rayne's eyes. They look dull, dun. The horses' snorts and sneezes don't perk her up. She has something on her mind, imagines Elora.

Before they start for the bench, Elora says, hesitatingly, "Something wrong? You don't seem too chipper."

"I'm not. I need to talk to you about something."

"What?"

"When we get to the bench, we can sit and chat." Then, to the horses, "No one more sugar today, guys. Maybe tomorrow." One of them sneezes their thanks and shakes his flanks.

Elora's stomach tightens. She hates to "talk." Talk means pain. She's cannot handle pain now. On top of everything else. Especially coming from Rayne. Not today. *We need to talk* is an ambush, right, Elora. I want to talk to you about something you should have seen coming, but you did not. And now it will hurt you. Talking = hurt, she sees in her mind. Never a way around it. And it's never *guessing what? I have a check here for you in the amount of one trillion dollars.*

Ahead, the bench where they sat before, a cheerier moment.

They sit.

Elora saying, "It's starting to become our bench now."

Rayne looking at the treetops, the clouds, the sky. *Guide my hand.*

Silence for several seconds, and Rayne saying, "Have you ever imagined riding into town atop a white horse in a suit of armor, saving everyone from the biggest catastrophe of their lives?"

"Maybe."

"Or pulling a boat ashore on a river just seconds before it slides over a waterfall?"

"No. Never thought of that one."

"Or, how 'bout saving democracy in the United States. Or saving countless lives of people from coast-to-coast? Cleansing the nation of all the scum and muck that has prevailed for too long."

"What—?"

"I'm saying, you want to be your own person? To break from your father. His money?"

"Why are—?

She's coming after me.

A colossal breath, Elora, take in a huge breath.

You do know where this is going, El, do you not? Be honest. Elora wanting to listen to Rayne. But not hearing Rayne.

Then Rayne stands and paces slowly, pensively back and forth in front of the bench. The only sound the crunch of shoes on gravel. Her hands in her pockets, glancing at the treetops.

Seeking the courage, Rayne? Haven't quite nailed it, have you?

So, what's the lynchpin here?

Saying, "Some animals caught in a trap, you know what they do? Sometimes they chew their leg off to save themselves. And Aaron

Ralston, 'member him? The hiker. Canyoneering in the Bluejohn Canyon in Utah. Fell into a crevasse in the desert. His arm stuck in a fissure. Could not extricate it. Tried and tried and tried. Five days—*five whole days*. Finally, he got out his pocketknife—his *pocketknife*! —cut off a portion of his arm to survive. With a *pocketknife*! To move on. So he could live."

"What is this? A National Geographic special?"

"Can you imagine? —stuck there in a crevasse—arm wedged between two boulders—had to drank his own urine—amputated his arm with a dull pocketknife! —made his way through the rest of the canyon—rappelled down a sixty-five-foot drop—hiked seven miles to safety—all there in his book, *Between a Rock and a Hard Place*." Taking a breath. "We all pay a price for change—for escaping what we hate. Especially amputation."

"Where is this going, Foster? Because you are *creeping* me out."

"Big price sometimes. That's what you have to pay. That's you, Elora, right now—here—between a rock and a hard place. Down in a crevasse. And no one helps you but you."

"What rock? What hard place."

"And you know what, sitting here, you're trying to figure out how did Rayne Foster figure? How'd she figure *me*? How can Elora extricate herself from a *really*, *really* bad situation? Answer is, I know how *you* can. And you know how *you* can. Want to hear it?"

Elora jumps up, stares down at Rayne sharply— "I don't want to hear anything from you. Anymore! This is terrible, what you are doing to me."

"Sit down!" shouts Rayne, her irritation swelling. She spins around and faces Elora. "Because there's a lot more to the survival story and the young man cutting his arm off. A *lot* more."

Elora sits. "*Stop* lecturing me, Foster. I don't know why you're doing this. You're *really* upsetting me. What is your point? I thought we were buds. What's all this mumbo-jumbo nonsense about? Tell—no, wait, don't tell me." Five-second pause. "You know what, Foster—sometimes you are *weird.* I mean, I know you, and I *don't* know you? I thought—"

"You thought what? Thought a kiss and a passionate embrace—"

"That was more than a *passionate* embrace, Foster."

"—in a *hallway* was a pact for the future? That the fever was a strong song, felt forever? Sustainable?"

"I'm a fool, I am. For allowing myself to be *drawn* to you. A moth flying around Rayne Foster—charming and strong, attractive, fun. You are not who I thought you were. You're someone else. You *don't* want affection. You *don't* want to be loved—by *anyone.* You always have to know which way to turn the screwdriver because if you don't, then you are vulnerable."

"No one is who they think they are."

"Some other woman is talking to me, and I don't know why."

"Yes, you do. Just let it out."

"*I have nothing to let out.*"

"In a minute, you're going to have a lot to say."

"What the hell does *that* mean?"

"It means you have got to grab your pocketknife and start amputating."

"What? *What the hell, Foster*? Amputating what?"

"You know."

"Hey, stop screwing with my head! Okay? I have no secret to keep from you."

Rayne's patience vanishing. She stands abruptly, slams her foot on the bench next to Elora's thigh, reaches down to her ankle holster, and takes out her Sig-Sauer.

Elora: "What the hell is *that* for!?

Rayne: "Encouragement."

Elora: "*What is it you want me to say!?*"

"If you say it, if you voluntarily say it, it will be easier for both of us. Please don't let me force it out of you. I want to hear it now." Then she *screams* to the trees: "*Tell me*! *Tell me*!"

Nothing.

Elora, the widening eyes, the anger swelling, trying to clamber around inside Rayne's head without a map.

Rayne cocks the hammer.

The muzzle pressing Elora's pubic bone, harsh.

Elora saying, "A gun! That hurts! *Who the hell are you*?"

"Tell me. Right now. If you don't, I'll pull the trigger. You'll start to bleed. I'll stand here and watch you bleed out. Ralston, in the canyon knew the clean but painful way out. If you tell me, your conscience will be clear—you'll see the brightest light of your life—you'll finally be free."

Elora shakes her head— "You won't do that. You won't."

"I won't?" Rayne presses her forehead to Elora's, says softly. "I have."

"What do you mean *have*?"

Rayne pulls her head back. "I have—end of story. You want a kiss now? Huh? Now that you know who I *might* be, the woman with the gun, the ankle holster, the secrets. Who I *could* be? Who I *am*? With *this*," she says, wagging the pistol in Elora's face. "Now you know more about me. More than who I was in a dark hallway in a hotel?"

"I know why now, why you're acting like this—because *you*, Foster, have something to keep from me, to tell *me*. You have a secret. About me. Let's trade secrets. You go first."

"I have no secret to tell you, Sinner. Zero."

Now, Elora, go ahead. Stick it out there. Let it flow. All of it. She knows, she does. So just stitch the words together, and for God's sake, Elora, forget that she pressed a 9mm in your pussy just a minute ago. Go ahead. Tell Rayne everything you have in your heart.

Elora saying, "There at the bar the first time I met you, when you turned around and faced me, I knew in my heart my life just began. My heart beat faster. My life came alive. The arms I wanted. Wanted to taste you right there, Foster. Wanted you as a friend. A mentor. A pal. A buddy. I wanted you to fall in love with me the way I had fallen in love with you at that moment. I wanted our lips to touch right there, to hear your heart beating. I prayed at that moment that if we fell in love, it would last *forever*. And at that moment at the bar, looking into your eyes, I only had *hope*. That's *all* I had. You were a fragile bird in my hands. That I wanted to hold and cherish and adore and care for. *Forever*, Foster." Elora pauses, then her eyes glint and sadden, and she says, "So—now *you* tell *me*, Foster. *You tell me*! Tell me who *you* are and how you *feel about Elora*!"

She's turned the tables on you, Rayne.

She did it again—she gotcha, gotcha, gotcha, gotcha.

"I have nothing to tell you."

"Yes. *Yes, you do*!"

Silence.

"*Tell me*!"

Silence.

Elora saying, "Because when I looked into your eyes at the bar, I knew. I *knew*, at that moment. And in the hallway before the German tourists interrupted, I *knew* then a hundred and ten percent, I *knew*."

"You knew *nothing*, Sinner."

"I did, I knew—and don't' *dare* tell me what I know or *don't* know."

"I can't—"

"What? *Can't what!* Tell me? Tell me what you've been *wanting* to tell me."

Silence.

Rayne says, "I have nothing to tell you!"

"Of course not—you know why? Because you don't *want* affection. You don't *want* to be loved. You don't *want* to be cared for. Because—they make you feel vulnerable, and then you can't be *strong* anymore, and you *can't* carry on."

"You have no idea who or what Rayne Foster is. If you did, you'd vomit."

"I know one thing," Elora says, "I know that you are falling in love with me."

Rayne stands up straight. Then straighter. Then as straight as she can. She seems offended.

Knocked back.

Inhales.

Something's got her throat.

Something peculiar.

Rayne stops breathing.

The world spins hubbly-bubbly off its axis.

There is no air anymore.

There is not a scrap of sky left to shine.

No heaven to praise

No hell to loathe.

No misery to scorn.

No pain.

Nothing.

Just Elora Sinner staring into Rayne's eyes.

Waiting, Rayne.

And Rayne on a carousel with a million multicolored exuberant snickering ponies. Feeling Rayne's weight on them. The moon and the planets she loves and who love her recede. All vanished. And Rayne thinking the only thing she sees is Elora on the bench, her green eyes, the lines of her lips, beckoning, and all this spinning with the leaping, laughing ponies looking over their tresses to see Rayne hanging on, the ponies saying, *hey, who is that on the merry-go-round with us? Does she know where she is? What she wants? Where she's going?* No! She is like *all* the others when they saddle up, exuberant, hopeful—going round and round in circles seemingly happy. But do they ever grab the golden ring?

And Rayne uttering to herself, *damnit*. And then silently mouthing Elora's name in her mind, and just for an isolated second, smelling the *scent* of her—the first whiff of her *Iris Tubereuse* cologne drifting to her. Wanting to hold it inside forever. One of the first memories.

Yes, yes.

Go ahead. Admit it.

And then …

No.

I can't!

I can't!

Rayne Foster slips the pistol back into the ankle holster and sits next to Elora on the bench. Their knees touch. Nothing to hear. Except their deep breathing. The only sound is the bumblebee buzzing from one posy to the other.

Rayne saying softly, "Use the pocketknife."

Elora throws her head back, and her silky auburn hair flutters down, touching her collar, and she shuts her eyes tight, and, bruised and hurt, she says, "The red phone. That's what you wanted from me. That's all. Nothing else."

* * *

At the same minute down *Wolfacherstrasse,* less than a mile from the Ochsenwirtshoff, the Magician halts his Passat on a cutout on the road. Turns off the engine. Fingers drumming the steering wheel.

Hans Kesten, in the passenger seat, unbuckles his seat belt, reaches inside his jacket. He slides out his pistol. He gives the slide a sniff. Like he would a peach. Likes the smell of the fresh gun oil. Presses the release button, and the magazine falls onto his lap.

The Magician says, "*Was tust du*?" What are you doing?

"*Ich prüfe meine Waffe.*" I am checking my weapon.

Hansi yanks back the slide, and a 9mm pops into the air and lands on the Magician's thigh.

"*Warum tun Sie das jetzt*?" Why are you doing that now?

The Magician hands Hansi the ejected round, and he presses it back into the magazine.

Hansi saying, "*Denn ich will vorbereitet sein.*" Because I want to be prepared.

"*Wozu? Zweiter Weltkrieg*? *Das Vierte Reich*?" For what? World War III? The Fourth Reich?

The sun has about vanished, and it is getting dark in the car. The curve ahead separates them from the hotel. Hansi turns on the overhead light, pulls down the vanity mirror, and looks over his clothing. A Black Laponia Lederhosen with suspenders, Plattler length. A blue checkered shirt. Knee-length socks and hiking boots. A light gray Trachten jacket with matte gray buttons.

The Magician asks, "*Und warum sind Sie so gekleidet*?" And why are you dressed like that?

"*Tarnung. Also übermischung ich.*" Camouflage. So I blend in.

"*Zu was? Eine Bierhalle.*" To what? A beer hall.

Hansi shrugs his shoulders.

"*Du bist wahnsinnig.*" You are insane, the Magician says, shaking his head.

Perhaps a lack of sleep has confused Hans Kesten. All he has to do tonight is grab his flashlight and walk along the shoulder of the road to the *Ochsenwirtsoff* and get the lay of the land. See where the girls are, what they are doing. The Magician will wait here in the car until Hans comes back. They both have walkie-talkies but have agreed that they will not use them unless necessary.

The Magician says to Hansi, "*Und wenn Sie zurückkommen, legen Sie diese Automatisch in den Rücken und beginnen, einen Revolver zu tragen.*" And when you come back, put that automatic in the back and start carrying a revolver.

"*Warum*?" Why?

"The shell casings. Unless you want to shoot someone and then go around picking up the shells. They could be traced. *Verstanden*?"

"*Ja.*"

"I am sorry for yelling at you. We must be cautious."

Hansi checks his flashlight. The Magician shakes his head and grins. He says in English, "Who do you think you are, James Bond?"

Hansi smiles. "Yes. I am. For the moment. If I have to walk down this dark road with just a flashlight and the stars and nose around the hotel for the two women, I have to pretend to be someone else. *Ist das okay mit dir*?"

"*Ja.*"

The Magician glances at his watch. "Now," he says, gazing through the windshield, at the curve, "go into the lobby. Look around. Look into the dining room. It is dinner time. They might be there. Or at the bar. Be subtle. Try to blend in. Be observant—*Aufmerksame*—then walk back here. *Kompliziert*?"

"*Nein*. Not complicated."

"*Gut*."

Hansi holsters his pistol, reaches into the backseat of the car and grabs his carved walking stick—a collector's piece he paid $660 for at a Berchtesgaden antique shop. He calls it his hearty stick. Why? No one has any idea.

He starts walking, asking himself why Schumer did not make the scout himself. Why me?

The plan is—well, what the hell is the plan? Hansi has no idea what the approach is on this event. He never does. Not until they scout every detail and then get themselves into the end phase. Till then, Ernst does not speak. The Magician, he knows, is assiduous and thorough. He respects him. He does not like him anymore. He plots these events (that's what the Magician calls them) like he would a space launch. But he keeps Hansi out of the loop until he is certain Hansi can unquestionably fulfill his role.

Hansi walks slow. He's not going to knock himself out walking on the shoulder of the road to the hotel. The Magician did no say anything about walking speed. Can you remember, Hansi asks himself, in the past year when Ernst treated me like a friend? No. Always shouting. Never laughing.

The night air is pure, the stars and a russet moon illuminate his tracks, leaving the Magician behind until he goes around the curve and can't see the VW anymore. Hansi thinking, Sometimes it is good to be out at night by yourself with a hearty walking stick.

* * *

At that moment, Rayne and Elora at a booth in the *Oschsenwirtshof* Hotel dining room. They have drinks standing in front of them, Margaritas, extra salt. Wine coming too.

Rayne sips her drink. Sets it down on the napkin, flattens the damp edges, and looks into Elora's eyes. "I'm sorry about before."

"About?"

"The pistol."

Elora tastes her drink. "Well, it was an unexpected *intrusion*."

"Oh, so you never had a pistol in your pussy?"

Elora throws her head back and laughs the loudest she has in a long time. "You're funny, Foster. Wry funny. That's why I think I'm—" Then, Elora suddenly silent, saying, "Look at me. I want to see your blue eyes—so I'll remember them when I'm in jail."

"Hey, maybe not."

"What did you do with the phone?"

"Nothing. I have it here." She taps her pants pocket."

"You have this thing mapped out, don't you?"

Rayne nods her head. "If you can do what you said the phone's codes could do, you'll be saving the United States—and probably a lot of lives. And because you did it voluntarily, you could be avoiding jail time."

The waitress arrives and Elora orders a Bavarian cheese board with brie, camembert, gruyere, and Swiss cheeses with grapes and butter.

After the waitress leaves, Elora says, "My father will never speak to me."

"Elora, I have no sympathy for that. Your father and his money are responsible for Deadlight, no one else. So, you need to focus on that."

"Speaking of focus, you never really told me what you do. You have a law degree and don't practice. And you have a camera and say you are a freelance photojournalist, and I have not seen you take any more than six pictures since the first day we met. I know you're not who you say you are."

"I told you enough," says Rayne abruptly. "At this moment, you don't need any more Rayne Foster facts. You have enough."

And suddenly, Elora remembers.

It was one of those stories that make the rounds in a bistro in Paris, or someone relates quietly in a whisper to you in a Pub in the Strand, then there are several versions, and the facets change colors in conversation in a *boite* in London or Cairo. Then it floats around on different languages, drifts off, and it becomes what it is: a fanciful legend. The trade full of them, and most are invented claptrap.

This one about a woman called Half Face, a beauty born of the Devil. She had two faces, and she could disguise herself simply by turning her head. And any man, so goes the legend, would be a fool to take her to bed because she carries death between her legs. Some legends survive; some sources are forgotten, some never known.

Rayne slices the camembert, spreads it on a piece of toasted bread.

Then Elora picks up her napkin and taps the corner of her mouth, and she says softly, "There is a legend about you. Do you know about that?"

Rayne laughs softly, looks into Elora's eyes. "Is there? Has to be incomplete. One day I'll write the ending. One calm day."

"And there's something else I have to tell you."

Rayne asks, "Something you have wanted to tell me for a while?"

"Yes."

"Why'd you wait this long?"

"I didn't want our relationship to go off track. Because what I am about to tell you can be very disruptive and endanger both of us."

"Don't forget—Rayne and her big gun."

"But there's no turning back now, so everything should be out there."

They stare at each other briefly, sip wine—impatience chilling the air.

Rayne puts her glass down, leans over her plate a bit. "So. Let's clean things up."

Elora says, "We know who you are."

"Who I am?"

"We work for the same company."

"We work for the same company," Rayne repeats.

"Yes. I am attached to the political affairs department at the CIA's Berlin Station. I've been there two years. And you, you have been working almost exclusively for Lee Upchurch, black ops, and his Special Operations Group. In the CIA personnel files, there is no Rayne Foster. I looked. She does not exist. Upchurch and your father were close friends. You graduated in the top three of your law school class at Columbia, worked at your father's firm. Were on the Columbia undergraduate swim team. From there, you went on to the Summer Olympics. Won one bronze, one silver. Your father had a heart attack on his sailboat in Bermuda. While he was receiving emergency resuscitation at the dock, your mother had an attack. They died the same day at the same hour. Then you left your father's firm and started your own one-person shop. That did not suit your tastes, so you began freelance photojournalism."

Rayne laughs, recalling all this. Entertained. This compressed Wikipedia life-tour.

Rayne asking: "Where did you get this information?"

"It is part of the legend of Half Face."

* * *

At this moment here stands Hans at the hotel's reception desk, lifting a heart-shaped mint from a tray. He gently unravels it and then watches the crumpled foil fall into a wastebasket. He savors the mint. It has an honest taste.

No one here at the desk. Hans not realizing that Juta, the owner, is a one-person show: owner, receptionist, overall manager, bartender, maître de, sometime-cook (good one, too).

Then he and his hearty stick saunter to the entrance of the dining room and he peeks in and scans around. Nice atmosphere. The menu smells good—Glenn Miller music on the speakers.

He spots Rayne and the other woman.

And maybe I should walk in and shoot her at the table over, this Rayne woman.

Who needs plans?

You just shoot and run into the night. No car to track. Those are plans. Simple. The Magician and his plans are always convoluted, and maybe that's why we are always looking over our shoulders. Running through the pines. *That's* a plan. The Magician might appreciate that, Hansi. Or he might not. Hansi spinning the crooked notion in his brain. A spider stumbling around his own intricate bouncy web trying to avoid getting his feet stuck. Looking over his shoulder.

He steps toward the cozy dining room bar, takes a stool, orders a double Johnny Walker. Sniffs and sips. From the bar's mirror, he sees himself, and there behind him in the mirror, Elora and Rayne. How terrific. All three of us are in one place. Ernst will love this. How do they look to you, Hans? Not too happy? *Mürrisch.* What is that word in English? Ah, he remembers quickly: *sullen*, that's it. He will have to pass that along to the Magician (to show how observant he is).

On the restaurant's speakers, Dr. Buzzard's Savannah Band singing *Cherchez le Femme*. He smiles at himself in the mirror over the bar. *He loves this song*! One of his American favorites. Been a while since he heard it. What's the translation? *Look for the woman*.

But Hansi knows much about this song. The French use it as s*eek the woman.* A cliche in detective fiction, used to suggest that a mystery can be resolved by identifying a femme fatale or female love interest.

The French implication: no matter what the problem, if something has gone wrong, a woman is often the cause. Look for the mistress, the jealous wife, the angry lover: A woman at the root of each problem. That, Hans imagines, is the challenge here tonight. That he could solve this challenge in a flash and ingratiate himself to Ernst. He has looked for the woman. He has found the woman. She is there in the booth sipping wine. And she is so beautiful. He has detected their mood. Good job, Hans!

So, yes, he would be helping Ernst.

Or so he thinks.

Just throw back the scotch, grab the pistol and kill the woman.

Then walk out the kitchen door.

Go back to the Magician and declare your sacrilege. You *might* be forgiven.

But finish your Johnny first.

Almost in a whisper, Elora says to Rayne over the breadbasket, "It doesn't matter anymore, does it?"

"What?"

"That I know who you are, that you know who I am.

"You have a philosopher's hat on now?

"Because we're on the same team now."

"That's because you did the right thing—you jumped ship. You turned over the phone."

"I wanted to tell you about that for a long time. Now what."

"I have some ideas," says Rayne softly.

Hans allows the fiery Johnny to flow over lip and teeth, and throat. When it paints his stomach, he cringes slightly. But the Johnny is gone, and before Hans spins off the stool, he fingers his Walther PPQ M2 Coyote autoloader. Rubs the serrated back, the customized wooden grips with HANS carved in the mahogany wood. Maybe one more Johnny, right, Hansi, To give you an explosive edge for the task you have so diligently assigned yourself.He orders another double, downs it, and mellows on the images in the mirror—himself, the two women. The Johnny now making an impression on his brain aberrant brain cells. Hansi feels warm. Hansi thinking it could be difficult to blow a hole in such a beautiful head. But he will do it.

Hansi, do you think it smart with Johnny rolling around in your gut, coiling through chicanes and S curves in your brain, and disrupting all those neurons and synapses, to take on an adventure like this now?

Yes, I am good.

Who says so? The Magician?

Nein!

Then best you think it over, no?

Leave me alone. Go 'way.

Hans steps off the stool toward his target, Rayne Foster.

Taking his trickeries with him.

Then stands still for a moment, tests his balance, firm he is, and maps the room. He has to take the long way to Rayne Foster if he wants a back shot. Coming front on, no good. Rayne will spot him coming to her, uncoil, pull her weapon with the speed of a cobra. The long way then, shot to the base of the skull: walk parallel to the breakfast table, left before that table for two, then left, past one booth with four people eating their salads.

And then there you are, Hans, you with your friend, Mister Coyote. Toothy smile, whiskers bristling right now in his bespoke cozy holster resting near your heart. Eager.

Hansi starts from the bar.

The sound of the room a crescendo, a peculiar din: cutlery, subdued laughter, dining plates landing on tablecloths. Beer laughter. Snippets of conversation

Hans continues navigating.

Arrives at Rayne's table.

And then he hears behind him, "*Entschuldigung.*" A waitress with a large tray and two entrees. *Excuse me.*

Hans going for his Coyote.

The waitress bearing two entrées—one for Rayne, one for Elora.

And they look delicious, Hans noting.

"*Entschuldigung.*"

He watches for a second as the waitress settles the plates down.

He starts pulling out mister Coyote.

And then he turns for the exit, saying to himself: Maybe some other time.

Knowing that when he gets back to the VW he won't invoke the Magician's anger. At least not tonight.

* * *

Over their dinner, Rayne feels a tremor of inquisitiveness. She wants to hear more about herself from Elora's point of view.

Rayne saying, "How did you learn about me. Through—?"

"Simon Lane."

"The tree stump with the red quiff. Do you know him?"

"I do. He is eccentric. The mad scientist. His company is floundering. And I think—and this is conjecture—he's looking for something massive to draw attention to himself—his drones and other aircraft he designs and builds. You have to understand. I don't know as much as you think I might know. My father asked me to participate in this because he trusted me. Fact is, he never made me raise my hand to secrecy—it was assumed."

"Who else?"

"A man named Meese Van Der Leeuwen. Know him?"

"Tell me who he is."

"Who he *was*. He's dead. Simon shot him two nights ago in the bunker. I was there. I saw it. Almost busted my eardrums."

"What? Where?"

"In the bunker. Simon was taking us on a happy-go-lucky walking tour, singing his own praises. Proud of what he had achieved with the drones. Said Meese was cheating him. Meese was—"

"Your fiancé."

"Yes."

"Should I extend my condolences? I suspect not."

Elora grins, pauses, lifts her wine glass. Says, "Here's to the end of this nightmare."

Their glasses click.

Elora saying, "Everyone was compartmentalized—need to know. I have only one task."

"Which is? So far, you have not really laid it all it."

"Ok. Simple. The red phone everyone's in love with contains an app written by Simon Lane. That's all's on it. One app. And too complicated to decrypt quickly. A code is necessary to access the app. Which I have in my head. Once launched, two things can occur: they can be immediately aborted and flown back to the bunker. Two: the flight can be aborted, and the drones will self-destruct—but they can't be over a land mass."

"Why?"

"If they are destroyed over a land mass, wreckage will fall to the earth and then through forensics traced back to Simon and his company. Then it's light's out and jail time. Which could also include the death penalty for Meese's death."

"And once over the United States and mission accomplished?"

"Once launched and mission accomplished, they fly on to the Pacific ocean. A few hundred miles beyond California, they destroy themselves leaving no physical evidence. That's all I know."

"So, you are the codes girl?"

"I am the codes girl."

"And never happy with your role."

"Never. Doing it out of stone-cold loyalty to my father. Which I have been doing all my life and hating it." Then Elora looks down at her dinner plate, says, "And that is one reason I am so glad I met you. You changed my life, Foster. Can you appreciate that?"

She squeezes Rayne's hand.

Rayne hesitates, then says, "I think I can."

20
WHERE THE POTATO CHIPS AND FRIES AND HAMBURGER MORSELS REMAIN FOREVER.

Out here, the sound of evening crickets.

The night stars copious, and the moon's glistening white azimuth drifted since Hansi left for the hotel forty-five minutes ago. Now hear him, the faint crunch of his hiking boots on the gravel and the tap-tap of his hearty walking stick,

He opens the VW passenger door and flops in, drops the walking stick onto the back seat. Then he sniffs the air, a hound he is, of course. The Magician has drawn the last deep poke on what was a chubby dooby, pauses, blows the smoke out the window, and watches the wisps vanish against the tall pines.

Ernst saying, "*Also*?"

"They are there. Both. Elora Sinner. Rayne Foster."

"Doing?"

"Eating. Chatting."

"At what stage?"

"*Was? Was meinst du*?"

"I mean, what were they eating: An appetizer? An entrée? A dessert? An elephant?"

"*Ach*! Yes. I was leaving, and they were glancing at their entrees. Delicious ones."

"Anything else?"

"Yes, I had two double Johnny Walkers."

"*Was*? Drinking on the job."

"And you? Look who's talking. Blowing a joint."

"Anything else?"

Now think twice here, Hans, really give it some thought before you open your—

"Yes. I thought for the sake of the mission, I would expedite things—I was going to shoot Foster right there in the dining room then escape through the kitchen door. But—

Like a whirlwind, the Magician twirls in his seat and his hand comes around like a steely scythe.

"*What*! *Are you crazy*!"

He grips Hans by the throat, a vice launched from hell. Hans gags.

"*Why*? *Why would you do that*? *Asshole*! *You wonder why you piss me off*! *This is why*. There is a plan. You follow the plan."

He releases his grip.

Hansi says, "But I have heard no plan from you. I thought I was doing us a favor. Less work."

"Yes, you *have* heard the plan! The plan: we drive to the hotel. We are at the hotel. That's a plan. You go into the hotel. That's part of the plan. You observe the woman. Also, part of the plan. You come back to me and tell me what you saw. So far, all this is the plan. *Verstehe*?"

"*Ja, ja.*"

"*Gut.*"

"Now, listen to me," says the Magician, taking his hand away from Hansi. "You want the rest of the plan? Okay. Here is the plan. Can you remember it, though?"

Hans is insulted: "I think I can."

"I think you better. Now, this is what we are going to do. And you are a big player. Does that make you feel better? Important?"

"Yes."

"We put her on the little motorboat at the lake."

"*Ja.*"

"You start the engine?"

"*Ja.*"

"We move out to the Sinner yacht. *Erinnern Sie sich an den Namen der Yacht*?"

"*Ja.*"

"*Es ist*?"

"*Corsair* is the name."

"*Gut. Dann*?"

"Then we board the transom. We take her aboard and tie her up. Tape. Ropes."

"*Gut*. Now, do you have the Silvercup detonators and timers?"

"In the back. Two of them."

"Semtex explosive—one pound?"

"*Ja*. One pound."

"The masking tape and the rope?"

"*All* in trunk."

"The GPS unit with the preprogrammed coordinates?"

"*Ja, ja.*"

"Excellent. Now you know *most* of the plan."

"I feel better."

"Do you know what we will do with all the parts of the plan?"

"*Ja.*"

"*Was?*"

"We string them together. We take her to the dock, to the motorboat, to the yacht. When we get to the dock, we tie her up. We disable the yacht. We remove the ignition coils. Then we split the Semtex into two parts. Insert the detonators. Set the Silvercup timers, and *boom.*"

"*Wie viel Zeit*"

"Four minutes each timer."

"Good. Now we execute the plan."

Then Hans scratches his head.

Which was not part of the plan.

* * *

Elora and Rayne step out of the Ochsenwirtshoff Hotel, walk to the little garden and look up to heaven. They take deep breaths. Efreshingout here. The stars are bountiful. A dome of glittering brilliants.

Elora says, "My gosh, I've never seen so many bright stars. I wonder what all the people up there are doing?"

"The same thing we are doing," says Rayne. "Mucking things up."

They walk along the parking lot, up a short hill to a bench and picnic table just outsde the indoor swimming pool.

Elora settles back in the bench. She's starting to feel cleansed. She says, "You know what's better than star-gazing—star-gazing with a beer."

Rayne says, "I'll get us a couple."

But Rayne can't stand up.

She tries to lift her body, but she can't come off the bench. She tries again but goes down harshly onto the chair.

And now she can't see the stars anymore.

Or the moon. Or Elora. Where would they all go?

Oh, dear.

A soft chamois sack over your head, that's what it is. That's the venom right now with a drawstring tightening around your neck.

And then Rayne hears a male voice with a German accent.

"This is a bit eerie, isn't it—that we find ourselves in the same place again," says the Magician. "Remember? You? Me? Sunny Miami? Six months ago?"

Through his strong hands, he can feel her rage, sense, and feel the scream boiling up inside her.

"Don't raise your voice, please, for your sake. If you do, you will make it difficult for all of us, okay. We are simply going to take a stroll to your car. Nice and slow. No hippity-hop like the Easter Bunny, please. And before we get there, Hans will remove the sack." They start walking. "Be careful. I don't want you to trip and fall." Rayne nods yes. Then she hears Elora say, "Please, don't hurt her." And then she hears Elora repeat it. And once more before they reach the car.

Hansi says, "Not to worry. Elora is your name, I know. Simon Lane said that you are on our team. This is good. I like you. At the very least, we would like you to keep us company. Maybe you can drive some of the way?"

Elora says, "To where?"

"Lake Constance. Your father's yacht. Maybe some food and some drinks when we arrive? And a freshen up?"

Rayne Foster guided by the deleterious hands of one of the

world's most wanted hazards, a demonic lizard. The Magician moves her this way and that way down the inclined grassy path adjacent to the parking area. When they get to the bottom, they stop. Hansi removes the sack, and the Magician guides them to Rayne's car and opens the rear door and shows her the way in (he is such a gentleman). Then he slides next to her. Gracious enough to snap her seatbelt. "I don't want you flying around and hurting someone," he says. Hansi takes the driver's seat. He slips into a pair of black skin-tight driving gloves, which he believes raises his level of sinisterism. He raises his hand and says, "The keys." Rayne wiggles, finds them, drops them in Hansi's waiting gloved palm.

He turns the ignition, and they drive away from the hotel to Lake Constance.

Rayne Foster figures she has about as much fear in her head that her head can hold.

She's afraid of the unknown—why are they driving to Lake Constance? What could possibly be there that—then it hits her. They can weigh you down and drown you there, Rayne. No matter how good your swimming skills, a fifty-pound weight tied to your body will take you all the way down to the bottom. The End. She's afraid of Hans Kesten. She saw evil in his eyes. Psychotic monkeys doing gymnastics and cartwheels inside his skull. She's afraid for Elora. She thinks Elora is safe, and they have been told not to harm her. And most of all, she's afraid of Simon Lane. And he isn't in the car. Afraid of what he told the Magician to do to Rayne. Through their resources and informants and leaks they know who Rayne is. Simon so connected in the military establishment that he can find people that would provide him with the intelligence he needs. Rayne figuring, they have her nailed: she's a secret agent. She has the power to stop this operation. And, Rayne imagines, Simon wants to obliterate her. The only way she will be null and void. Eradicated.

And most of all, she's fretted about her own judgment, remaining here in the Black Forest. Why? Why did you stay? Why didn't you book a First Class ticket, drink a few Bloody Marys on the flight, and go home to New York? You'll never figure it out, Rayne, so give up on it, dunce brain. If you get out of this, treat yourself to a brain scrub, please.

Twenty minutes pass in silence. The Magician can't think of anything to say. He's staring through the night stars, lingering on the moon's hypnotism, half asleep.

Then Rayne probes the dark air with a prickly question. "What do you want from me?"

Ernst, eyes closed, says, "Me? N*ichts*."

"Then what I am doing here in this car driving to Lake Constance? Touring Germany?"

"I am only doing what I am told. What I am paid to do. You understand? It's part of the capitalist spirit I frequently enjoy."

"By whom?"

"It would not help you if you knew. Best for you to remain calm. And keep quiet."

"Do you know who I am?"

"I do. I know the legend."

From the front seat Hansi chips in: "I do too," he says cheerfully. Like they are driving to some wonderful picnic in the woods.

"Who am I?" asks Rayne.

Ernst says, "A seraph. A dark mystery few have ever encountered. You are the renowned legend. The least known. The least understood. The most beautiful and attractive Rayne Foster. You are made of steel. You are made of asbestos. You are a flower. You are a stone. You are caustic. You are soft. You are belligerent and kind. Most of all, a survivor—your best trait. And if you don't shut your mouth, I would say you are stupid because you are *pissing* me off!"

"With whom?"

"What? With whom?"

"Who do you think I am with?"

"Not known with any confidence, but it would seem CIA, NSA Special OPs. Perhaps Disneyland. And you are—I really don't care."

"Then you might imagine what those boys from Virginia—CIA, NSA, whoever—will do to you if anything happens to me—they will go to the ends of the planet and put such a medieval hurt on you that you would wish yourself unborn."

Half a minute passes, and Rayne reaches down to her ankle holster.

She says, "So, it would seem to *bother* you to have kill such an attractive woman."

"Who said anything about killing."

"Your eyes. Your mouth. You are not good at containing intent, Ernst."

So dark in here Ernst won't see or sense what I am up to. Down there near my boot.

The idea: pull the pistol up. Click the safety down and spike two rounds into his face. Then, jam the muzzle into the base of Kestin's skull and tell him to pull over or she will kill him. It's a maneuver, that's all it is. Cleaver. Only if executed.

The Magician saying, "I am better than you think I am."

"I do not accept that. From the moment I read your file, heard about you through the rumor mill. Saw your picture, your face. The first time I saw you in Miami. I said to myself, now there's a real bottom feeder. A *remora*. Do you know what that is, a *remora*?" With reluctance, Ernst shakes his head. She says, "A remora is a suckerfish, or a shark sucker that attaches to a shark for food. Like you, they dwell on the actions of sharks. They don't initiate because they are mindless. They are thrilled when their shark friend kills, then they benefit from the morsels that drift here and there for survival."

Ernst says, "Let me put this to you, miss holier-than-thou: You have killed, I know you—that is part of the legend of Half Face. You are good with a gun. So, what makes the difference between you and me? Your sanctioned kills, or my hired for profit? *Nothing*. That is the answer. The only real difference is the pounds-per-inch pressure on the trigger and the weapon you choose. The only thing that would make a real difference would be if you taught kindergarten for a profession. Beyond that, you pull the trigger; I pull the trigger. The same way. Now, shut your mouth, close your eyes and imagine how accurate I am, and go to sleep. We have about forty-five minutes before journey's end."

Rayne sits silent. Maybe Ernst Schumer has a point? Perhaps I wouldn't be here if I told Lee I was going home?

In their zeal to get Rayne in the car, the two master criminals—particularly the one at the steering wheel—did not do a body search. The two males figuring the two females would never bear arms.

Says Rayne, "Well, cowboy, say what you want—I got a big news bulletin for you: I don't think you are better than you think."

"How so?"

"The Miami job for example. The treasure, the illuminated Manuscript, you sought in the Mafia Don's safe. You really screwed up that whole Miami job. A real Charley Foxtrot."

"A what?"

"Charley Foxtrot—a *clusterfuck*."

"Clusterfuck? What is this clusterfuck? What are you talking about? I got him into the mobster's mansion. I helped Stonecipher kidnap that man's daughter."

"But you *didn't* get the treasure. The target. That's what you were hired for. Your fault. You screwed the pooch, cowboy."

The Magician snaps his head around: "Not me, *cowgirl.* That FBI agent, Edmund Stonecipher. He was psychotic. Alcoholic. It was all *his* fault. Besides, I got him to you, didn't I?"

"He hired you to do a lot of things for him, and you didn't exactly ace the exam on any of them. So, what you did was you did the minimum; you kept below the parapet just enough to collect your fee. That's what you are going now. You just couldn't kick it up a notch." Then, with a chuckle, Rayne adds, "You *stole* from *him. You* owe *him.*"

"He's dead. I'm alive."

"You still owe him. In my mind. Your reputation's starting to smell like week-old fish, *Herr* Schumer."

Ernst does not think that is funny. He was bored before. Then he was amused. Now, Rayne's disturbing him. "I'm getting tired of your voice in my ear."

"Tired? Or Guilty?"

Lightning speed and the Magician's automatic is pressing Rayne's cheekbone.

Her fingertips, sweaty, nervous, clamp the butt of the pistol in her ankle holster. Start pulling up, Rayne.

Ernst, pressing her cheek hard: "You should think of yourself now, not the past. Hansi, please to tell Foster what our plan is."

Hansi starts to turn—

"Keep your eyes on the road!" Ernst rolls his eyes. "Go. Tell her."

"The plan?" Hans feeling a challenge, and exam.

"Now!"

"You mean the plan for tonight?"

"*Tonight*, yes. Not our summer holiday! *Please*!"

The pistol half up her thigh.

Hansi saying, peering through the windshield, "We will board *Herr* Sinner's yacht. Tie up and gag Foster. Set the timers and detonators to the Semtex and leave the yacht for the shore where will watch the fireworks go off." He chuckles.

Then the car hits a bump, and there goes Rayne's pistol onto the floor mat. Into the murky twilight zone of car interiors, where ice cream and cheeseburgers and French fries and packets of ketchup mingle.

Elora says, "And what of me?"

Hansi says, "You—you relax, you wait in the car for us. Take us back to the hotel. We leave in our car."

Ernst says, "Simple. No harm to you."

Rayne says, "If it works. And it won't work."

"And it won't work? Why you say that?"

"Because I won't let it work."

"Ha! How so, you arrogant bitch?"

"Because—my legendary skills, remember. The legend of Half Face."

"Not all legends are true."

"By the time you tie me up and activate the explosives and leave the yacht, something, someone, will disturb your plan. It could even be me. By the way, here's a little factoid for you: Every time a criminal commits a crime, he commits twenty-eighty mistakes. On the other hand, perhaps the dunce driving the car will destroy your entire plan."

Hans asks, "Dunce? *Was ist dunce? Ich habe nie von diesem Wort gehört.*"

"It means," says Rayne, "that you are as dumb as a soup spoon."

Hans shrugs his shoulders. *Suppenlöffel*? Whatever: "We are one mile from the dock."

Ernst says, "*Das is gut*. When you are half a mile out, lights go off, drive backward to the dock, *Verstehe*?"

"*Ja.*"

"And when we stop," he says to Rayne, "I will open my door, and you will slide out toward me. If you scream, I will shoot you right here in the head." The cold muzzle taps her forehead. "But before that—and listen closely—I will shoot your friend here," and he points the muzzle behind Elora's ear. Am I clear?"

Elora says, "Not as far as I'm concerned."

Hans says, grinning, "He's kidding you. Stay calm. That is Ernst's humor. His game." Hans kills the lights. The car stops. The vehicle backs to the dock.

Now, now, Elora, what are you going to do to save your friend? What? Push Kesten out of the car and drive away? Insane idea. Jump out and grapple with Ernst Schumer? Grab his gun. Oh, yeah, that's rich! Use your cell phone? Make a call? Who? Your father? Yes! Ask Ernst and Hans to give you a minute to make a call to your father in New York, to pardon Rayne. He's got all the money in the world. He could affect that. Sure! They're bound to be delighted with that notion, allocate a minute or two for a phone call to one of the wealthiest men in the world. That's about as brainless as beach sand, you moron!

Better yet—

Elora jumps out of the car and says to the Magician, "I'll give you each a million dollars if you let her go. And I will have sex with you both here in the backseat. Not a wham-bam-thank, you ma'am., but real sex."

Hansi likes that idea. He doesn't quite get the wham-bam part, but—

"Ernst? You hear that? *Eine Million*! *Stück*! Plus, a backseat tussle. A wham bam one!"

Hansi opens the driver's door, jumps out quickly, a hot-footed bullfrog. Seeing Rayne coming out the driver's side, so he opens the rear door then goes around to the Magician, pulling Rayne out the back, saying, "Ernst! You hear what she said, a million apiece *und ein Fick*!"

The Magician starts leading Rayne to the motorboat. "Ask her if she has it in her pocket."

"Do you have—"

Rayne steps into the boat, the Magician and Hans behind her. They fidget around sitting, balancing, and then Hans gives a tug on the starter cord, and he backs them away from the dock.

As they go, a gray hawk flitters low across the lake, his sharp wingtips snapping the surface, the only intrusion in this bleak, bewildering silence. Lake Constance, or some say Bodensee, is thirty-nine miles long and nine miles wide. Who knows where they will go once on the yacht? Or, maybe nowhere, Elora. So, settle yourself. There is nothing you can do. Rayne is gone.

Out there on the tranquil water, a silence Elora Sinner wants never to see or hear again.

She remembers what she said to Rayne a few nights ago: what will happen to us when we leave here, me my way, Rayne yours? Apart? No answer.

Through her tears, Elora watches the humble motorboat approach the gleaming black yacht, the *Corsair*, her father's. She steps closer to the edge of the dock, as close as she can to Rayne, the toes of her riding boots over the dock's edge. She wishes so much she had Rayne in her arms now, soothing her, protecting her. She has given me so much, and I want to pay back a lifetime of heartfelt lessons that no one else ever proposed, that she didn't tend to in herself. She can barely see them clambering aboard the *Corsair's* transom, can scarcely peer through her tears, dripping off her jawline. The silent kind. The deep kind. Hopeless, Elora, isn't it? She turns toward the car, the rear driver's side door Kesten left open. She ponders this for a moment. Then, Elora, close the door and leave here? Never turn back. Forget it. All of it. Douse Rayne Foster from your mind? Discard the memories. Go someplace, anywhere on the planet. Rayne has taught you so much about yourself. Keep *that* in your heart, Rayne's gift. She will always be near you. Not just today. Always. But where will all the question marks go that I saved in a precious box? That I culled and cherished like I would a diary of life's long unanswered questions. Maybe time to jettison?

Elora?

Whatcha think?

About Foster?

Yes?

She grips the doorframe, glances inside at the seat, the floor mat.

There, Rayne's pistol. Oh? The one she stuck in my pussy.

There where the potato chips and fries and hamburger morsels remain forever.

Gun in hand, Elora Sinner wonders not who she is or what she was or where she is but where she is headed and what she must do now to save her friend, Rayne Foster.

21
OH, THEY KNOW, THE TWO OF THEM. THEY KNOW.

Lake Constance, Germany, 12:30 p.m.

Elora standing at the dock, gazing at *Corsair* out there on the smooth lake. The Magician and Kesten have Rayne Foster roped and duct tape smeared across her mouth. They have disabled the diesel engines, removed the ignition coils. Now, they hasten to the transom and the little motorboat to take them back to the dock where Elora awaits.

A stupor of sorrow inside her head.

She paces off for the car again, Rayne's Walther PPK in hand.

She checks for a chambered round. Pops the magazine release; it's full. Slams the mag back. Building her courage.

Keeping the music playing.

They told you to wait here, then they would drive back to the hotel, and they would leave her there and depart on their own. She stops at the rear of the car. Turns and walks back to the dock. Back and forth. Back and forth. How many times are you going to do this useless exercise?

To the edge of the dock again, as far as she can.

She thinks about leaving them here. When they return, no car, no Elora.

But where would you go, Elora? What would you do? You could drive back to the hotel and wait for the launch order from her father. You would obey him after all, no? Yes?

At the dock, Rayne's gun dangling from Elora's hand.

She makes up her mind and turns for the Audi again.

This is it.

I'm leaving this mournful place. Leave them here, have them figure what do.

I can't bear it.

From the corner of her eye, that's where she sees it.

A flash of spray coming off from the back of the motorboat. Coming back to the dock.

Elora stands there at the dock waiting, watching. Before they come to her, she nudges Rayne's pistol into the top rear of her riding boot.

And then, simultaneously, the Silvercups close their electrical circuits.

She sees the explosive flash light the trees and cottages and the water and the shoreline. Light faster than sound. Then the blast travelling 340 meters per second—faster through water. Feels the concussive force, the massive ***whomp***, slamming her chest, knocking her back two feet. Her ears go numb. Half a second later, the night sky evolves into an explosive red. Several hundred feet in the air, spars, engine components, deck chairs tumble, leaving smokey white tendrils. The shoreline lights up. There, visible, a small cluster of little lakeside cottages.

The explosion lights the motorboat nearing the dock.

Elora walks back to the car, leans on the trunk, crosses her arms, assuring herself the engine's still running because she will need it soon.

At the dock, Kesten and the Magician alight from the motorboat and don't bother tying up.

Elora stands. Less than thirty yards from Hansi and Ernst striding toward her, coming off the dock, creeping over the mowed grass. Behind them, the fiery bloom continues to twist and blossom.

They stop a short distance from Elora.

She's just standing now, arms folded, glaring at them.

Something, a tenuous quiver bothers the air, catches the Magician's experienced criminal eyes—her attitude.

"Stop right there," she says.

Smiling, in German, the Magician asks: "*Was machst du dort?*"

"*Warten auf Sie.*"

"Ah, so kind of you. Waiting for us." And then to Hans, he says—"She is just waiting for us. How kind—*nett*."

But he is the Magician. He knows a trickery when he sees one. He does not believe Elora for one simple second.

Hansi, frozen. What should *I* do? Should I go for my weapon? He turns slightly, looks to his leader for some sign, but no signal is forthcoming. Hans, saying, "Maybe you should —"

Ernst asking, Elora, "Why are you looking at me like that?"

"I want to hear you say my name, Ernst. Just once more for me, give it to me one more time, so I don't ever forget what it is like to kill a criminal?"

"*Warum?*"

"I want to hear it the second it comes off your lips. Just before you die."

"*Was*? What are you talking about, you brain-dead fucking cunt!"

Simultaneously they scrape for their pistols.

But Elora going down the short way to the back of her riding boot. Smooth going for her.

But the Magician having a tough time coming around his back with his right hand clawing like an ugly crab for the pistol that his belt is most reluctant to relinquish.

The hammer, Ernst, the hammer has caught on your pants belt.

Ernst saying, "I don't mean, I mean, *I did not want to be cruel to your friend*. But perhaps we should talk about this? *Was halten Sie davon?*"

An inefficient cloud of apologies from Ernst dissipating in the air.

Elora: "Didn't mean to *what*? You stupid moron! She's probably all over the lake, a thousand pieces."

Ernst: "Maybe we can go and *look* for her? Get in the motorboat. She's a survivor."

Elora: "Oh, Ernst, my dear demented fool. A favor please, a big, big solid favor, for both of us?"

"*Ja! Ja!* Anything*!*"

Elora: "Do it gently, do it slowly, do it fast. But just go find a place in hell."

And Elora already has a specifically effective grip on Rayne's ready-to-go-safety-off pistol. Bending her knees slightly, the classic shooter's stance, her body, her hands, legs, now muscle memory, gripping the pistol the way A.G. taught her hour after hour back there at the Bedford, Connecticut, ranch while the horses hooves covered their ears.

Then, *WOW*!

Here's Ernst's 9 mill finally free. Coming around not as fast as he would like, asking, nor proffering any late-night favors. Just his thumb probing, depressing the safety.

And Elora's forward sight spots the Magician's breastbone.

And for some useless reason, Ernst brings his left hand up an inch.

Maybe hoping to stop a 9mm round flying at 820 mph. *Oh, yeah.*

And Elora pops three rounds. Cordite scorching her nostrils. The shell casings cartwheeling like mad bees from this madness.

And Schumer wishing, pleading for one more pure starbright second, *please, please,* give me a steady aim. And the other hand flim-flamming the air.

And Elora's 9mm rounds doing a butchery to his fingers, ropes of blood arching, a spray of red gruel, tendons exploding. Fingers somersaulting.

And Ernst seeing meaty anarchy. Then he sees his weapon. He is stupefied. What to tend to first? *Oh my*! Where'd the fingers go? Only *two* left, Ernst. The other little flying weenies have left the combat zone.

And then the Magician screaming, "*STOP! STOP! WHAT THE FUCK ARE YOU DOING! STOP*! *Why you do this*? *We are friends with you.*"

And now, the Magician, Elora sees, is a hazardous man because the muzzle of his weapon is aimed straight at El's heart.

And Hansi, a frog hip-hopping on a hot skillet, reaching for his shoulder holster, whirling in a nervous circle, going this way and that. Circling around himself.

The Magician firing one paltry round that cracks a pine somewhere. But his shattered hand has made him feeble and wobbly.

Elora caps one, caps two, caps three.

The first two goring the Magician's eye socket, spiking the back of his skull, exiting the size of an apple. Number two blisters through his jawline, and he tumbles toward the lake like he's blind caught in hellfire The Magician splattering one round after the other into the mud until the magazine runs dry and his bloody face splatters wet grass.

Elora canters left, at the frozen Hans Kesten.

"*Bitte*, *bitte*, *bitte*," he shouts. "We can work something. I like you *sooo* much!"

His plea does not shield him.

He's staring at her stupidly. Mouth open.

Then his right hand scurries for his Glock up and out from the bespoke leather holster. This does not endear him to Miss Sinner. She wants to leave here ASAP. She is impatient.

So, she aims, fires, and the round slaps Hans Kesten under his armpit, exits through his shoulder blade. And he wanted to use that arm to shield himself, but tonight it does not work. He is disappointed.

He drops to one knee.

"*Why you do this*?" and again, screaming in German. "*Warum haben Sie dies getan*?"

He starts spinning like the winged seed of a maple tree toward the grass and pine needles.

Halts on both knees and his Glock aiming, it seems, for the moon, and before he can get himself parceled out and organized, the next shot from Elora blows through his head somewhere. Hard to tell because of the blood spray. Then titling over, earthbound, and Elora trying to blow off a few more rounds but getting that ugly click-click of an empty magazine.

No more bullets.

She bounds for the Magician's corpse and scrounges for his SIG-Sauer, skimming through his pockets for magazines; she finds two. His blood lathered on her hands. She duck-walks to the hardly breathing Kersten, flips him, and grabs his Glock G-19. Finds extra mags in his pockets. She jumps away to avoid those blood-spumes, pump-pumping one after the other.

As she stands, she says, "Listen, Hansi, I know this is untidy, but the light here is deadly, no pun intended, and it has been a while I target practiced in Bedford. Because all that shooting annoyed our horses. Understand?"

And then she uses Hansi's Glock to shield her eyes and fires into his head, and that ends Hans Kesten.

When she rises, she thinks she sees small, silvery splashes out there on the lake's surface nearing the dock. Just enough moonlight to cause—could that be Rayne, *swimming* toward me? No WAY.

An illusion, hope, Elora. Get in the car and get out of here.

She slashes the shift lever into Drive, and then—she gazes into the rearview mirror. That could be Rayne nearing the dock.

Into Reverse. Tires spitting pebble and rock, pummeling the rocker panels.

Audi sliding through a long reverse skid, overshooting the runway, splintering a wooden fence pole, and the thing flailing, skimming, then sinking beyond the dock.

She stops the Audi at the threshold of the dock. And here comes a long arrow slick leg jutting out the driver's side, challenging the door swing-back.

Running *toward* you, Rayne.

Going to you.

Running!

To you!

Black leotards, the end of the dock, black turtleneck, riding boots.

Pistol in hand.

You know who! You do, Rayne.

Racing to you, Rayne!

Who is this?

But of course, Rayne knows who this is running down the dock toward her. To save her!

It is Elora!

Elora at the dock's ladder.

Enough moonlight to powder your faces.

Rayne climbing the mossy steps, soaked, quivering, and there's Elora's hand going for Rayne's, pulling her up, saving her. Embracing Rayne.

Embracing her!

And Rayne, feeling the heat of Elora's face. Her breath, her lips scuffing Rayne's neck, lingering, hesitant to move away. Taking in her scent. That scent. The press of their bodies unrelenting.

Like failed lovers newly conjoined.

Now Elora's hand with Rayne's Sig-Sauer arbitrarily pointing to Rayne's most favored star, Alpha Centauri A, beaming its radiance, its *affection*.

The Sig hot in Elora's hand. Aimed at Rayne's star chalice, her universe, and Rayne locked onto Elora's dazzling moon shiny eyes, teary. Neither saying a syllable, lips *so* close, wondering, is that the heat of lake water, huh? Or tears blending?

Oh, they know, the two of them. *They know.*

Tears, Rayne, tears. A deluge.

Rayne assured now who this is, her muscled body familiar. *That* perfume. The scent of her breath. Squeezing the air from the Rayne's lungs. Lips so close.

An archangel of the highest rank, Rayne, saving you from the hellion gods that were banished tonight by your beautiful star guards. Those star devils, they were disallowed imperial descent from your domed chalice. The archangel, *here*, look at her, *here* at the dock for *you*. Look how *beautiful* she is!

Elora Sinner.

In your arms.

Elora Sinner saying, "I killed them both, with this." Wagging the pistol.

Rayne, ignore Elora's words. Allow yourself instead a passionate consideration.

Or are you incapable?

Allow Elora to plow you away from the dock and head for the tree line where you can hide. Where you can catch your breath and your sensibilities.

They say nothing as they scrabble for the trees, Elora's arm around Rayne, embracing her, carrying her into the black line of pines.

Rayne saying, "Gotta stop. Can't breathe."

So, she vomits. And they stand there silent, still for a moment.

Then they flop to the pine needles. Bringing their knees up to their chests.

Rayne wants to say something temperate, a thank you, clement things, but not enough air to pump out the words. Elora's arm around Rayne's shoulder, sensing her shivering. Elora's hand comes up presses Rayne's head down onto her shoulder. A gift.

Elora saying, "I never, never thought I'd see you again." And grips her so hard, Rayne grunts.

Out there across the lake, the *Corsair* continues to toast off, lighting almost the whole lake.

"This lake," Elora says, "the shoreline covers Germany, France, and Austria. Recently two huge fireboats were delivered to the German Fire Department at Friedrichshafen, on the German side. In a minute, those two monsters are going to slice their way to the yacht. We should see them and hear them rushing to the *Corsair*. Then, this whole area's gonna flare up with *polizei*. And one colossal shitstorm's gonna fall. So? Rayne? Super spy. What do we do? Stay? Go? Rayne?"

Rayne shakes her head. *Give me another minute*?

Rayne saying, "I've never been so cold in my entire life. We can't afford to get rounded up."

The *Polizei*, the *Feuerwehr emergency* lights, blues, and reds, multiplying. Singing that distinctive *weeeee haaa, weeee haaa* ripping the night air.

A pause. The dim snapping of the *Corsair's* wood on fire. The scent of it drifting across the lake. Far away, a dog's bark. A car horn. A twist of a breeze scuffing their hair, fluttering it, stirring the scent.

Rayne, her head still nestled on Elora's neck, saying, firm, "I *never* should have told you, Elora, who I was. *Never, never*. What I do. *I never, ever, ever should have told you*! I could not help myself. But in the hall, after dinner, I almost died there in your arms against the wall. *A gift*! You started to kill me!"

Elora saying, "So. What. We have more than that."

"What?"

"A pretty friendship," with an extra squeeze.

Rayne saying, "They'll round us up, take us to the police station and start in. I'm not implicating anything like the old days. No. Not that. We just won't have a shot at stopping the drones, is what I'm saying. And you, they'll yank it out of you—these German police. They'll glue it all together. All of it. And then the entire country, the USA, will be a mouse, and a sledgehammer will come down and squash it."

"Rayne, the entire country is screwed anyway. No more rhyme or reason. A retreat from democracy. A turnabout from decency, from caring. No more hometown queens giving us their best smiles, prettiest dresses. It's all Starbucks and Dunkin' on every corner in every state. That's what we carry around in our fingers, in our cars. Now one knows who Benjamin Franklin is, and they don't care. Fish full of mercury. Forests diminishing. Icebergs turning into ice cubes. Dirtbags ten. Good guys, zero. Animals at the mercy of demons, uncaring, incapable of tenderness. In case you haven't noticed, things ain't what they used to be."

Elora takes Rayne's fingertips and presses them to her lips.

Slowly, she sucks each finger, kneading Rayne's palm with her thumb, her eyes closed. Savoring.

Saying, "You know the song, 'You'll Never Find Another Love Like Mine'? The singer? Lou Rawls. I've memorized it."

Rayne shakes her head *yes, yes, I do*.

Elora kisses Rayne's fingertips again, leaves them for an impossibly long minute of silence.

Then, saying, "'*all the magic we shared, just us two.*'"

Then brings them back into her waiting mouth. Their absence too much, and sucks, so slow. So meditative. Eyelids closed. The motion bringing comfort to both.

Rayne does not hold back. Elora feeling the tremble. The silent sob. Her head nestling Elora's neck.

All of it coming forth now. Spilling. The fear. The hope. The wanting.

Rayne shakes her head. She takes Elora's fingers from her mouth, kisses them.

Rayne saying, "I never should have listened to Lee. I should have dropped the operation and left you sad, crying, not knowing who this whacky Rayne Foster really is. And not the legend of Half Face. It would have been better. I should have dropped you on the spot when I saw that smile at the bar. I should not have allowed you to come so close to me, to my heart. So you couldn't be hurt by this."

"Why?"

"I should have just packed up my dirty laundry and left you. Left the hotel. Left the Forest. Left the sneezing horses and the bees and butterflies. Left Lee. Left the whole screwy operation. Gone home. Put my pillow over my face. Cried and cried. What I should have done. No more fight left, El. Gas tank's empty."

"But you didn't, Rayne. You didn't. We are still here. Alive. Breathing. Holding each other. No need to leave. Why should you have left?"

Rayne looking into Elora's glistening eyes—"Because can't you see it—I played *you*! I *played you*! *We* played you—*the United States* played you! Got that? We wanted the red phone! Not *you*! The red phone. That was it!"

"No, you did not. If you played anyone, Foster, you played yourself. Because I knew that all along, it was in your beautiful eyes. You haven't allowed yourself to be you. Rayne played Rayne."

"Not true," disbelieving herself now.

"Hey, I don't believe that for one squirrely minute," Elora says, almost whispering. "Let's just get out of here, come back some other time. Just before Juta serves Wiener schnitzel and black forest cake for dessert. Just sit at a bar and get pie-eyed and tell each other funny stories."

In the distance, the Lake Constance fireboats, sirens shrieking, and their brassy fire nozzles gaining on the *Corsair*, washing the flames.

Rayne saying, "The police are going to swarm this whole lake. Five more minutes. All over the thirty-nine-mile shoreline from Germany to France to Austria. All of it. Not have a clue what the hell they're looking for. Terrorism? Hooligans? Accident? But you know what," Rayne says, standing, extending her hand for Elora's, "We can't wait around to find out."

They hasten to the Audi, Elora hearing the last of the lyric in her mind:

All the magic we shared, just us two.

22
SAY IT'S NOT OKAY FOR FOSTER. SAY IT. PLEASE.

At this hour, Rayne and Elora speeding away from the lake and the scream of sirens. Lots of night stars and an abundance of moonlight.

Down in the bunker with the drones and at the urging of his aberrant scientific instincts, Simon Lane sets down an old, collectible Wehrmacht field table left beyond after WWII that he found in some storage room here.

He adjusts the table so that it faces the four drones. He unfolds a portable wooden chair, sets it before the table, and sits. Reaches into a shoulder bag on the floor and takes up a cold, classic bock beer bottle: *Einbecker Ur-Bockthermos*. Pops the cap with a bottle opener and then reaches for the long tin foil log.

A midnight snack with the drones attending.

He unwraps the tinfoil and reveals a bratwurst with sauerkraut, mustard, and curry sauce, his favorite, and an ample helping of crispy *Bratkartoffeln* (fried potatoes). No plastic fork or knife is needed. Simon only uses stainless-steel cutlery, which he has in hand. He digs in.

The drones are yards away watching.

They wonder: Is he going to fire up our auxiliary engines and check our systems now? Please, Mister Lane, we're anxious to fly. To fulfill our design parameters that you set down years ago. They stand eager, the drones, arrogant—all that designed into their frames by the man savoring the bratwurst and fried potatoes. Simon occasionally grunting a *yummy*, a sound the drones cannot comprehend.

They are so intelligent, Simon thinks, gazing at them, tapping his mouth with a linen napkin he stole long ago from a Munich restaurant. The drones know what I am doing. They know I am here. I console them. They console me. We are communicating. Each to watch over the other. Brothers and sisters of aggression. Eat Mister Lane, but please tend to our codes and algorithms as soon as you finish your strudel. We are eager

Simon happens to look down, and there it is, the bloodstain, the faint red juice that made Meese Van Der Leeuwen an untruthful thief, as he was all his life. That fluid that Meese inconsiderately left behind in such abundance before he left for the ionosphere. Simon ponders it for a moment, then moves on.

He pulls up his laptop from his shoulder bag, flips the cover, orders a voice command, and the laptop screen lights with a multitude of colors.

A big sip of the *Einbecker Ur-Bockthermos* as he waits for the drone checklist program to initiate.

He shakes his head and then goes dipping back to his bag. He almost forgot.

He pours *the Einbecker Ur-Bockthermos* into the stein. Inevitably, the beer always tastes better, quenchers better coming from the stein. The drones understand. They sit; they wait with patience.

The checklist finally arrives on the laptop screen. Simon pauses between bites, stares at the screen. He presses the C key; the screen refreshes. He puts the app into Test mode, a replication of the mission. Now the entire mission from launch to destruction will show on his screen, but not in real-time, slow enough for Simon to observe all the checkpoints, fuel levels, exhaust temps. He lets the program whirl on, running itself because if there is an anomaly along the route somewhere, the program will freeze for Simon to inspect.

* * *

On the E54 speeding from Lake Constance, from the blazing *Corsair*, Rayne at the wheel of the Audi. Elora leans toward Rayne for a peek at their speed: 277 km/h, 172 mph.

Elora saying, "Obviously, you are not trying to shatter a land speed record; how come? This the thing can do faster than this."

"It can, but we have less than a quarter of fuel. The faster I push it, the more gas it consumes."

"Let's take a chance."

"*Oh, shit!*" Rayne shouts.

"*What?*"

"The cell phones!"

"Where are they?"

She jams her foot on the brake and pulls into a rest stop.

"They're in the trunk, hidden."

She jumps out of the car and pops open the trunk lid. Crawls halfway in. Her hands searching, probing under the rear package tray where she hid the phones earlier. Then, yes, thank you, here they are, Rayne's and the red phone.

When she starts to pull out of the trunk, she spots two gun cases under a matt.

There, under the matt, two new 9mm Heckler & Koch SP5K-PDW machine pistols, thirty-round mags in place.

Rayne slams the trunk lid down. Jumps back into the car.

"The red phone," she says and drops it into a beverage holder. "And here's my phone; please check for messages." The screen lights with a long list of unanswered texts and messages; Elora scrolls through them,

Rayne notches the gear lever into D and accelerates, her foot pressing down to the floorboard until the car is spearing down the autobahn at 130 mph.

Elora saying, "Here, something from Upchurch: 'where are you?' Deadlight could launch in less than three hours. Am heading for the bunker area.'"

Rayne says, "Type: 'Will be there in thirty minutes.'"

And El says, "And here's a lengthy one from a Christian Largo."

"*What*?" The word thick with shock. "Are you sure?"

"Positive. Old friend?"

No answer.

"Old flame?"

"Too many questions, El."

And too many memories coming back now, Rayne? Disallow them, all of them. You don't need to listen to excuses about unanswered love. Rayne, you don't need to feel hurt renew at this moment. Rayne, you don't need to see his face light up in your mind. Christian there at the dock in Miami for the last time, watching you leave in a helicopter for another horizon. That's the last sliver of him you should allow. And then kiss the memory and let it go its way, Rayne, you don't need him to tell you what he feels because you won't believe him if he did. Just say goodbye.

"Please read it to me."

"Are you sure? Here? Now?

Rayne nods *yes, here and now*, just to get it over with.

Elora reads the note from Christian Largo:

"I'm sorry for not writing sooner. But my heart did not have the courage to write to you before now because what I have to say is so very hard for me to put down. I got your last note several days ago—God knows where you were, where you are now? Remember, I used to answer within nanoseconds. And this is the part of the problem for me. A big part. A one-sided relationship. We often tried to talk this through. I tried several times to get the words from head to hand to respond, but it always seemed I had an excuse to stop me from writing or calling you. I had to sharpen my pencils. I had to do laundry. I thought when we met in Miami the first time that there was no mountain I could not surmount. Your face, your bluer-than-blue eyes, your beauty, all of you set me back. And I started falling in love with you. I'm still in love with you. To have you in my arms was a gift from heaven that is seldom if ever given out. It is too precious. The problem, Rayne, is that you are never around. What an adventure we had. My heart aches. Remember that song we loved so much and played so often? "Here's That Rainy Day?" Well, Rayne, my love, that rainy day is here. I am so glad I saved all those leftover dreams. I'll always have us. And now I know not which is thicker, my tears or the raindrops. The world is your home. You are here for a few seconds. Then, I look around, and you are gone. For eternities. Here's that rainy day they told me about, and I can't live like this—with less and less of you. I want someone around to share popcorn on Saturday nights. To take walks whenever. To kiss and hold hands. To make love to. Now, I don't know how to end this note.

If you ever want to talk in person, please let me know. Keep safe and happy wherever you are, and whatever you are doing, think of me. Eternal love.
Christian

A moment of nothing passes. Dead air. Oh gosh. What can we say? The two of us here in the car. And that big elephant in the backseat. A vacuum of no thought, no motion. No reason. No sound, pleading for everything to step aside, please; we have some questions here. And so, the planet has been ordered to, please, please, stop rotating. A tone of conflict that they can feel. The conflict inherent in Christian's note. The elephant. It's tone, it's meaning leaping off the phone and disallowing words between Elora and Rayne. Because somewhere in all of that El and Rayne see the words affecting them. The air rushing over the Audi's surface louder and louder. That hissing sound that goes with you wherever you go. Reminding you that sometimes destinies are never known just because you are moving forward.

There are no other vehicles ahead at this hour. They are the only humans on the planet, and the Earth has generously abided by their wish to stay still, not forever, but for a few wistful moments while the note settles in. For the time it takes to take a breath. To respect what must be mulled, and then when all their thoughts—Rayne and El's—are silently exhausted and the request fulfilled, they will open their eyes again and see that more choices need to be made.

Particularly Elora. With her wounded heart and her multitude of questions, this email has provoked. And the certainty that not all the questions will have answers. Isn't that the way it always is, El?

Saying, "He loves you, Foster, I mean, my, God. It's apparent: he's bluffing too. He doesn't want to let you go." She stops for a moment, thinks hard, then says, "I wouldn't let you go. Not me. I'd figure something. But, this Christian Largo, his note, all of this. It's okay, Foster. I understand this. You don't have to explain this," she says, wagging the phone.

Rayne takes Elora's hand. Rests it on her thigh.

She waits half a minute, says, "No, El, it's *not* okay. It isn't okay." And she squeezes El's hand. "Say it's not okay for Foster. Say it. Please."

Elora leans over, whispers into Rayne's ear: "It's not okay." And then again. "It's *not* okay."

* * *

Simon right now is in the control room of the bunker, wiping away the remnants of his meal from his lips. He taps his monster quiff, making sure there are no pending landslides. This business makes the drones happy, seeing Simon in the control room in charge. They are like dogs, the drones: lift and shake their leashes; they know it is walk time.

Then he saunters into the Utility Room and rolls out an air compressor and spray gun. He wheels it to the nose of **Meese, Dear, Meese.** Slips into latex gloves. Grabs a can of DuPont paint specifically mixed for fighter aircraft. Pours one liter of USAF Gray #42 aircraft camouflage paint into the compressor's paint jug. Flips the compressor switch. The motor's electrical hum swells throughout the hangar.

Then he starts spraying, obliterating **Meese, Dear, Meese** on the nose. Using this time, a spray gun instead of a handgun to kill off Van Der Leeuwen one more time. (What is the difference, Simon?). Going slowly, fastidiously with such pleasure. Feeling the threat of Meese thawing. Left to right, right to left, slow. Until Meese—he's vanished! A bucket of woe has disappeared. Amazing, the power of an airbrush. He allows ten minutes for the drying process, abiding by the paint manufacturer's precise instructions.

And using the time to clean up his buddy, the Beretta Centurion.

Because, very soon, my drone friends will go airborne. And the potential for chaos here could undoubtedly be boundless and require a well-oiled weapon, right Simon? Hope not, but—.

Now, washing his hands thoroughly, wiping them. Then checking Signal and seeing a text from A.G. Sinner: pls check voicemail.

I will respond, A.G., but first, I must tend to something personal.

Something history will need to see somehow. To understand our purposes here.

Simon Lane reaches into his jacket pocket and pulls up a chubby black Sharpie. He approaches Meese, the drone, and in Latin painstakingly writes in script words he has wanted to write for a long time:

IGNE NATURA RENOVATUR INTEGRA
Through fire, nature is reborn whole

Excellent job, Simon says to himself. He can sense the drones' unbound appreciation, too. This extends their sense of purpose, this sense of holiness that he has instilled in them since their childhood CAD/CAM days. Those complicated, hardworking days of trial and error. A gift Simon has given them toward their birth. One of understanding. One of purpose. One they deserve for their years of patience, loyalty, trust. And all those endless hours of flight tests and doubt. And no ground loops!

He takes three steps back, holds up his phone, and snaps half-a-dozen pictures of his artwork. His desire.

Then he dials his voice mail and hears A.G.'s first coded message.

"*Launch Go One.*"

The drones see this in Simon's eyes. Those words.

If they could, they would cheer. Instead, they stand dutiful.

Waiting.

Rayne and Elora wait in the darkness on the dirt road extending from the Hotel-Ochsenwirtshof to the bunker area.

They arrived two hours ago. Rayne doused the Audi's lights and parked under a droopy Norway Spruce. Then she duck-walked to the trunk and took out a pair of lightweight night-vision binoculars, military-grade, that Leland had left there for her. Unpacked the Heckler & Koch machine pistols and thirty magazines containing thirty rounds per mag.

Now they sit on a soft bed of pine needles leaning against the Audis nose.

Elora glances at the red phone, says, "A.G. sent a text to Simon saying, 'Launch Go One.'"3

"And that means?"

"He will want him to launch at"—she glances at her watch—"in fifteen minutes."

Along the valley and up the short hills of tall trees, windows are dark, horses and dogs and chickens asleep. No cars rush along *Wolfacher Strasse.*

Through the binoculars, Rayne imagines she sees two men. From here, she can't distinguish who they are. They duck into a shallow ditch not far from the bunker's main entrance. Then, on the other side of the vast grassy field, she sees six men in camo gear, armed with automatic weapons. They stop, form a flanking fire position, and blend into the surrounding area.

Elora whispers, "Another Text from A.G.: Launch Go."

"Which means Simon's churning up the launch, checking all systems for an imminent start. Should have all the auxiliary motors off and is running on the main batts now."

“Are we close enough for you to use your app?

“No. We are more than eighty-five feet away for the Wi-Fi to connect. I can't pre-abort. Have to wait until all five are airborne. But I think we should move up closer.” Then she pauses, says, “Hey, you and Leland, you've got connections—call in an airstrike?”

“Are you kidding me! We'll have World War III on our hands. Kill innocent people. Destroy everything around here. Really continue our relationship with the German government.”

“How 'bout troops. Penetrate the bunker Not an option?”

“Not an option. That bunker is so secure an atomic bomb wouldn't dent it. Why do you think Simon picked this spot? It's impenetrable. Simon wanted a spot like this, remote, not desolate. The only thing that will stop the drones is Elora Sinner and her fancy red phone.”

In the control room, Simon picks up a microphone: “Sensors detecting intruders within the perimeter. I am sending you a video feed so you can see where they are. You need to eliminate all of them before getting closer to the entrances and the take-off ramp. Copy?”

“*Roger that*,” comes a response.

Rayne's Blackphone screen lights up.

A text from Leland:

I am at the south end of what I think is the spot the drones will take off from. The only weapon we have is Elora's red phone. I will tell you when the ramp opens. Once it does, one by one, the drones will ascend from the open ramp. Do not attempt to enter the bunker through the ramp. You will not overcome thousands of pounds of thrust from a drone. Stay where you are. Do nothing till you hear from me. I assume you have found the H&Ks in the trunk. Prepare them. Use them.

In the control room, sitting before an array of computer screens, Simon starts the startup process, one drone at a time.

The first is *Tommy Tells Tales*. The Simon Lane customized SS4-ML engine powers up quiet as a household vacuum cleaner. Wingtip indicator lights, other position lights glow. Simon flips a switch, and the lights go off.

Then Simon initiates the startup process for *Oh, Gosh Golly*.

The process goes on for the next ten minutes until all the drones have moved and settled into their startup positions.

Each drone's dimensions are the same: 38 feet long. A 62-foot wingspan (thirty feet folded). Height ten feet. Another feature that attracted Simon to the bunker is the ceiling height, fifteen feet. Max takeoff weight 4,000 pounds. Each drone has a fuel capacity of nearly 1,600 pounds—range 2,400 miles with a capacity for air refueling. Simon has them configured to a ceiling of 42,000, but most of their flying will be on the deck. Cruise speed: Mach 0.9—about 700 mph.

Simon's security force on the far side of the grassy field has moved out. A.G., having hired the best military commandos he could hustle. They are heavily armed with an abundance of camo and inter-radio gear. They thrash through the brush and trees and scrub and grass. Point their Sig-Sauer's like knight's lances. Driving for blood. Against Rayne and Elora.

Rayne has them moving toward her and hearing their snorting and spitting and huffing. Big guys, muscled, combat boots, and their gloves with the fingers cut off at the tips.

Rayne Saying to Elora, "We have got to get closer, closer to the Wi-Fi zone, or you won't be in range for the red phone.

Elora stands and—

A shot fires past her head, and she drops to the dirt.

"Damn! Firing at us."

Rayne picks up an H&K, hands it to Elora.

"Know how to use it? Better before they get here because I'm sure that Simon has ordered them to take away our heads on spits."

"Sorta."

"It's like a pistol: here's the safety, click it down it's ready to fire; this lever selects single or auto fire. Press this button, and the empty mag drops out. Slap another one in, pull the slide back, and the weapon is ready and racked again. This is one of the best automatic machine pistols in the world. Use it right and you will kick some butt. Because, if you don't, were chopped beef."

* * *

The Control Room: Simon Lanes has the drones in-line for a silent, powerful launch. The vacuum brigade he calls them because of the sound they make.

This plan, he thinks, is coming together like honey and vanilla ice cream.

Gimme a few more minutes, okay, and we'll have this clash working smooth as silk. He looks out the window of the Control Room.

Tommy tells Tales is first to launch. Poised at the base of the ramp. Simon smiles: *Tommy Tells Tales*, he hates to admit, was always his favorite done. Can't explain why.

Ah, let the music play! I will dance all night long.

I will dance on the spot where I spilled Meese Van Der Leeuwen's cheating blood. That spot, yes! I know, I will. No wonder, Simon Lane thinks, that all the professors thought I was the best. The coolest. Some thought I was nutty as a fruit cake, but where are they? And look what it produced. You, Simon. Not your brother Myles. You! Do not *ever* relinquish that thought.

Half across the fields, security force guys are looking like they jumped in from Mars, searching for targets of opportunity. Obeying their orders.

Rayne sees the line, eight of them walking toward her.

She pops up and lets a ten-round burst snap the air.

Hears a scream. One guy flips up high, a circus act. Drops with two 9mm's in chest and thigh.

Rayne's phone vibrates. It's Leland.

Saying, "*Rayne, goddamnit! Are your returning fire? I told you to chill down there. Now we have to finish this! You are getting us into one big shitstorm. One day, you are going to listen to me, and by that time, I'll be gone.*

"Can't talk, Lee. They're coming for us. Seven or eight. Can you take them down? Please! And you," she says to Elora, "how 'bout you pop up over the parapet here and start spraying that H&K. You got enough bullets; you could stop an invasion of France."

The operatives are slinging grenades, fragmentation type, somewhat ineffectual because of the lighting and not seeing their targets.

Around the immediate area, the pines are lighting up white and blue with gunfire.

In the Control Room, Simon presses the Ramp Open button. Slow, it ascends,

Tommy Tells Tunes rolls a few feet closer to the base of the ramp. The ramp appears like a vast cheese wedge, thin edge on bunker floor, thick edge at the top where it leads out to the grassy field.

The operatives pause now. Intense gunfire coming from two shooters. The area crisscrossing with 9mm rounds hitting trees, bringing down branches.

Beyond the grassy area, Leland is firing down at the shooters. They are stuck in a vice now: Rayne and Elora in front of them, Leland and his colleague behind them.

Tommy Tells Tales launches into the night sky, a sliver of exhaust showing it's way toward the stars.

Then, quickly following:

Elora.

Dear Elizabeth Anne,

Oh, Gosh Golly, and the final drone, *Igne Natura Renovatur Integra.*

They are all gone. Less than five seconds after *Igne Natura Renovatur Integra* has grabbed the night sky. The ramp shuts up.

More gunfire now from Leland, Rayne, and Elora firing back.

Now Simon Lane's force is down to one man. He decides he wants to be a hero.

He almost makes it.

When he stands, he only has half a mag left, and four rounds pop off ineffectively.

The fifth and last bullet hits Elora.

Rayne aims at the shooter, fires. A 9mm splatters his breastbone, and he smacks the grass with his face.

"Hey," says Elora, stumbling, "I think I've been shot." She starts crawling to a pine tree.

In the dim light, Rayne can see Elora. The left side of her face and shoulder are blood-covered. She runs to her, but before she reaches her, Elora collapse

"Shot in the shoulder."

She slides down the pine tree and rests there, and gazes at the stars. Right now, the only thing Rayne can do is stop the bleeding. She takes off her blouse and inspects Elora's wound.

Rayne saying, "You've been hit in your acromion—that's the lumpy bone there on top of your shoulder—got nicked. You'll be fine."

"Not going to die? There's so much blood."

"You bleed more every month."

Then a specter appears—here's Simon Lane standing above them.

"Thought you'd disrupt up my plans didn't you," he says to Elora, noting his Beretta hanging loose in his fist. "And you, Rayne Foster, cowgirl of the CIA—agent without portfolio, strong desire to change the whole world—like all of us. Laudable it is. But misplaced."

Then Simon crouches down, the pistol swinging slowly between his thighs.

Saying, "I hate to be the bearer of bad news, girls, but all those plans of yours to abort my plans, to haul them back using the codes in your silly little phone. The drones on their way to the United States. Deadlight will proceed. The United States will soon be toast. By the way, El. where might that phone be?"

"In my pocket."

"Please, take it out."

She hands it to Simon.

Simon says, "Look at the screen." He faces it toward Rayne and Elora.

PROGRAM TERMINATED

"Even if you got within two centimeters of the Wi-Fi antenna, your phone would not have affected the plan you thought your father wanted. I guess he changed his mind. So—"

Simon stands.

He says, "It might have worked. But your father, he was getting a bad vibe. It seems Mister Van Der Leeuwen served a good purpose after all. He visited your room yesterday and noted an alarming rate of mistrust in you—which he related to A.G. And that information, my dear, was related to *me*. So, *I sabotaged your phone*. On daddy's orders.

Electronically that is. In essence, what you have here"—he shakes the red phone— "is nothing more than a boat anchor. Check your local Apple store, they might honor the warranty."

Rayne says, "Why don't you just shut up and do what you have to do—you and that whack-a-doodle plant thing you have growing out of your demonized brain cells."

Simon doesn't laugh, says, "I have a bit more. Then a nice surprise ending for both of you. First, my lovely boy and girl drones are on their way, unencumbered, I might add. Deadlight, the purveyor of a new dawn, goes as planned and will succeed. That was always the plan anyway—and there are contingencies. To the best of my ability, I know of no antidote, no magic United States Air Force wand that will bring them down. They fly too low, are too stealthy. In less than a day, the United States will be immobilized, and Deadlight will be in place. And your father, Elora, will replace the government himself and govern the country. So, Elora, you and your generous father might be headed for some very long walks in the woods to figure out little things like inheritance and fatherly love."

Simon stands.

Elora says, "What are you doing?"

"I'm about to present you with a pleasant surprise, particularly since you have so many unpleasantries ahead."

"He's going to shoot us," says Rayne.

"*What*!?"

Simon says, "Not as bad as it seems cause it's over at the drop of a shell casing."

Simon pulls back the slide on his Beretta. There's a round in the pipe.

Elora says to Rayne, "In situations like this, I usually offer to screw the daylights out of the guy. Any chance you can jump in and double the offer? A *ménage à trois* might save the United States."

Rayne does not have time to make a counteroffer.

The gunshot loud enough to do harm to their ear drums.

And Simon's face a mask of appalling surprise.

His face splatters.

And, look at this.

Simon's tattered head is next to Elora's shin. A mess it is and part of his jaw resting near Elora's lap, blood soaking the soil.

When Elora takes her eyes away from Simon, a shadow standing a few feet from her takes a step closer and glances down at dead Simon.

He stands there, silent. Savoring his kill shot.

He has an automatic weapon of some kind dangling from his hand.

He is tall and trim and spidery.

Standing there in soiled tennis clothes and rumpled baseball cap.

And he stands so straight, too, so close to Elora and Rayne and so still that they hear his raspy breathing, Elora grinning, whispering the tennis guy's name. Knowing who he is.

"Fucking Saxby."

23
MORE OF YOU

Rayne, sitting against the bark of a tall pine. Head resting on Elora's shoulder. Still breathless.

Rayne waiting for the echo of gunfire to fade. For the harsh scent of gun smoke to dissipate.

Leland and Saxby stand before them. This is as close as they will come. They must leave the area immediately.

The *Bundesnachrichtendienst* (German Intelligence) and the *Bundespolizei* or BPOL (German Federal Police) will be swarming up this hill in minutes.

They squat down.

Saxby says, "I know it didn't work but, in the end, you tried, you did the right thing. And for that, we're all better off." He lifts Rayne's blouse off Elora's bloody wound. "Nothing to it. Nothing a Band-Aid won't tend to. Lee and I have to get the hell out of here. I'm sure you understand why. We both busted about five hundred Federal and International regs getting into this."

Elora shakes her head slowly, looks into Saxby's eyes, smiles, and says, "Fucking Saxby." He gives her a wink and his best grin ever. Takes their guns and stands.

Leland saying to Rayne, "Gotta run. We did what we could. The elephant keeps marching. The parade never stops, Rayne. Remember the shovel and the pail So, for now, farewell, America—for now. There'll be a new one. Democracy is renewable, and it will need us to follow the elephant. There is a VW sedan about fifty feet down the road. As soon as you can, get back to the hotel and lay low. I figure about ten minutes before the police arrive here and try to sort this out. They're going to be pissed that some American has hidden drones here in an old WWII bunker. Will talk later."

They vanish into the darkness, and Rayne closes her eyelids.

She will open them soon. But first, she wants to remember how beautiful it was to see Simon's face in shards and his blood befouling the forest floor. And the valley begins to speak. A distant siren ululates. The German Shorthaired Pointer barking. Lights coming on. Distant shouting rising. No rhyme nor reason here, only the peculiar fragments of sounds waking the night. And that harsh, guttural stone-cold-clatter of this local German dialect hollering. But before she opens her eyelids, she wants to listen to the braying horses once more. Remember their kind faces and puffy cheeks. Remember the bumblebee and the bench she sat on with El. That fly. The cackle of the irate chickens. More of this soft chalky moonlight through my eyelids. She pulls in Elora. She wants to feel her this close. I want to run my fingers along this faint fuzz on your temple so that it tickles, and we giggle so loud that we cannot stop laughing. Run my fingers along your lips and your jaw and pause behind your ear and linger in your hair. I want to suck your fingers too. Linger on that image of your face. *That* face. *Those* eyes. Smell your *Iris Tubereuse* once more. Take the scent in and hold it and never let it go. And then, right after, before I open my eyelids, more of that unimaginable ruckus surging. More of that dog barking. A breeze through the pines. More of all of what I can gather that is pure and wonderful. More of the posies and the sunflowers bowing their welcome. More of those horses sneezing. More of you. A moment or two more.

ACKNOWLEDGMENTS

Thanks to the team that made this happen. To Maryann Karinch for her patience, understanding, and diligence in making this book become real. No effort, hard work, or dedication to her craft could equal what she put into it. Mostly, I want to award her the highest accolade in publishing: The Greatest Agent in the World. Danke! I also want to extend my appreciation to Judith Bailey, my acquiring editor at Armin Lear Press, and to the amazing team at Albatross Book Company, specifically C.S. Fritz and Emily Fritz whose design and technical talents and skills have made the book beautiful.

VINCENT DEPAUL LUPIANO is the author of two novels under the pseudonym Christopher Sloan, In Search of Eagles, and The Wings of Death. Writing as Vincent dePaul Lupiano, he has written three nonfiction books, It Was a Very Good Year: A Cultural History of the United States From 1776 to 1996; Exploring IBM's Bold Internet Strategy: An Inside Look at IBM's Vision for Network Computing; and Operation Tidal Wave: The Bloodiest Air Battle in the History of War published by Lyons Press. His international political thriller, One Minute to Midnight, was published in 2020 by Armin Lear Press.

Vince spent many years as program director, writer, and host of his radio program at WFAS in White Plains, NY. In New York City, he worked at WOR-TV and WOR-AM as a promotional writer and producer. At the American Broadcasting Company's WABC and WPLJ, he was a writer, producer, and editorial director. He also worked at IBM for ten years as a speechwriter to senior executives, editor of a management publication, producer, and director of corporate films and videos.

Born and raised in New York, NY, Vince currently resides in Franklin Lakes, NJ, with his dog, Chase.

www.ingramcontent.com/pod-product-compliance
Lightning Source LLC
Chambersburg PA
CBHW060814310726
48980CB00002B/301

* 9 7 8 1 9 5 6 4 5 0 1 1 8 *